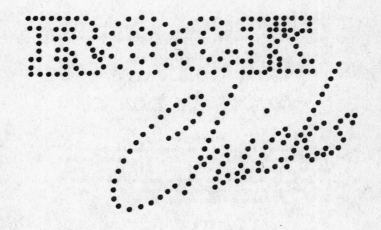

ROCK Chicks

RONNI COOPER

sphere

SPHERE

First published in Great Britain as a paperback original in 2010 by Sphere

A CIP catalogue record for this book
is available from the British Library.

ISBN 978-0-7515-4275-2

Typeset in Bembo by M Rules
Printed and bound in Great Britain by
Clays Ltd, St Ives plc

Papers used by Sphere are natural, renewable and
recyclable products sourced from well-managed forests and certified
in accordance with the rules of the Forest Stewardship Council.

Mixed Sources
Product group from well-managed
forests and other controlled sources
www.fsc.org Cert no. SGS-COC-004081
© 1996 Forest Stewardship Council

Sphere
An imprint of
Little, Brown Book Group
100 Victoria Embankment
London EC4Y 0DY

An Hachette UK Company
www.hachette.co.uk

www.littlebrown.co.uk

To J, B & C
More than words . . . always.

Endless gratitude to Sheila Crowley for believing in the Rock Chicks . . . and Emma Beswetherick for putting them on the stage.

A Note from the Author

Rock Chicks is set in another time, another place. Artistic license has been used with some of the events, dates, bands, geography and famous names. However, I would like to assure readers that no actual rock stars were harmed in the making of this book.

OVERTURE

1991. The Chateau Marmont, Los Angeles.

The Steel Spikes are in residence.

Last night, the puddles on the carpet were Jack Daniel's, sweat and water from the bath that had overflowed when one too many rake-thin blondes cast aside their handbags and headshots and climbed in to join Sly Rammer in the kind of bathing session that had more to do with getting dirty than clean.

In the main bedroom all the usual suspects were orbiting Planet Fucked Up. On the floor, the other band members, Dax, Spank, Tye, Strings and Muff, were all coked up, sexed up and letting the action come to them. And come, it did. The girls lined up to please them, desperate to inhale the stardust alongside the white powder that rose in snowy peaks from every surface. On the round, scarlet silk bed lay Marny Rammer, naked, stoned, her legs wide enough to accommodate the long brown locks that were undulating between them, completely oblivious to the fact that if she and Sly were a normal couple they'd be having dinner right now to celebrate the sixth anniversary of the day they met.

Over at the huge mahogany dining table Coco LaBiba was

performing her party trick – all it took was flexibility, an open mind and three dicks. Tonight two of them belonged to the band and one to a journalist who would for ever consider this the most incredible night of his life.

No one paid much attention to the first gunshot – the music was so loud that everyone thought it was a sound effect on 'The Law Don't Matter', the Spikes' global hit that was blaring from the sound system.

It was only when the music stopped and another shot rang out that they were forced to pay attention. Lori Wyatt held the smoking gun; over six foot in her steel stiletto heels, a leather catsuit adhered to every inch of her body, her hair scraped back into a two-foot-long black ponytail that reached the small of her back. She had their attention now.

'If I don't know you then fuck off,' she announced, her clipped voice perfectly calm, raised barely above conversational level.

Ten minutes later the suite was empty of everyone except the core players: Marny, Coco, Dave, Diana and the band, a few of them wondering aloud when their manager was going to find a new party trick. It wasn't the first time Lori had shot up a hotel ceiling but shit, there had to be an easier way to clear a room.

All that had happened last night.

This morning the room is silent and the numbers even fewer. One man lies slumped against the window, his pulse long stopped. Near the door, another body, perfectly still. On the bed lies a woman, her motionless limbs splayed like a broken starfish. Only her shallow, sporadic breaths give any clue that she's not already destined for the morgue, an occasional rasp audible over the tinkling sound of the music coming from a wooden box that lies open on the floor.

Rock-a-bye baby . . .

A bored Honduran maid walking by with a large pile of eight hundred thread-count Egyptian cotton sheets stops, listens, smiles, remembers.

On the tree top . . .

Her reminiscence is cut dead by a sudden realisation. As the fluid seeps out under the door and spreads across the deep-pile, monogrammed carpet to the white canvas of her shoes, she understands . . . and the only sound now is the sound of her screams.

Because this morning, the puddles are red.

TRACK 1

ONE

1985

Invisible. Marianne Tucker was invisible. The family sitting in the corner, joined by clutched hands, their faces tear-stained and drawn, didn't even register her existence as she walked by their table. The group of nurses over by the door didn't pause in their conversation when she cleared their plates. Even the hospital chaplain, normally good for a libidinous leer, didn't take his gaze from the young, puffy-faced, PVC-clad woman next to him. Another hooker for Father Sean to save just as soon as he got a good eyeful of those naked, creamy white thighs.

Invisible. Nothing to look at. Nothing to see.

The shapeless brown uniform that she'd pulled on at the beginning of her shift counteracted every physical plus point that she possessed. It drained her complexion, making her look pale, washed-out and older than her nineteen years. The A-line, mid-calf-length cut of the fabric shrouded her full, pert breasts in cheap cotton while camouflaging her tiny waist, slender hips and shapely legs. The hairnet constrained and concealed her ponytail of fine blonde hair. The flat, battered espadrilles that completed the ensemble were a size too large and scuffed as she walked, adding to the general demeanour of weary defeat as she pushed the trolley between the rows of tables, clearing away half-eaten plates and crumpled cardboard coffee cups.

Invisible. And that was just how she wanted it to be. In fact, she was counting on it. Her eyes flicked to the large clock on the wall above the door. 11pm. She wasn't due off shift until midnight but she'd already decided that it was time to leave. Who would notice? The cooking staff had already clocked off for the night, leaving Old Abe, the lifelong pot wash, behind the counter to finish clearing away the dried, congealed food from the row of steel bain-maries.

The swing doors to her right opened and a tall, baby-faced doctor strutted through, scanned the room, then made for the family in the corner, every one of them now staring at him with expressions that were a tortured mix of fear and hope. A few seconds later, it became clear which emotion was the more appropriate – a traumatised scream came from the middle-aged woman in the centre of the group, an almost feral noise thick with pain and devastation. The young doctor looked apologetic now, the family stunned, the mother begging for a different outcome.

Marianne had seen it so many times: the news of the dead. No one ever sat in St Joseph's Hospital canteen late at night unless they were being paid, being solicited by God or in danger of losing a loved one.

The woman was rocking back and forth now, still wailing, the three twenty-something women that surrounded her gasping for breath between their own sobs, the one solitary teenage male in the group tight-jawed as he flicked a stirrer between his fingers and stared intently at his feet.

Marianne slammed the mental door on the emerging flashback, pushed her trolley to the back wall of the room and parked it behind the partition that concealed the stinking waste bins and boxes of sugar sachets, milk portions and napkins. No more. Time to go. She pulled at the apron, feeling a surge of liberation cut through her nervous apprehension as the poppers flew open, then yanked off the hairnet and grabbed the bag that she'd left squashed in between the industrial-sized tins of coffee and the stacks of well-worn trays.

She could hear Old Abe banging away in the background, muttering to himself as he filled the huge dishwasher for what was probably the final time of the day. He wouldn't notice if she sneaked away early and even if he did the smell of Wild Turkey on his breath would prevent him from seeking out anyone to report her to. His mind was so addled with cheap bourbon and weed that he barely functioned, except to perform his duties and occasionally, in his more lucid moments, attempt to feel her up when she was bent over the battered old steel sinks.

Now dressed in a simple pink T-shirt and jeans, Marianne moved silently towards the exit, careful to stay out of the eye-line of Father Sean, who was now preaching his gospel directly to the partially exposed, bruised breasts of his companion.

It had to be now. Right now. And as she slipped out the door, she realised that her racing heart was an over-reaction, because no one had noticed the invisible girl leave.

Silently, her sneaker-clad feet padded down the drab green corridor to the staff exit, then slipped through the door to the alley that ran behind the ambulance bay. As she met the humid blanket of darkness, the first thing that hit her was the stench from the yellow and black bags piled high between the over-flowing dumpsters that punctuated the opposite wall.

Even at that late hour, an August night in Philadelphia was much too warm for goosebumps, but nonetheless Marianne shivered as she rubbed them away from her forearms and then turned to her right, thankful that her early escape wouldn't be caught on camera. The nurses' union had been calling for surveillance in the area since a spate of attacks on staff leaving after their night shifts, but the hospital management's answer had been to employ an extra security guard to patrol the area. It might have been an effective policy if the new guard had felt any compunction to leave the linen cupboard where he napped from 10pm until sunrise.

She was almost at the end of the alley when she heard the moan. Shit! A tramp? A junkie? Security? The scumball who had already put three interns in intensive care? Her stomach twisted as a jerking movement at the top of the dumpster only a few feet away entered her left field of vision. Her fight/flight reflex was about to opt for an urgent sprint, when she spotted the footwear: bright red Converse baseball boots, dangling from two black denim tubes draped over the rim of the large steel depository. An image flashed up in her head: Benny, her brother, the last time she saw him he'd been wearing red Converse. But that was years ago, before . . . She shook off the memory. That was a scab too painful to pick.

There was another moan, barely discernable over the noise of her thumping heart and the blood that was rushing to her brain.

Go. Just go. Quickly. But her feet weren't paying attention. Benny. It could be Benny. Before sense and reason could intervene, she acted. Years of regular exercise served her well as she clambered up the side of the dumpster then swung the top half of her body over the top. The stench made her retch, the sight made her reel. Of course, it wasn't Benny, and given the state of this guy she thanked God. He couldn't have been much older than her. Long, tangled brown hair was stuck to his face, his sallow skin unnaturally grey. A droplet of blood was smudged beneath his nose and a line of crusted vomit trailed from the edge of his pale blue mouth and spread over his black stain-splattered Aerosmith T-shirt.

His leg jolted as if a spasm ripped through it, the shock jarring her from her precarious position and sending her careering to the ground where she landed on a refuse bag stuffed with contents she'd rather not think about. She should go. This was nothing to do with her. None of her business.

If she ran now she'd still make it to the station in time for the bus. She'd been planning this night for months, she had a schedule to keep and she couldn't let some fool in the garbage distract her from it. But . . . he didn't look good. This man/boy looked sick and if she left him . . .

Nope, she couldn't do it, she decided as she headed back in the direction of the hospital to get some help.

Marianne had turned her back on someone once before and the consequences would last a lifetime. It was a mistake she wasn't going to make again.

Colette Belmont was in heaven. The strings on Nikki Sixx's guitar counted the beat that took her step by step up the butt-clenching, clit-throbbing path to an orgasm. Faster, pounding faster, her nerve endings prickling with bliss as Vince Neil burst in with that howling, grating vocal that had given her rush after rush since she'd discovered the joys of masturbation.

But tonight she wasn't relying on her own manual dexterity.

'That's it baby, I told you I'd fuck you real good.'

Immediately, the urge to come began to dissipate. 'Don't speak!' she hissed to the hulking form between her legs. Determined to get back to that intoxicating, ethereal place, she pulled her stomach muscles in hard and switched her focus back to the sounds of Mötley Crüe. Tommy Lee was pounding out the beat and Sixx was warming up now, going into the bridge of 'Too Young to Fall in Love', the section that always made her lips smile and her nipples harden.

She pushed back her damp waves of ash blonde Christie Brinkley hair and pursed her bee-stung lips as she pushed back against the third participant, who sat behind her in the rear seat of the Oldsmobile. His back was pressed against the side window, his beautifully defined abdomen a firm support for her head and shoulders, his rock hard thighs wide open to let the top half of her torso nestle between them. His arms cupped around to her front and he squeezed her tits. Hard. The way she liked it.

'Fuck, I'm going to come!'

The voice came from the other end of the back seat, followed

11

by several grunts as Dale Lawson pounded against her, only the constraints of the condom preventing him from filling her with his hot sticky liquid.

Exhausted, spent, he exhaled noisily as he slumped into the corner, his legs numb from kneeling in such a cramped space for so long. But it wasn't long enough for Colette.

All anticipation of an imminent orgasm now gone, she slid her long, coltish legs down from Dale's shoulders and switched her attention to his brother who was still kneading her tits, his hard-on pressed against her back. Colette flipped herself around; head slightly crouched to avoid matting her hair on the roof of the car. She'd discovered months before that good posture was one of the casualties of having sex in the Lawson family car. She didn't mind.

Facing him now, she climbed on to the upright cock of Mack Lawson, and leaned forward to slip a rigid nipple in his mouth. His hands found her buttocks and he squeezed them the way he knew turned her on. In the years that this *ménage à trois* had been a regular occurrence, Colette had told them everything that she liked, and when words failed her, she'd simply given them a step by step demonstration. Three things never varied: she liked the music loud, she liked the boys silent and once was never enough.

The air in the car was sticky and thick with the smells of sex and sweat as she rode him, slowly at first, concentrating on nothing but the sounds that were still oozing out of the car stereo. Gradually, she allowed her other senses to return to the present, her thigh muscles easily taking the strain as her pace increased, her hand behind her now, reaching downwards and cupping Mack's balls. She smiled as she felt a movement behind her and realised that Dale had rejoined the proceedings. Ah, the joys of fucking boys her own age. She'd screwed a few older men but none of them could shoot and be ready to get going again just a few minutes later. And none of them had a twin brother with an equal amount of energy.

Without turning around, she knew what Dale was up to

behind her. His hand was in her wild mane and he was tugging it while simultaneously tugging himself. It was a familiar scene that sent a wave of excitement rushing down to her clit. She loved that she got them so hot and she'd realised long ago that it was nothing to do with lust. No, this was power. Pure, unadulterated power. Inside her she felt Mack throbbing quicker now as she rose and fell on his cock. This was bliss.

Vince Neil was still singing to her, creeping under her skin and making her pupils dilate with the raw sex in his voice. In her mind, that's who was fucking her. It wasn't the two physically perfect star quarterbacks from her high school football team. It was Vince Neil and Nikki Sixx, one behind her, one beneath her, both of them worshipping her, adoring her, both completely powerless to do anything other than what she wanted them to do. Over the musical soundtrack, she could hear their whispers in her head now, telling her she was the best ever. They'd never had anyone like her. So sexy. So hot. So . . . Her back arched and her vaginal muscles squeezed like a vice as she climaxed, her screams of sheer ecstasy all it took to make Dale and Mack follow suit. The three of them shuddered to a halt a few seconds later, then collapsed in a tangle of limbs that was suddenly too excessive for the back seat of the Lawson family car.

After a long enough pause to let her pulse rate return to something near normal, Colette disentangled herself and stretched over the passenger seat, popped the cassette out of the stereo system, flicked it over and re-inserted it. A large Diet Coke on the driver's seat, all that was left of their drive-through dinner, gave her an idea that she couldn't resist. As the first bars of 'Shout at the Devil' burst out of the speakers at either side of the dashboard, she turned around to face the boys again and repositioned herself above them, balancing herself against the top of the front seats and stretching her legs so wide that they almost touched the windows on either side of the back seat.

The cup lid slid off easily and slowly. Provocatively, she tipped what was left of the drink down her body, excitement surging once again as a cold trail of ice coursed down her chest and abdomen and soaked the thin strip of hair between her legs. She grabbed her breasts and began to massage them, before leaning down and taking it in turns to flick her tongue across each nipple. God bless huge tits, she thought, before slipping one in her mouth again and performing her latest trick. It had been a long, happy, revelatory night when she had discovered that she had both the voluptuousness and the flexibility to tend to her own needs in that department.

The temperature in the car notched up another few degrees, the air suddenly heavy with anticipation and longing. Dale Lawson unintentionally groaned, making Colette smile. Sitting side by side now, intently studying her every move, there wasn't much to choose between them – they were both identically gorgeous, blonde haired, blue eyed American boys, both perfectly formed, and their gradually re-erecting dicks might not be the biggest she'd ever had but they were impressive nonetheless. Dale's little outburst was enough to convince her that he should win the prize. She beckoned him towards her with her index finger and when he was close enough she pushed her fingers through his hair and pulled him towards her pussy.

Fun. Music. Sex. That was all she needed to get through the day.

As his tongue found her clit and started to work it just how she'd shown him, she tuned out of Dale Lawson and back into the sounds. It wasn't the high school jock who was licking her out – Nikki Sixx was playing her like the most precious Stratocaster. And Colette Belmont was just about to sing.

Ashes to ashes. Dust to dust . . .

Right on cue the heavens opened and the minister and collective gathering were drenched in a summer shower.

Lori Wyatt rolled her eyes to the sky, thinking that even in death, the old bastard she'd had the misfortune to call her father had a sick sense of humour. If by some miracle the drunken waster had made it to heaven, he had probably turned the tap on personally and was right now slugging Jim Beam from the bottle while cackling at the freak show below. And freak show it was.

A minister. A daughter. And ten yards away, two aging ex-hookers in leopard print and lamé and four dishevelled old drunks, huddled together on a barren patch of brown earth under a cypress tree, counting the minutes until the service was over and they could get to the wake. If the turnout at a funeral reflected the life that had been led then this pathetic gathering, Lori decided, was just about right.

Slowly, jarring off the sides as it was lowered into the freshly dug hole by four glum-faced cemetery workers, the cheap pine coffin disappeared as the minister wrapped up the service. Lori nodded to him, acknowledging that God's work had been done and he made off in the direction of the shelter, ostensibly to comfort the other mourners, but in reality to escape the downpour. The rug manufacturer offered a two-year guarantee against rain shrinkage, but he didn't want to push his luck. The episode with the severe winds at the garden wedding had proven that inclement weather was not a friend to the follically challenged.

Slowly, the stiletto heels of her black leather boots sinking into the turf, she walked to the very edge of the graveside and waited until the workers had retreated to the dry haven of their nearby van, one of the younger ones receiving a surreptitious thump across the back of the head for a glance that lingered on Lori for a few seconds too long.

The rain was thundering now, infusing the air with the scent of freshly cut grass and sodden earth.

It was just her. And him. The way it had been since their mother had taken off in the middle of the night when Lori was six years old, pushed over the edge by one too many drunken brawls and public humiliations. Lori had never seen her since but she'd heard stories that her ma had headed east to New York, presumably figuring a city with almost five hundred murders in an average year still had to be safer than living with Jack Wyatt.

But this wasn't the time for reflection or for memories that still cut like a scalpel along a vein. It was a time for last words and for bidding farewell.

'Goodbye Pa,' she whispered quietly, tossing a mound of earth into the hole. Then she pulled herself up to her full height, straightened her back, and spat on his coffin. 'I hope you rot in hell.'

Her black dress clung to every curve of her athletic frame as she crossed to the squad of desperados tweaking for their next shot or their next smoke, a shambling embarrassment of dregs and scum. Just her old pa's kind of people. The minister gaped open-mouthed as she tucked a hundred dollars into the wrinkled, crêpe cleavage of Rita Mae, the sixty-year-old tramp who still turned a trick if the guy was too loaded or too desperate to care. 'There won't be a wake so take this for your trouble,' she said in a voice that made it clear her announcement wasn't up for discussion. Not that they cared. A hundred dollars would keep them all mighty happy for the rest of the day and even better, they could go wherever they wanted and avoid any pretence of loss over the death of Jack Wyatt.

With another nod to the minister, Lori headed off to the late Jack's old Chevy pick-up and hot-wired the ignition. No keys. It was another one of fate's cruel little games. They'd been missing since the day he had been found dead almost a month before. He'd been discovered by the cleaner who'd opened up Jack's Alehouse first thing in the morning on a seemingly normal August day. When Maria had seen the broken chairs and the smashed glassware, she'd realised that nothing about the scene in front of her was normal, least of all the state of her boss. He'd been lying behind the bar, his face unmarked and eyes closed. It wasn't the first time she'd found him flaked out, but this time the frozen expression, blood-matted hair and stillness of his chest told her it would be the last. Her first call had been to 911, her second to Lori, her third to her cousin Emilio. She ordered him to collect her and get her out of town before the cops passed her name on to immigration and she found herself on a one-way ticket back to Havana.

Lori had arrived at the same time as the cops and despite her protests they'd insisted that she stand to one side as they swept the bar to make sure the perpetrators had left the scene. The broken window in the stinking gents' toilets had told them that Jack's killers were long gone. Waiting by the door, Lori had noticed that the till lay open, the takings from the night before cleaned out. Bottles of spirits were missing from the gantry and the door through to the back office had been ripped off its hinges. Through the hole, she'd seen that the safe was lying wide open and empty. It was a mess – even by the Alehouse standards, where hygiene and decor were low on the priority list and the clientele spat, vomited and passed out on the floor on a nightly basis.

Lori had shuddered, prompting a young female cop to rest a sympathetic hand on her forearm and give her a kindly smile. Murders in Rackstown, Pennsylvania were rare, and although Jack was well known to every cop in town as a violent drunk and a vehemently vocal bar-room anarchist, as far as the rookie was concerned, he didn't deserve to die like this. Lori had returned the gesture with a sad smile that dissipated as soon as the sheriff re-appeared from the direction of the toilets.

'Lori, you know it's not procedure, but before anyone else gets here you can go on over. Just don't touch anything and I'm sorry Ma'am but that includes your pa.'

Lori had smiled at the formality of the 'Ma'am'. Sheriff Donnachy had been a good friend of her mother and had known her all her life, regularly stopping to give her a ride on a wet day and frequently dropping in to check on her every time her father had been slung in the slammer. At least that would be one community service he could cross off his list from now on.

Being careful to avoid the debris and the spatters of liquid that were splashed randomly across the floor, she'd edged over to where he lay. Bile had risen in her throat when she'd reached him and she'd inhaled furiously, an action that the young female cop had interpreted as a distraught gasp of grief. Jack's eyes were wide open and his face was contorted into an angry scowl, his standard expression, for Jack Wyatt had been mean-assed furious since the day he was born. Lori had knelt down, ignoring the tense vibes from the cop who still stood beside her and who had no desire to be hauled over the coals in court for allowing the crime scene to be contaminated. The officer needn't have worried. Lori had no intention of throwing herself on the body in a hysterical demonstration of grief, or sentimentally running her fingers through his blood-matted hair. She crouched until her face was only twelve inches from his chest and then paused, perfectly still, staring straight ahead. After a minute or so she was reassured. Jack Belmont was finally, indisputably, very definitely dead.

Only the fact that they'd broken procedure by permitting Lori anywhere near the body stopped the rookie from telling her colleagues back at the station about the peculiar reaction of the bereaved daughter.

Lori Wyatt had smiled.

TWO

'Hi.'

His voice sounded exactly as she'd imagined. For two days Marianne had spent every possible minute next to him, watching his face, willing him to wake up, wondering what he'd sound like, what he'd say. After the doctors had pumped his stomach and stabilised him on that first night, they'd warned her that he'd already ingested a massive amount of opiates so a deep, prolonged sleep was inevitable. She didn't mind waiting. Instead of whiling away her breaks in the suffocating, nicotine-coated surroundings of the staff smoking room, all her spare time had been spent in the sanitised atmosphere of his hospital room, sitting on a big old leather chair by the side of his bed, talking to him, asking him questions that went unanswered. Naturally shy, she was surprised to discover that it was actually easy to talk when there was no one awake to listen.

There had been no other visitors. Right now, somewhere in the city, was a mother frantically looking for her son? Was a father begging God to bring his boy back to him?

Everything he'd had in his possession when he was found now sat on top of the teak veneer table next to his bed. One packet of Marlboro cigarettes, one Zippo lighter, one Sony Walkman (batteries dead), one cassette, unlabelled. It wasn't a lot to go on. John Doe. Smoker. Likes music.

Now he was staring at her with eyes that belied curiosity rather than fear. Suddenly embarrassed by being there, by her tatty brown uniform and her chewed-up nails, Marianne flushed as she leaned over towards him. 'Hi,' she answered, her speech thick with self-conscious apprehension. 'I'm Marianne.'

'Are you a nurse?' His voice was hoarse, the gravelly tone dipping out on the words that were too much of an effort to form.

'No, I er . . . found you.'

Confusion contorted his beautiful features. She could see now that his eyes were dark brown, framed by sweeping thick black eyelashes. 'Where?' he croaked.

'In the alley at the back of the hospital. You were . . . out of it. They had to pump your stomach.'

He groaned, understanding now why his throat felt like he'd swallowed razors. 'Fuck. What day is it?'

'Sunday.'

'Shit.' He thumped the bedspace beside him.

Marianne flinched; her eyes widened, then instinctively fell to the floor, the hunching of her shoulders adding to the outward reflection of her inner discomfort. Anger scared her. Especially when it seemed to be directed at her.

'Sorry, I didn't . . . Sorry,' he croaked. 'Married. I was supposed to be getting married yesterday. Shit, she'll kill me.'

'Do you want me to call her for you? Your . . . girlfriend?' Her stomach twisted just a little more. This was suddenly becoming too real, too messy to deal with and for the first time since she climbed up on to the dumpster she felt a rising surge of regret. What had she been thinking? Hadn't she learned that the only way to live was to keep yourself to yourself and stay away from meddling in other people's business?

A rueful smile crossed his face as he shook his head. 'So first you save my life and now you want to get me killed – you're like

20

a regular superhero,' he laughed, and then buckled as racking coughs overtook his amusement.

Marianne grabbed a blue plastic beaker of water from the side table and held it to his mouth to let him sip. When she replaced it she realised that he was still holding on to her other hand.

'Thank you,' he whispered. His dark eyes were wide now, sad, maybe even a little scared.

'S'OK,' she replied, trying her best to keep her voice steady. 'Is there someone else I can call for you?'

A puff of air escaped from the pillow as his head fell back into it. 'No. Somehow I don't think many people would be too happy to hear from me right now.'

An inherent sense told her not to argue or cajole. He'd been through a lot and the most important thing was that he was going to be OK. Everything else could wait. An alarm sounded on her Casio digital watch.

'I . . . I have to go now – my break is over.'

'Your break?'

'I work in the canteen here. I was just leaving on the night that I found you.'

'Lucky for me,' he whispered softly, finally releasing her hand, his gaze still surveying her face as if there were answers to something there.

'Will you come back again?'

She hesitated. This was ridiculous. Why would she come back? She didn't even know this guy. And there was no point striking up a friendship because . . .

'Please?' he asked, with just a hint of something between desperation and panic.

'OK. Tomorrow. My break is around six. I'll come back in then.'

'See you then, Supergirl,' he joked softly.

Walking to the door, she pulled her hairnet out of her uniform pocket but then changed her mind and shoved it back in, deciding to put it on outside. Her fingers were already on the handle when she realised the first question that she should have asked. Turning back, she was surprised to see that his eyes still hadn't left her.

'Your name. You didn't tell me your name.'

'Sylvester. But everyone calls me Sly. Like the *Rocky* guy.' The grin was there again and something in Marianne responded to it. Two days ago this guy was pulled out of the trash, he'd missed his wedding, had his stomach pumped, woken up to a stranger's stare and yet he was acting like this was just another day on easy street.

For a fleeting moment she wondered what her mom would have made of him and the unexpected idea brought more goose-bumps. She hadn't thought about her parents for a long, long time but now a mental vision flashed up of her mother. Dorisanna was sitting in the backyard of their apartment block in the area of Philly that nice folk avoided, surrounded by deadbeat neighbours, berating her eldest daughter for her shy, sensitive nature and pointing out her children's faults to anyone that was sober enough to listen. Marianne wondered if the angels were listening to Dorisanna now.

A flush of colour rose from the top of her uniform as she returned his smile. 'I'll let the nurse know you're awake.'

'Marianne?'

The door had almost closed behind her so she pushed it back open.

'Yes?'

'Thanks babe.'

Mack Lawson didn't understand it. As star quarterback of the school team, he'd talked his way into a few of the cheerleaders' panties and they'd all been almost comically similar. They wanted sweet words, soft loving and declarations of love. But not Colette – this chick was wild. As he pulled up outside her front door, she kissed his cheek and then stretched over to repeat the gesture to his brother Dale, who was still lying across the back seat, before giving them a breezy smile and strolling inside with

22

a casual wave that gave no indication whatsoever of the night's activities.

But that was Colette's style.

The first night they'd got together was at a major-league party to celebrate her sixteenth birthday. His mother had been stoked when the invitation had come in, thrilled that she could boast at the cross-stitch club that her twin sons had been invited to the Belmont estate, former home of J.J. Belmont. The property baron had been one of the richest landowners in the Tri-state area until the heart attack that ended his life just a year before that pink invitation had dropped through the door of the Lawsons' tidy, white clapboard house.

The Belmont parties were legendary. Since Mack was a little boy the townsfolk would gape and gossip as the Gulfstreams flew overhead bringing politicians, European royalty, rock stars, dignitaries and even, it was once rumoured, President Ronald Reagan. They would fly in, landing their jets on the airstrip that slashed across the dense forestry on the outskirts of the ranch that occupied almost a thousand acres of prime Connecticut land.

His mother had badgered his dad Ed into taking a day off from his dry-cleaning business to get the boys fitted for suits, so it was a very smart Mack and Dale Belmont who had boarded the bus that was leaving from outside Conn Liberty High to chauffeur their classmates to the soirée.

Inside, it was clear that any residual mourning had been suspended for the day. The party was held in the west wing of the house, where they'd converted a huge dining area into a disco by blacking out the windows and laying a temporary dance floor. On a stage at one end, a suited band blasted out covers of hits from bands like REO Speedwagon and Huey Lewis and the News.

They'd just broken into a soulful, enthusiastic rendition of Tears For Fears' 'Everybody Wants to Rule the World', when Mack, on his way back from the john, stopped on a balcony above the action to watch the teenagers take to the floor below.

So far it was just pockets of girls, most of them nervously shuffling on to the dance floor, pretending not to care if they attracted the attention of the boys who stood in groups around the periphery. Conn Liberty High pupils congregated at one end of the hall, with what he presumed were Colette's friends from her posh Catholic school keeping to themselves at the other.

It was almost an hour into the party, but so far there had been no sign of the birthday girl. Until now.

'Sooo, Mack Lawson, does it meet with your approval?' The playful voice had whispered in his ear as a body pressed against his back. Mack's erection was as swift as his blush. Shit, he wished he could control either or both, but it seemed like lately parts of his anatomy were unilaterally deciding on their own actions.

Turning around, he added his gasp reflex to that list.

'How fucking embarrassing is this?' she grinned, gesturing to the revelry below. The mouth was pure locker room, but the face and body were about as stunningly feminine as it was possible to be.

The white strapless leather dress looked like it had been painted on as it clung to every curve from her incredible tits to the top of her long, bronzed thighs, and the gold zip that ran from top to bottom had been left open an inch or two giving a mesmerising view of her cleavage. Almost two feet of dark blonde curls cascaded down over one shoulder, the other side pulled back and secured with a diamond clip, holding her locks away from a trail of glitter than ran from her cheekbone to her collarbone. There was no way that the girl in front of him looked sixteen.

For the last few weeks Mack had been jerking off over a *Playboy* with a ten-page spread of Kim Basinger. The actress was white hot, but something told him he wouldn't need to rely on magazines from now on.

Regaining his composure, he leaned back against the balustrade, keen to maintain eye contact in the hope that she wouldn't notice the bulge in his new pin-tucked black pants.

'Hey, you got the right brother this time?' he joked, referring to the pranks that he and Dale had played on her for years when they were children. His mom used to work as a seamstress for Mrs Belmont and the boys had visited the ranch almost daily for weeks every summer, playing with Colette while their mother fashioned new drapes and soft furnishings for every room in the house. Over the last few years, though, since Mrs Belmont started using one of those fancy interior designers from New York, the extent of their interaction had been the occasional conversation at town fairs and Sunday service.

'It's the mole,' Colette grinned, running a purple nail very lightly along his cheekbone, stopping at the small brown spot that sat just under the outer corner of his eye. Explanation complete, her gaze flicked over his shoulder as she checked out the scene below and groaned.

'I begged my mother not to do the whole party thing, but would she listen?' Hormone-induced confusion and sleight of hand prevented Mack from noticing from where Colette produced the pack of Camel Lights that she was now opening. She pulled a cigarette and a pencil-slim gold lighter from the pack. Whoa, she was smoking! If he went home smelling of nicotine his mother's delight at her son's newfound social status would be temporarily postponed while she invoked the wrath of God and beat him with a broom.

'I mean, look!' she gesticulated to the crowd of teens that Mack didn't recognise. 'I've no idea why she thought inviting anyone from my last school would be a good idea.'

'Last school?' he asked, the testosterone surge still making it difficult to keep up.

'St Mary's expelled me,' she answered glibly. 'Apparently no amount of money can make up for getting caught at a rock concert with a joint in one hand and some guy's balls in the other.'

Mack momentarily wondered if it was normal that his windpipe seemed to have swollen to a point that made breathing impossible.

'But thank God at least mother is allowing me to start at Conn Liberty after the summer, thus this little introductory, break-the-ice bash. I know some of the Liberty girls from church and I figured it had to be better than starting all over again from scratch. What do you think? Are they all going to be bitches to the poor little rich girl?' she asked, in an amused tone that hinted that this wouldn't bother her in the least.

'Probably,' he shrugged, still struggling with the mental picture of the whole joint/balls scenario.

'Great. Then at least it won't be dull. I hate dull. So . . . I'm going to need a friend when I come to your school,' she giggled, 'and I've decided that you're it. Can you handle that?' She was teasing now, and he was finally starting to relax and play the game. Come on, he was Mack Lawson, he told himself, of course he could handle it. There wasn't a female downstairs who would say no to the town's rising football star. Reminding himself of his own importance, he felt his confidence restore itself to its naturally inflated level.

'Sure,' he shrugged, throwing caution to the wind by taking the cigarette from her lips and slowly inhaling on it, praying that he wouldn't react the same way that he did on the one and only other occasion when he'd experimented with smoking. Buckling over at the waist and choking so violently that he puked would definitely put a bit of a downer on the current situation.

'Ooooooh, a bad boy – I like that in a friend.' A sexy pout dissolved into a wide smile that revealed a perfect row of porcelain-white teeth. He handed the cigarette back and there was a comfortable pause as they stood side by side, both watching the action below while mentally adjusting to their newly restored connection. Colette was the first to speak.

'God, I don't want to go down there. It's my birthday; I'm supposed to be having fun.'

Mack's ego took a momentary hit. This was like nothing he'd ever dealt with before. Fun? Usually the chicks had fun just being around him, but this one was a whole different ball game and obviously his very presence wasn't enough to satisfy her amusement quota.

The five-inch steel heel of one of her white stilettos finished grinding the cigarette out on the marble floor and suddenly her hand grabbed his.

'Come with me.' It was more of a gregarious command than a request.

'Where?'

They were halfway down the hallway before she answered by opening a door and pulling him inside. It was the most incredible bedroom he'd ever seen. White silk fabric covered the walls, contrasting with the shocking pink, thick-pile carpet. The bed was a huge mahogany four-poster with blood-red satin sheets and a six-foot square heavy gilt mirror balanced behind an overstuffed gold chaise that was thick with silver and red cushions. But it was the pictures that really made it stand out – huge, black framed posters of Van Halen, Twisted Sister, KISS and a couple of other bands that he didn't recognise.

'Mother's refusing to pay the decorator's bill. She gave him a brief but I managed to persuade him to add a few of my suggestions.'

'How did you do that?' he asked with his very best cocky jock smile.

'You want me to show you?' she teased, taking a swig out of a beer bottle she'd picked up from her dresser.

Oh, dear Lord, he prayed – I don't know what I've done to deserve this, but thank you.

Colette playfully pushed him back a few paces, then without breaking eye contact even for a second, she slowly pulled down the zipper on her dress and let the rectangle of leather fall to the floor.

'Like this.'

Mack's gasp reflex sprung back into action. He was no virgin – he'd screwed three girls already, two in the school changing rooms and one on her sofa while her parents were at a bible rally in the church hall – but it had always been a fully clothed, panties-to-one-side, rushed fumble, so he'd never actually been presented with a fully naked woman.

And Colette Belmont was definitely standing in front of him in nothing but a pair of white high heels.

He made a mental note to torch the *Playboys* because he'd definitely never need them again now that his memory had a real-life image of a female who was 100 per cent cock rod.

Jeez, she was beautiful. Her huge breasts sat high above the curves that met at her waist and then spanned out to gloriously generous hips and firm, perfectly shaped thighs, with a small round bush of blonde wiry hair contrasting against the dark, golden tan. Slowly, she turned around 360 degrees, giving him a perfect view of the most gorgeous, pert ass he could ever have imagined.

Mesmerised, he'd watched as she walked towards him, unzipped his fly, and flicked out his dick, massaging it as she gently guided him backwards to the wall behind him, then pulled herself up onto his solid cock. Only after he'd come – an embarrassingly short period of time later – did he realise that he'd fucked her in between Van Halen and KISS.

That had been two years ago, and now, as he and Dale got home, handed the car keys back to his dad and confirmed to their mother that yes, they'd had a good night at the mall, he remembered the words she'd whispered on that first night as they belatedly and reluctantly joined the other party guests.

'I think we're going to have a great time being friends,' she'd whispered. 'And next time, wanna bring your brother?'

Religion was a big thing with the Ramones. Everyone within fifty yards of the payphone heard the thankful prayers of Sly's mother when he called her to let her know he was OK. A few seconds later, he had to hold the phone three feet from his ear to avoid certain deafness as a result of the hysterical, incomprehensible hell and damnation rant of fury when he refused to tell her where he was. He figured that the last thing the rest of the sick folks in this hospital needed was his mother, father and four sisters storming the corridors with huge pots of spaghetti carbonara – and not to mention Gloria, his fiancée. Or should that be ex-fiancée? Fuck, her old man would have his guts, if his mother didn't get them first.

The matriarch of the Ramone family had told him in no uncertain terms that now she knew he was still alive, she planned – in the name of the blessed Madonna – to punish him for the rest of time. Such was the shame and pain that he had wreaked on the parents that had done nothing but cherish him since the very day he was pushed from his mother's womb. And yes, he would be paying her back for the wedding hat that had 'cost a hundred bucks of her sweat, blood and tears!'

The world then heard how the havoc caused by his actions didn't stop there. Apparently, Uncle Sol was so distraught he'd had to take a double dose of his angina medication, Aunt Maria Christina had taken to her bed for two days and his father had taken a chainsaw into the garden where his fury had resulted in the destruction of two huge oak trees that had been there for decades. Oh, and two of his fiancée's cousins had been sitting in a beat-up Mustang at the end of their street all week and the neighbours were whispering.

Jesus, Mary and Joseph, how could she have raised such a son? How could any child of hers leave a girlfriend, her belly swollen with a gift from God, and take off like some two-bit slimeball?

He said sorry. And then sorry again. And again. Then another sorry just in case she hadn't heard the first twenty. In fact if there was a world record for saying freaking sorry then he reckoned he'd just about broken it.

'I'll make it up to you Ma, I promise. I'll make it all good and I'll sort it out with Gloria. Keep the hat, Ma, you'll still be wearing it.'

Eventually, after another ten minutes of abuse that cost him almost two dollars to hear, she grudgingly hinted at forgiveness as long as he said three Acts Of Contrition and visited Father Domenici as soon as he got home.

'And when will that be?' she demanded.

'Soon, Ma. I'll be home soon.'

As he hung up the phone and wearily wandered back to his room, Sly Ramone realised that right now an anonymous hospital bed on the other side of town from everyone who loved him seemed like the healthiest place for him to be.

Lori handed over a cheque to the beer delivery driver and saw him off with a cheery wave, then stepped back down into the backroom of the bar and kicked the trashcan so hard it split in two.

'Motherfucker!'

She reckoned she had about five days before the cheque bounced and he was back, a little more hostile this time, to demand cash. He would look at her the same way that the liquor supplier, the water company and the soft-drinks rep had looked at her the day before, when they'd all shown up demanding to be repaid for the bad cheques that Jack had written in the days before his head had a meeting with a baseball bat. Whoever had raided the bar that night had cleaned out the previous weekend's takings that Jack had been too lazy or too drunk to take to the bank – and the days when anyone within fifty miles of Rackstown would give the Wyatts credit were long gone. She just hoped that the next few days would bring in enough money to keep the bar open for another week. Week to week. That's how her pa had lived for years, and nothing was going to change now.

It had occurred to her that she should just pull down the shutters and leave – after all, what was there to keep her there? But the truth was that she had nowhere to go, no money to pay for the journey and no roof over her head when she got there. Staying and somehow finding a way to make this shithole work seemed like the best option.

It was an hour until opening time so she picked up a mop and bucket and headed for the ladies' toilets. That damn maid hadn't been seen since the day Jack died and finding new help who were willing to work for intermittent cash in hand had so far proved impossible. No one wanted to come near The Alehouse, at least not until they'd had vaccinations against the vermin that frequented it. And she didn't mean the rats.

The front door banged and Lori's heart sank. If this was another enraged creditor then she wouldn't be responsible for the destination of the mop pole in her hand. Dear Lord, she said a silent prayer, if that old bastard somehow made it to heaven, then please round up your biggest guys and order them to beat the crap out of him once again. Amen.

The deadbolt on the door put up a fight but eventually she wrestled it open to be greeted by a sweating, fat middle-aged man with a nasty combover and a cheap suit.

'Councillor Gorman,' she sighed, stepping back to wave him in. She'd been waiting, but had fervently hoped that the fact that she'd been robbed, abandoned and effectively orphaned within the last month would have been enough payback to whatever gods of fucked-up karma were playing with her life.

She re-bolted the door, grimacing as the stale smell of sweat from his body made her gag.

'Well there, Lori, I was mighty sorry to hear about your father. Mighty sorry.'

'I must have missed you at the funeral,' she countered dryly.

'Ah, you know that the work of a public servant leaves little personal time, even for someone as close to the community as I am,' he sneered, his smug, leering grin almost as nauseating as his personal hygiene. Lori moved behind the bar, figuring that putting a couple of feet of thick wood between them could only be a good thing.

'I'll have two fingers of bourbon since you're asking.'

'I wasn't.'

'Well then I'll still have them all the same now, won't I?' he baited, flicking a fat cigar out of his pocket and lighting up. This guy was slime. He was abhorrent. But . . .

'I thought it was about time we had a little chat about the

licence for this here bar.'

. . . a degree of amiable behaviour was called for because Councillor Gorman was also the head of licensing for the district.

Two fingers of her cheapest bourbon were delivered in the pause that followed. 'Why that's mighty kind of you, Lori.' The sarcasm dripped from every elongated vowel. Still Lori said nothing, determined not to buy into this piece of crap's twisted, vile little world.

'The way I see it, Lori, this bar is now operating illegally. The licence was in your daddy's name and since you're still a minor in the eyes of the law you can't take it over. And even if you are of age, you would still require the support of your local councillor. That creates a problem right there now, doesn't it?'

And once again, Lori thought, today's performance was taking place thanks to the kind sponsorship of the fucked-up karma gods. A big cheer for the sponsors, ladies and gentlemen!

There was no getting out of this one. There was only her, and she alone was going to have to fix this.

'So what do you intend to do about this problem then, councillor?' she asked, her tone as conciliatory as she could manage.

The smug grin conveyed his pleasure that she was coming round to realising just how important it was to be nice to the man who could control her future.

'The way I see it there are three possible solutions,' he said, before pausing to take a long draw on his cigar and wash away the taste with a swallow of bourbon. 'You can shut the place down. Or we could close it temporarily until you find another partner who is an authorised licensee. Or . . .'

There was no mistaking where this was going.

'Or what, Councillor Gorman?' she asked, putting on her very best sweet smile and endearing expression.

'Or . . . Let's just say your local councillor could make the licence problem disappear.'

Lori's eyes widened and her heart picked up just a little bit of pace.

'You could do that for me Councillor – you could really fix this?' The relief in her voice puffed his chest out just a little bit more.

'I could, little lady, yes I could. Of course, we'd need to come to some . . . arrangement.'

Lori decided not to even pretend that she didn't know what he was talking about – hadn't she suspected that it would come to this? And hadn't she already realised what she would have to resort to when it did?

Bourbon and cigar were forgotten as the town official watched her slowly slip one hand up and undo the top two buttons of her red shirt, allowing him a full view of the black lace bra that concealed her apple-firm breasts.

'An arrangement?' She was in full survival mode now, playing with him, leaning over the bar, giving him a spectacular view as she shot another couple of inches into his glass.

'I always knew you were a smart girl, Lori.'

'Oh, I am, Councillor,' she giggled. 'I'm real smart.' She opened the rest of the buttons and tossed the shirt on to the ledge behind her. 'Now why don't we just get everything out in the open and let's get on with fixing this "problem"'.

Lori leant over, gently took hold of his tie and pulled him towards her, forcing him to stand on the bar stool's footrest to reach her. With a playful smile, she slowly ran one nail down his chest.

'Why don't you get it out and let me see what I can do for you,' she purred seductively, instinctively knowing that what she was about to do was the only way to hang on to the one thing she had left.

His face now red and his breathing heavy, he winked at her as he hastily unbuttoned his fly, wobbling slightly as he struggled to balance on the narrow strip of wood. He exhaled heavily as he flipped his semi-flaccid penis onto the bar top.

'Oooh, now what shall I do with this?' she asked playfully, making the cock grow just a little more in the process. 'I think

'I'll have to . . .'

The elected member didn't even see it coming. While he was still playing out the best damned sexual experience he'd had in years, Lori lurched towards him, grabbed his lapel with one hand, and with the other snatched up the bourbon bottle and brought it down hard on his dick. The screams could be heard all the way to Pittsburgh.

Pulling her shirt back on, she jumped across the bar and stood over the pathetic lump of crap that was now buckled in two and writhing on the bar floor.

'Let me tell you something, Councillor Gorman,' she spat, giving him a swift kick in the kidneys just because she could. 'I turned twenty-one today, and I think my local councillor just decided to support my appliation so I'll expect that licence to be in my name by the end of the day.'

'You. Fucking. Bitch. I'll. Have. You. Fucking. Jailed.' He could barely get the words out between the screams. The next kick didn't make that situation any better. She was six feet and four inches of solid, athletic muscle, he was five foot ten inches of unconditioned lard – he didn't stand a chance.

'I don't think so, you fat, spineless fuck. Because see that up there . . .?'

She grabbed what was left of his hair and twisted his head to see the newly installed camera with the flashing red light in the corner of the room, the one that had caught every single moment since he entered.

'A present from Sheriff Donnachy – he said it would protect me from the trash. I guess he was right. Now get your dick back in your pants and get out of my bar and let me tell you this – if I ever, ever get another little "problem" from you, two things will happen: the whole town will see that tape and then I'll track you down, wait until we're alone and then slowly, painfully, slice that fat, useless dick from your body. Are we clear?'

Eyes blazing with pain and fury, he tried to spit in her face, but missed and gave himself a new stain on his shiny suit instead.

34

Using both hands, she dragged him up, shoved him to the back door and threw him out into the alley, where he landed in a heap next to the empty kegs and crates.

Then for the second time that day, she stepped back down into the back office and kicked the trashcan across the room.

It was only then that she felt the tears creep up to the back of her eyes, forcing her to lean back against the wall and swallow hard. Lori hadn't cried since the day after her mother left and she wasn't going to start now.

'Hey Mama,' she blurted, knowing that only the termites and those gods of karma could hear. 'Happy Birthday to me.'

THREE

'Doctor Callow says I'm getting out today,' he announced as soon as Marianne slipped into his room on the sunny morning of the fifth day. He looked so much better now and she had even noticed a couple of the younger nurses coyly flirting with him as they filled up his water jug and checked his temperature and blood pressure. She didn't blame them. She'd never had a boyfriend, but if she had, she'd have wanted him to look exactly like Sly. His hair was clean now, thick and shiny as it fell to below his shoulders. His jaw was angular and he had the kind of high, defined cheekbones normally seen on women, yet the end result was resolutely masculine. But it was his eyes that had her hooked, huge brown pools that Marianne – if her shyness would have allowed – could happily have stared at all day.

Instead, she sat in the chair beside the window, her gaze downwards, her stomach tight. She'd known this would come soon. The last week had been like a stolen episode in time, an unnatural detour from the outside world, where all that mattered were the two of them.

Other than her day off, when prior plans made visiting him

impossible, she'd dropped by every few hours. He'd managed to acquire new batteries for his Walkman – she suspected they came from one of the young nurses who seemed to think he needed extra care and attention – and often he wouldn't hear her enter, so she'd watch him for a few seconds, hesitant, unsure of what to say. His head would bob up and down in time to the music, his fingers drumming a tune on the wheeled Formica table stretched over the bed.

It was his music, he'd told her. Songs he'd written. Marianne knew nothing about popular music – where she lived, tunes were never high on the priority list. Neither were friends. Perhaps that's why casual conversation had never come easy to her. She naturally avoided questions about herself, convinced that she had nothing of interest to say.

'So tell me about your family,' he'd asked her during one of her earlier visits. Marianne wasn't sure if the lurch of her stomach or the heat in her face had come first.

'I don't have one,' she'd shrugged, surprised by the sudden constriction of her vocal chords. Why was she getting emotional about that now? It wasn't like it was a recent development. 'My parents are both dead – a car crash when I was ten. My brother too. Don't have any other relatives.'

'Shit,' Sly whistled, followed by a silence that was long and excruciating.

'So you live . . .?'

She finished his sentence for him, 'Alone.'

'Do you want to talk . . .'

'No.'

That was it. Over. The sum total of Marianne's contribution to their personal disclosures. It was exactly how she liked it. Years of solitude had blocked her ability and desire to share on any kind of personal level.

Thankfully over the next few days her shy awkwardness was balanced by Sly Ramone's easy stream of chat, a consequence, he told her, of coming from a large Italian American family who were only ever silent for the two hours every week that they were in mass.

Now the time had come for him to return to them. For the first time in years, Marianne felt the sensation of tears welling behind her eyes and chided herself. Hadn't she learned that tears achieve nothing? They were wasted, useless. Maybe it was good that he was going. He'd distracted her from her plans, taken her mind off her goals. Now she'd come to the end of the temporary delay, she could reschedule her move and get on with the new life that she'd been planning for as long as she could remember.

'Marianne, I'm not going back home.'

His voice cut through her thoughts and as she looked up at him she saw that his fists were clenched and his jaw firm in resolution. 'If I go back then it's over. The wedding will be back on, we'll live in the apartment over Uncle Sol's garage while Gloria busts my ass every day because we don't have our own place, I'll work twelve-hour days in the restaurant and that'll be it.' He shook his head. 'Can't do it, man. That's fucking death. I mean, don't you think that ending up whacked-out in a dumpster on the night before your wedding should tell you something?'

Marianne nodded. Over the last few days they'd speculated as to how he'd ended up there but with no conclusion. He remembered knocking out a few songs at the local bar, then going outside to smoke some hash. A while later all the male relatives of both the bride and groom had descended and they'd tanked down a serious amount of shit in the back of his uncle's pizza joint. That was as far as he got – the journey between there and waking in a hospital was still nothing but blackness.

'That shit's not for me. Gloria even goes nuts when I turn the music up too loud, says it could damage the baby. I mean come on . . . like Keith Richards ever had to keep the tunes on low.'

'So what do you want?' she blurted, an edge of impatience in her voice. It was a toss up as to who was most startled at the outburst. Until that moment, Marianne's modus operandi had been listening, comforting, caring.

'I want to get out of here. I want to make music. Man, I want to rock the fucking world.'

'Then do it,' she challenged him, her eyes glinting with tears. So that was it then. It was time to move on with her life.

He swung his feet on to the floor and in three paces was crouching in front of her. He slipped a hand around her neck and pulled her head towards him, landing his beautiful, pillow lips on hers. Her hands stayed by her side, her whole body rigid with a terrifying mix of thrill and fear. Marianne Tucker was nineteen years old and she'd never been kissed by a boy. Now she had a tongue darting into her mouth, running along the side of her gums, flicking against hers, and a strange sensation that seemed to be flooding her stomach and making her nipples harden against the cheap brown fabric of her uniform.

Suddenly, he pulled back, his eyes latched on to hers, his hand still woven into the back of her hair.

'You're gonna come with me Marianne.' It was a half question, half statement.

Slowly, hesitantly, Marianne Tucker nodded her head. And changed her life forever.

Sweet Lord, when would it be over? Colette counted the number of students in her row who were still to collect their graduation certificate. Another eight, including her. She instinctively felt a stare burning into the back of her head and turned to see Dale Lawson grinning behind her. She gave him a wink and turned back to face the front, relishing the little flutter of excitement in her chest. Dale and Mack had been her favourite discoveries of the last two years and her time at Conn Liberty High wouldn't have been half as much fun without them. Sure, she'd made friends among the girls too, but although she acted otherwise when she was with them, the truth was that they really didn't have too much in common. They were just too . . . *intense*. Too uptight. They were on a whole different wavelength that Colette just found exhausting and frankly didn't understand.

Kimmy and Cindi, her two closest girlfriends, could spend hours, no *days*, analysing the behaviour of their boyfriends or the guys they had the hots for. They'd talk until the end of time about a flirtatious discussion or kiss. And dear God the weekend that Cindi had finally let her boyfriend Colt have a feel of her bush would go down in history as the most hysterical event of all time. The tears, the recriminations, the declarations of love and then the overwrought regret when he didn't call her the next day . . . And although Colette had been appropriately sympathetic and supportive, she only got through the forty-eight-hour marathon of emotional hysteria by promising herself that as soon as she got home she'd roll the biggest joint since Woodstock, have a cold bottle of beer and then play something hot on her video recorder until she mellowed again. A music video she'd taped off MTV had restored her equilibrium – a new Australian band called INXS and their song 'Love is (What I Say)'. It wasn't the hard rock that she usually preferred, but she had never limited herself to only one genre and got off on the rush that came with discovering new bands. And besides, their lead singer was so damn sexy she could watch him all day.

Seven more to go now.

All eyes swung to watch the next candidate mount the side of the podium, causing the town mayor in the front row to veer swiftly to one side to avoid collision with the extravagant black hat of the woman next to him. Colette was thrilled that her mother had taken her advice and worn it – this whole repressed, conservative town needed a little bit of ridiculous now and then. Of course, no one would dare criticise her mother's choice to her face. Oh no. The same women who espoused sympathy for the tragic loss of the Belmont widow would haughtily pass comment behind her back, and the men . . . well, the men were too busy salivating to notice what was going on above eye level. With her patrician, Grace Kelly looks and her long limbed, beautifully postured frame, Darcy Belmont had always been the most stunning woman in any room. It was the happiest day of Darcy's life when she'd won Miss Tri-State South in 1965 at the age of nineteen. J.J. Belmont, the forty-eight-year-old, multi-millionaire land baron had been one of the judges, and within three hours of putting the crown on her head she was on his private jet and headed for the Bahamas. It could so easily have been just another young virgin for the legendary playboy to indoctrinate into the ways of the world, but a combination of a Presbyterian upbringing and a fair measure of intelligence had deemed otherwise. Darcy had played it perfectly. She'd wandered around in sheer chiffon sarongs. She'd worn nothing but the tiniest of bikini thongs and a lick of sunscreen. She'd been fun and beguiling and utterly adorable. But despite his efforts she had never let the man who was used to getting his own way get past a glancing brush of her nipple. Three weeks later they were married and ten months later Colette was born. Darcy's middle class parents had been ecstatic. J.J. Belmont was a pillar of the community, an illustrious businessman and thanks to his service in Vietnam (volunteered, not conscripted) he was an American hero. An American hero that had died of a massive heart attack while driving their fifteen-year-old daughter to the pony club three years ago.

Six more to go.

As was often the case, songs pushed any thoughts out of Colette's mind and Bruce Springsteen's rasping vocals were in her head now. As the opening line of 'I'm on Fire' consumed her the weight of the music slowed down her breathing and pulled her eyes closed. She'd never get bored with that song. She'd been playing it over and over now for months, letting the Boss's poetry speak to her, soothe her.

Five more to go.

Colette imperceptibly shifted her weight from one buttock to another. Shit, her ass and thighs felt like they'd been in a rodeo. Riding the Lawson twins the night before had been a better workout than three hours with those Jane Fonda tapes that everyone was talking about. Who needed leotards to feel the burn when you could have a red-hot night with two of the most gorgeous boys in the state? Apparently sex burned off five hundred calories an hour, so by rights doing it with twins should burn off double. The flutter of excitement was back, this time accompanied by a tightening in her groin – just thinking about those boys got her horny.

Four more to go.

Bruce was still singing to her, telling her that she was the only one he wanted. Wanted to see. Wanted to feel. Wanted to fuck.

Three more to go.

Springsteen would understand her plans. He knew about the small town upbringing. He knew about wanting to change the life you were born into. He knew that at the end of every day nothing mattered more than love and the sounds that were created by truly great musicians.

Persuading her mother had been tough at first. Years of conditioning had moulded Darcy's dreams for her daughter – university, European travel, a fine husband, a family. That was all she'd ever wanted for her little girl. But after months of fighting, friction and sulks, she had finally, reluctantly, conceded to her daughter's wishes. Colette didn't know why. She had no idea that one quiet Sunday morning Grey Masters, the ranch manager who had been with the family since he rolled up straight out of school twenty years before, had wisely pointed out to Darcy that she herself had lived in constraints her whole life. She had been held first in the suffocating bubble of the expectations of her parents, then in the suffocating bubble of J.J. Belmont's life, standing and reputation. He had told her that she had to let her girl run free, let her find her own way. And then he'd kissed Darcy and made love to her all over again.

Two more to go.

Cindi, Kimmy and the Lawson twins didn't need to know what was going on. She'd leave them a note. What was the point of discussing it? The emotional drama of it all would be just too tiresome for words. They'd try to change her mind, try to persuade her to join them at university or in internships, prisons of conformism and normality. Her mind's cassette ejected the current track and inserted another, the song that had inspired her, driven her to the point of such conviction that she knew, absolutely and without doubt, what she wanted to do with her life.

One more to go.

Suddenly, Jon Bon Jovi strutted into the camera in her imagination. The ass-kicking truth in the first verse of 'Runaway' kick-started the adrenalin that surged every time she reminded herself that her future was so close she could almost taste it. Or listen to it. Or screw it.

Ladies and gentlemen, Colette Belmont!

She turned the internal volume down and approached the stage, the claps of the townsfolk echoing her steps. Somehow she didn't think they'd be quite so enthusiastic if they realised that the reason she walked just a little slower than the other graduates was because of a three-way workout in the back of an Oldsmobile the night before. Her mother met her gaze and returned it with a smile of love and hope. Only the very perceptive would realise that it was also tinged with sadness. She mouthed a message that her daughter immediately understood.

'I love you, Coco'.

Tears of surprise sprung in Colette's eyes as she returned the gesture. 'I love you too, Mom,' she mimed gratefully, making all the elderly women in the audience well up and sigh wistfully. Taking the steps one by one, she mounted the stage and turned to face the audience, just as Jon turned the decibels up again and took it to a chorus that could have been written just for her.

Colette had been Daddy's little girl, but life had taught her a lesson. Now she was about to live up to the story in the song. Colette was going to be the runaway.

She bowed slightly to acknowledge the applause then scanned the room, taking in her friends, her teachers, her neighbours and her lovers.

And she hoped to God that she never saw any of them again.

FOUR

Rock–a–bye baby . . .

The tune kept playing for as long as she left the lid up on her music box. Every night she fell asleep to the sounds and then when she woke up in the morning it had stopped, the lid down, waiting silently until the darkness came and it could come to life again.

She pulled a hand out from under the pink blanket and pushed back the drapes that hung at the side of her bed. There were so many stars tonight and the moon was a full circle, like a round plate of shimmering gold or the locket that hung around Mama's neck. She'd asked her once what was inside, but Mama said that it was a secret. She didn't understand that. Didn't Mama also say that they should never keep secrets from each other?

Rock–a–bye baby . . .

She closed her eyes really tightly. It was time to go to sleep. Her head was getting heavy and Miss Molly, her favourite doll, had been sleeping snugly beside her for ages now.

Sleep. But . . .

Sleep.

Her eyes wanted to open but she wouldn't let them.

Sleep.

Because if she opened her eyes again, then it might come back and she had prayed and prayed and prayed that it wouldn't.

Rock-a-bye baby . . .

Because she didn't like it when the shadow came.

TRACK 2

FIVE

1987

Eyes wide with rage, spittle spraying from his mouth as he roared, he summoned the strength drawn from adrenalin and a dozen shots of cheap tequila to thrust the heavy steel ashtray down towards his fiancée's head. The roar picked up volume as a base-ball bat crashed down on his forearm a split second before he could deliver the blow, forcing the ashtray to change trajectory and ricochet off, causing a minor graze instead of a major con-cussion or worse. He hadn't even seen Lori coming. Her second hit, this one to his groin, elicited an even louder yell, and several sniggers from the onlookers who were prepared to witness the spectacle, but not to intervene. Hell, if they got involved in every fight at The Alehouse then they'd never be done scrapping.

'Jimmy, come pick up some trash from the front of the bar,' Lori shouted into her radio mic, straining to be heard over the sound of the music blaring from the four-piece country band on the small stage in the far corner of the room.

'Callie, come on down to the office and I'll patch up that head. Unless of course you want to press charges this time? Got plenty of witnesses – not that they're worth a sack of shit.' The spectators didn't even flinch at the insult, too busy knocking back another slug of beer and watching the bottle-blonde in front of them shaking her head in protest. Three years Callie Jones had been engaged to Billy Deaver and she'd lost count of the number of times a night had ended in pain, bruises or blood. But she loved her man. That's why the tattoo on her shoulder said *Callie and Billy Forever*. That's what was going to be, even if for ever meant taking monthly trips to the ER.

A small trickle of blood dripped onto her false eyelashes and she pulled up her red vest to wipe it away, giving everyone a flash of her sheer white bra. Modesty had never been high on Callie's agenda and that's why she was a firm favourite of most of the scum in town – another four or five drinks and she'd have been on top of the bar gyrating along to 'Sweet Home Alabama', the layers on her short little pink ruffle skirt swaying to give everyone below a real interesting view.

True to form, no one paid any attention to the drunken moans that were coming from the floor, just as no one stepped in to help as Billy was half carried, half dragged to the door by two large bald men wearing black T-shirts with SECURITY on the back.

'Thanks Lori, but I'm fine. I'll just get him on home and put him to bed. Sorry, hon.'

Lori shook her head and jumped back over to the other side of the bar, put the baseball bat back under the counter and served the next customer. Just another day in paradise. Over the two years that she'd been running the bar on her own she'd learned not to judge, condemn or get involved in the lives of her customers. Billy Deaver, presently holding his bruised balls in an alley, would sober up tomorrow morning, sheepishly wander in to apologise to her and then buy Callie whatever wilted flowers had been marked down to clear in the buckets outside 7-Eleven. She'd learned right from the start that barring them wasn't the answer – they'd just take their tempers and their violence somewhere else. At least here she could keep an eye on them and intervene before it all went too far. Jaded? Absolutely.

Scrupulous? Probably not. But then, morals were something that Lori had long learned she couldn't afford.

The bar was paying its way now. Those first few months after her father was put into the ground to rot had been hard-going as one by one she'd ejected the old clientele – the leeches who got tanked up on credit and thought they could settle their bills with welfare cheques that often didn't materialise. A hundred dollars in the hardware store had bought the russet paint that now covered the walls and the ebony varnish that concealed twenty years of grime on the floor. The toilets had been spruced up so they no longer smelled like hell's sewers and the wooden bar had been sanded down and re-painted. It would never be a class joint but it was clean and it was fit for purpose.

If only she could say the same for the customers.

The Alehouse attracted a younger crowd now, drawn in by the bands that played every night. The females were mostly under thirty, came in all shapes in sizes, and the only thing they had in common was a seemingly mutual devotion to wearing their Spandex dresses as tight, low and short as possible. Oh, and the hair. The smaller the dress, the bigger the hair – that was the law in Rackstown. The males that propped up the bar and surrounded the pool table weren't complaining. Tits, ass and music – it was more entertainment than the town had seen in decades.

Lori had put a poster up on the door advertising an open night for up-and-coming musicians and groups. The response had been slow at first but now she pretty much had an act on most nights, guys who played for free because it was cheaper than renting rehearsal space and it gave them the opportunity to reveal their musical brilliance to the world.

Most of them sucked.

The boys who were playing now were murdering Kenny Rogers' 'Tomb of the Unknown Love'. Sounded more like tomb of the unknown tune. Thankfully, the crowd were mostly too drunk to care, happy to just dig the beat while they concentrated on their crusade to get legless and laid.

As long as the money was coming in over the bar, Lori didn't mind. The three bar staff she'd recruited would need to be paid at the end of the night, as would the bouncers on the door. For the first year every penny of profit had gone to settling the debts and restoring credit with her suppliers, after that she'd finally started to see a small reward for working fourteen hours a day, seven days a week. Homeless since the bailiffs turned up at Jack's house barely a month after he died, she'd been living on a camp bed set up in the back office. Now she had enough money to convert the small loft upstairs. It had never been used for more than storage, but when she'd cleared it out and discovered an old rusty shower and toilet at the back, she'd realised that with a bit of work and the addition of a small electric stove, a fridge, some units and a bed, it was just about habitable.

She had a house, a truck and a job – but she didn't kid herself that this was any kind of life. That's why there was a long-term plan. The profits every month now were being tucked away and in another two years' time there should be enough to quit the lease on The Alehouse and set off for New York. That was as far as the plan had been developed – jobs, dreams and aspirations would come later because Lori knew that if she allowed herself to become too embroiled in the glorious details of the future, then she'd never be able to deal with rank monotony of the present. It was enough to believe in her heart that this was only temporary. There was another life out there for her and she'd get to it eventually, just as soon as she'd paid her dues.

Between customers, she realised that the country band – thank the Lord – were winding up now and the next act was about to take the stage. She didn't hold out much hope for this one either. The kid had appeared out of nowhere that afternoon, guitar in hand, and begged her for a slot that night. Usually she'd have fobbed him off with a Monday or a Tuesday when it was quieter and there were fewer people in the crowd to start throwing things if it got really bad, but the guy had been insistent and frankly she was too beat to argue. If nothing else, he'd please the girls in the audience. His long chestnut hair, huge hazel eyes and the muscular frame that was evident under the black skintight jeans and T-shirt would have them shaking their tits at the stage – a good voice and a decent song would be a bonus.

He plugged an electric guitar into the beat-up amp that was chained to the floor at the back of the stage and adjusted the microphone to his height. And then, without saying a word, his fingers started pounding out a hypnotic beat. It was a great choice. 'Addicted to Love' had been the biggest hit of the previous year and before he even got as far as the bridge, half the heads in the bar were nodding along with it, caught up in a collective rush that came from the down and dirty sex vibes of a great song.

Three and a half minutes later, Lori realised that not a drink had been ordered, not a fight had been started and not a female in the room wasn't imagining herself getting up close and orgasmic with the guy on the stage.

The chicks were starting to visibly sweat by the time he slid into the opening bars of U2's 'With or Without You', and when he added his low, haunting vocals even the drunkest, most abusive rednecks paid attention.

This guy – crap, what was his name again? – was good. In two years no one had ever grabbed and worked the crowd like this. Stu. Stan. Steve . . . Goosebumps rose on Lori's arms and she suddenly realised that she was grinning. And she never fucking grinned. Sly! It was Sly. Like the *Rocky* guy.

Sly . . . Lord, he could move as well. His hips undulated to the rhythm of the song, his wide shoulders counting out every beat of every line. Ramage. Ramses. Ram . . . Ramone! Sly Ramone.

However, Lori knew, instinctively knew, that for her he was called something altogether different – her passport out of Shitsville.

He had them and fuck, it felt good. Two years of travelling, going from town to town, bar to bar and every stain-crusted mattress in a cheap motel was worth it for this feeling. Time for another tempo change as he racked up the energy again with 'You Give Love a Bad Name'. The place was going wild, the atmosphere hot and thick with sweat as everyone jumped to the music, hands in the air, expressions exultant. It hadn't been like this in the beginning. Back then he'd played his own stuff, tunes he'd picked out on his strings in the afternoons and then tried out on late-night drinkers in late-night dives. Mostly they'd been too drunk or too jaded to care. Gradually over the months it had sunk in that when he played cover versions, people started to listen. Sure, his artistic satisfaction was suffocated under the weight of the hit-song-juggernaut, but it was worth it for the adulation, the buzz and the fifty dollars that the owners inevitably tossed his way at the end of the night.

Playing The Alehouse had happened more by accident than design. He'd had a two-week gig in a bar twenty miles away that had ended with him and Marny in the back of a van with two construction workers, some decent grass and a drive-through chicken bucket. Rule number one on the road: you had to take food, shelter and decent weed where you could find it. Unfortunately they lost all three the next morning when they woke up in Rackstown and were ejected because the workers needed the space for the load of timber they'd come to collect. He'd been pissed off, but as always Marny had taken the edge off his irritation. Looking back, almost dying in that dumpster had been one of life's little bonuses, because it had brought Marny to him and there wasn't a day that went by that he wasn't glad. When it came to the female species, she was the most extraordinary woman he had ever known. His mother, his sisters, Gloria – they'd all been strong, loud, dominant forces that commanded attention and doled out demands. It was their way or death by outrage. And the guilt . . . Jesus, he'd been made to feel guilty since he was born. Growing up, a smart-mouthed comment would result in the clutching of chests and wails of 'How can you do that to your mother?'

His resistance to being an altar boy? Oh dear God in heaven, what had they done to deserve such a son?

His love of loud rock? Did he have no consideration for other people? Had they not brought him up better than those long-haired imbeciles parading about, spreading promiscuity and filth?

The day that he'd announced he wanted to be a singer, his mother had screamed and put an immediate SOS out to God, the angels and Father Dominici. By the end of the night, the combined forces of heaven and earth had railroaded him back to an acceptable career. And once he'd got past the illicit gropes of her tits and the promise of sex in return for an engagement ring, he'd realised that Gloria was just a younger, prettier version of his mother – intent on dictating every move and controlling his life, doling out guilt and making him feel like a loser when he disappointed her.

Marny couldn't have been more different.

She let him breathe. She let him take charge. She never criticised, never judged or complained. She made him feel like he was the most interesting, talented man on earth. He adored her vulnerability, her sweetness, the way she demonstrated her faith and confidence in him by following his lead, no questions asked, even when they ended up getting kicked out of a van in the insalubrious surroundings of Rackstown.

Wandering down Main Street they'd stumbled across The Alehouse. Other bands on the circuit had talked about how the hot chick who owned it had it rocking at the weekends, with over two hundred people squeezed in on a good night. Apparently, the regulars were fierce, but the risk of assault by a flying object was worth it for the chance to play to a serious number of people.

They were right on both counts: the hot owner and the heaving mass of people that were staring at him right now, drinking in every sound and movement that he made. This was the best gig yet and he was in no rush to end it. Maybe he'd stick around here for a while longer. He'd promised Marny that they'd settle in one place for a while sometime soon, so maybe this could be it. They could get casual day jobs for a couple of months, play this gig, introduce a few of his own numbers, and build up a decent-sized following. With any luck the hot-chick owner would help out with finding somewhere to stay – just temporarily of course, because as he rocked the house with his cranked-up version of Van Halen's 'Why Can't This be Love', Sly closed his eyes, imagined that there were twenty thousand screaming bodies in front of him and swore to himself that he wouldn't stop until that was a reality.

Marianne was grateful for the raw, heaving, sweating crowd for one reason – it camouflaged the undeniable truth that she stank. It had been days since she'd had a shower – a hasty, danger-fraught affair in a Pittsburgh train station rest area, in a cubicle that still hosted the previous occupant's syringe and blood-soaked bandanna.

She swayed her hips and watched the man she loved doing what he did best. The familiar pride swelled and her adoration surged, but in moments of brutal self-honesty, she acknowledged that hidden among those feelings was a tiny bud of resentment and fear. Sly was hers but from the minute he stood on that stage she had to share him with everyone else, she had to watch as other women lusted after him, desired him, begged him for more than just another song. Most of the time she could just about handle it but on nights like tonight, when she was dirty, hungry and exhausted, she felt every word he sang just chip away at her soul. That guy up there was the public Sly Ramone, the one who was fearless and talented and hot. The one she slept beside every night was the real one. He was the guy she would listen to as he sang her a song he'd been working on all day or read her a poetic line that he'd come up with while they were making love. Being on the road, forcing his way towards success was Sly Ramone's dream – she'd known that from the start and she'd been prepared to follow him to every hick town and filthy train station to pursue it. And the only motivation she needed was the feeling of his lips on her neck and the sound of his voice whispering her name. Not Marianne – he hadn't called her that since the day they boarded the Greyhound out of Philadelphia. Marny. She was Marny Tucker now. And she fell more in love with the man on that stage with every passing day.

That's why, when most of the females in the room were saying a silent prayer that the guy at the microphone would undress them with his teeth, Marny was wishing for something entirely different – a home, a shower and a settled life with just her and her man. She didn't need to be with a star or a musical genius – Sly was already more than she could ever want. Her lips would never vocalise her true feelings, but her heart knew that she would be happy to give up on the music, settle down and live the rest of her life with just her, Sly and a family of Ramone juniors. A real family, a real home, a stable life of love and contentment – was it really too much to ask?

SIX

Crack. One. Two. Three. Four. Crack. One. Two. Three. Four. Crack.

Ari Covet liked to count the pauses in between the lashes. Crack. The anticipation of each beat heightened his excitement and kept his eight-inch dick harder than the marble pillar he was strapped to. Crack.

He felt the welts rise on his buttocks and the sensation made him whimper. He would have screamed but the gag that was slicing into his gums made that impossible.

'Do. Not. Make. A. Sound.' The voice behind him screamed. 'Do. You. Hear. Me. You. Pathetic. Piece. Of. Crap.'

Her command made him whimper even more. Yeah, she was good – this bitch was definitely worth the five hundred dollars an hour he was paying her.

Crack.

Tiny blood pools were forming on the floor now, dripping from his wounds, yet he felt no pain, only the ecstasy of the pure, raw sexual arousal that was reaching an almost unbearable level.

He sensed her approach him and then watched as she unbuckled the leather ties that imprisoned him, pulled him away from the pillar and then refastened the straps so that his hands were tied in front of him.

'Lie down,' she ordered. 'On your back.'

There was no need to tell him twice. He knew what was coming and squeezed his eyes shut as the sweet agony of it consumed him.

The black leather boots kicked his shackled hands above his head and then forced his legs apart. When he finally looked up it was to the most thrilling view of his life. She wasn't tall, but then what did height matter when she was built like a goddess, one that was wearing a black rubber cupless bra and matching crotchless panties. Oh, and the accessories that no decent dominatrix ever went to work without: a black leather cap and matching boots with six-inch steel heels. She was directly above him now, one foot on either side of his head, facing towards his feet, giving him a full view of her bare ass and the shaved lips that protruded from the crotch of her costume.

'It's time you gave me what I came for, isn't it, asshole?'

The whip was being used as a teasing prop now, and he groaned as she bent over and slowly trailed the leather tip of the hand grip up and down the shaft of his erect dick. 'You know what I want, you rancid freak, don't you?'

He nodded frantically and she rewarded his eagerness by pulling off the ball gag and tossing it to one side.

Holy fuck, he didn't know how much longer he could stand it, but he had to hold on, he had to wait for the . . .

Her knees bent as she started lowering herself so, so slowly, her snatch inching down towards his face while the handle continued to rub against him, still torturing his solid, purple dick.

'You're going to give it to me,' she demanded, as she lowered, closer now, the whip moving just a little faster. 'Give it to me now!'

No, not yet, just a little . . . just a little . . . Her moist, pink lips and that gorgeous ass were less than twelve inches from his face now.

Another second, another second until . . .

'NOW!' she screamed, at the very same second as he bit into the crevice at the top of her thigh, an act that caused him to explode and shoot his spunk high in the air. She fell to the side, one hand automatically going to the searing pain between her legs.

'Fuck, Ari,' she spluttered in outrage, 'did we not agree to stop with the biting! Honestly, a shrink would have a field day with you, ya twisted prick.'

His eyes blazed at the insult. He paid her good money to abuse him, but as soon as his spunk left his body he was back in charge and he wasn't going to listen to some jumped-up whore give her opinion of him or his sexual predispositions.

He slipped one hand out of the leather manacles and tore the gag off his mouth.

'I pay you to work, not to talk, so shut your face and get the fuck out of here.'

Mistress Damage scrambled to her feet and hissed as she strutted off to the guest bathroom to put her clothes back on. The anger didn't last for long. She had a standing arrangement with Ari: once a week, regular as clockwork, and he paid her four times the going rate for her time, her tolerance and her discretion. Secrecy was expensive in Hollywood and Ari Covet was prepared to pay.

Ari heard the guest door slam as he pulled on a black silk robe and went into his en suite to splash some water on his face. He'd shower later. The scent of sex would give him a semi for the next hour or so and he got off on making business calls with his penis large and throbbing against his stomach.

The cold water didn't refresh him, but the line of coke on top of his marble vanity unit certainly did.

The door at the opposite end of the john led to his office and Ari hit the speed-dial button as soon as he sat down. It was time to rouse the troops, all those parasite bastards that were taking his money every month and then claiming even more on bogus expenses and what did he get in return? Jackshit.

A&R they called themselves. Artists and repertoire. Well, they hadn't brought in any decent new artists and their repertoires weren't worth a damn. They were slipping, getting lazy, feeding off history.

He'd built AC Records from scratch and he'd made millions from finding the next big thing, the red-hot act that the world would adore and it was he who would incite them to transfer a large portion of their disposable wealth straight into his bank account. In the old days, he did the scouting himself, living in the underground clubs and pubs, chasing up any fledgling band that came on to his radar and nailing them long before the competition got so much as a sniff of their talents.

That was how he found both Decomp and Nuclear Fear, two of the biggest hard rock bands to hit the scene in the last ten years. They'd been bigger than Aerosmith, grossed more than Mötley Crüe at the ticket office, sold more albums than KISS, and both had imploded at the top in a rock 'n' roll suicide of heroine, coke and PCP. There were a whole lot of rehabs that owed their swelling balance sheets to the star-making powers of Ari Covet.

Fucking drugs – in the hands of musicians they were the worst enemy of commerce and profit.

The top drawer on the left-hand side of his mahogany desk slid open and he leaned into it, picked up the 24-carat gold straw and snorted another line, dabbing the residue on the square sheet of mirror adhered to the inside base of the drawer with his finger and rubbing it on his gums.

There were another dozen bands on the books that were doing well, in the black and making their keep, but it wasn't enough. AC Records needed their next megastar act, the one that would shoot into the stratosphere of fame and make them all a fortune.

Mercury Records had Bon Jovi and *Slippery When Wet* had been fucking huge for them last year. The smart bastard David Geffen had signed Guns N' Roses, the result of the merger between LA Guns and Hollywood Rose, two bands that Ari had told his A&R guys to keep their eye on. The useless cretins had watched them all right . . . all the way to Geffen's office. GN'R's album *Appetite for Destruction* had just been released and every fibre of his money-making gut told him it was going to be massive. Over at EMI, there were some punks with a fucking crazy name, the Red Hot Chili Peppers, who were set for greatness, despite the rumours that Kiedis and Slovak, their core guys, were on their way to becoming hardcore dope freaks. Those other dope freaks, Mötley Crüe, had put out *Girls, Girls, Girls* on Elektra. Meanwhile, Poison were building well over at Enigma and RATT were still doing a turn for Atlantic.

Covet didn't have a single act that was making waves in the genre and that made him want to spray down a shower of piss on the assholes who were supposed to be out there working for him.

'Yes, Mr Covet, how can I help you?' The orange button dialled straight through to Rita May Combs, his fifty-something secretary who had been with him from the start. People often wondered why she was still there; after all, middle-aged women were as rare as God-fearing virgins in the music business. The truth was that it suited Ari to keep one person near him that he didn't want to fuck – it kept the business flowing without all the emotional shit that invariably arose when hormones stopped and feelings started.

'Honey, get me the A&R guys, all of them, right now.'

There was a pause.

'Please,' he added. Rita was a stickler for manners and it amused him when she bust his balls.

Less than two minutes later his phone rang.

'They're on the line, Mr Covet.'

'Thank you Rita. OK, who've I got?'

They knew the drill and fired off their replies.

'Jeff Craney in New York, Mr Covet.' Sleek, seedy, lazier that a coyote in the afternoon sun.

'Bill Dyvor in Detroit.' Big on talk, short on delivery.

'Casey Alder in Memphis.' His only female and in a fight to

the death with the others he'd put his money on her coming out on top.

'Dan Temple in LA.' Too stoned to work, too stoned to care – one joint away from unemployment.

'Dave Lopez in Philadelphia.' New recruit. Brought on to focus on the Philly/New Jersey area. Jersey had already spawned Frank Sinatra, Dionne Warwick, The Four Seasons, Whitney Houston, Springsteen and Bon Jovi, so there was definitely something in the water out there.

'Anyone got anything for me?'

There was a burst of activity as they all started speaking at once.

'SHUT THE FUCK UP!' he roared. The line went silent. 'Let me rephrase that. I don't want to hear about "potential" or "vibes" or "hot tips". I want to know which one of you mother-fuckers has a sure-fire, guaranteed, stake-your-life-on-it act that is going to put you down in history as the genius that discovered the noise of the fucking decade.'

More silence.

'What the fuck am I paying you for? One month. One fuck-ing month and then I want to see you all in my office and every one of you assholes had better be clutching a tape that will give me a fucking hard-on. Is anyone under any confusion as to what that means?'

More silence.

'Good. Oh, and if any of you bastards dares to fly business class, it's getting docked out of your wages. Now fuck off, get off your asses and go do your jobs.'

He hung up before any of them had a chance to reply and sat back, his jaw set in a grimace. The blood was pounding through his head now and the emergency line of coke he snorted from his top right-hand drawer just made it even worse. Deep breath, deep breath. As he moved his head from side to side to stretch out the knots that had formed in his neck, his robe slid open to reveal a decidedly unimpressed organ. Shit, all that money and he was hanging like a gay in a chick's whorehouse.

He pressed another button on the phone and it was immediately answered by his houseman, Lenny.

'Len, has the hooker left yet?'

'No, Mr Covet, she's standing right here – I'm just settling your account.'

'Then sling her another five hundred and send her back upstairs.'

SEVEN

'Baby, if you'd have told me that we were coming this far out into the sticks, I'd have made sure I got good and oiled before we left.'

Dax Rice slid his hand up his girlfriend's thigh and under the silk of her thong. 'Honey, you're always good and you're always oiled,' he teased.

Coco laughed as she slapped his hand away. 'Keep your eyes on the road, you deviant, before you get us all killed. So how far have we got to go anyway?'

''Bout an hour. Rackstown, PA and I'm sure my hometown will be just thrilled to see ya,' his amusement clearly suggesting that the opposite was more likely true.

Coco shrugged and turned up the volume on ROCK fm. The year before she'd seen Van Halen live at the Nassau Coliseum in Uniondale, New York, their first tour since Sammy Hagar took over from Dave Lee Roth on lead vocals. Now Sammy was in the cab of their truck, filling it with the intoxicating sounds of 'Love Walks In'.

Out of the corner of her eye, she glanced at the man sitting next to her. A year now she and Dax had been together and he still turned her on every bit as much as the night they first met.

Back then, a relationship definitely hadn't been on her agenda.

She'd been living the single life in New York for a year and she'd loved every decadent, exhilarating, liberating minute of it. Her mother's monthly cheque was more than enough for a one-bedroom flat in Greenwich Village and she'd quickly become a familiar face on the scene, earning pin money that she didn't need by handing out flyers and putting up posters for new bands and club managers. Her allowance would have been enough to give her a comfortable existence, but she liked the thrill of being involved and enjoyed the connections and social life that it brought. Her old girlfriends at Conn Liberty High would have a stroke if they could see her friends now: an eclectic assortment of musicians, strippers, drag queens and artists, none of whom could hold down a 9–5 job if their life depended on it. Coco loved every one of them. Gone was any attempt to conform to the life or appearance her privileged upbringing demanded. Her hair was a wild mane of excess, teased, curled and sprayed into the size of a large bush. The eyeliner was thick, the pout glossy and anything more than a sparkly bra, matching shorts and sui-cidal heels was considered overdressed.

The rejection of her old identity was complete when she inherited her new title from an outrageous black ladyboy who decided to change his stage name from LaBiba to Sheedy in trib-ute to his ultimate goddess from *The Breakfast Club*. As they celebrated his new moniker with bourbon and Cokes, Coco decided it would be a blast to take on the old one.

So it was Coco LaBiba who had been cruising around the East Village, dropping into her regular haunts and riding on the vibe of her neighbourhood, when she had walked into The Eastside, a cool little club that had an open mic on Friday nights for rock and metal bands. The words spray-painted on the drum kit announced that these guys were called 'The Steel Spikes'. Cool name. Most eyes in the room were on Cami Steed, the lead singer, a muscular white dude with waist-length wiry platinum hair, prancing across the stage in nothing but a pair of denim cut-off shorts, but Coco's gaze had immediately been drawn to the guy on lead guitar. While the other members of the band were giving out high energy and playing to the crowd, Dax Rice was down on his knees, eyes closed, stretched back like a viper about to pounce on its prey, completely and utterly inhabiting another world where only he and his guitar existed. Coco felt the familiar rush as every chord reached into her, setting her nerve endings on fire and causing that swell of hormones that invariably ended in a long night in a strange bed.

At the end of the hour-long set, Coco had taken Dax back to her apartment and, almost twelve months later, he still hadn't left. And neither had most of his bandmates. Yep, Coco's one-bedroom, quaint Village apartment was home to an heiress from Connecticut and a motley collection of mongrels called Dax, Spank, Tye, Strings and Muff. They lived as a collective, throwbacks to the sixties ethos of free love and communal possessions and that heiress from Connecticut loved every caring, sharing minute of it.

She loved Dax most of all. Every inch of his body was dark and chiselled, his incredible physique a testimony to a Native American heritage that his white mother had never elaborated on in the dilapidated Rackstown clapboard house he grew up in.

But the attraction was more than that. Sure, he was a wild boy, but he had an inner calm, a quite confidence that came from an almost spiritual sense of who he was. He treated everyone fairly, never bitched, never sweated the dramas. Growing up, his mother has supported them by singing in lounge bars in hotels all over the state, her sleeping son looked after by a grandfather who would wake him in the mornings by strumming softly on a beat-up guitar he'd bought at a flea market a dozen years before. His whole life had been set to music, so his career choice had been obvious, and anyone who watched him could see that he didn't play for the money or the adulation, Dax played because music was part of his soul.

'Hey Coco, are we nearly there yet?' The voice came from behind the curtain that separated the cab at the front from the body of the van. Coco giggled as she spun round on to her knees and pushed it to one side, immediately encountering a wave of dope fumes. 'What am I, your mother?' she laughed, tossing an empty can of Coke in the direction of Muff. 'Baby, you can be my mama anytime,' he sang in reply.

'Yeah, and your daddy will kick your ass,' Dax jumped in, faking fury and causing the rest of the group to break into peals of laughter.

Coco turned back to the front and giggled as she ruffled her boyfriend's jet-black hair. 'Ooooooh, hello Mr Protective. You're a year too late, but nice to see you anyway.'

Dax grinned. He couldn't get enough of this chick. She was the most uncomplicated, open, funny, wild, life-embracing girl he'd ever met. He was entirely convinced that she was a woman born after her time. Coco lived by the ethos of the flower power generation – free love and plenty of it. He could do exactly as he pleased and so could she, and as long as they came back to each other at the end of the night then that was just fine. Relationships didn't get any better than that.

'So what about this woman we're going to meet then – have I got a rival?' Coco teased, loving the way that his deep brown eyes burned with intensity on a permanent basis. Shit, he was fine.

Dax shook his head. 'No way man, Lori's not that kinda deal. She owns a bar; let us play there whenever we wanted last year, helped us get our shit together. Says she's managing a new singer now that needs a band . . . we're just checking him out.'

A surge of hope tingled in Coco's stomach. The band had been looking for a new lead since Cami got himself strung out on angel dust, arrested and committed to Bellevue Hospital for the third time in five years. They didn't reckon he'd be joining them again any time soon.

Night was falling when Dax pulled the truck into a parking

space outside a bar with a neon sign above it announcing it was 'The Alehouse'. There was a long queue outside and from the noise levels it was pretty obvious that the inside was already jumping. Security waved them through with handshakes and nods, causing a barrage of objections from the bodies on the street. Dax gave them the finger and moved on in.

Coco laughed as she took in the chaos. 'I tell you, this guy had better be something special because there's every chance we're going to get killed before we leave here.'

An Amazonian female, a formidable sight in her black leather cowboy boots, greeted them as the band on stage bid the audience goodbye. 'Hey Dax, thanks for coming,' she said, giving him a friendly punch on the side of the arm. 'I'll shout up some drinks for you and the guys.'

'No problem Lori. Good to see ya.'

'And you. He's just setting up now . . .'

Coco turned to face the direction of Lori's nod. Well, the guy definitely had the right look: the long hair, the beat-up black leathers, the black vest and the biker's cap was a cool touch. But the look was just part of it – the most important thing was the voice and if he didn't have that then this was going nowhere.

She watched him as he threw his guitar strap over his head and winked at a pretty-looking blonde at the side of the stage who seemed to blush under the spotlight.

'I'm gonna start with something a little slower tonight – just to get all you guys in the mood.'

The crowd roared in response. Shit, he had them in the palm of his hand already. Sure he was cute, but what did he have that could turn a whole room of small-town rednecks into a heaving mass of adoration?

The first note made the hairs on the back of her neck stand up. After four chord changes tears sprang into her eyes. When he started to sing, there was no one else in the room – not a single other person existed or mattered other than her and the man on that stage, because he was singing to her. He was doing a breathtaking cover of 'I'm on Fire' and, like Bruce, he was saying that every beat of desire was for her only.

Colette Belmont was the past, Coco LaBiba was the present, and right then she realised that the singer piercing her heart with his voice was her future.

'S'cuse me, I'm looking for Lori.'

'You found her.' A few things struck Lori as strange. One: she'd never seen this guy before in her life. Two: his suit and tie, admittedly a little dishevelled, were completely out of place in a bar full of blue jeans and T-shirts. And three: he was the only one in the room who wasn't caught up and transfixed on Sly Ramone's performance. If this was some debt collector from the beer supplier, she'd kick his ass all the way down Main Street because she knew for sure that she'd sent their cheque off weeks ago.

'Dave Lopez. I'm in A&R for AC Records. That means . . .'

'I know what that means.' Neither her voice nor her expression conveyed the sheer fucking exaltation she was feeling inside. Yes! She'd sent demo tapes to every record company official on the Eastern seaboard and she'd heard nothing back from anyone. Until now . . .

'So you manage him?'

'Yep.' Still stone, still not giving him even a glimmer of interest.

'He's incredible.'

'I know.'

'Name's a bit of a cliché, though – inspired by the Ramones?'

'Nope, it's his real name.'

'No shit! That's genius, man. Anyway, I think we should talk.'

'So talk.'

Dave Lopez was beginning to feel decidedly uneasy about this one. This wasn't the usual response that he elicited from bands and managers. Usually they'd be falling over themselves, gushing pathetically in excitement and desperation.

'I think he's got huge potential and I want to hear more. Not sure about the solo thing though . . . Is he always a one-man gig or does he have a band?'

Lori flicked her gaze over to where Dax and his crew were standing, every one of them transfixed on the stage, entranced in the music, and shit, the stunning half-naked chick with them had been crying for the last hour.

'Yeah,' she told him, relishing the thrill of a good plan coming together, 'He's got a band.'

'Then I think we need to make some arrangements. Because there's a man in LA that I want you to meet.'

EIGHT

Marny's breath deepened, coming in short, rapid rasps now, as her nails dug so deeply into Sly's flesh that his jaw clenched to stop him screaming out loud.

'*Ladies and gentlemen, the captain has now switched off the seatbelt signs . . .*' announced a voice from God knows where. Marny fixed her stare on the woman in front of her, watching as her perfectly painted lips widened to a grin as she spoke to her colleague. How did women get to be that glamorous? The glossy black hair tied back in a chignon, the flawless honey complexion, the perfect white teeth that glistened in the dim light. Watching her was almost enough to take her mind off the . . . oh dear Lord, what was that?

'For fuck's sake, Marny, you're going to scar me for life. Chill, baby girl. It's just a bit bumpy 'cos we're going through the clouds.'

Looking down at his hand she realised that this time she'd drawn blood, tiny rivulets of red running down the side of his hand and on to the navy plastic top of the armrest.

'Hot towel madam?'

The beautiful one was standing next to her now, balancing a

tray of white rolls of fabric on one hand and clutching a pair of metal tongs in the other.

She had no idea how to answer. A hot towel for . . .? What? A red flush of embarrassment crept up from the neck of her T-shirt and she squirmed uncomfortably as Sly leaned over and took two towels and then dropped one in her lap. How did he know what to do? He'd never been on an airplane before either but as always he was just rolling, just going with the flow while she oscillated somewhere between terror and mortification.

Why was she doing this? The hot breath followed by a nuzzle to the side of her face as he gave her a reassuring kiss reminded her why as a wave of love surged through every pore. He was everything. It was that simple.

There had been very few moments in the last fortnight that she hadn't had a churning, sick feeling in her stomach, but Sly's constant presence made all these new experiences – the crippling shyness in the face of all these strangers, the worry that she was saying the wrong thing, doing the wrong thing – Sly made it all worthwhile.

'*Good morning, this is Captain Will McKenzie, welcome to flight 2323 to Los Angeles.*'

Her hands shot to the armrest again, sending the white towel flying to the floor. The beautiful one quickly bent down and picked it up with a sympathetic smile in her direction.

The red flush covered her face now, deepening as embarrassment and self-consciousness replaced the fear. She shouldn't be here. Someone like that air hostess should be sitting next to Sly Ramone, someone beautiful, cool, calm. That's who he deserved and that – she was sure – was who he would end up with. After all, what did she have to offer him? Just a whole heap of insecurities and he could definitely live without that. For the first time in her life she had someone who cared, a real relationship, and now she understood what it was to love someone, to have another person there to share the days with. It was almost like all the crap, all the pain that she had gone through, living a life with no family, no love, had been the price she'd had to pay to appreciate how incredible being with Sly was. And now she was terrified that she was going to lose it. Sure, he pretended like he loved her but she knew it wouldn't last. Nothing ever lasted. Why would he stay with her when there were so many other . . .

'Whoa, sorry sweetie!' Coco giggled as she swayed so wildly in the aisle that she almost landed in Marny's lap. Standing behind her, Dax snatched her back just in time before she body-surfed the entire row – something that might not be a problem for Marny or Sly, but may have upset the suited, stone-faced businessman pretending he was absorbed in a crossword in the window seat.

Another ping took Marny's attention back to the panel of lights above her head.

'Ladies and gentlemen,' announced the female voice, 'The captain has switched off the no smoking signs. Please note that smoking is only permitted in rows 18–32 and is strictly forbidden in the aisles and the toilets. Thank you.'

The cheer from the rows across from her was raucous and punctuated by the sound of four Zippo lighters flicking in perfect synchronisation. Despite Marny's anxiety, a tiny wedge of amusement permeated her tension as she watched the remaining four members of the Spikes take deep, desperate puffs on their cigarettes, therefore fulfilling what she'd learned was half of their dietary requirements for the day. Spank, Tye, Muff – nope, hang on, that one wasn't Muff, that was Strings – Muff was the one sitting behind, next to the seats vacated by Coco and Dax. It was easy to confuse them – twins with identical red hair that reached their shoulder blades and was as wide as it was long, shooting out from their scalps like flames suspended in mid-air. The airport security guard who had checked their bags before boarding, a middle-aged guy with the flat-top and demeanour of ex-military, had made a point of holding up the three large cans of hairspray that he'd pulled from their bag and gesturing disapprovingly. If he was looking for a reaction from the guys then he must have been disappointed because they both just laughed and shrugged. 'You should try some, dude,' Strings told him in a lazy, gravelly slur. 'The chicks really dig it.'

Sadly, the security guard didn't dig them and the result was rubber-clad fingers inserted into orifices that were not necessarily in the mood to party. It had been two unusually subdued guys who'd taken their seats ten minutes after everyone else, but they seemed to have made a recovery, aided by the bottle of Jack they'd taken from Coco's bag and had been surreptitiously slugging back since the plane doors shut. That was the second component of their daily diet. No wonder they all – with the exception of the ultra-toned gym freak Dax – looked like they were on the sick side of skinny.

These guys were like no one Marny had ever met. Muff and Strings were so laidback they were almost horizontal. Literally. They smoked so much weed that getting them to a standing position was sometimes a challenge, one that was invariably conquered by Dax kicking them in the ass until they were roused from their stupors and picked up their guitars – Strings on a twelve-string rhythm and Muff on bass. Tye was the drummer, an overexcited, hyper guy with a Hendrix afro who banged on anything he could touch: tables, bar tops, and the current surface of choice, an airplane fold-down table. Spank was different and the hairs on the back of Marny's neck stood up just looking at him. He was . . . dark. Foreboding. Quieter than the others, he rarely spoke, and made eye contact even less. While she'd watched the rest of the band on stage in their cut-off vests and then – when they were into the set – naked from the waist up, Spank was covered from neck to toe: jeans, messed-up biker boots, long-sleeved T-shirt, his sallow face and jet eyes almost completely concealed under the black fedora that he never took off. The only part of him that was clearly visible was his hands and they made Marny's skin crawl. As he picked out the music on his keyboard she'd stared, transfixed, as the blood seeped from the dozens of scars and scratches that covered the back of each hand. The events of her life had made her ultra-sensitive to picking up danger vibes and when this guy was around her alarm bells went off like a liquor store during a looting spree.

He scared her. This whole scene scared her. Two weeks ago it was just her and Sly, moving around, making music, making love, getting by. Now they were a collective, multiples of dysfunction welded together, motivated by the words of the A&R guy from the record company. He said he was going to take them to LA and make them stars. It was the moment Sly had been dreaming of since he was a kid and Marny knew better than to argue, object or reveal that she didn't want to go.

Because she didn't want to find out whether Sly would choose opportunity or love.

Sly hadn't been sure at first. That night in Rackstown, he hadn't even met these guys and the bar-owner chick was already presenting them to the record company dude as a band. But that changed when they'd met again at The Alehouse the following morning, walked through the vomit and piss of the night before and jumped on to the stage. Dax had pulled a gleaming Les Paul from the hard black case beside him, strapped up and immediately launched into the opening solo from the Scorpions' 'Rock You Like a Hurricane'. And man, he rocked it – no drama, no antics, nothing – he just stood there and let the strings sing and by the end of it Sly knew that while he might have the voice and he might be hot on lyrics, neither he nor anyone he knew could touch this guy on lead. Dax was Sambora to his JBJ, Slash to his Axl. He nailed it and Sly knew right there that it was going to work. They'd jammed the rest of the day – played around with some Cheap Trick, New York Dolls, Bowie, Hanoi Rocks, Aerosmith and it just worked. It was only at the end of the session he realised that his beat-up Starburst was still in its bag and he'd decided that when it came to performing it would stay there. Dax played guitar, Sly sang, the other guys provided the rest and together it was fucking genius. Like it was pre-ordained by God.

'So are we doing this?' Lori had asked as night fell and she got ready to open.

Sly looked over at Dax, naked now except for a pair of denim cut-offs and a bandanna around his head. He saw his decision mirrored there.

'Yeah, man, we're doing it.'

He knew it was going to be one of the most important partnerships of his life.

Much as he adored the girl who had sat in the corner watching him all day, it hadn't even occurred to him to ask what Marny thought.

'Wider baby, oh yeah, that's it, give your pussy to Daddy . . .' Dax slammed into Coco and laughed as a crack started in one corner of the mirror behind her and with every thrust worked its way further across until there was a diagonal gash running from top to bottom. Coco didn't see it or care. She was right where she wanted to be – sitting on the metal sink of an airplane toilet with Dax's dick inside her, her legs stretched up over his shoulders, her feet touching the wall behind him, forcing her to tilt her pelvis upwards so that every thrust felt like it was going to split her in two. She put her hands out at each side of her, pressing against the other walls of the john, then gasped as he grabbed her nipples, bent down to take one into his mouth and bit so hard that the pain made tears spring to the back of her eyes. It was all she needed to come, hard, fast, and gripping his dick like a vice until he had no choice but to shoot inside her.

'Welcome to the mile high club baby,' she purred, as he licked a line of sweat all the way from her neck up to her forehead then flopped his head down on to her shoulder.

'I love you Coco,' he murmured. 'And you are the hottest fucking chick I've ever met.'

'Yes I am,' she said with a smile, 'and don't you forget it when all those LA girls are throwing themselves at you. Just remember who you're coming home to, lover boy.'

'Always,' he replied, his voice thick with emotion as he whispered the promise they'd repeated to each other daily since their first meeting.

'Always,' she whispered, re-confirming her side of the agreement.

Her relationship with Dax was a forever thing and she knew it. It transcended sex, fidelity and restrictions and all the other bullshit that normal people lived by. They were free spirits but two halves of the same soul, one that could never be broken no matter what other stuff got in the way.

However that didn't mean that a girl couldn't look, couldn't touch, couldn't get off on someone else. God had blessed her with an insatiable sex drive that was fuelled by three things: music, excitement and danger. Music had been part of her life since she was old enough to slip 45s on the record player that her daddy had bought her for her fifth birthday. Surrounded by adults, protected by security and the barriers of wealth, sometimes rendered lonely by the intense, almost obsessive adoration that her parents had for each other, her record player had become her best friend, her entertainment and her soother. As she got older, it taught her about love, about connecting to the beat, about letting a rhythm dictate her mood and take her to somewhere unrestrained by her name or environment.

And when she hit her mid-teens, it taught her about sex. About excitement. About danger. Now, the combination of all three was enough to keep her aroused long after other females had feigned a headache and rolled over to sleep. For her, sex was all about those exquisite physical sensations, nothing to do with love or relationships. The lessons she'd learned in her bedroom from guys with long hair and pounding tunes had taught her that sex and love were not connected in any way, and that day, that horrible fucking day that she'd watched her daddy die had been a tutorial she would never forget.

But this wasn't the time to go there. Her father was gone and Coco LaBiba didn't look back, especially to events that she'd long ago chosen to forget. She lived in the present. Hendrix had his guitar, Lennon had his lyrics, Coco had sex. And it was an activity that was best enjoyed when set against the screech of a guitar or the screams of a shit-hot vocalist.

Sly Ramone.

His face came into her mind and immediately her nipples hardened again. That boy could sing like no one she'd ever heard and just thinking about him made her juices start to flow again. She knew she had to fuck him and she would, just as soon as she'd sussed out the scene with his girlfriend. So far she was getting the vibe that they were tight and not looking elsewhere. Understandable. She'd only known Marny a couple of weeks but she liked her; she was sweet, shy. They'd chatted a bit, shared some make-up, swapped stories while the guys jammed. One of these days she'd ask her how she felt about sharing Sly – nothing heavy, nothing personal.

'I need some Jack,' Dax announced, pulling his flaccid penis out of her and lowering her legs off his shoulders. Sinking her ass further into the sink she turned on the tap and watched as a pool of cold water seeped up to wash her pussy. It should have been enough to cool her down but the image of Sly Ramone was still in her head and her clit was throbbing.

'Aw, baby . . .' she tugged at his hair and pouted, landing a kiss on his lips. 'One more time.'

His laugh reverberated off the walls. 'Later, babe. Let me get some Jack and . . .'

Not good enough. Her head was already shaking from side to side. She needed to get off again and she needed to do it now. And that meant that there was no other option than to go to their occasional fall-back strategy.

Opening her legs wide again, she took a breast in each hand and began to massage them, alternating slow circles of each nipple with the tight pinches that never failed to make her clit throb even harder.

She needed to come again and if Dax wasn't up for it then hey, it was time for another member of the band to join the mile high club.

'OK, my love but as soon as you get back to your seat, send Muff up here.'

There was a reason he got his name. Looks had never been the twins' strong point in school, so while Strings had concentrated on perfecting his musical talent, Muff had worked hard on developing other skills to compensate. As a result, he gave the best head she had ever experienced.

Slipping his cock back in his pants, Dax responded to her order with a knowing grin.

'Tell him to hurry, babe,' Coco added, slipping a finger down between the lips of her pussy.

'We don't want his breakfast to get cold.'

Lori didn't give a damn. She pressed the button on the armrest of her chair and pushed it back as far as it would go, choosing to ignore the indignant tuts and sighs from the fat, florid-faced guy in the cheap suit behind her. Nope, she didn't give a damn. She'd watched as Dax and his . . . his . . . what would you call her? Girlfriend? Partner? Slut? Anyway, she'd watched as they'd sneaked into the bathroom, she'd heard him screw her all the way across a state line, she'd seen him leave and then observed as the bass player replaced him. And nope, she didn't care. Whatever got them through the day. She wouldn't have batted an eyelid if the passengers in the entire three rows that seated her new discoveries stood up, stripped off and copulated all the way to California. All that mattered was that she'd found them, she knew they were the real deal and they were going to change her life. This was the opportunity she'd dreamt about all those years growing up slaving in a cesspit with an absent mother and a cruel, sick fuck for a father and she wasn't going to pass it up. Failure, doubt, worry didn't come into the equation.

At least, not for her . . .

Out of the corner of her eye, she noticed that Lopez, the

A&R guy sitting beside her, was staring at the washroom door, his face a little flushed, his expression nervous. Maybe Dax's lady friend could do him too to take the edge off. The guy was so uptight in his button-down shirt, pencil-thin tie and crumpled suit – not the kind of gear you'd expect a twenty-something music scout to be wearing. He looked like the fifth Beatle, the one that got screwed over and left to pay the cab fare after the others had taken a ride to world domination.

Taking a deep breath, she rejoiced in the sensation of the air she inhaled. It might be filtered, it might be thick with bacteria spewed from the lungs of everyone around her, but it didn't stink of the shit and sweat of the scum that populated The Alehouse. It hadn't been hard to extricate herself from her tarnished inheritance. Sheriff Donnachy had suggested that a cousin called Slick, who had spent ten years running a nightclub in Philly and had returned to Rackstown, could manage it for her until the six-month notice period on the lease expired. She'd thought he'd take one look at the place and bolt back to Philly but luckily, on the two nights that Slick had come to check The Alehouse out big football games on the TV had kept most of their regulars away. Slick would find out the truth soon enough but by that time she'd be on the other side of the country. There was no doubt he'd be disgusted, annoyed and would rob the till blind, but she didn't care. She had no intention of returning to that hellhole anytime soon, if ever. The Steel Spikes were the future, the fifth Beatle would lead them to it and on the way the band and their hangers-on could do whatever they wanted as long as it didn't interfere with her plans.

Lori didn't give a damn. She stared at the clouds, sending out a silent prayer to the usual destination. 'Help me, Mama – help me make this work.'

It was a superficial gesture, because Lori knew damn well that this was her only chance and there was no point turning to anyone but herself to make this work. So no more. She decided there and then that this was the last time she'd even think about her mother or the past. From now on, it was all about the future and it was all down to her. She was going to learn this business and do it fast, and she wasn't going to let doubt, fear, inexperience or other people bring her down. This was her game and she was going to play it her way – and she'd shown before what happened to anyone who tried to stand in her way.

Lopez was trying his best not to look shocked but he had a horrible feeling he wasn't succeeding. It was 9am, and already these guys were tanked up and partying. In fact, he was pretty sure that they just hadn't stopped partying from the night before. He'd been in the music business for exactly 121 days, having gone via accountancy school to keep his mother happy and the college football team to please his dad. Unfortunately his move into the music business had disappointed them both. He wasn't too bothered. When it came to occupations that allowed him to listen to music all day while smoking his way through one or two of his favourite herbal roll-ups, it was either the music business or serving cold drinks from a shack on the beach. As far as he was concerned, he'd made the most sensible choice – and he had complete faith that he could make something of it.

A two-year fling with a British psyche major had instilled in him a true appreciation of the Stones, the Beatles and the legions of bands their legacy had spawned. Now his taste in music was truly eclectic; he listened to Whitney, loved Robert Palmer, the Eurythmics, Bryan Adams, George Michael, Heart and Madonna and every night he went to bed wondering if the next day was going to be the day that he discovered the next pop sensation. In fact, the only genre that left him cold was the heavy rock scene. All that had changed when he'd listened to the cassette that sent him to Rackstown, PA. Beginner's luck? Absolutely. In fact, he wasn't even sure whether the brilliance that his gut told him was there really did exist until, with some trepidation, he'd couriered the demos and some photographs to Mr Covet and received a phone call that night ordering him to get them on a plane to LA immediately. Oh, and the cost of the courier was coming out of his wages – apparently the US airmail service would have been sufficient.

The thrill of having his instincts confirmed had even surpassed the trepidation at entering the lair of Ari Covet. OK, maybe not completely – the very prospect made his mouth dry and his sphincter contract, but he was trying to dwell on the positives. If The Steel Spikes made it big, he'd go down in history as the guy who discovered them. Yeah! That felt great. 121 days of slog and already he might have made the discovery of his career – how lucky (or talented) was that? Almost made up for the fact that this was a beast he had some serious anxiety about unleashing.

His eyes darted to the air hostess who was now passing him with a pot of coffee and a little tray containing milk and sugar portions. Ever the professional, she didn't even pause when a low, indisputably sexual moan could clearly be heard coming from the direction of the door across the aisle from his seat. The lead guitar player and his girlfriend had gone in there as soon as they'd got into the air and there was no mistaking what they were doing. Not that he was jealous or anything. OK, well maybe just a little. That Coco was the most beautiful girl he had ever seen. Movie stars didn't even come that perfect. From the thick mane of dark blonde hair to the incredible body . . . put it this way, if he ever had a girlfriend like that he'd want to make love to her in airplane toilets too.

But that wasn't the point. The fooling around and the drinking and the drugs he'd seen them smoking he could just about handle. After all, he'd puffed marijuana every day since his babysitter rolled him a spliff when he was twelve. But come on, was he imagining it or had Muff now taken over where his mate had left off? Shit, that was so sick. Like, seriously twisted.

The stories about the rank decadence and debauchery that went hand in tattooed hand with the rock scene had been doing the rounds for years. The Stones built legends on that kind of behaviour. Ozzy Osbourne's antics crossed the line between wildness and insanity. The guys from Aerosmith had gone about as low as it was possible to go. Truthfully, though, he'd thought that there were as many urban myths as there were exaggerated claims of hedonism. But now . . . now he was feeling the heat and just trying not to look like the shocked, small-town guy from Milford, New Jersey, that he really was. Nonchalant, that's how he had to act. If he wanted to attain any level of credibility he had to act completely indifferent to anything that these guys got up to.

Waaaa. Waaaa. Waaaa. Waaaa.

Dave shot bolt upright and frantically scanned the cabin to find the source of the screaming alarm. Crap, they were going down! Where were the oxygen masks? Where were the life jackets? Shit, what had they said in the safety briefing? He'd been too engrossed in *Rolling Stone* to pay attention.

Waaaa. Waaaa. Waaaa. Waaaa.

WHERE THE HELL WERE THE AIR CREW?

Waaaa. Waaaa. Waaaa. Waaaa.

He grabbed the nearest arm for support, not caring that it was attached to Lori, the woman whom he'd already realised was tougher that the collective might of the Eagles' defensive line. She was kind enough not to look too disgusted, but neither did she look in any way concerned. 121 days and he was going to die before anyone even knew about his new discoveries – they'd just be names on a passenger list of the deceased.

Just as the amount of oxygen his ribcage would allow into his lungs was plummeting to a level that could cause him to faint at any moment, the gorgeous air hostess with the tight skirt made a reappearance and strode towards him, her standard American Airlines smile momentarily replaced with an expression that was more akin to acute irritation.

Her heels made a sudden stop when they reached his row, allowing her to flick a switch on the toilet door, then bang it in the centre, causing it to fold open in one swift action.

It was then that he noticed the small green light flashing above the cubicle, and the sign beside it saying, 'In the interests of passenger safety, these toilets are fitted with a smoke alarm.' The air hostess took one step to the side, allowing everyone a clear view of a (thankfully) fully dressed Coco, a large cloud of smoke and a bewildered Muff, both of them clutching Camel Lights.

'Hey man,' Muff muttered from beneath his shock of red hair (that had somehow escaped being ignited by either one of two cigarettes in a three-foot by two-foot space). 'Can't a guy even have a smoke after getting off any more?'

To the sound of roaring applause and a drum roll played out with stamping feet, Coco and Muff returned to their seats and Dave watched as Dax reached up and ruffled Coco's hair.

'That's my girl,' he announced with a grin.

She dropped down on to his lap, flicked back those stunning waves of spun gold and kissed him with very obvious tongue action.

As he fought to restore his pulse to anything near normal, Dave Lopez realised he had a long way to go before he would ever manage to pull off nonchalance in the face of the mayhem that came free of charge with The Steel Spikes.

NINE

It wasn't often that Ari Covet got a hard-on without paying for
it but this was one of those rare occasions. There had been a definite tingling in his loins when he'd listened to the tape that had
saved Lopez's ass from the welfare queue. He hadn't heard vocals
like that since . . . shit, never. This guy could snap from a low
range that was almost guttural to a pitch that sounded like Vince
Neil with his balls in a vice and he could do it without slipping
even a fraction off key. It was almost like listening to a synthesiser
but it was real and raw and fuck, he'd graduated to a semi now.
The final steps to the boner of the week came from the second
tape (hastily recorded a few days ago somewhere south of
Hicksville) that had put those vocals over a band with a guitar
player that was insane, a rhythm section that kicked ass and a
drumbeat that pulled the whole thing together. And the material
was nothing short of dynamite. There were four songs on the
tape – a cover version of Van Halen's 'Panama', two original
amp-busting anthems that he could already hear being sung by
80,000 kids in a stadium and one low, husky ballad that would
have the girls coming in the aisles. This band could write and
they could play and it didn't get any better than that. The result

was a musical hard-on that he'd only felt twice in his career – once with Decomp, once with Nuclear Fear, two bands that went on to be his label's biggest hits and who were in the top five earners in rock over the last decade. Until, that is, those old favourites – ego, women and drugs – had combined to give them new awards for being two of the biggest fuck-ups in rock over the last decade.

That had been nothing to do with him though. He was a star maker and he'd been in the business long enough to know when the slots were about to hit jackpot and that time was now – he just had to make sure that he got these guys before anyone else.

Swinging his chair around, he stared for a few moments at the view. His building was in one of the best spots on Wilshire, with CAA directly across the street, ICM a few hundred yards away, Trader Vic's diagonally to his right. From his office on the thirty-ninth floor he had a 180 degree vista of Los Angeles and on a clear day like today could see all the way down to LAX. That was the direction he was looking in now. Lopez was flying them in and they'd be here within the hour. Barring any major problems, and it would have to be real serious – earthquake, sudden death, Martian fucking invasion – he wanted them signed before the day was out. He'd already had his lawyers draw up the contracts – a few thousand upfront to keep them sweet, a ten-year lock in, publishing rights sewn up and a royalty rate that was just below the market standard. What would they know? They'd just been plucked from obscurity and been offered the biggest chance of their lives and he, Ari Covet, was the man who was giving it to them. According to Lopez, they were being managed by some bar owner from Hicksville. Weren't they fucking all? He'd lost count of the number of bands who'd walked in here with their pals, their cousins, some lowlife club scene asshole managing them and not one of them had made it into the final deal. Things got done Ari's way around here and that came with full control. He'd install a management team of his choosing, bring in producers who knew the score and they'd have an album out before the end of the year. It was all money in the bank, baby.

A surge of adrenalin coursed through him. Yes! He was back. He was hard, he was on fire and he was a fucking genius.

He pushed his chair back and strode over to the punchbag that hung in the corner of his office. After hanging his jacket (Savile Row, cut by a London tailor who could make a suit that flattered and concealed a slight paunch better than any flash designer label ever could) on a wall peg and rolling up his shirt sleeves, he launched himself at the target. Every punch meant something: a left hook – Bon Jovi, you're fucked. A right roundhouse – die Mötley Crüe. Left jab – Queen, kiss my fat ass. Yetnikoff at CBS and Clive Davis over at RCA went down with a left/right combo. Those punks had been lucky over the last couple of years, lording over him, making him feel like shit.

It was time for the king to reign once again and everyone in this damn town was going to know about it. But first, there was a very pressing anatomical matter to be addressed . . .

Swaggering back over to his desk, he snorted a five-inch line of coke that was prepared by his secretary every morning in anticipation of his arrival, rubbed his boner like a proud daddy, then pressed a button on the intercom.

'Rita May, can you call my special friend and ask her to send a couple of my regulars over. I've got something that needs taking care of.'

The limo that collected them at the airport was a nice touch, Lori decided. Make the boys feel special, like they mattered and all for a couple of hundred bucks.

'What hotel are we staying in?' she asked Dave Lopez and then watched as he checked his notes with hands that were definitely shaking. She'd give him the benefit of the doubt and choose to believe that the trembling was the result of the long plane ride combined with sleep deprivation, but she had a hunch it had more to do with his stress over the antics of the band as they crossed from one coast to another. After the smoke alarm incident came the Jack Daniel's incident (every miniature removed from the galley by Muff, Strings and Tye while Dax and Sly distracted the stewardesses by chatting them up for twenty minutes somewhere above Kansas). Then there was the fight incident (Muff and Strings in a whole 'What was the best Led Zeppelin classic' dispute that led to a full-on scrap in the aisle – an even more bizarre sight because the two of them were identical so no one had any idea who had won or lost). And finally there came the strip incident. Surprisingly this involved not Coco, but Dax – who stripped to the waist and challenged a big-mouthed, arrogant marketing director from Poughkeepsie to an arm-wrestling competition, with the loser buying drinks for the rest of the journey. She had no idea how that guy would explain his expenses report this month.

Through the whole trip, she sat back, didn't interfere, just kept an eye on proceedings. Choosing her battles was second nature to her and she knew that sometimes you had to let the reins loose a little or resentment built, and it was far too soon in their relationship to allow that to happen.

Mr Lopez, on the other hand, obviously didn't have the same calm faith in the universe working things out by itself. For him, the whole journey had been a tension-filled nightmare that had ended with him begging the stewardesses not to press charges for any one of at least a dozen federal air offences that he was sure the guys had committed. Lori chose not to inform him that legal action was never a possibility. The reason she'd sent Dax and Sly to chat to the crew in the first place was to keep them sweet and it was just bad luck that those two lovely girls would show up at a pre-arranged club tonight to find that they'd been stood up by their new bad-boy dates. Not her problem. At least they would have a great story to tell their friends when the guys made it big. She was just glad that Sly's little blonde sparrow had been asleep when it all went down (thanks to the little yellow pill that Lori slipped her after ten airborne minutes of watching pure fear on her face) because that could have caused a scene. There was something about that girl that made Lori uncomfortable. She was damaged. Fragile. Like her nerves were on the outside of her skin.

And of course, at the other end of the scale was Coco, who stood for many things Lori despised yet who was actually kinda likeable. There was a carefree optimism and a wild enjoyment of life that was difficult to criticise and besides, the band loved her and she kept them happy . . . in many ways and countless positions.

'The Vinewest Hotel in Hollywood,' Dave answered her question with an instruction to the driver, 'and then on to AC Head Office.'

The where? In all the research on LA and on the music industry that she'd done in the last two weeks she hadn't come across even a single mention of The Vinewest. She supposed that wasn't exactly a surprise. What had she expected? The Mondrian? The Beverly Hills Hotel?

Those were the kind of places that she knew she was destined for – but it was just going to take a little bit of time, some hard graft and some smart thinking to get her there.

After a ten-minute stop at the hotel to unload the excess baggage (of both the human and suitcase variety) only Sly, Dax and Dave made the final part of the journey with her, every mile passing in total silence. Dax had nodded off to sleep, Sly was engrossed in some music mag, Dave looked like he was focusing all his energy on not shitting himself and she just stared out of the window, absorbing her new city, taking in the vibe. It was such a contradictory place. The area that the hotel was in was dark, even in 75-degree sunshine. There were tramps on the corners, dumpsters in the street, boarded up shops and the limo driver had scanned the streets warily the whole time they were there. Now it was a different story. Driving along Wilshire, the Porsches, the Lamborghinis, the Ferraris, even a Rolls Royce were passing her by, all driven by people in smart clothes and dark shades, clutching carphones to their ears. Carphones. What the hell would they think of next? On either side of her the buildings, tall shards of glass and metal, gleamed in the sun. Every crack in the scrubbed pavement oozed money and power – and Lori was determined that she was going to get herself some of both.

The secretary who greeted them at the elevator on the thirty-ninth floor was a surprise. Lori had expected a body-beautiful with vacant glamour and tits you could see from space, but the reality was a fifty-something, friendly-looking soccer grandma who was obviously no stranger to Denny's buffet. Maternal figures had never been much of a comfort to her, but in a bizarre way, it took the tension down a notch, and given everything she'd read about Ari Covet, she guessed that was his intention. His tales of excess and ruthlessness filled countless articles and books and those were just the ones that she'd come across over the years in the music press or managed to find in the last fortnight in the woefully inadequate Rackstown library.

There was no doubt about it, this could turn into a dog fight and Lori had done as much preparation as possible. In front of her, and in accordance with her strict instructions, Dax was pumped and looked incredible – faded Levi's topped with a white tank stretched across his body revealing every single inflection and curve of a torso that looked like it had been carved from steel. His jet black hair fell like a sheet of black ice down his back, parted in the middle and emphasising his Cherokee heritage. Sly on the other hand, was the male model-esque rock boy – tall and skinny, incredible cheekbones and the all-American square jaw framed with a mop of brown waves, wearing black boots and a black vest and jeans so tight they left not one area of his anatomy to the imagination. Individually, they were remarkable – together they were orgasmic.

Lori had played it a little more down-key. The whole power-dressing *Dynasty* shit wasn't her scene so she'd gone for a pair of guys' Levi's (they didn't make them long enough in girls' sizes), a plain black shirt, cowboy boots and a silver cross around her neck, hair caught at the back of her neck with a simple bone clasp.

As they walked across the thick, green and gold mono-grammed carpet (AC repeated in ten-inch cycles across hundreds of square metres), she realised that Dave had now gone from a worrying shade of pink to a deathly shade of white and the trembling was getting a whole lot worse. 'Am I going to have to give you CPR anytime soon?' she whispered.

Without breaking his stride, he leant in close so no one else was in earshot. 'There's every possibility.'

'Good to know.'

It was hard not to feel sorry for the guy. In an industry notorious for its sleaze, its debauchery and its hardened, shady players, they'd been found by the one A&R man who could double as a Sunday-school teacher. But in Lori's eyes, that was all good. A lack of experience on Dave's side lessened the probability that he'd have the balls to shaft them. It also gave her the chance to catch up on the business without judgemental eyes watching her every move. The last two years had taught her about promotion, about image, about balancing profit and loss sheets and keeping her eye on the bottom line. But what she knew about the inner workings of the music industry she could write on one inch of Dave Lopez's skinny tie.

But that was OK. She'd learn fast. And meanwhile, it was reassuring to know that someone else was shitting themselves far more than she was.

When the secretary knocked on Ari's door, there was a sharp intake of breath from Dave's direction and Lori made a mental note to brush up on first aid.

The first thing that surprised her about Ari Covet was his height – maybe five foot seven – and it was obvious those shoes had lifts. The second was his pupils. They were huge, covering almost the whole retina, showing that the guy was clearly loaded. The third was his charm.

He greeted Sly and Dax like they were long-lost relatives, all rambunctious handshakes and pats on the back, then took her hand and kissed it. 'God, you're beautiful,' he told her, his expression slightly puzzled as he looked to Dave Lopez for clarification.

'Lori Wyatt, the band's manager,' Dave announced in a voice that suggested his balls were in a vice.

Lori tried not to smile as Covet whistled. 'Well, well, well – the manager. Have to say I was expecting someone . . .' he struggled to complete the sentence.

'Male?' Lori suggested with a beauty pageant grin.

'Older,' he said, recovering admirably. Good – he was on the back foot, off guard. It was a small victory but she'd take all she could get.

They settled in the four seats placed in front of his huge black onyx desk and Lori smiled when she realised that his chair was set to a higher position, allowing him to look down on his subjects. Little Man Complex, 101. There was a few minutes of small talk (yes, the flight was fine, yes, they looked as good as in the pictures Dave had sent and yes, they'd seen all those gold and platinum discs that lined the walls of the outer office), before Covet's attention span snapped and he switched abruptly to the purpose of the meeting.

'Listen boys, I ain't gonna beat about the bush. I want to sign you guys and I'm prepared to give you a deal that you won't get anywhere else in this town.'

Listen boys? Her beauty had obviously had a very momentary effect on Covet because he was now completely blanking her and speaking directly to Sly and Dax. Good. Let him run with it.

'Contracts are here and I'll just get someone up from my legal team to witness them and then let's talk about how I'm going to make you guys fucking superstars. This time next year your name will be on a gold disc out there, I guarantee it.'

It was all she could do not to laugh. Now he'd moved on to Hollywood Big Shot, 101 and was treating them like they were small-town jerks. Or maybe he was just acting out a scene from the manual entitled *Full of Shit*.

Sly and Dax picked up the sheaves of paper in front of them and – as they'd been told – wordlessly passed them directly over to her. For the second time in ten minutes, Lori knew she'd caught Covet off guard. And by the frequency of the breathing on her right, she also knew that the time until Dave Lopez might need medical help was getting shorter.

To a backdrop of complete silence, she skimmed through the first couple of pages until she got to the important stuff.

'$50,000.'

Her voice was steady, betraying not a hint of emotion. 'Yep,' Covet responded with a grin, then paused to light up a large fat Cuban cigar.

'$10,000 up front,' she added.

'You got it.'

The silence was excruciating, punctuated only by the noise of the pages flicking over as Lori scanned the rest of the contract. The boys' faces stayed blank, again just as she'd primed them, despite the fact that she knew they'd chew their own dicks off to sign this. A deal with AC Records was the Holy Grail, the big deal, and to Sly and Dax this was the miracle they'd been look-ing for, yet they hadn't reacted at all. Again, they'd played it out just as instructed. If these guys didn't make it as musicians they'd sure as shit make it as actors.

'Do you have a pen, Mr Covet?' Lori asked sweetly. Cigar in one hand, he passed her a pen with the other, clearly elated that this little session was all going exactly to plan.

Lori took it and filled in the dotted line on the last page, then leaned over and put it back on the desk.

'Now that's what I like! Smart move missy!' he bellowed, then pressed a button on his intercom. 'Rita May, can you get your ass in here with some champagne.'

'It's Lori,' she replied, her tone even, calm. 'Guns N' Roses got $250,000 over at Geffen, just under $40,000 upfront.'

As he spun around he swayed slightly, whatever chemicals were in his bloodstream obviously affecting his balance.

'I know you're a legend Mr Covet, but you're past it. You need a hit as much as we want a deal.'

Lori's years of practice at suppressing emotions in the face of fear came into play, giving her a demeanour of assured confidence that she definitely didn't feel. His eyes were widening now, fury written across the lined, bloated face. 'But unlike you, we've got nothing to lose. I've written on the back page what we want. Call us when you're ready to agree.'

Sly and Dax stood up, taking their cue. 'Oh, and there's no mention of management in there. I'm part of the deal and authorised to sign and make decisions on their behalf. Lori Wyatt. Let me know if you need help with the spelling.'

Without a further word they turned and left the room, passing a tray of champagne coming in the other way.

They hadn't gone more than a few yards when there was the unmistakable sound of a bottle smashing against a wall and a deafening roar. They didn't look back. In fact, it was only when they got into the lift she realised that they'd left Dave Lopez behind.

And she had a feeling Rita May was already on the floor giving mouth-to-mouth resuscitation.

Coco dumped her bag on the bed and jumped straight in the shower. Actually, 'shower' was a little generous – it was more of a trickle that came from a rubber hose attached to the taps in a pink grime-rimmed bath, the one that matched the pink grime-rimmed sink and the – oh holy crap – she didn't even want to look at the pink grime-rimmed toilet. God, if her mother could see her now she'd have a fit; hanging out with a shambles of stoned rockers in a stinking hotel in an area of Hollywood where even the cockroaches had fleas. Coco had never been happier.

LA. She could already sense that this was her vibe. New York had become too glam, all New Wave and yuppies and sanitised chic, but Mötley Crüe were scattered in houses across this city. Guns N' Roses came from these streets. Dave Lee Roth lived only a few miles away. This was the epicentre of the hard rock world:

the Whisky, the Rainbow, the Troubadour, the Cathouse – the rock scene was legendary here and now she was going to be a part of it and she couldn't be happier. That was her definition of suc-cess – waking up feeling happy, going to bed the same way. It was all about living for the day, because life had taught her that you sure as hell didn't know what was going to happen tomorrow. Maybe, she thought with a smile, she should become a Buddhist. Weren't they all about that karmic appreciation of life stuff? If only they endorsed daily sexual encounters she'd sign up tomorrow.

She threw on a yellow neon Lycra mini and a Rolling Stones T-shirt, pulled on leather biker boots and grabbed her bag, fig-uring that if she left it there was every chance it wouldn't be there when she got back. The hotel didn't bother her. Sure, she had the money to go check into somewhere that the bathrooms didn't come with hot and cold running vermin, but she never would. Pulling the cash card wasn't Coco's thing. Material shit like cars and houses didn't matter. Her father had spent his life accruing those and it amounted to a pile of nothing when they put him in the ground. What was important was the band, the interaction, the music, the sex, getting high . . . and making it. She had no doubt that the Spikes were going to crack this busi-ness – she had complete faith that Dax and Sly were going to pull in this record deal – and if they didn't? Hell, there would be another one. The excitement, the raw brilliance of the Spikes, was undeniable and she'd been around bands long enough to know that they were special. For them, it was only a matter of time before everyone else saw it too.

On the way down the corridor she knocked on Marny's door.

'Hey, Marn, I'm going out, gonna have a look around, want to come?'

No answer. Another few hard thumps on the wood and the lock fell off. Convenient. Coco pushed the door open to see Marny lying naked and spreadeagled on the bed. Girls had never been her thing, but hell, if they were then this would be a place to start.

How had she never noticed that Sly's girl had a body to die for? Probably because Marny kept it well masked, wearing baggy pants and shapeless jumpers a couple of sizes too big for her tiny frame. The posture didn't help either, always round shouldered, head down, like she wanted to disappear into the background. How had someone so introverted, so shy, ever managed to hook up with Sly Ramone?

'Marny? Marny?' Coco moved over beside the bed and pushed some wisps of blonde hair back off Marny's forehead. 'Marny, I . . .'

The scream was so piercing the window rattled, although it said something about this hotel that absolutely no one came running. Marny shot bolt upright, flailing, lunging out at Coco until . . .

'Marny, Marny!' Coco grabbed her wrists, then threw her arms around her, pinning Marny's elbows to her sides, all the while shushing her, talking to her. 'Marny, honey, it's OK, it's me, it's Coco, come on babe, come on . . .'

It took a long, long twenty seconds or so, but eventually the noise and the chaos diminished and Coco let go just enough to pull back a little and get a look at Marny's face. She wished that she hadn't. It was pale, her eyes huge and terrified, yet still uncomprehending of what was going on.

'Marny, honey, have you taken anything?'

Marny stared at her for a moment, until her brain started pulling the brakes on the rollercoaster of confusion that she was riding.

'Coco? God, I'm sorry.' True to form, Coco watched her shrink back to type: the eyes went down, the head followed, the back curved and Marny was once again a tortoise retreating into her shell.

'Did you take anything?' Coco repeated, letting go enough to reach down and pull a filthy blanket around Marny's shoulders, covering her nudity. Coco could march down Hollywood Boulevard butt-ass naked and love every step of it but she'd already gathered that Marny didn't share her penchant for exhibitionism.

'No, I . . . I didn't. But I've been feeling really weird since the flight,' she whispered, shaking her head as if trying to clear away a blanket of fog.

Despite the evidence to the contrary – the shakes, the hysteria, the disorientation – Coco actually believed her. In the couple of weeks that they'd been hanging out she hadn't seen Marny take any more than a single toke of a joint and only then it was because Sly coaxed her into it.

'OK, then come on.'

'Where?'

'We're going out and we're going to get you something to eat and then we're going to see what this town has to offer the girl-friends of two sexy guys who are just about to land a record deal.'

Marny jolted back, embarrassed, pulling the blanket tighter around her shoulders. 'No, it's fine, I'll just stay here and wait . . .'

A heartstring tugged in Coco's chest. Shit, this girl was in a bad way. She was quite literally afraid to breathe, terrified of everything. How the hell was she ever going to survive here in a world that was legendary for being wild and dangerous and straight-up crazy? With Sly around she could just about function but the minute he left the room she just shut down, closed off completely.

Lifting Marny's chin so that they made eye contact, Coco smiled at her. 'Honey, I know this has all been a bit wild lately but it'll be OK. The guys will do great, I promise you. And . . .'

She stumbled, not sure how to say it and then deciding that blurting it out was the best way forward. 'Babe, I know you're only digging Sly right now but the rest of the band are good guys and you know, I'm here to be a friend if you want me to be.'

That was the thing about Coco. Outsiders took her to be a guys' chick for understandable reasons, but she was an equal opportunities girl at heart – a definite throwback to being born in the sixties when all that peace and love stuff was going down.

'So come on hon, let's get you dressed and get out of here. It's time for us girls to do a little shopping.'

Marny wasn't even given a chance to object as Coco pulled her up, grabbed a pile of clothes from the floor beside the bed and thrust them in Marny's direction. Big material shit didn't matter but some of the finer little things in life were necessities that no girl should be deprived of. It was time for the little mouse to learn to live a little. And Coco was just the girl to show her.

'We'll take them.'

'Which ones?' the teenage shop assistant gave them a smile that was as wide as the piercings that ran all the way along her top lip would allow. They'd been in this little boutique on Robertson for the last three hours and – to the ear-splitting sounds of Zeppelin, Floyd, Blondie and Bowie – Marny was fairly sure that she'd tried on every outfit in the shop. And she was completely sure that she looked ridiculous in all of them.

This was, Coco had informed her, the best place to pick up cool, custom clothes and T-shirts and she was right – on Coco everything looked great. On the teenage assistant with the tattoos and the metal hanging from her face it all looked great too. On Marny? Not so much.

But she didn't want to hurt Coco's feelings by arguing so she just went along with it. In truth, it had been impossible to resist Coco's enthusiasm or excitement and Marny had watched her with a mixture of awe and admiration as she had chatted to the shop staff like they were old friends, treated the racks like they were her personal wardrobe and thrown on multiple pieces that invariably combined to make an outfit that looked stunning.

Marny had gone for the most conservative choices available – which still left her with a selection of clothes that she'd never, ever have dared to buy herself. Skintight bleached denim jeans that flared at the bottom and came with tears in the fabric that exposed inches of her thighs, glimpses of her butt and hung so low that her hip bones jutted out above them. Cropped tops in a hundred colours, all of them clinging to every curve and ending just below her breasts, some of them with such a deep V that there was only an inch or so of fabric between her and indecent exposure. Lycra miniskirts held together at the side with nothing but thin strips of clear PVC at six inch intervals. Jeez, if she twisted the wrong way the whole world would see her bush. Then there were the leather pants that came with laces instead of zips and looked like they'd been painted on. Oh and the gloves – ones with only half fingers. Most of her anatomy would be hanging out on public display but hey, at least her knuckles would be covered. Finally, after the closest Marny came to asserting authority and making her own choices, there were a few longer T-shirts, most of them in primary colours – scarlets, purples, canary yellows, emerald greens, all of them with scooped necks so that they fell off one shoulder. Some were decorated with a retro insignia or artwork. Marny had no idea what some of them meant – who were Deep Purple? Black Sabbath? – but she took them anyway figuring that what they lacked in style, they added in coverage.

When Coco pulled out her chequebook and paid for it all Marny was mortified.

'I'll pay you back,' she whispered as the girl behind the counter put the cheque and a card in a machine then swiped it from one side to the other.

'Forget about it, my treat – and besides, we deserve it. We deserve nothing but good things,' Coco had giggled, grabbing the bags and slipping an arm through hers as they headed out of the shop.

The objection that was on the tip of her tongue got swallowed back as the one thing she'd learned was that there really was no point in arguing. Coco was like a wave that just took you along with it. A bit like Sly, really. In fact, now that she thought about it, Sly and Coco were a lot alike – both so comfortable in their own skin, both bold, fearless, with a passion for life and music that determined every minute of their waking day. Her thoughts were interrupted when they ducked into a home-style shop a few doors further along.

'OK honey, we might have to stay in that hotel but it doesn't mean we can't fix it up a little. I like my little luxuries – when I'm in bed I want to be fucking Dax, not wondering whose dried spunk I'm lying on.'

Marny almost spat a mouthful of Coke across the room, causing Coco to crease into a fit of the giggles.

'What? Shit, you're like, angelic or something? It's OK to talk about this stuff, hon. And if I was doing Sly I'd be talking about it all day long.'

Marny knew Coco was teasing, just joking around but the familiar panic started to rise once more as she realised that she didn't know how to react. Was this what females did? Was this how girlfriends talked to each other? Did they swap sex stories and talk about their boyfriends?

Marny had absolutely no idea because the truth was that her life had become a whole big melting pot of firsts: this was the first time she'd had a boyfriend and on that first night with Sly she had bled all over the rough, stained sheets in some run-down motel on the outskirts of Philly. Now this was her first time out of her home state, first time on a plane, first time in LA, and absolutely the first time anyone had ever bought anything for her. Over the years there had been acquaintances, people she'd lived alongside, co-existed with – but no one ever got too close to the orphan girl who spent most of her time staring at her feet. Sly had crossed that line. Now Coco was the first female who had come even close to anything resembling a friend. Marny had gone from solitude to intimacy and that came with a whole new set of fears and boundaries that she was still to learn.

Coco had a cart now and she was storming up the aisles, taking multiples of two of everything she needed off the shelves. Sheets (satin, cream), blankets (chenille, white), candles (vanilla, jasmine, cinnamon), soap, towels, washcloths and then over in the disposables section, toilet rolls, cleaning fluids and j cloths.

At the checkout, she paid again, then split it equally into two bags, before handing one to Marny. 'Like I said, hon, we deserve it. Life is just going to be all good from here on in.'

Marny swallowed back the lump that had appeared in her throat.

They 'deserved it'. 'All good'.

According to Coco it was as simple as that. And maybe now it was. But that state of mind was going to take a while to get used to because Marny had learned a tough lesson when she was a little girl and it was going to take more than a few nice-smelling candles to unlearn it. It was the root of her insecurities, her apprehension about Sly and her wariness about relationships. She knew that just when you thought you were safe and that life was OK, something incredibly bad could come along and take it all away.

No one had said a word for the last five minutes. They just all sat, unflinching, staring out the window, watching the buildings of Wilshire go by outside.

Dax Rice was feeling chilled but not in the mood to get into a whole post-mortem scene. This was exactly how Lori had said it would play so it was going to plan and that was a good thing, right? He took a large reefer out of his back pocket, rolled it in his hands to convert it from flat to round, then lit up, leaned back and closed his eyes. Stressing the small stuff wasn't his thing and anyway, there was a lick going off in his head that he just wanted to focus on for a while – it was a real cool low-down number, eight notes, just going round and round and all he wanted to do was get back to the hotel, get his guitar and play it out.

Sly Ramone was a little less at peace with the world. Fricking hell, he'd been almost there! He'd almost had it. Ari Covet, record deal, the money and HE'D WALKED AWAY! A knot of tension was tearing Sly's stomach so tight there was a good chance he would puke any minute now. He reached over, took the joint from Dax's hand and took a long, desperate drag. He'd walked away. From a record deal. What the fuck had they done? This broad better know what she was doing because otherwise they were well and truly fucked before they'd even got started. The Steel Spikes – the band that, in ten years' time the world would still look at and say 'Who?'. Ari Covet had been seriously pissed and everyone knew that he wasn't the kind of guy that you fucked off because he took it personally. And Sly had grown up around enough Italian women to know that you didn't want to be around when people took things personally.

What if that was it? For the last two years of starving and mooching around dive bars just trying to get enough to survive, all he'd thought about was getting a record deal and now he'd just walked away from one. *He was fucking nuts.* Dax was relieved of his joint for a second time. *He'd put all his faith in some twenty-three-year-old bar owner who knew jack about the music industry!* Fuck it, Dax wasn't getting the smoke back. If Sly was going to get through the next five minutes without smashing his own head repeatedly off the car window, he was going to need all the herbal intervention he could get.

Lori could sense the opposing energies in the car and she filed it away for future reference; knowing how someone was going to react when things hit turbulence was always worthwhile. If she were to 'fess up to how she was feeling, the truth was that she was somewhere in the middle. This wasn't her fighting for her livelihood against some small-town councillor back in Rackstown. This was the big leagues right here and she was the new girl in town who was getting in the game before she'd read the rule book. The guys in the band were depending on her to make their dreams come true and right now she'd say it was probably fifty/fifty that she'd blown it. Just as well confessionals weren't her thing.

'Lori, I have to ask you . . .' Sly was tapping his foot nervously, twiddling his fingers, shaking his head. The guy was a frigging bag of nerves and frankly Lori wasn't surprised. In the short time that she'd known him she'd realised that he was a dichotomy, a finely tuned balance between arrogance and insecurity and on any given day at any given time the balance could tip one way or another. Right now a metaphorical fat bastard was sitting on the insecure end of the seesaw.

'. . . do you think we blew it?' Another nervous inhalation of Jamaica's finest.

Truth or dare? Confess or cover up? Lori was weighing up the options when the smoked glass screen between the driver and the passenger seats slid back, and without taking his eyes off the road, the driver passed back a large black telephone that didn't even have a cord. Lori looked at it for a moment before sussing it out – she'd heard about these new cell phones but never actually seen one up close – and putting it to her ear.

'Hello?'

The driver, the passengers and probably all pedestrians within a three-street radius heard the shouts, which went on for at least a minute. Lori didn't say a word.

Finally, the phone went quiet, only a vague mumbling sound indicating to Sly and Dax that the person on the other end of the line was still speaking. After a few moments there was complete silence, and Lori, still not having uttered a syllable, leant over and tapped the driver on the shoulder.

'Here you go, Ed,' she said as she handed the phone back. 'Oh, and sorry, but can you turn around and take us back to the AC building please – seems Mr Covet has some new contracts for us to sign.'

TRACK 3

TEN

'You do know that you're actually supposed to participate in that?' Coco laughed. Of all the things she'd ever caught the guys from this band doing, watching five skinny, tattooed, long-haired rock guys drinking coffee while watching a Jane Fonda exercise video tape at two in the afternoon was possibly the strangest. Hang on, there was the time that Spank got messed up on PCP after a gig in upstate New York, stole a goat that he was convinced contained the soul of Jimi Hendrix and sang 'Purple Haze' all the way from Westchester to Manhattan, before finally being persuaded to release it into Central Park at 5am. Yep, it was close, but the goat came out top of the weird list. Jane, however, was a close second.

'I want to fuck her four ways to Sunday,' Strings whistled at the screen, before chugging back a healthy dose of Jack straight from the bottle, completely ignoring his brother who at that point lost both his balance and consciousness, keeled off the arm of the beat-up couch and landed with a thud on the floor.

'It's research, baby,' Dax replied, grabbing her hand and pulling her down to her favourite resting place on his knee.

'Research for . . .?'

'A track. We've watched everything else – it's all that was left.'

Coco checked out the pitiful pile of videos scattered beside the TV: *Beverly Hills Cop, The Terminator, A Nightmare on Elm Street, Rambo, Rocky IV, Platoon*. Hell, they'd even caught Muff watching *The Muppets Take Manhattan*. How rock 'n' roll was that? Coco fell silent and nuzzled into Dax's neck. If this was some kind of weird creative process then she was happy to shut up and let it flow – anything that would get them out of here. Her first month in Los Angeles had been nothing like she'd expected. They'd stayed in The Vinewest for three days after the contracts were signed, most of that spent recovering from a celebration on the first night in the Troubadour where they'd watched the Stone Temple Pilots play a blinding set that had taken her somewhere very close to orgasmic. Afterwards, Lori, Sly and Marny – who, incidentally, looked freaking gorgeous in her new clothes – had split back to the hotel. The rest of band had scored some serious coke from a guy whose purple velvet trilby was as oversized as the pistol in the shoulder holster that he flashed as he took their money. They'd hit four or five other clubs on the strip, ending up in a backstreet strip joint where they'd watched as two skinny white girls performed a sixty-nine and attempted to convince the crowd that they were seriously getting off on it. Only the desperados chugging at their dicks under the tables chose to believe it.

As the sun came up they'd all headed back to the hotel, taking a few strippers from the club with them. Coco had picked the two prettiest and taken them to her room where they had found every permutation of a foursome that existed and several that they could possibly have trademarked. Girls weren't her thing. However, watching Dax get off on her playing around with some hot chick definitely was. It was all good. And she didn't even mind that when she'd woken up twelve hours later half the clothes she'd bought when she arrived were gone. The girls deserved them for services rendered. Dax was still there, they still had some coke that they'd stored in the heels of her boots and they had nothing that they needed to get up for. So they'd put some Zeppelin vinyl on Dax's old record player, left the repeat arm up and slept, smoked and screwed their way through the next thirty-six hours, occasionally managing to eat something vaguely identifiable from room service, until Lori had banged on their door and told them it was time to clear out.

The excitement had run high. Dave Lopez had told them that they were moving to a five-bedroom house with a studio that AC sent all its artists to when they wanted them to make a record. Nuclear Fear and Decomp had both composed and recorded every album there. When the van had arrived to collect them Dax had been absolutely psyched to be following in the footsteps of his heroes. As soon as they'd hit the Pacific Coast Highway and headed north past Malibu, excitement had bubbled over and they'd broken into a jamming session that started wired and frantic and then slowly diminished as the milometer clicked over.

'Hey man, did they say this pad was in Canada?' Strings had asked nervously as he'd realised his weed situation was diminishing in inverse proportion to the mileage they were racking up. One hour later, Dave Lopez had to leave their van and move to the luggage truck behind them because Spank was threatening to disembowel him with a craft knife. Three hours later they got to The Shack – a barn-cum-rehearsal space-cum-recording studio that was so remote it had its very own zip code.

On the way in Coco spotted the other inhabitants of the area and shouted over to Spank, 'Hey honey, best keep away from those goats. No point you finding love when you're just about to embark on a transient life.'

In a testimony to the fact that she was one of the very few people on earth that he didn't want to kill (so far that numbered the band, Coco and his grandmother – the jury was still out on Lori and Marny) he just picked up a boulder and went for semi-serious injury instead. Luckily it missed, causing the rest of the guys to snigger and the mood to lighten. Mission accomplished.

Four weeks later Sly and Dax had played everything they'd

ever written to the assembled team and they'd pulled out eleven songs (six of them Sly's, five of them old Steel Spikes numbers written by Dax). Watching the two of them work had given Coco an almost permanent turn on. Sly was genius on the lyrics, especially when his brain had been oiled by a combination of liquor and pot. Dax, on the other hand, could pull a riff or a melody or a harmony out of nowhere, add it to Sly's lyrics and suddenly there was a song. When Sly got uptight, Dax calmed him. When Dax's mind was wandering to pleasures like chilling out or the exploration of Coco's love areas, Sly pulled him into focus. They challenged each other, pushed each other, and the result was a relationship that was based on mutual respect and co-dependence . . . with just enough ego and competition to keep it edgy. They clicked – and the result was a fluid, dynamic process. As soon as the lyrics and the tune were down, the rest of the band would add their instruments to the mix, often inspiring more development or variation to the track. When it came to music, it took a lot to impress Dax, but Sly was hitting the mark every time. And no, Coco didn't mind in the least that her lover was devoting more time to his new partner than he was to her. Every note of every finished track made it worth it.

But now, eleven songs later, they were exhausted and all out of ideas. Covet had sent in a couple of producers with orders to come back to him when they had the rough cuts on twelve tracks. For number twelve they were going to have to write something new, and results were proving elusive for two main reasons: they'd all brought everything they had to the table where only the very best had made the cut, and they were now completely out of drugs and had drunk every liquor store within a twenty-mile radius (which totalled a pathetic three) dry. Despite the adrenalin rush of the record deal, a combination of pressure, cabin fever and lack of chemical stimulation had kicked in and it showed. Over the last few days all creativity had evaporated and there had been more fights than Coco could count. Sly had retreated away from the rest of the guys – behaviour that she had a hunch was caused by a mixture of frustration and embarrassment. Muff and Strings were scrapping on an hourly basis. Spank was sporting new red welts on his arms every day. Tye was banging on everything within touching distance. Even the incredibly even-tempered Dax had freaked and put a coffee table through a window. And still no track twelve.

Coco was as bummed as the others. Dax was so tense he didn't want to play around and he'd asked her not to have any music on because he felt it was scrambling his brain. When there was no sound, her world went flat. It was like a prison sentence. No music, no sex, no thrill of getting turned on and then getting off to an amazing soundtrack. Torture. Coco couldn't wait to get back to real life.

She wouldn't have to suffer for much longer.

At the other end of the couch, Sly's fingers suddenly started tapping out a piano sequence on the armrest, then he grabbed a piece of paper and started scribbling.

'What you got?' Dax asked, his voice a mixture of eagerness and optimism.

Sly put his hand up. 'Hang on, hang on – thinking. Strings, turn that fucking thing off a minute.'

Reluctantly, Strings stretched over and pushed the button on the TV.

Sly was humming something, a melody, going from e to c to f to e minor in a frenetic, rhythmic beat.

Twenty years older, no shame in getting high
Livin off her body doing anythin' to get by

Tye picked up the drumsticks that never left his side and matched the beat by leaning over to where Muff was lying comatose and playing his sticks on the back of Muff's leather jacket. Sly was repeating the phrase again and again, trying to find the next line. Waiting for the song to take him there. Dax was drumming it out now on Coco's thighs, his eyes shut, every inch of his body

111

moving and pulling the beat in. *Mmmm, mmmmm, mmmm, mmm, mmmmm*. He was feeling it, adding a harmony to Sly's melody line over and over again, until . . .

> *She doesn't ask his age, switches off her soul to keep*
> *The only time she cries is when she shuts her eyes to sleep*

Coco's jaw dropped. Shit, it sounded incredible. It was just . . . freaking incredible. Sly and Dax were both working it now, putting the lines together, their heads moving in perfect synchronicity, legs counting out the beats.

In one swift movement, Dax removed Coco from his lap and put her on the floor, then grabbed the battered Echo acoustic that was sitting beside the sofa and started to play, picking out the riff immediately.

Sly was doing it, Dax was doing it, Tye was in there, Strings was digging it and even Spank managed to raise an impressed eyebrow. Even while unconscious, Muff was playing his part. Those guys didn't write, never had, probably never would, but they'd been around Dax when he'd put together other songs for the band and they'd never seen him as hyped as this. It was almost like Dax on his own was brilliant, Sly was fierce, but together – shit, this was like watching genius. Suddenly a huge grin crept across Dax's face as he led them out of the verse again, but this time didn't immediately wrap back to the start. Coco felt a rapturous stirring in the pelvic area as she watched him ramp up the volume,

'*Wanna fuck her fo-o-ur ways till Sunday,*' Dax sang. Several things happened: Strings leapt up, punched the air and screamed, 'Yes!' then managed to lose his balance, stand on his brother, who then woke up, reached out, pulled Strings to the floor and started beating him about the head. Tye dived over to the TV and started drumming on that instead. Spank raised another eyebrow in the Spankworld version of delight.

And Sly came straight in with, '*Minds apart, a broken heart, gonna make me pay*'.

Dax's adrenalin roared. *'Wanna fuck her . . .'*

'Fo-o-ur ways till Sunday,' all the guys were singing now, Sly and Dax harmonising beautifully, Dax's tenor weaving in and out of Sly's grating alto, once again repeating the lines, feeling them, creating something that was . . .

Magical. Coco knew right there that something very special was happening here. This was the first song that had been brand new, not derivative of anything that the guys had brought to the studio. It was the first true Ramone/Rice composition. These two guys who could already play like nothing she'd ever known had found their fit, had worked it out and the result was nothing but magical. Dax already rocked every bit of her world with his playing and his talent as an artist, but now . . .

The atmosphere and sheer brilliance in the room was making her nipples harden and her snatch wet. She couldn't take her eyes off him. She wanted to fuck him right there and then and she didn't care who watched. Jane freaking Fonda could have a ringside seat if she wanted. His voice, his face, every sinew of every muscle . . . Her stare just refused to be broken. That's when she realised that she wanted to watch Sly Ramone until the end of time.

Marny looked at herself in the mirror and watched as a stranger turned around in front of her. Who was she?

Coco had cut her hair in one fierce, blunt chop and then she'd shown her how to mess it up so that it fell in sharp white shards to just below her chin. Coco had also given her a make-up bag full of lotions, blocks and sticks and had then spent an unseasonably rainy afternoon showing her how to apply it all. In the space of a couple of hours Marny had been transformed from looking like an awkward schoolgirl to . . . to . . . an awkward woman. But a beautiful one. Her cheekbones seemed even higher with the band of dark shade below them, her eyes were a smoky grey and her jaw looked slightly squarer, like Debbie Harry but without the confidence or attitude. For the first time

113

in her life she felt she was learning what it was like to be normal, to be young and into stuff like clothes and make-up.

The clothes were next. She pulled on a pair of red panties, then black jeans that were decorated with bleached-out vertical stripes. Careful not to smudge the bright Revlon Red on her toenails, she breathed in as she wrenched the lace that fastened them as tightly as it would go. She slipped straps of the red bra (again donated by Coco) over her arms and then leant forward before joining the two clasps at the back. When she stood up she saw that it had achieved the desired effect. Her breasts sat higher, rounder, supported by the underwires and pushed together to look like two tennis balls on a rack.

The black vest top was the final touch, cut lower than the bra so that the red lace peeked provocatively over the neckline.

The first time Sly had seen her in her new clothes – on that night in LA before they headed out to celebrate the record deal – he'd given a low, dulcet whistle and then taken every item right back off her one by one, leaving just the bra and panties. He'd pulled down the cups of the bra letting her breasts spring free, latched on to one of them, sucking hard while he pushed the panties to the side and entered her hard and fast. When they'd met back in the hospital something in their minds had connected, but now their bodies did too. He'd told her he loved her again and again and again, whispering it with every thrust. For the first time, the lights stayed on, her eyes stayed open and the apprehension she always felt seemed a little lessened. Maybe one day she'd feel no more worry as to whether she was doing OK, if she was pleasing him, turning him on. Or maybe not.

Now, a month later, the routine of fixing the hair, applying the make-up, wearing the clothes, was one she performed every day and the effect on Sly was still the same. She might still look like a stranger but she was a stranger that Sly seemed to love even more than the girl who'd been there before. And that was all right with Marny – if this was who he wanted her to be on the outside that was fine by her. If only there was a bag of lotions, blocks and sticks that could make her bold and fierce on the inside too.

Living in someone else's world might be preferable to living alone, but it brought the scariest feeling of all: the fear that it might all disappear. Her jaw set as she felt the familiar itch of terror. He could tire of her. He could meet someone else. He could decide he wanted to be young free and single. And now that she'd experienced what it was to have someone, she knew that she didn't want to live without it. She didn't want to live without Sly.

The bedlam coming from the TV room downstairs broke through her thoughts. Rhythmic banging, the guitar, and then Sly's voice slicing through the noise. A few minutes later, she heard the thumping footsteps of high heels on a wooden floor and then Lori, shouting, 'Right you shower of deadbeats, get into that studio and don't come out until that's down.'

It was taking a while for her to get used to Lori's personality: the raw, razor-sharp humour and the no-nonsense, unemotional approach to everyone and everything. Sly seemed to like her though so she supposed that was all that really mattered. Marny found her terrifying.

'Hey, baby girl, you're looking gorgeous,' Coco purred at her from the doorway. Marny automatically blushed and her eyes went straight to the floor. 'OK, remind me the next lesson is going to be on self-confidence and the acceptance of compliments,' Coco smiled encouragingly, coming over and throwing an arm around her like it was the most natural thing in the world.

'I just thought you might like to know that our boys are freaking incredible down there today – wanna come watch?'

'Sure,' Marny replied, thankful that her internal voice, the one that didn't know how to deal with this community life, couldn't be heard. Staying in the bedroom for the rest of the day would have been her first choice but she knew that Sly would expect her to make an appearance. Why were groups of people so hard for her to deal with? None of the band had ever been nasty to her, yet she still burned white hot with self-conscious embarrassment when she had to sit with them all, even with Coco at her side being supportive and friendly and giving her a running commentary on the technicalities of everything they were doing. That was the thing about Coco that had surprised her most – she knew so much about music. All the bands, the hits, the lyrics – everything that they played or heard, Coco knew who sang it, when it was released, how many copies it had sold. Whereas she'd missed all that – didn't have a clue about popular trends, or music genres or anything that had been out prior to the night that she climbed up that dumpster. A chill ran down her spine as the metal gate slammed closed on her memories.

'Ready hon?' Coco asked.

'Ready.'

Down in the studio the energy buzzed off the walls as the guys prepared to go for the first live run through of 'Four Ways Till Sunday.'

The studio space was a disarray of equipment, instruments and half-naked men playing instruments (Spank being the exception as always). The original Spikes members all had cigarettes either burning beside them or in the case of Dax, hanging from his mouth.

'Wow, check out Dax – he's sooooo Joe Perry,' Coco purred. Marny didn't feel the need to confess that she had no idea who Joe Perry was.

Sly spotted her through the glass on the production booth, winked and beckoned her through. He liked her beside him, sitting on a stool against the wall just to the left of his mic stand and had insisted she was there through the laying of every track. 'Hey, my good luck charm is back,' he whispered, as – head down – she slid into her nominated spot. His good luck charm. Is that why he was with her? Because she'd once saved his life and now he thought she was lucky? She hoped that was true because that meant he would never let her go.

A thin film of perspiration glistened on his bare chest, all the way down to the open button of his Levi's and the wiry tuft of black hair that protruded above the teeth of the zipper.

'Hey, what's with the blushing?' Sly whispered, kissing her neck, her shoulder, her arm. She snaked her hands around his neck.

'I missed you,' she whispered so that only he could hear, and was rewarded with the sensation of his hands sliding down inside the back of her jeans. 'You missed me?' he murmured playfully. Even though no one else was paying them any attention, her face was scarlet now, but she didn't care. What mattered was keeping him happy, letting him know how much she loved him, proving to him every day that his life was better with her in it . . . because maybe that way she'd never have to face the alternative.

'OK, guys let's do this,' came an enthusiastic voice from the speaker system that Marny recognised as belonging to Dave Lopez.

Dax launched straight into a solo riff, a hypnotic tune that built and built until bang! The other instruments came in and Sly opened up his voice on, '*Twenty years older, no shame in getting high . . . Livin' off her body doing anythin' to get by.*'

The hairs on the back of Marny's neck stood up. Through the glass she could see Coco, eyes shut, nodding her head in time to the rhythm. Even Lori was smiling as she stood, arms folded against the back wall.

Three minutes, forty-one seconds later, Dax played the last note of the song, a screeching sound that came from high up on the fret board and left the ears ringing long after it had faded. Then silence. Complete silence for a few seconds as everyone on both sides of the glass processed the last four minutes of their lives: the pain, the angst, the fire, and for some, the sheer gut-wrenching emotional connection of a song that had ripped straight through their psyche.

The bedlam unleashed. 'Man, you are a fucking hero,' Dax laughed, as he grabbed Sly in some weird handshake, back-thumping thing.

Suddenly everyone was cheering, punching the air, kicking amps, banging walls, every gesture fuelled by undiluted euphoria. The madness was a welcome distraction from her reaction, until Sly broke away from the others and came to her, looking at her tenderly as he kissed away the tears that were sliding down her cheeks.

He was staring at her now, the two of them safe, protected in the eye of the storm.

'What? Tell me,' he begged softly.

As always she shook her head and shrugged off the moment with a shy smile. What could she say? That she loved him? That the song had moved her like nothing she'd ever heard? Or that he'd somehow written a story that was so close to her mother's life that it hurt.

The door flew open and Coco burst into the room and jumped Dax, wrapping her long, bare legs around his waist, throwing her head back and shrieking with laughter when he pulled up her T-shirt and buried his head between her bare breasts.

'How do I get one of those? Is there, like, a mail order hot babe service?' Strings asked his brother. Muff shrugged. 'If there is, put me down for two that look like that.'

Legs still tight around his waist, Coco released her hands from behind Dax's neck and allowed herself to fall back so that her torso and head fell upside down, hair spread across the floor, her breasts sliding so that they dangled somewhere close to her chin.

'No chance boys, I'm one of a kind,' she laughed.

'Thank fuck,' Lori retorted wryly as she strode in the door, 'Or we'd never get any work done.' Coco pulled herself back up and slid her hand down the front of Dax's pants. 'You're absolutely right,' she murmured.

Marny's face flushed yet again. How did Coco do that? How could she be so free, so bold, so uninhibited? How could she just ignore digs, fly in the face of disapproval, embrace every moment as if it were designed for nothing but pleasure?

Dave Lopez came in at Lori's back. 'Ladies and gentlemen, our very professional gentlemen on the desk,' gestured to Tom Coffe and Jake Simms, the producers that Ari had sent up to work on the first set of tracks for his new signing, 'have informed me that, for now, that's a wrap.'

Spank, Muff and Strings immediately stormed over to the glass, dropped their pants and mooned the gallery in appreciation.

Dave caught Lori's eye and she shrugged and gave a reluctant nod. He obviously took that as a signal to proceed. 'And as a token of our humble appreciation and in light of the fact that you've been in solitary for four weeks now, please accept this gift on our behalf.'

Marny watched, intrigued, as he slid his hand into the satchel that was strapped across his shoulder and pulled out a small, clear bag filled with snow.

The room went into rapture once again.

Spank was the fastest off the mark and he snatched the bag, emptied it and spread the contents on the back of his Yamaha keyboard. Without a hint of hesitation, he took the razor blade that hung on a chain around his neck and cut up the powder with all the art, precision and ceremony of a Japanese chef at a teppanyaki grill. He then pulled a silver cigarette case from his back pocket, flipped it open and extracted two little silver straws. Muff decked Strings in the rush to grab one first, resulting in their second fist fight of the day. The others stepped over them on their way to the Colombian altar.

The band's natural hierarchy kicked in as Dax and Coco went first, taking a line each then moving out of the way to let Tye and Strings step up. Ever the gracious host, Spank looked to Sly to partake before him. Marny held her breath. Sure, Sly smoked weed and a couple of times she'd seen him taking coke but it wasn't a regular thing and it made her nervous. It made him hyper, really jittery, he talked and ranted and sometimes made no sense at all. It also made him want to make love all night long but without the snuggling and the softness that made the whole act matter for her. Say no, Sly, say no. But of course, she'd never say that out loud.

He dropped his arm from around her shoulder. He was going. Time to psych herself up for a long, long night ahead. But he didn't leave her side. Instead, he took her hand and gently tugged her off the chair. 'C'mon baby, time to party.'

She froze. 'But I don't . . .' No more words would come out because at that very second she realised that everyone in the room was staring at her expectantly. Every synapse in her brain collapsed in paralysing fear, causing her mouth to snap shut and her motor functions to relinquish control. Sly led her across to the keyboard, took two straws from Spank's outstretched, scarred hand, gave one to Marny and then leant down and snorted up a four-inch line of the white dust. Marny watched as the muscle on the side of his jaw spasmed, then he rubbed his nose furiously and grinned at her, stepping back to allow her to move in.

'Go baby,' he whispered. And that's when she realised that there was absolutely no choice. If she refused everyone's attention would be on her, judging, questioning, laughing at her. If she went ahead, then at least she was joining in with the pack. There wasn't an option. Fear of being in the spotlight outweighed apprehension over trying something new. Stepping forward, she bent down, and held one nostril closed as she'd seen Sly do. Ignoring the thudding of her heart and the stomach that was churning with anxiety, she inhaled a line and . . .

BAM! The explosion inside her head was like no other feeling she'd ever experienced before. The fizzing sensation came immediately afterwards, like blood was rushing to every nerve ending, every pore, pure liquid fire that was setting her alight from the inside out.

Spank took the straw from her as Sly pulled her over to the wall at the back of the studio and positioned her against it, his hips pressing hard against hers, and that's when it came, the wave of . . . of . . . God, she'd never felt like this before. Or rather, it was more about how she didn't feel. Gone was the fear, the

120

embarrassment, the crippling shyness. She felt alive. She felt free. She felt . . . good! The lifelong craving for invisibility lifted for the first time and what was left was contentment, confidence, joy.

She'd found it. It didn't come in a lotion or a block or a stick. The thing that had finally shown her a way to change how she felt on the inside came in powder form. And for Marny Tucker, it was the second time in two years that she'd fallen deeply, hopelessly in love.

Lori dragged the suitcase out from under the bed and flipped it up on top of the patchwork blanket. Thank fuck they could finally get out of this place. Sure, it was better than being stuck in Rackstown with a bar full of Neanderthals who downed a dozen beers and then experienced a chemical reaction that turned them into Rambo, but there had been times over the last month when even that would have been preferable to the boredom and tension here. With the exception of Sly, she could see now that these guys didn't do solitude. They didn't do discipline. They were a party band, guys that got off on having a good time and used that energy in their music. This environment had sucked the life out of them and there had been a few occasions that she'd had to come down hard on them to head off a mutiny. Thankfully, Sly and Dax had seen that they had to suck it up and get on with it and they'd helped to keep the rest of the band under control – those guys were already tight, already working together as if they'd been knocking out tunes for years. There seemed to be a natural fit with them and they'd pretty much dug deep, found a mutual respect and kept their focus, despite the fact that Dax made no secret of the fact that he spent half his life fucking and the other half playing his guitar while thinking about fucking. And Sly . . . she hadn't worked him out yet. She couldn't get him away from the little blonde mouse long enough to find out what made him operate. But she would. Only a matter of time. Drugs, alcohol, chicks, sex – like the rest of the band whatever made him tick would be a balance of at least three of those.

The other guys in the band had been easy to read. God knows what drugs Muff and String's mother had taken while she was pregnant but they'd definitely left a legacy with those two – one minute they were comparing the sizes of their dicks and the next they were trying to set fire to each other's pubes. Tye took hyperactivity to a level that could benefit from medication and Spank acted like he was Satan's emissary on earth. Shit, why couldn't she have discovered the next clean-living, bible-thumping, teetotal pop sensations? At least the chances of destruction and death would have been lowered to a level that reduced the probability of her having an ulcer by twenty-five.

Drugs had never been her thing. She needed to be in control, understand what was going on, spot danger, see opportunities and, much as there had been many times in her life when oblivion would have been the option of choice, she was smart enough to know that she could only fight her way through life with a clear head. Money. Success. Power. None of that was gonna come if she was lying junked-out in a corner. Let the boys do what they needed to do – they were musicians, not saints – but it wasn't part of her deal.

Screwing with Ari Covet, however, definitely was.

She picked up the telephone and punched in seven numbers.

'AC Records, how can I help you?'

'Lori Wyatt for Ari Covet.'

She spent the next five minutes listening to 'I'm Gonna Get You,' by some middle-of-the-road soft-rock band that AC should have dumped years ago. Yep, Ari Covet definitely needed The Steel Spikes.

'Lori! What a pleasure to speak to you my dear,' he bellowed and Lori was sure she could hear the slime dripping from every vowel.

'It's done.'

'So I hear. Mr Lopez has already called in the good news.'

Damn him. Lori made a mental note to keep an eye on Dave Lopez. He wasn't smart or experienced enough to be a real pain in the arse but he was so amenable that it was sometimes easy to forget that he danced for the organ grinder.

'I'm taking the boys back to LA tonight and I've found us an apartment on Highland – nothing too flashy so your accountant shouldn't balk when the bill comes in.'

She knew she was chancing it sticking Covet with the cost – strictly speaking they should be paying for living expenses out of the advance they'd already received, but Covet was so vile that she went to bed at night pondering new ways to piss him off.

To her surprise she didn't receive a profanity-littered tirade of the type that she'd become accustomed to when she'd given the progress reports he'd demanded over the last few weeks.

'Don't you worry about that my little sour tits – they won't be there long.'

This was the first she'd heard of it and Lori hated surprises.

'They're going out on the road with Decomp,' he told her, obviously enjoying pulling the strings.

'No way. Decomp are over, out of it.'

'They got out of rehab last week and they're back on form. They've sold over a hundred million albums over the last ten years and they're not fucking over till I say they are.'

Lori weighed it up. Sure they were huge, but the stories of their demise were legendary – a typical, Aerosmith-like descent into debauchery, that for Decomp culminated in two very naked, very dead hookers in the pool of a Santa Monica beach house, both of them concealing household objects inside their vaginas and the skin of Randy Storm, the lead singer, under their finger nails.

That aside, though, Covet had a point. Decomp were huge in their day and if he was going to put them out again it would be in decent-sized arenas, not the kind of grotty little clubs that the Spikes had been playing for the last two years and that most newly signed bands started off in. This was actually an incredible opportunity for them. Even if they were playing to twenty, thirty thousand at each venue – and she had no doubt that

Decomp could still pull in those kind of numbers – that was still massive exposure and the perfect platform to promote the album. Covet might reside in the gutter, but the old bastard still knew what he was doing.

'When does it kick off?'

'Six weeks. Don't want to give them time to relapse and OD with their heads up some hooker's ass this time.'

'Compassionate man,' Lori retorted dryly, ignoring the smug laughter on the other end of the line. 'I'll call your secretary in the morning and get the agenda.'

'No you won't – you'll come in personally and see me. I wanna listen to the Spikes tapes with you. I'm a hands-on kinda guy.'

The shudder was as violent as it was sudden. Fuck, he sickened her, the insidious little bastard. What had she done in life that God had rewarded her by littering her path with evil, vile, sleazy fucking assholes? But she knew she couldn't push it. She might have worked with a load of bands over the last couple of years, she might have done her research on the industry, but she knew she still had everything to learn and not much time to do it. Hanging out in the orbit of Ari Covet, if his stink didn't kill her first, would be the best way to learn it.

'OK, I'll be there.'

'At three.'

'OK.'

The blood began to thunder in her head, once again belying the cool exterior and steadiness of her voice. She hated taking orders from him. Who the fuck did he think he was?

'Oh, and Ari, don't ever keep me hanging that long again. One minute. The next time I call I'll wait for one minute and then I hang up and you'll have to kiss my ass to find out what's going on with the guys that are going to save your label.'

She wasn't sure who slammed the phone down first. Ari Covet may think he ran this show but he didn't. This was about power and possession and she had both: The Steel Spikes did what she said and they belonged to her.

She just had to make sure that it stayed that way.

Blood pressure returning to normal, she detached the key from the bracelet she wore around her wrist, slid it in the padlock on her suitcase and watched as it popped open.

As she undid the zip around all four sides of the metal case, the last of the anxiety was replaced by a calming wave of comfort as her mind tuned in to what she was about to see. Flipping back one half of the case, she smiled and snapped open the compartment that held the only material thing in the world that meant anything to her. The child's doll was old, tatty. It was her mother's sole contribution to her life; the only thing that she had left of the woman who had walked out and left her six-year-old daughter to live a life in the hell that was created by Jack Wyatt.

It was the key to her past and despite vowing that life would be all about looking forward, somehow she just wasn't ready to let it go and maybe that wasn't such a bad thing – a reminder of her old life was sure as hell the best motivation to change her future. She tucked it back into its resting place and lay back on the bed, the strains of the last few weeks dissipating with every exhalation.

This is what mattered. Here. Now. Her. And the success that was so close she could almost taste it. Contemplating failure wasn't an option. A thin smile played on her lips as she visualised what that would feel like. The power. The rush of never being on the crap end of the stick again. Calling the shots. A sexual charge kicked in as she channelled that feeling – the confidence that she knew would come with control and power. She'd seen it in Ari Covet, the insidious prick. But he was an insidious prick that had conquered his world – and she was all about following him to the top.

Power. Her nipples hardened at the thought. Money. A tingling in her clit. It was the first time in months that she'd had any awareness of the physical needs of her body. Sly, Dax, the other guys left her cold, didn't do it for her. But then, no one ever had. Sex had always been a zero priority when every day was about surviving the shit at the mercy of an old drunk who farted, raged and screwed his way through life.

She pulled back from the memory and fought back to the feeling she'd had just a moment before.

Success.

Success was what did it for her.

She pulled her T-shirt over her head, slid out of her jeans and then lay down, caressing her body, rubbing her nipples, gasping as they reacted to the touch. Slowly, she moved downwards, her fingers tracing their way from side to side like they were probing every inch of her. By the time they reached the thin strip of black hair that sat above her pale white thighs, her pulse was thumping like Tye's drumming: hard and furious. Only when she couldn't stand it for another second did she succumb, opening her legs and slipping her fingers inside her, torn between coming and keeping the excruciating thrill alive for just a bit longer . . . Just a bit longer . . . Just a bit . . .

With a scream that she muffled by biting down on her tongue until it drew blood, her back buckled, her legs clenched together and every muscle in her pelvis and buttocks spasmed again and again as the most devastatingly perfect orgasm ripped through her.

ELEVEN

Rock-a-bye baby . . .

The minister said in church that hating someone was a sin, so she tried really, really hard not to hate him. What was it that God's servant on earth had said this morning? Forgiveness is the road to redemption. She didn't know where redemption was, but it sure sounded a lot nicer than the fires of hell. So that was what she was going to do — she was going to forgive. And she was going to make Miss Molly forgive too so that she could take her along to that redemption place.

Rock-a-bye baby . . .

She was just about to close her eyes when she heard the noise and pulled her knees up so sharply that she almost threw up. With a trembling hand she pushed back the drapes and saw the shadow. Forgiveness. Forgiveness. Forgiveness.

It was no use — the hatred was too strong and it was winning. 'It'll be OK,' she whispered to Miss Molly, and then she turned her over and pushed her under the covers.

There were some things that Miss Molly didn't need to see.

TWELVE

Rock Out magazine, October 15th 1987

Decomp Come Back To Life – by Bobby Sofranko

You can't say that they don't have a sense of humour. In a gesture that sticks two defiant fingers up at the world, former rock gods Decomp have announced that they are going on the road again with The Rehab Tour: Twelve Steps to Chaos.

Frontman Randy Storm announced today,

'On behalf of the band I'd like to thank the fans who have supported us while we were healing and finding our way back from the lost world of excess that we'd gone to. Every one of us has now completed a rehab program and for the first time we are a clean and sober band who want to look to the future and who are committed to lives of sobriety. Kids, don't take drugs. If just one person learns from the mistakes that we've made then everything we've gone through will be

worthwhile. We've made the mistakes so that others don't have to. God bless you all and see you on the tour.'

Astonishing words indeed from the man who one said *'Fuck everyone who says that we're gonna crash and burn. Decomp won't be done until they're tossing the dirt on my grave.'*

Decomp's return after the tragedy that appeared to have ended their career has been met with no comment from the parents of Mary Jo Taylor or Candy Rays, the two nineteen-year-old prostitutes who were murdered in the grounds of Storm's Santa Monica estate after a party in June of last year. No charges were ever brought for the crime despite evidence that confirmed both girls had had sexual intercourse with Mr Storm, who had an alibi for his whereabouts at the time of the girls' deaths.

Many had predicted that this, combined with the descent into drug addiction of all members of the band, had closed the book on one of the biggest selling groups of the last decade.

Now it seems that those predictions were somewhat premature. Decomp lives on . . . even if those around them sometimes don't.

Decomp, The Rehab Tour, kicks off on December 1st in the Long Beach Arena. Tickets available from all standard channels. Decomp will be supported on the tour by AC Records' latest signing, a New York band called The Steel Spikes. No information is available on this act at present. Stay tuned . . .

THIRTEEN

Sly Ramone was psyched. Shit, it was Rammer. Sly Rammer. The new name still hadn't sunk in. It had been Ari Covet's decision – apparently Ramone sounded too derivative, like he was being clichéd by using the name of icons from the seventies. Well, fuck it – that was his name. Objections had been futile though – it was clear that when Ari Covet made a decision then that was it and there was no point in arguing, especially when Covet had already instructed the lawyers to make the name change official. The guy was a premium-grade cunt, but he was a premium-grade cunt who had given them their break, so Sly wasn't up for going to war with him on something as simple as a name. Lori had been prepared to go to battle for him, but the newly monikered Sly Rammer had told Lori not to sweat it. He'd appreciated her having his back though. Meeting her had been destiny and she'd come through on everything she'd ever promised them. Shit, she was the fiercest woman that he'd ever met and that was saying something considering he'd been brought up at the bosom of Isabella Ramone, formerly of Naples, and proud owner of the loudest voice in the Bronx.

Many times over the last couple of years he'd considered calling home and then his nerve had crashed the minute he picked up the phone. Pathetic. He was a grown man, twenty-three now and a member of a band that was about to go on its first nationwide tour. The family might even be proud of him, shake his hand, visit him in the emergency room after his mother whipped his ass from one side of the street to the other for leaving a pregnant fiancée and disappearing off the face of the earth. Nah, no point in going back there. He couldn't face his ma, he couldn't face Gloria and he couldn't face the thought that he now had a kid out there somewhere. His kid. A boy? A girl? Kids had never been part of the plan. Gloria was supposed to be on the pill and he was too grateful to be getting sex on tap to check. Dumb fuck. How stupid had he been? A kid that he'd never wanted, to a woman he'd never loved. No doubt Gloria would already be telling it what a no-good deadbeat its dad was. He couldn't argue. Definitely no point in going back there. This was for the best.

He was Sly Rammer now, lead singer in The Steel Spikes, with a girlfriend who was hotter than she could ever realise. He slipped his arm under the covers and tightened it around Marny's waist, smiling as he watched her exhale softly and nuzzle further into his shoulder. She was his good luck charm, she'd saved his life and then helped him turn it around until it was facing a crowd of twenty thousand screaming fans. He loved her and he loved the dream and he was smart enough to know that he might not have made it on his own. He needed Marny, he needed Lori and he needed Dax. Every incredible band that had ever rocked had a duo up front and he knew that together, him and Dax were un-fucking-stoppable. In only a few months they'd already developed an almost silent communication, based on some kind of instinctive understanding of how the other one worked. They just got each other, man. It was like poetry, like love, like some pre-ordained fucking act of God.

Pre-ordained act of God.

He slipped his free hand out from under the sheets, grabbed the pen that lay on the bedside chest and wrote 'Act of God' in blue ink on his chest. His mind was already ahead of him, setting it into a chorus, playing with a riff, picking out the beats of a bridge that he knew Dax would hear just the way that he did.

This is who he was now.

Sylvester Ramone, son of Isabella, ex-fiancé of Gloria, child of the Bronx, oppressed, caged, guilt-laden, upstanding citizen in fully paid family employment was long gone.

He was Sly Rammer, singer, musician, free spirit, leader of The Steel Spikes – about to take the first step onto that stage that was waiting for him.

And he knew it was where he belonged.

Lori had never heard anything like it. Long Beach Arena, over thirteen thousand fans screaming for a band they'd never even heard of. For the first time she understood what Coco meant when she said that the music turned her on. For Lori the aphrodisiac was the cash that every one of those kids had paid for a ticket. She wasn't looking at a rock crowd, she was looking at zeros on a bank statement and it was definitely giving her a thrill in the deposit area. She got 10 per cent of everything the Spikes made. That was looking like 10 per cent of a whole lot of incredible potential right now.

The isolation up at the recording studios had given her time to think about many things, and in some ways acted as a decompression chamber between her old and new lives. The Lori who went in was a bar owner from Rackstown – the one that came out was someone who was on the inside of the music industry. She might not have everything about the business sussed yet but she was a fast learner and if anything, her lack of pre-conceived limitations worked in her favour. When the marketing department at AC told her something wasn't done in a certain way, she asked why. When the accountants in finance were vague, she drilled down to the details. Every aspect of her business mattered to her, she wouldn't be fucked with, and she was smart enough to know that had to show.

The image overhaul had also been interesting. Gone were the jeans and the shirts and the cowboy boots and in were the leather pants, the thigh-high boots with stiletto heels, and the body-moulded jackets that screamed menace. Coco had hooked her up with a back-street boutique just off Sunset that made bespoke pieces. She'd ordered half a dozen pairs of pants, basques and jackets to start: all black, all a combination of leather and rubber, all frigging amazing. If she was going to be the manager of the next big rock band she was going to look the part and having to peel her clothes off every night with talcum powder was a small price to pay.

Her next move was to organise a bus that would get the band from gig to gig in something resembling comfort and safety. She'd found a school bus at an auction in South LA, then driven it down to a garage in a ghetto near Compton. There, she'd given them clear instructions as to what she wanted and promised them that there'd be more work if they got this one right. It was a gamble. Either she'd never see it again or it would come back looking like it had been designed by a pimp on crack. Thankfully, the latter became the reality.

The outside was a black gloss, and some of the best graffiti guys on the streets had painted the name of the band along both sides, each letter punctured with a steel spike that came from a random direction. It looked incredible and the inside matched. All the seats had been pulled out and replaced by black faux-leather sofas that were bolted to the floor, the walls and ceiling painted silver and a plastic film placed over the windows that allowed the passengers to see out, but concealed the inside from prying eyes. The rest of the world didn't need to see Coco fuck-ing Dax all the way from Hollywood to Long Beach.

The guys had been stoked when it had been delivered, with Muff and Strings near orgasmic. 'Cool work boss, cool work,' Muff had whistled. It was progress. It was the first time that he'd managed to give her a compliment without offering to give her head as an extra bonus.

Talking of which . . .

'Boss, can I get a hundred? Want to head out after the gig and don't wanna be . . . you know . . . financially embarrassed.'

'No problem Muff.' Lori pulled a wad of notes from the inside of the soft black leather jacket that was moulded to her frame and pulled off two fifties. 'Thanks,' Muff grinned. 'You know you're looking smokin' tonight and there's one thing that can make a smoking woman even more smokin' . . .' The wink that punctuated the sentence made the cringeworthy come-on even more toe curling.

She sighed wearily, but was faintly amused. 'Muff, have we not had this conversation many, many times? I will let you eat me out only when I require the heat of your body because hell has frozen over. Do you understand, my furry little friend?'

'You have absolutely no idea what you're missing. I have written references.'

'And I have a large gun that I could kill you with,' she replied, deadpan. It was the truth. A couple of grand had paid for the bus, a couple of hundred had paid for the Colt with the rubbed-out serial numbers that sat under the floorboards, courtesy of her vehicular wizards with a sideline in small arms. It made sense. When it came to protecting the goods, it was smart to take precautions. There were a lot of lunatics out there – and then there was the one who was still standing in front of her.

Muff dissolved into laughter. God love him, Lori thought. He was so gormless that he was actually pretty adorable and she loved that he didn't even have the sense to be wary of her.

Her soft spot for him did not, however, require to be enhanced by testing out his proficiency in the cunnilingus department.

She tucked the roll of money back into the inside pocket of her jacket. Holding the band's cash was another decision she'd made in the last few weeks. The guys had been pretty pissed when she'd told them but she'd talked them around. Periods of inactivity were deadly for a group of guys like the Spikes – if she'd released all their cash to them she knew that the lot would be snorted, smoked and fucked away within a week. Being on tour could be even worse. There was a dealer in every city just waiting to swap cash for chemicals. This way she kept a little control and kept them from killing themselves. Despite their protests they'd agreed on a compromise – do it her way until the end of the tour and then they'd review it when they had a longer-term vision of their financial picture. They'd heard the stories; they knew that it could take years for the next instalment of cash to come in so they were prepared to bend. She just wondered how long it would be before the egos took over the decision-making and they became a nightmare to deal with. It was coming and she'd handle it when it did. All part of the job – dealing with that shit was what she was paid her 10 per cent for.

A tightening of her pants around the hips distracted her and she realised that it had something to do with the hand that was now heading down towards the crack of her ass. Instinctively, she lifted one foot and thrust it backwards sending a steel stiletto heel straight into the shin of Ari Covet.

He didn't even yell. Interesting. In fact, he returned her gesture with a smile. Fuck, he must be coked out of his head.

'Like the outfit. Not exactly the hick from Hicksville any more now, are we?' he leered, breathing the sweet, cloying smell of expensive brandy into her air space.

Lori wondered if there was a precedent for a band manager to vomit on the head of a record label chief. Yeah, probably, and she didn't want to do anything that had already been done. She was just going to have to carry on planning to cut off his penis instead.

He was right, though – her new look was definitely different. Covet was still leering at her, waiting for her to spit back a reaction. He was so fucking smug she could scream, but she wouldn't give him the satisfaction of seeing her riled.

'So still think your boys are up for it?' he asked teasingly.

'You know they are. You heard the edits.'

Only that morning the edited tracks had come back from the producers and she'd watched Covet's ugly little face break into an even smugger expression than normal when he'd realised that he'd been right. Every song was worthy of being there, there were at least five out of the twelve that could be singles and calling Sly and Dax back in to re-do some of the vocals and guitar work had been right on the money – it was brilliant before, but now it was off the scale. This was their *Slippery When Wet*. Their *Appetite for Destruction*. Their *Permanent Vacation*. It was the definition of who they were as a band and it was going to make them huge. She just hoped Covet hadn't lost his touch and still knew how to turn talent into sales.

'They're good,' he answered, 'Passed the hard-on test.'

Was he trying to shock her or turn her on? She wasn't sure which of the two freaked her out most.

'Glad to hear that's still a possibility for a man of your age,' she said innocently.

He nearly choked on the big fat Cuban cigar that was dangling from one side of his mouth.

'Honey, you know, one of these days that smart mouth of yours is going to get you spanked.'

'You've absolutely no idea how many times I've heard that before.' The innocent smile was still there, still levitating the conversation above what they both knew it really was: a power-play and a challenge to his authority. Ari wanted rid of her so that he had full control of his new cash-making machine. She was staying where she was and planned to squeeze him for everything she needed – no expense spared – to make her band a success.

As far as both of them were concerned there was only going to be one winner. But Lori knew now wasn't the time to get into this so she did the last thing he would expect: dipped her head down by a foot and kissed him on the cheek.

'I hope you know how much we appreciate everything you've done for us, Ari.' For a moment, watching his face twist from arrogance to surprise, she thought he looked like he was about to have a stroke. Now there was a happy thought that could get a girl through dark days and rainy nights.

The visible little pulse in the side of his jaw told Marny that Sly was nervous. At the sound-check that afternoon he'd been wired, on the edge, demanded that they went over everything again and again until even Dax, the band's resident perfectionist, told him to stop. Sly had ignored him and demanded that they do the first track, 'I'm Into You' all over again. Back in the dressing room, he'd blocked out everyone by flopping out on the floor in a corner, his head on her lap, headphones on, listening to their tracks on repeat, the line between his eyebrows deep with concentration. Anxiety was easy for her to understand so she knew how to be there for him: stroking his face, loving him, but stopping short of polluting the air with clichéd words of reassurance or bullshit. He got enough of that from everyone else.

Later, when the room started filling up with an assortment of people that Marny didn't recognise she watched in awe as Sly flicked off his nerves and switched on the confidence and the charm. Travelling in the opposite direction, Marny just shrank further back into the background.

Invisible. Best to stay invisible. Which, it would seem, wasn't too difficult, because the only person anyone wanted to talk to was Sly.

'Sly, come and meet Anthea Jackson – she'll be looking after your publicity.'

'This is Don Verasano – he's in charge of West Coast distribution.'

'Bobby Sofranko, *Rock Out* magazine. So Sly, how does it feel to be supporting Decomp and what's the message that The Steel Spikes want to get out there?'

From her vantage point in the corner, Marny watched him mingle, charm, and joke his way around the room and she thanked God once again for letting her find him.

'Soulmates,' he'd whispered that morning, as he'd made love to

137

her as the sun came up. Nerves and cocaine had made sleep impossible, so eventually they'd given up, pushed the bed over to the window of the hotel room and made love against the cold glass while LA stretched awake. He was right. Soulmates.

His back was turned to her now, his shoulders wide in the tight grey T-shirt that he would pull off after five minutes on stage, his ass squeezed into white leather pants that Lori had picked up for him only that morning.

There was a sudden commotion at the door and as the crowd parted, Marny could see that Randy Storm had strutted in, closely followed by the rest of Decomp.

'Clear the fucking room,' he screamed, sending dozens of minions scurrying out. Marny immediately pulled her knees up to her chest and made herself as small as possible. Shit, if this was him sober, she'd have hated to have met him when he was high. After a few minutes, only the two bands, a couple of guys who were with Decomp, and Coco and Marny remained. Storm checked out Coco and pulled the rock star grin. No wonder. Much as Marny felt exposed in just jeans and a tiny white cropped T-shirt and matching four-inch white stilettos (they had taken her several days of practice to master), she was conservatively dressed next to Coco's blue PVC hot pants and bra top.

Sly made the first move, walking over to Storm and shaking his hand. 'Hey, man – thanks for having us on the tour.'

'No problem,' Storm replied gruffly. On the face of it he looked great. He was trim, lean and pumped, his face and body was tanned and his peroxide white hair slid down in shiny waves to his shoulder blades. Only when Marny focused on his face did she notice the dark circles under his bloodshot eyes.

'This is Bob McAllister, our recovery counsellor. We wanna just let you guys know that we're grateful that you signed the sobriety contracts.'

The Spikes, even Spank, acknowledged his words with a nod and mumblings of encouragement.

Bob McAllister, way over six-foot tall, just as wide, and with the beard and dress of a Canadian lumberjack, spoke up. 'It's important to us to reaffirm our commitments every day so we'd like you to join us in doing that.'

OK, now this was getting a *little* uncomfortable. Dax and Sly looked at each other and gave almost indiscernible shrugs as they stepped forward, Spank followed with a mumbled 'Fucking dickheads' that Marny was relieved was out of earshot of the others. Tye followed and behind him Muff and Strings were already dissolving into a scrap that was accompanied by mutters of, 'Not fucking holding your hand, you homo.'

It was an incongruous sight – a dozen long-haired rockers all standing in a group holding hands, head bowed. Marny didn't move and no one beckoned her into the circle. Suited her fine.

'Dear Lord, we stand here tonight . . .' Bob McAllister's deep baritone reached every corner of the room. '. . . and we thank you for giving us the strength to walk the path that brought us here. We thank you for this second chance, this opportunity to prove that we have the strength to overcome the obstacles that were put in front of us. We thank you for taking the liquor and the drugs from our lives and we reaffirm to you that we are dedicated to making today and every day clean and sober. We ask for your help in doing this Lord, in Jesus' name, Amen.'

There was a group hug at the end that lasted for several moments until Muff slapped Strings across the back of the head for playfully feeling up his ass and Strings retorted with a karate kick that missed and ended with him rolling on the floor clutching his thigh, screaming, 'Aw, you fucker!'

No one bothered to ask if he was OK.

Instead, with much hand-shaking and some self-conscious, cool-man-type-hugs, Decomp headed off to prepare for the gig. Randy Storm famously required an hour of complete solitude and silence before he went on stage, but according to *Rolling Stone* magazine, that was because in the old days it took that long to find a vein.

The door slammed behind the main act and there was a moment's stillness in the room.

'Where's Lori?' Sly asked.

'I spoke to her half an hour ago,' Muff replied. 'She's up at the side of the stage watching the stadium fill up. Fucking crazy out there, man.'

Sly had already lost interest. He stuck his head out of the door, told the AC records minion that was standing there to keep everyone out, then flipped the key on the door to lock it.

Marny watched as, unusually sombre, he addressed the rest of the guys.

'Gentlemen, I don't have to remind you that this is fucking it. One chance. And we can't mess this up. We need to keep it in line and fucking kill out there tonight.'

There were murmurs of agreement from the others.

'And we need to honour Decomp by sticking to the sobriety pledge . . .'

'Fuck!' It was a pretty unanimous sentiment from everyone except Dax, who was watching proceedings with a wry smile.

'At least . . . unless we're behind locked doors.'

Grinning playfully, he took the key out of the door, slipped it down the front of his pants, before nodding at Dax, who in turn winked at Coco.

'OK, babe, get them out.'

Marny watched as Coco unhooked her bra top, slipped it off, and pulled off a large packet of coke from inside each cup.

Dax pressed the button on the boombox in the corner to cover the noise of the cheers. For the first time that afternoon, Marny had a reason to come out of the corner and just a few minutes later she felt that rush that had become her favourite part of almost every day over the last few weeks. Dax opened up his guitar case and pulled out a bottle of Jack Daniel's to wash it down. No one thought to mention that they hadn't eaten all day. There was a priority scale when it came to nutrition and food was way down the list.

'You OK honey?' It was Coco, delivering a second helping of coke via a tiny silver spoon that had also been concealed in her breast area.

Marny nodded gratefully and snorted it like a pro, before rubbing the spoon along her gums to siphon off the last few tiny grains. It was amazing how quickly you could develop a technique. She and Sly might be soulmates, but the little pile of white powder had become her new best friend, one that wiped out a lifetime of shyness and fear with every long, nerve-jangling sniff.

Happiness descended in an ever-increasing wave. She was fine. She could handle tonight. All those fans, the band, the record people – not a problem. She could deal with the whole scene.

'Fifteen minutes, people!' the banging on the door was delivered with a prompt from the stadium security. Dax tucked the bottle of Jack back into the guitar case and Spank licked the last of the coke off the table top.

Just in time.

'Open the fucking door!' Lori's voice this time. And yep, Marny decided, she could even handle Lori. It was all good. All fine. No nerves, no apprehension. Marny was in control of her life and everything in it and it felt *sooooo* good. Nothing could spoil her mood. Nothing.

'Hey Sly,' she heard Coco say, her voice low and husky, 'you want me to get that key out of there for you?'

The heat was unbearable. Humid. Sticky. Rank with the stench of human sweat.

It was what Coco had dreamt of her whole life. Over the years she'd been to hundreds of concerts and she'd seen some incredible bands – Bon Jovi, Van Halen, Nuclear Fear, Twisted Sister, KISS, Poison, even Decomp – and after every single gig she'd dreamt about being part of the action, imagined what it would feel like to have one of those songs sung just for her. Now she knew.

She'd stood in the wings for the whole concert, sang every

141

word along with Sly, burned with excitement as Dax had turned his back to the audience and stared straight at her as he sung '*You're the one I'd die for baby*,' – the last line of the chorus on 'Suicide Now'. It was her favourite track on the album – a story of love and death that Dax had written for her a few days after they met. It had always sounded amazing, but now, with Sly on vocals and Dax harmonising, Coco was sure that there wasn't a female in America who wouldn't get wet just listening to it.

'They're pretty good.'

Coco could feel the breath on the back of her neck. She didn't have to turn around. She knew the voice – had fucked to it many times and got off by herself many more.

'I know.'

'But they're nothing. Why's someone like you wasting your time when there are bigger things around the corner?'

'Maybe I like this corner,' she replied, with more than a hint of amusement.

'Well if you ever wanna try moving up in the world, just gimme a shout.'

Coco turned to look at the face that had stared down at her from posters on her walls for years. When the scandal of the dead hookers in his pool had broken she'd been horrified. That kind of violence was so far removed from everything that she associated with music. It was about passion, love, sex, getting high – not fishing two dead girls out of a swimming pool and telling their parents that they weren't coming home. Reading that Randy Storm's alibi had proved he had nothing to do with it had been a major relief. It was reassuring that one of the icons she'd grown up with hadn't turned out to be a murdering piece of crap. Hopefully, one day they'd find the scum that did it.

But for now . . . The guy in front of her might have found sobriety. He might have found God. But he'd also found her and fuck it, he was still Randy Storm.

'Which one do you belong to?' he asked her, motioning to the Spikes.

'It's 1987 – I don't belong to anyone,' she replied.

'Ooh, she's sharp. I like that. OK, so which one are you *with*?'

'Dax. Guitar,' she pointed out the love of her life, who was in the middle of a solo and lying flat on his back on the stage, oblivious to the screams of a crowd that were going wild for him.

'Well if you ever feel like changing . . .'

'All OK?' On the surface it seemed like a perfectly innocent, free and easy question, but Coco knew Lori well enough now to realise that she didn't do innocent, she didn't do free and she didn't do easy. Lori stuck her hand out in Randy's direction.

'Lori Wyatt – I'm The Steel Spikes' manager.'

'You're fucking kidding me! How come we get a baldy, fat little bastard and they get you?'

Lori smiled. 'They're just lucky.'

Randy was saved from attempting to steal his supporting band's skirt and management in one night by the appearance of the aforementioned baldy, fat little bastard, who shouted him over and walked him back in the direction of the dressing rooms.

'Cool or dickhead?' Lori asked Coco.

'Cool, I think. But then, I'm biased – he's Randy freakin' Storm!'

'You are so easily swayed, it's pathetic.' The words were harsh but the delivery wasn't. Coco and Lori had found a banter that made their relationship work, made them rub alongside each other without judgement or jealousy. Coco didn't want negative vibes and Lori didn't need tension in the band. Friendship was perhaps a step too far, but they'd both realised that if they were going to be in the same orbit 24/7 for the foreseeable future then it was easier to get along.

'You're absolutely right,' Coco laughed. 'Good to see your people skills are improving.'

Lori smiled ruefully. 'It's the pants. I'm too busy worrying about friction burns on my snatch to be truly evil.'

Coco was still laughing when the band broke into their final number.

'Spotted any possibles?' Lori asked.

Coco nodded in the direction of the audience.

'Front row, the four bleach-blondes and the two brunettes. They've all had their tits out since the guys walked on stage.' The six girls in question were screaming adoringly at the stage, all of them dressed only in miniskirts and heels now. Hell, Coco couldn't blame them. Sly and Dax had the same effect on her.

'And Dax will love the Asian girl at the end – he's got a whole oriental thing going on just now.'

'You two are so fucked up,' Lori said, shaking her head.

Coco feigned surprise. 'Why? Don't all girls line up hot chicks for their men? I thought it was in the contract.' Lori's teasing didn't bother her one little bit. It didn't take spectacular insight to see that her relationship with Dax seemed outrageously dysfunctional to the outside world, but what they didn't get was that it was honest. True. It wasn't about forcing each other to be monogamous, or trapping each other in some warped, conventional restraint, it was about accepting the other for who they really were, encouraging them to explore and live every moment unshackled by expectations or rules.

She loved him enough to let him be exactly who he was and the superfluous, physical stuff like sexual fidelity didn't even factor in their connection to each other. The sex was free, the love exclusive – that was how it was for them. Emotional and spiritual fidelity was what counted. He would only love her. She would only love him.

That was their deal.

'Always,' in her mind she heard his voice whisper his promise.

'Always,' she replied. And she meant it . . . just as long as she ignored the other voice that had been creeping into her thoughts. The one that was taking it back to the chorus, making six girls in front of her swing their tits at the stage. Lori's reply pulled her back to the present. 'Cool. Then feel free to go make their night.'

Coco nudged the huge security guard that was standing in

front of her and he stepped aside to let her make her way down the steps at the side of the stage. Slinking along the front of the cordon that was holding back thousands of screaming fans, she weaved through another four or five guards before slipping in front of the half-naked blonde nearest to her. She leaned over to talk to her and after a few puzzled expressions, the blonde screamed and then, arms flying in rhythm with her boobs, she passed the information on to her friends.

After getting the OK from Coco, the nearby guards stood aside, opened the steel fence a few inches and let the girls slip through. A few minutes later they'd been deposited back in the dressing room, with a roadie on guard to make sure they didn't steal anything, while Coco returned to the side of the stage to join Lori for the final encore. As she watched the audience go insane, she realised that they'd done it. The Steel Spikes were officially here. All those years of slogging in clubs, the practice, the work they'd put in since they all got together, all of it led them here and they'd done it – they'd got the break. And the thirteen thousand, five hundred new fans that were now screaming at them, surging forward to the stage in a wave of frantic determination to get closer to the band proved that they'd rocked it.

Music. Excitement. Danger. It was her axis of bliss.

Coco slipped her arm around Lori's shoulders and shouted so that she could be heard over the noise. 'You've no idea how turned on I am right now.'

'Sorry, love, you're not my type,' Lori retorted with a smile.

The boys were walking towards them now, all soaked with sweat, fired up and ecstatic. Dax and Sly bumping knuckles, their mutual adrenalin highs mirrored in their expressions.

'Look at them! Doesn't this get you off?'

Lori shook her head. 'Ask me again when we get paid and I'll show you what gets me off.'

It was only then that Coco noticed that Marny had appeared behind them. She reached back and pulled her closer so that both Sly and Dax had a welcome party as soon as they reached them.

Coco wrapped her arms around Dax's neck and tasted the sweet salt of the sweat that completely covered him. His eyes were wide, pupils huge, his energy and adrenalin pumping out of every pore of his body.

Grabbing her, he nearly took out Tye and Spank as he swung her around, finally stopping by slamming into the door that led back down into the bowels of the stadium.

'Hey, baby, wanna go fuck a rock star?' he whispered.

'Right here, right now,' she grinned.

'Dax!' Lori's call interrupted them. 'Great set. Way to go there guitarman.'

Dax acknowledged her with a bow and then booted the bar on the door behind them and pulled Coco with him. The rest of the guys followed behind, Sly with his arm around Marny, Lori pulling up the back to make sure that Muff or Strings didn't manage to get lost, injure themselves, or kill each other during the two-hundred yard walk back to the dressing room.

All around them techs and roadies were darting backward and forward, shifting equipment from one place to another. It was like a swarm of ants all playing a part in the greater good of the rock gig colony.

And Coco knew exactly what her part was.

At their dressing room, the guard stood aside to let them in.

'Freeze!' Lori yelled as Dax's hand went on to the handle. She pushed forward, grabbing Strings and Muff by the scruff of the neck and pulling them to the front, before letting them go.

Dax looked at Coco quizzically and got a beaming smile in return. Lori made the announcement.

'Guys, you were incredible tonight. And to say thank you, Coco and I found you a few little presents.'

The door swung open and there, directly in String's and Muff's eye-lines, were twelve naked tits and six eager expressions.

Coco watched the guys' faces light up and realised that it was as close to heaven as they'd ever been. And she was right there with them. This was her family now and it was one that lived on sex, drugs and rock 'n' roll.

Coco had no idea why anyone would choose any other life.

TRACK 4

FOURTEEN

'Fifty-thousand copies.'

'Fifty-thousand. In six months. That's fucking shit, Ari.'

'Don't bust my balls. Look, Decomp have gone platinum on the back of this tour so don't sweat it. Your boys' time will come.' He couldn't keep the self-satisfaction out of his voice. He could never have foreseen how well Decomp would have been welcomed back. Stick that to all those fuckers who said that the whole heavy metal scene was finished.

He'd made a fortune from them, it was a moment of glory and now it was being spoiled by Miss Sour Tits who was in his face and riding his ass about the Spikes. Who the fuck did she think she was?

'We need a video. MTV. Come on, Ari – where's the exposure, where's the buzz? They're killing it on stage every night, but we need more.'

Such a shame she had to speak because he was enjoying just taking in the view of her rubber-clad buttocks as they paced up and down his office.

The tour had covered 112 dates, moving over as far as the

151

Tingley Coliseum in Albuquerque, and now they were back in California for one last gig at the Forum in Inglewood. Then there would be a three-week break before they moved over to the East Coast. It was the kind of exposure that most new bands could only have wet dreams about, yet this bitch still wasn't satisfied.

Fifty-thousand copies wouldn't exactly keep him in whores in his old age but it was a solid start. Now he had to weigh up whether it was worth spending the cash on a video for this album or waiting until they had the next one up and ready to go. He hadn't become a very rich man by throwing money away and making rash decisions. And to be honest, he'd been a little distracted from the fate of the Spikes by Decomp's success. Fuck, they were selling off the shelves again and that got him thinking that if they could do it, maybe his priority should be getting those pricks from Nuclear Fear out of whatever sewer they had crawled into, straightening them out and getting them back on the road too. Ah, he loved a happy ending.

The rubber buttocks had stopped now and were positioned directly in front of him, only a large slab of black onyx separating his teeth from that pussy. His jaw started to grind at the thought of it. He'd bet fifty-thousand record sales that she'd be monu-fucking-mental in the sack. For a start, she was stunning – cheekbones you could snort a line off and the biggest green eyes he had ever seen. And that body . . . only strippers, models and high-class hookers had bodies that hard. Where was she from? Somewhere near Philly as far as he could remember. He made a mental note to get someone at the East Coast satellite office to check if she'd ever done any porn shots. Those were the kind of pictures he'd pay serious money for.

Her voice was getting louder now – but he'd zoned out for so long he had absolutely no idea what she was saying.

'Hey, hey, hey! I said I'll think about it, OK? Now unless that gorgeous little ass of yours wants to get over here and make itself useful by sitting on my dick, then this meeting is over.'

The noise as Lori slammed the door on the way out shook every window on the floor.

He leaned back in his chair and put a lighter to the end of an illegal Cuban cigar the size of a hot dog then checked his watch. 2pm. He pressed his intercom.

'Rita May, call my car and have it outside in ten minutes, then phone Lenny and let him know I'm on my way home. Tell him I'm looking to do some damage.'

Once again, he couldn't help but be amused by his own cleverness. Decomp were back on top. He'd get Nuclear Fear back there too. The Spikes were waiting in the wings. And Lenny, his butler, would understand what he had to do when he got Rita May's message.

His favourite Miss Damage was probably already on her way.

Life was good. In fact, if only he could blow his own cock it would be perfect.

'Hey man, would you shut that fucking noise up?' Spank growled.

The baseball went flying across the room and hit Tye's boombox right off the table, sending it crashing to the ground, pieces flying everywhere. Tye took another drag on his joint before answering. 'Chill out man. Fuck, time of the month or something?'

Lori got in the middle of it before Spank drew a weapon. He'd already threatened to disembowel Muff for stealing his valium stash and mutilate Dax for stealing the eighteen year old that he'd picked up after the gig last night. Dear God, it was a sad day when Coco wasn't enough of a woman for one man. As Lori regularly reminded her lead guitar player and his girl, she didn't pretend to understand the dynamics of their relationship but she had to admire their capacity for enjoying themselves at every opportunity.

However, the enjoyment was definitely starting to sag now. The guys were tired. 112 gigs, together 24/7, and it was a relentless cycle. Wake up around two, bus to the venue, sound check, gig, travel on to the next city, arrive sometime during the night, party a little if there was a strip joint or a nearby bar still open, screw, sleep at dawn, wake up around two and do it all over again. What had seemed like living the dream in the beginning had turned into a hard, exhausting slog, albeit one that that most of the guys were still digging big time. But there was no denying that fuses were getting shorter and the coke lines were getting longer.

Meanwhile, she was getting frustrated.

That tight, dickless bastard Covet was stalling on the video and Lori knew that they needed it now to really ramp up the momentum. So far the crowd reaction had been fantastic, the reviews were positive and Sly and Dax were already getting up quite a following, but it wasn't enough and she had run out of ideas on how to make Ari Covet take his finger out of his ass and get on with it. Didn't he realise that this wasn't a fucking game to her?

The gig with Decomp ended in a few weeks when they went off to Europe and the Spikes were scheduled to return to LA to start writing album number two. That would be the perfect time to shoot the promo but would require the organisation to start now. Ari might be ready to pull the curtain down on the first album and move on, but she wasn't. It hadn't reached its total audience or fufilled its potential and there was no fucking way she was gonna give up on it without a fight. The big sales were still out there to get. In the last couple of years, CDs had taken off and were selling off the shelves now, opening a whole new revenue stream. Dire Straits had sold over a million of those little discs with *Brothers In Arms*. U2 and Michael Jackson were in there shifting phenomenal numbers too. Like others in the industry, Ari had made a fucking fortune by re-releasing all his back catalogues in the new format. Well, he could damn well spend some of that cash on a video for her band.

She ground a Marlboro out on the floor with the tip of her heel and kicked the stub. Unfortunately, it landed in the mop of hair belonging to Strings, who was lying on the floor in front of her, either sleeping or in a coma. It was hard to tell which. They'd no doubt find out when they attempted to wake him to get ready for the show.

She yawned. Exhausted. Every one of them was just dog tired.

Over on one couch, Sly was sleeping off the dual effects of last night's Jack Daniel's and whatever chemical enhancements he had managed to score, steal or borrow. He'd been playing the part of the wild rock 'n' roll bad boy just a little too well lately. Next to him, Marny sat, eyes wide, chewing the nails off her fingers after snorting up yet another line, this time from the mirror that she'd taken to carrying around with her wherever she went. It was a disaster waiting to happen. Her eyes were bloodshot, her nose ran constantly, she was jumpy all the time and if she didn't get a fix she reverted to the terrified, anxious woman–child that she was when Lori first met her, latching on to anyone she thought might be able to score. Spank had never been so popular.

Dax and Coco were flaked out on the other couch – Dax snoring softly, while Coco lay with her eyes closed and a faint humming coming from the headphones that were on her ears. Lori could tell she wasn't sleeping because her nipples were like bullets – her standard reaction when she was listening to some-thing that she was digging. It was a bizarre phenomenon – a female with a libido that was directly connected to her auditory senses. Coco should donate her body to medical research. While Lori was watching her, Coco's eyes flicked open and a moment later she climbed up on to her four-inch platforms.

'Lori, can you tell Dax I'll be back later, hon?'

'No problem.'

Lori watched as she disappeared out of the door and had a feeling Randy Storm would get a knock on his door any minute now. It wasn't a big secret or a big deal.

Over on the other side of the room, Spank was busy carving his initials into his forearm with a craft knife and Muff was valiantly trying to score with the only groupie in the history of the world who had refused to put out. It had become a standing joke with the rest of the guys. Muff had picked this chick up six nights ago and still hadn't got past putting his tongue down her throat, despite his calling up three ex-dates and asking them all to tell this new girl how he could give head like no other dude on earth. Lori was pretty sure she was holding out because she had the hots for Sly and was waiting for him to notice her. She'd be waiting a long time. As far as she could see, Sly didn't fuck around on Marny, but then, that might just be because she was pretty much surgically attached to him at all times.

The door to her left opened and in walked Dave Lopez, looking as always like a physics student who'd got lost on his way to class.

'Hey,' Lori greeted him. 'Any objections to me killing your boss?'

'None.' Dave replied with breezy nonchalance. 'Just don't stick me with the cleaning bill for disposing of the body. No doubt they'd deduct it from my salary.'

It was only then that Lori noticed the stunning black girl who was walking in behind Dave: breathtaking face, dressed in killer heels, tight jeans and a white jumper that slid off one shoulder, backstage pass around her neck.

'Lori, this is Diana Delatto – Ari asked me to bring her back to meet the guys.'

'Tell me you're not related to Mr Covet in any way,' Lori replied dryly. She knew she shouldn't be mouthing off about Ari in public – this chick could be anyone: a reporter, a new recruit to the record company or – God forbid – his daughter.

'No, I'm definitely not related. They remove the children of evil at birth.'

Lori laughed. 'My kind of woman. Come on, grab a seat. Sorry, the guys are all kind of out of it just now but you're welcome to hang for a while. So how do you know Ari and what can you tell me that will help me ruin his life?'

Diana Delatto grinned. She'd heard of Lori Wyatt already. A

few of the papers had done features on her using the 'female in a man's world' angle. She'd heard her interviewed on a couple of radio stations. And that afternoon Ari Covet had shouted Lori's name just as he'd sunk his teeth into Diana's pussy.

'Come on baby, just close your eyes and let me do it to you.'

Coco was beginning to think it was a mistake coming to see Randy Storm but the atmosphere had been so down back in the Spikes' dressing room and she'd been listening to Decomp's new single on her Walkman and well, the rest was inevitable, really. Jon Bon Jovi or Axl Rose would have met the same fate if they'd been within a hundred yards and unencumbered by chicks or security.

But now she was here it just seemed too kinda *heavy*. Sex was 100 per cent pure pleasure for her. Sex. Music. They went together, intrinsically connected, inseparable in her mind. Love was what she had with Dax. Sex was what she'd been having for the last couple of weeks with Randy Storm. Dax didn't mind. The Asian girl was long gone but he was so wiped out that he was glad of the rest.

It was the perfect solution – a practical example of why their outlook on free sex worked perfectly for each of them.

Or at least, it had been working for her until the last couple of days with Randy Storm. The day before she'd found it hard to get in the zone, especially when he'd insisted on telling her all about his newfound religion beforehand and then expected her to stay and hang with him afterwards. She didn't particularly want to know how the Lord was with him every step of the way. She definitely didn't want to hang afterwards. She just wanted an incredible fuck and then to mosey right along afterwards.

So far, today wasn't looking like it was going to be a particular high spot either. She was lying on the pool table that sat in the centre of his dressing room and he'd just produced an insanely huge dildo and wanted to watch as she got up close and intimate with it. Not her idea of a great time, but hey – better than staring at the walls waiting for the action to start back at the Spikes' hangout.

'Baby don't go, you know you're the light in the dark . . .'

Night after night for the last six months she'd listened to Randy Storm sing those words. He'd written 'Light in the Dark' while he was in rehab, the fans on the road had loved it and now they'd just released it as their new single and it was pretty close to freaking genius. Incredible. Moving. Gut-wrenching. A massive power ballad that had production values like nothing else she'd ever heard. There were strings on there, a whole classical section that worked with the rock to produce . . . *OK*, now we were getting somewhere. As the music flooded through her head and raced through her veins, she felt her shoulders relax, her smile return and her legs open.

A completely naked Randy Storm took that as a signal to proceed and twelve inches of vibrating synthetic purple, courtesy of a Taiwanese plastics factory, was now bobbing up and down on her clit, just working her up, getting ready to move right along inside.

Storm put her hand around it then let go, leaving him free to add the finishing touches. Coco watched as he reached under the table and came back up with four scarves. Quickly and efficiently, barely glancing at her, he used two to attach her feet to the bottom pockets of the table, then moved upwards to her free arm and tied that up at the top. Leaning over, he reclaimed the vibrator and slowly pushed it inside. Coco's pupils dilated as the sensation of utter pleasure made her scream. Storm leant over her, taking one nipple in his mouth and sucking hard, then suddenly breaking off to tie up her remaining limb.

Starfished now, she watched eagerly as Storm grabbed the top of the dildo and worked it out and in a few times, each stroke going deeper and deeper until all but the very base of it was inside her.

Her breaths were shallow now, quick gasps that were punctuated with cries for more. Oh fuck, that felt good. So good. The
chorus had broken into the bridge now and those strings were
getting higher, fiercer. Then the drums came in – a deep, pounding, rhythmic beat that smashed the fragility of the sound and
twisted it to somewhere dark, somewhere raw.

'Harder! Oh, fuck, baby do it harder!' she gasped, but Storm
had let go again, leaving the dildo inside her to do all the work.
Now he had climbed up on to the table and was above her,
standing with one foot on either side of her hips, looking down
on her hungrily as he jerked himself off.

Coco could feel the orgasm coming, the delicious tingle that
started deep in her pelvis and spread like an explosion of sheer
ecstasy to every nerve ending in her body.

'Yes! Randy . . . Randy . . . Randy . . . Oh, fuck yes!' she
screamed, almost disconnected from reality by the excruciating
perfection of the orgasm.

Suddenly he threw his head back and roared some guttural,
indiscernible noise as he shot his spunk all over her.

It was over in seconds and he slumped to his knees, exhausted
and soaked with sweat, then bent forward to let his head fall on
her chest.

The music had stopped now and she was back in reality, back
in a dressing room in some stadium, with the rest of the Decomp
guys next door, the Spikes down the hall and thousands of frantic teenagers already lining up outside. She waited for the familiar
rush of endorphins to follow the orgasm but they were slow in
coming this time. Of course, that might be because of the physical complications.

'Randy . . .?' she whispered softly.

'Yeah?'

'Could you take it out now?'

'Shit!' he laughed, as he gently retrieved his favourite new sex
aid and switched it off.

'And?' Coco gestured to the ties around her wrists, and he

stretched over to un-strap them. Despite the shaky start, she was glad she'd come to him. It might not have been her thing, but it had turned out to be pretty enjoyable and she'd already learned that these days she took the good times where they were offered because she didn't know when the next opportunity was going to come along. Decomp might be travelling from gig to gig by limo and jet, but her poor Spikes boys were strictly bus only and it was really taking it out on their energy, their social lives and their stamina.

Sliding off the table, she pulled her denim shorts and bikini top back on. Over on the sofa, Randy was slouching, still butt-naked, legs splayed, his dick and balls dangling as he took a long drag on a cigarette. Now there was a vision that the majority of the planet's female contingent would die to see.

'See ya . . .' she reached down and kissed the end of his nose.

'Hey listen,' he drawled, his expression curious, 'How's the sobriety thing holding up with your guys?'

A chill ran all the way up the back of her spine. What had he seen? Had he heard rumours? Has someone grassed them up? Noooooo. This wasn't good. They were only halfway through the tour and if they broke the agreement they'd be out and that would be it. Over. Done. Finished. Dax would be devastated.

Deception went against everything that she stood for, but there was a time to lie and it was now.

'It's going great. The guys are really committed and they've stayed straight the whole time.' Randy nodded his head thoughtfully. She detected an underlying reason for the question and knew that she had to dig a little deeper. If there was anything going on that could jeopardise the Spikes she had to find out what it was and do something about it.

'Why do you ask?' she said as casually as she could manage.

He shrugged his shoulders. 'No big deal. Just thought you were trippin' a little today.'

What? She was trippin'? He was the one that had tied her up and screwed her with twelve inches of purple plastic. If he wanted to see who was tripping he should be looking in a mirror.

'Why would you say that?'

'Dunno . . . you just seemed a little . . . *disconnected*.'

What could she tell him? That she thought he was a self-obsessed Jesus freak? That purple plastic didn't do it for her? That the whole bondage act wasn't her thing?

Or should she admit the truth that she didn't even want to confess to herself – that the whole time he'd been fucking her she'd been thinking about another singer altogether.

She'd been thinking about Sly.

Diana Delatto untied the top of her pale blue halter dress and let it slip to the floor. If the cop who'd stopped her for speeding on the way over here had known what she was concealing, she'd have got more than a couple of chat-up lines and a telephone number. Four times she'd been stopped for travelling too fast and not one ticket. It was a record she was proud of. If they ever upped the quota of female officers in traffic division then she'd be screwed. The irony of that thought wasn't lost on her. Diana Delatto got screwed every day of her life – and that was no one's choice but her own. Travelling to Hollywood from Dallas had seemed like a great idea once. She'd won Miss Black Teen Texas and gone straight from there to the oldest cliché in LA – the young girl arriving off a bus, determined to make it. Her parents had tried to talk her out of it but their words had more effect on the flock in their church than they'd ever had on Diana. Shit, if her dad could see her now he'd be on his knees praying for forgiveness for her until the end of time. But they'd never know. The jump from failed auditions, to escort work, to offering specialised services, had been a direct one for her. Sure, she could have taken work in a bar, or waitressed her life away for minimum wage, but earning great money while being her own boss suited her better.

And now, she'd finally found the break that she'd been looking for.

She had an offer on the table . . . and it didn't involve taking that bus back to Texas. From now on, the only Dallas she wanted to see featured JR, Sue Ellen and the most over-populated ranch-house in the south. Unlike this place.

She checked out her appearance in the bathroom mirror. Actually, it was more of a dressing room than a bathroom – two hundred square feet of marble and mirror (more than half the size of her apartment) and it didn't even get used. It was the Jill bath-room to Ari Covet's Jack. So of course, it lay empty because no woman could ever live with the sick son of a bitch.

The leather bondage straps wrapped under and around her breasts, cup-less harnesses that let her voluptuous, firm tits swing free. The leather then snaked down around her hips, joining together then separating again to leave her snatch exposed. There were two reasons that she couldn't wait to walk away from Ari Covet for ever. The first was that he was a twisted freak who deserved nothing but a slow painful death. The second was that she could let her bush grow back and be done with the bald thing. Did he not realise the discomfort and maintenance that it took to keep it the way he liked it? Sick bastard.

Hat on. Ankle boots with a chain of metal spikes around the top to match the five-inch steel heels. Ball gag. Whip. Nipple clamps. Handcuffs. The sleazeball who owned S&M Paradise down on Sunset probably put his kid through college on her earnings.

But not for much longer. Oh no. She had found a way out of this and she was going to grab it with two hands – hands that were no longer going to be handcuffed to a sweating, middle-aged millionaire with a pain fetish.

Striding into the room, she placed her bag of tricks in the corner and saw that he was ready and waiting for her; naked and on the floor, one thumb in his mouth, his flaccid dick flopped out under his bulging stomach. From this angle she could see the hair plugs that hadn't taken after the last transplant. Urgh, he was gross. Vile. And it was that disgust that made her so very, very good at her job.

Unable to restrain herself, she cracked the whip in his direction and watched as an angry red welt immediately flared up across his chest. His head flipped up in surprise and he opened his mouth to object.

'Get against the pillar NOW!' she spat, flicking the whip again but this time falling just short of contact with his saggy flesh. He used his hands to push himself backwards across the floor until he made contact with the marble pillar behind him.

'Are you going to . . . hurt me?' he asked in a little boy voice.

She had never hated him more. Her voice was low, deadly.

'I'm going to fucking kill you if you speak to me again without my permission.'

And there it was – the trigger that made his dick stand to attention and colour up in a split second.

She moved around behind him, tied his hands behind the pillar and then strutted back to the front. He knew the drill. He'd designed it. The first time she'd come here, new, naïve, only six weeks into working for the escort agency, he'd spelled it out, step by step, every little detail of his fantasy. For the money he was paying she'd been willing to do it. Five hundred dollars, no penetration? She'd take that any day of the week. But then the biting had started and the last two times he'd drawn blood and it was seriously freaking her out. She wasn't going to let this pathetic old bastard scar her, not when she had plans to get out of this line of work and go make a decent, law-abiding life for herself.

Ignoring his salacious stare, she walked back over to her bag, crouched down and pulled out the other tools she required at this stage in the game.

She gripped Ari's hair as she shoved the ball gag in his mouth. No wonder his damn plugs hadn't taken when she was pulling on them twice a week. Working swiftly, she latched the steel nipple clamps on and got a small sense of satisfaction when he writhed in pain. Unfortunately, his prevailing hard-on demonstrated that it was the kind of pain he liked. That upset her. The loud crack as she slapped his face resounded around the room. His wide-eyed look of surprise was rewarded with a repeat action.

Springing back up, she grabbed her whip again and then flicked it above his head. He was trembling now and hell, it looked like his dick was just about ready to burst. OK, back to the script.

Crack. One whiplash, then she growled the first insult.

Crack. Another one, followed by a handy rant as to what a piece of scum he was, all delivered in a high volume, furious shout.

Crack. More filth, more venom.

Return to the beginning of the scene and repeat.

Stage one over, she released his hands from behind the pillar, tied them in front of him and moved on to stage two.

As she squatted down in front of him and rubbed the handle of the whip along his shaft. He threw his head back, causing a thud as it met with the cold hardness of the marble. One of these days the daft bastard was going to do himself a permanent injury and she had absolutely no idea how he was going to explain that to the paramedics.

Slowly, but without letting up on the pressure, she took the handle back along the other side of his cock, trying to block out the sound of his groans. Last time. The very last time. She wouldn't have to do this ever again.

Another couple of passes with the handle of the whip and she knew he was ready. Standing up, she straddled him and, looking down, watched as his brain processed what was going on.

'You want me now, don't you, sweetie?'

He nodded, but at the same time he was struggling, trying to understand why she wasn't sticking to the routine. Slowly, she began to lower her pussy towards his face and she could see that he was getting real furious now.

It was hard not to smile. Yes, Ari, you fat prick, I'm not playing it your way this time – the ball gag is staying in.

If he was ever going to have that heart attack the time would be now. She knew he was freaking out. His instructions had always been clear: remove gag, sit on face. Not difficult. Not easy to forget. Just a little . . . well . . . *unpalatable* for her today. *Unpalatable*. Great word. Ari Covet was an unpalatable piece of shit.

With every inch that she lowered, his eyes grew wider with sheer fucking fury.

Lower.

'Come on baby, you know you want it this way,' she purred.

Lower.

'Oooooh, what's the matter? Is little Ari not getting what he wants?'

Lower.

'And look at that beautiful pussy just ready to . . .'

Aaaaaaaaaaargh.

His explosion as he came was as violent as it was prolific. But she knew him too well. By the time his fluid was about to leave his body, she'd already darted to the side, and now he lay there, furious, wild-eyed and covered in his own cum.

Miss Damage stood and surveyed the scene. She should release him. She really should. But it wasn't over until the fat man sang and this fat man sure as hell wasn't singing yet.

'Interesting. Certainly a novel way to make a living.'

Diana flicked her head back and made eye contact with the new arrival. From the increase in squirming and muffled screams, she could see that Ari had spotted the visitor too.

The footsteps headed over towards the bag that was still sitting in the corner off the room, in – she would later discover – the absolutely perfect position for the concealed camera to catch every bit of the action.

The new arrival lifted the camera from its hidden position and flicked the off switch. Ah, it was so perfect when a plan came together. So sweet when justice is done.

The noise of heels crossing the floor was the only sound until a face moved in so that it was only inches from Ari Covet's sweating, fetid brow.

'So here's the deal.' The voice was pragmatic. Almost flippant.

'The Steel Spikes need a video and they need it now. And unless they get it, then the official promo to publicise their next release will feature a twisted asshole quivering on the floor covered in his very own spunk. Not much of a story but I'm thinking the novelty value will make it a smash.'

Ari was raging now, straining against his ties, thrashing his head from side to side, his teeth grinding so hard against the gag that the gums began to bleed.

'I'll expect to hear about the arrangements tomorrow morning.' With that parting shot the intruder stood up so that all six foot four inches of her was standing over him. She put one five-inch heel on his chest and slowly traced it all the way from his collarbone down to his matted pubes.

'And, my little mogul friend,' she added in a sweet, breezy voice. 'If anything negative happens to me, my boys, or the lovely Miss Damage over there, this little home movie goes on general release. Do you understand, darling?'

A thin trickle of blood ran down from the corner of his mouth to his chin, his eyes crazed, insane with fury and frustration. It didn't help that she blew him a kiss before turning and heading in the direction of the door.

As she passed Miss Damage, she winked.

'Sure you don't want to try your luck as an actress? I can definitely see talent there.'

Diana laughed as she shook her head. 'Think I've had enough of pretending to be someone else to last me a lifetime.'

'OK, if you're sure. I'll see you Monday, our place, 9am. Don't be late.'

'Oh, trust me, I won't be. Think I'll be doing my best to keep on your good side.'

They'd clicked the moment they met and the easy banter amused them both.

As Lori headed down the sweeping marble staircase, she couldn't help but feel a little surge of satisfaction. Councillor

Gorman in Rackstown. Ari Covet in Los Angeles. Worlds apart but both so, so alike that it made perfect sense to use similar tactics when bringing them down. They had the same weaknesses: both arrogant, both sleazy, both had egos that ruled their behaviour and their dicks. She knew the type. She'd grown up with it.

And if there was one thing that Lori knew it was that when she came up against someone with a weakness, she would always come out on top . . . Because she was never afraid of using whatever means necessary to make sure that she won in the end. No matter what shit she had to go through to get there.

Wasn't that what she had always done?

FIFTEEN

Rock-a-bye baby . . .

Miss Molly's hair was looking nice today. She'd brushed it and brushed it until it was shiny, just how Mama had always told her to. Had to be nice for visitors. Had to put on a nice dress and brush her teeth and pull her hair back in a bow, just like Miss Molly's.

Must never ask for anything, must speak only when spoken to, must remember to use nice words and never ever to cuss. Visitors didn't like to hear cussing. That made them sad and run away and then she'd have to come back to the dark room and then God would be angry. And when God was angry bad things happened.

Rock-a-bye baby . . .

But tonight God wouldn't be angry with her, because today she'd be a good girl.

She giggled as she hugged herself tightly, careful not to crush her pretty white cardigan. The pastor said that God knew everything but that wasn't true because he didn't know that she had a secret that only she and Miss Molly knew about. A special secret. She couldn't think about it right now but she would plan it more when she came back to bed and the lights went out because that made the dark less scary.

She didn't want to be scared any more.

And she knew exactly how to make it stop.

She was just waiting for Miss Molly to tell her when the time was right.

SIXTEEN

'Marny? Can . . . can I ask you something?'

'Sure.'

'Are you OK?' Marny turned to face Dave Lopez and saw a concerned expression. Sweet boy. OK, so he was a grown man but to her he still seemed young, clean – an altogether different breed from the guys in the band and the roadies and the rest of the crew that had become spectators to their existence.

She wasn't even entirely sure what his role was now. He'd become their day-to-day guy – their go-to man from the record company, always around, always working to make sure things went smoothly.

Which, of course, they never did.

They were now banned from every Howard Johnson in the country because back in San Francisco, Spank had gone on a drugged-up cutting session with two sixteen year olds that ended up with them deciding that it would be a great idea to decorate a wall in his hotel room with their own blood. One of the girls' fathers was still threatening to sue.

Tye needed emergency dental work in San Diego after his front teeth were punched out during a fist fight with Chuck, the security guard Dave had posted at the door to make sure they didn't leave the hotel to score in the hours before they left for the gig.

In Palm Springs, Dave had to bail out Muff and Strings after they got arrested for urinating out of the bus window. They still claimed that they hadn't noticed the motorcycle cops that were riding alongside at that very same moment. After one of the most dampening experiences of their lives, the cops were probably still on antibiotics but thankfully, Diana Delatto, their new bus driver and assistant, had gone down to the station with Dave and somehow persuaded the officers of the law not to proceed with charges.

The parties, the craziness, the drama: everything that happened, no matter how bizarre or unexpected, Dave dealt with it and somehow got them out the other end. Everything they needed, he came up with the goods.

And luckily for Marny, that included the small brown paper bag that Dave was now handing over to her.

'Yeah, 'course. Everything is er, good. Yeah. Everything's good.'

There was no way to tell if he was convinced by her assurances as she'd been looking at his feet the whole time. She hadn't had her little snort of confidence yet that morning and she'd noticed that somehow dealing with people when she was straight was even more excruciating now than it had been before.

Without staying to elaborate, she tucked the bag into her jacket pocket and headed back to her room where Sly was waiting, lying on top of the crumpled bedsheets, naked, his eyes still heavy with sleep.

If it was possible, she loved him more now than she had ever done.

'Hey baby girl,' he croaked, giving her a lazy smile. 'You giving room service today?'

Marny held up the paper bag and nodded. 'Yes, sir – breakfast is right here.'

She tossed the bag on the bed and shrugged off her jacket, not even stopping to unzip it first. All her clothes just fell off her these days and she hated to catch sight of herself in the mirror. She'd always been slim but now she was downright scrawny and found it was best to avoid large reflective surfaces altogether – looking at her own ribs sticking out of thin, transparent flesh had no appeal at all.

It never occurred to her to wonder when they had last eaten a meal.

Sly had become her skeletal twin. His cheekbones and jawline were like scaffolding over which a papery layer of skin had been stretched. From the neck down he had a whole Steve Tyler/ Mick Jagger look going on and she was sure it was because, like them, he worked that crowd, night after night, a hyperactive bag of bones that didn't stop from the first note that was played until the last beat of the encore.

Every night he left the stage exhausted, drained, fired up, buzzing – a raging conflict of feelings and emotions that in the beginning had been calmed and reconciled with a bottle of Jack, some partying and then a long night of love. Now they'd found a different way.

A pill as soon as he came off the stage to bring him down.

A few lines of coke a little later to bring him back up again.

A dose of speed to give him the energy to get through the night.

A vial of amyl nitrite to fuel the most incredible sex they'd ever had.

A couple of Valium to send him off to sleep.

A few uppers to wake him back up again.

The mood swings and the volatility that had become part of their everyday existence were a small price to pay. Some people saw arrogance and attitude in his outbursts but Marny knew it ran deeper than that. Back when they first met she'd realised that there was an edge, a thirst for danger in there and now she saw that there was a flip side to that; a melancholy that could bring him down without warning or reason. He could switch from happy to morbid in seconds and she dealt with every stage on the mood spectrum in the same way: by being there for him and doing whatever he needed her to do. It was no hardship. If anything those layers of complexity ramped up her love for him.

To her he was still everything.

He was the one up front, the one that was dealing with the pressure, the fans, the attention. The fact that he could even do that was amazing to her. And still the fact that he did it all with her at his side amazed her even more. She'd seen the options that were laid out before him. Her stomach would twist with fear before every concert when the girls would strut into the dressing room looking for autographs and photographs and often much, much, more. During the performance she'd see them in the front rows, frequently half naked, showing him what he could have if he just nodded in their direction.

There was a repeat performance after the show. Girls in the hotels, on the tour bus, in the clubs, all throwing themselves at the band, but yet he stayed with her. 'You know why, don't you?' he'd told her once, when her insecurities had floated to the surface. 'Because you're the only person who ever let me breathe.' She wasn't sure what it meant, but she'd take it.

She knew about the guilt he'd felt growing up, the alienation of living in an environment that suffocated and stifled, where you were never made to feel like you were good enough to be there. In the early days he'd talked about his family a lot – his Italian parents, his sisters, the crazy aunts and the uncles who lived for their food, their families and their businesses. It was so obvious that he missed them, yet the umbilical cord that led back to them appeared to have snapped.

She got that – had felt the same pain.

'Is that enough?' she'd asked him once. 'Me – am I enough?'

He'd nodded, his fingers playing with the wisps of hair that framed her face.

'Yes, my little co-dependent one. You. The band. That adds up to enough.'

Almost all of her believed him. There was just a tiny doubt. Every now and then she'd glimpse something in his face, a sadness, a longing, and she knew. He might think he was happy. He might even have convinced himself that he had all he ever wanted. But there was something missing for him and he was filling it with the contents of Dave's little brown bags.

For her, the pay off was confidence, happiness. Sly claimed that for him it was all about the trip. Sex, drugs and rock 'n' roll, baby. Marny wasn't convinced. More and more she saw that he relished the numbness, the disassociation with reality and she was sure that it was because, unlike her, there were doors to the past that were left just a little open in his mind.

Now they'd come a full circle. They were in another faceless hotel, grey skies outside matching the bland, generic interior, but today was different.

'Are we here?' Sly asked, pushing back the sheet as he sat up. If those groupies could see him now, naked, beautiful, they'd go wild.

He emptied the brown bag onto the bed, sorted the pills into a pile in the middle and then deposited the coke on the bedside table for her to cut it up on her trusty mirror. Instructions weren't necessary. This was their standard morning routine. The only thing that made today different from any other day over the last few months was . . .

'We're here.'

Philadelphia. The city they'd met in. They were back in their home town for the first time in three years. Marny needed a line before she could even bring herself to think about it.

'Are you gonna go see anyone?' Sly asked.

'No.' There was officially not a single person in this place that she wanted to see. Plenty she wanted to avoid, though. The worst days of her life had been spent here. The last day she saw her father. The last day she saw her mother. And Benny. Her brother. The last day she saw Benny.

'Hey, hey – what's wrong?' Sly leaned over and wiped away the single tear that was running down her cheek. It was only then that she realised that she was crying. Served her right for letting her mind go back there. Hadn't she learned that those things should be kept in a box, sealed, removed to a part of the brain that was as far away from the pain receptors as possible?

'Tell me . . .' Sly urged. 'I want to know. Tell me.'

Marny shook her head, shrugged off the tears and busied herself chopping up another line on the bedside table. 'There's nothing to tell. Old news. Other folks have had it much worse.'

It was her standard reply and she knew Sly wouldn't push it. In the first few months he'd asked her often about her life and the answer was always the same: there was no family.

Her parents and brother had died in a car crash when she was ten. Nothing to tell. Nothing to see. Move on along and start a new life and leave the past where it belonged.

He understood that and let it be, just like she'd always done for him.

Soulmates. Two souls connected by trust and understanding.

That was why she'd never pushed him to open up or examine his demons, but lately those fleeting moments of sadness she saw in Sly had been coming more and more often. Perhaps it was the drugs. Maybe it was a need to share the incredible things that were happening to him. Or maybe . . . maybe that door to his past needed to be re-opened.

'What about you? Gonna go see your family?' Her heart beat just a little faster as she said it and it wasn't the after-effects of the cocaine.

'Can't do it. You've no idea, Marny. I'll be dead to them by now. Pulling a stunt like that . . .' he paused to throw back a couple of Quaaludes that he washed down with some Jack straight from the bottle. '. . . that's like, serious shit, man. You don't do that in a family like ours. The shame has probably killed my mom by now,' he choked out the last few words. There it was – the pain, screaming out from the frownlines on his forehead, the tension in his jaw. Marny instinctively crawled over the stained blue blanket and climbed on top of him, strad-dling him as she took his face in her hands. 'Go see them, Sly. You're their son, they'll forgive you.'

That familiar pulse in the side of his temple told her that his anxiety and temper were rising. It didn't take much to make him snap these days and this was definitely way too deep for him to deal with.

There was a sudden explosion as the bottle of JD went shoot-ing out from beside her and smashed against the nearby wall. 'I can't fucking do it. I'm dead to them by now. Don't you get that? Don't you fucking understand that? I'm like, fucking evil to them.'

The smell of the liquor on his breath assaulted her as he spat out the words, making her reel backwards. He snatched out and grabbed her wrist.

'Do you get that, Marny? Do you?'

It wasn't Sly that was talking, she knew that. It was the pain. It was the pills. It was the grief that was making him jolt his legs to the side so that she slid right off the bed and landed with a thud on the brittle grey carpet.

There were only two ways to deal with him when he did this – sit quietly until he calmed down or leave him alone for a little while until the happy pills kicked in and took the edge off.

This time she chose the latter.

'Where the fuck are you going?' he spat. The aggression was still there but she knew he didn't want her to go, didn't like her being out of his sight for too long.

'Just gonna get you some more Jack, baby. I'll be back in a few minutes.'

He snatched three Valium pills from the pile and tossed them back dry, then turned to stare out of the window at the city he'd grown up in.

She was dismissed. By the time she got back he'd be mellow again, he'd be sorry, he'd whisper how much he loved her and she would shush away his pain.

Without further explanation, she grabbed her jacket and slipped out. A little way along the corridor she stopped and rapped on a door.

'Marny! Hi sugar, you OK?' Diana Delatto answered with her usual cheer and affection. In many ways she was like a less scary, more low-key version of Lori – strong, sassy, with a sense of humour but dangerous when riled. She'd already threatened to castrate Dax for sneaking strippers on to the bus and leaving them there for her to find in the morning.

'Hi Diana – Lori there?'

The door opened wider and Marny saw that Lori was sitting at a small wooden desk by the window, a pile of paperwork in front of her.

'Lori, can I have some money?'

Lori's eyes narrowed a little, not unkindly, but she was clearly wary.

'More?'

Shit, she forgot she'd taken that hundred dollars last night to pay Dave up front for the score.

'Yeah, just a few things that I need to pick up today. Y'know – toiletries and stuff. And Sly wants me to get a couple of albums that he's been hearing about.'

'I can get those for you,' Diana offered.

'No, s'OK. I come from Philadelphia so I kinda know my way around here.'

Lori got up from behind the desk, took her wallet out from inside her jacket and handed over the notes.

'No problem, Marny. Everything OK?'

Jeez, what was it with everyone today? Did she not look OK? Why did anyone care? Why did everyone need to know what was going on with her?

A sudden shiver made her tremble and at the same time she realised that her nose was running. She sniffed, pulled the edge of her sleeve down and wiped her nose. She caught a look exchanged between Lori and Diana but couldn't read it.

'Marny, I'm not going to get into your business, but go easy on the coke hon. I'm starting to worry about you.'

A heat rose from her neck and Marny chewed the inside of her gum as she felt her face start to burn. 'It's just a little . . .'

Lori put her hand up. 'Marny, I'm not your boss and I'm not telling you what to do. I'm just concerned, OK?'

Marny shrugged, self-consciously. Thanks, but everything's fine. Really.'

Wow, major discomfort. Time to leave. However, her hand was on the door handle when she suddenly realised she didn't have everything she'd come for. It was either ask here, or face the strangers at reception. She turned back.

'Sorry, but do either of you have a couple of dimes?'

Diana fished into her back pocket and handed a couple over. Perfect.

Now she had everything that she needed. She just hoped that she was calling this one right, praying that those dimes would heal Sly's pain . . . and they wouldn't cost her a future with her soulmate.

'You really worried?' Diana Delatto raised an eyebrow in Lori's direction. It was rewarded with a pensive shrug.

'Not worried, just aware. She's an adult, and I sure as shit wouldn't appreciate anyone messing in my life, but you know, I just don't want her to get in too deep. Just need her to know that I can see them going down the path and I'm going to have to bring them back before they get way too far along. After the shoot I'll talk to them again. Got a couple of weeks' break, so maybe they need some time away. I've heard rehab is nice at this time of year.'

'Think they'll go?'

Lori pondered that for a few moments. 'Not Sly. Fucker is so self-obsessed he can't see that he's messing up. Messing both of them up. I'll sort it, don't worry. No way I'm going to let Sly's little habit affect my bottom line.

178

'Can't believe you're watching that stuff again.' Lori changed the subject, gesturing to the mute TV where Bruce Willis and Cybil Shepherd were arguing about something on *Moonlighting*.

Diana laughed, pressed the off button on the remote, then moved around behind Lori's chair, leaned over and took the pen out of her hand. Never before had she met someone as focused and dedicated as this chick. Lori ate, slept and breathed The Steel Spikes. As far as Diana could tell there was nothing else, just business. 24/7. No love, no fun, no play, no guys, no drugs. Just focus. What drove people to be like that? Sure, she knew all about sacrifice – hadn't her dignity been the first thing to get put on hold when she needed a way to make a living?

But Lori was different and in the few weeks that they'd been on the road together, Diana's gratitude for Lori taking her on-board had morphed into admiration. And awe. And something . . . else.

Lori looked up, surprised. 'Hey, what's . . .?'

Without speaking, and ignoring the voice in her head that was screaming, 'Don't fucking do this, she'll kill you!' Diana leaned over and kissed her on the lips. Soft. Tender. Shit, Diana's heart was thudding out of her chest. What the fuck was she doing? This was the best job she'd ever had and now she was potentially screwing it up by . . .

The chair flew back, cracking against the window behind them, as Lori shot up and pulled away.

Diana threw both hands up. 'I'm sorry. I'm sorry, But, shit Lori, it's just . . .' How could she say it? It was just that Lori's performance at Ari Covet's house had impressed the hell out of her? It was just that every time Lori opened her mouth, sorted out a problem, Diana fell for her just a little bit more? It was just that Lori was so fucking impressive that she'd started to fantasise about her when she closed her eyes? This was her high school cheerleader crush all over again only this time it was more about deep attraction and respect than just wanting to hang with the cool crowd.

Although the truth was, Lori was the coolest chick she'd ever met – if she ignored the fact that she was standing in front of her right now, eyes blazing, making it clear that a violent rejection was imminent.

'It's just that . . . I get you.'

Lori pushed her away. 'You *get* me? What the fuck do you know about me? Huh? What the fuck do you know?'

Diana realised that she had a fair point. Perhaps in hindsight having the whole 'fancy some girl-on-girl?' conversation might have been useful before she slipped her tongue down her boss's throat. Shit, she was in trouble. And the last thing she wanted was to lose this job because she loved it. She wasn't going back to Hollywood and servicing depraved pricks six nights a week. She couldn't do it. But maybe she should have thought about that five minutes ago.

Time for apologies, soft words of atonement. 'Lori, I'm sorry, girl – won't happen again. I've just been feeling . . . I like you. I like you so much and I just got carried away. And I couldn't stop . . .' Damn, this was excruciating. She uttered a silent prayer. Ground. Open. Up. Make. Me. Disappear.

'I couldn't stop myself, but hey – now I know. Won't happen again. Sorry, babe.'

And don't fire me, she thought. Please God, don't let her kick my ass right out of here.

'You don't know me,' Lori whispered. 'You don't know anything about me.' Her tone took Diana by surprise. The fury was gone, the rage calmed, replaced by something that sounded more like sadness.

Suddenly Diana was torn.

Try again. Or bail out. Try again. Bail out. Self-preservation and the need for a job told her to bail, quickly. But there was something there, something in Lori's eyes . . .

'I'd like to know you.' Fuck, Lori still looked like she was about to punch her out but yet Diana *still* couldn't stop talking. 'You do it for me. Just thought you should know that.'

'And if I don't want to know?'

Diana laughed, more out of tension than an attempt to break the glacier that had formed between them. 'Then just don't fire me until we get back over to the West Coast 'cos I ain't got enough for the airfare home.'

Lori was still standing, only a few feet from her, staring out of the window now. Five seconds. Ten. Her silence told Diana everything she needed to know.

'You know what, it's cool. I'll pack up. Be out of here in an hour.'

No point delaying the inevitable. Congratulations, Diana, you've just fucked up the best job you ever had and for what? Because you couldn't keep it together and keep your feelings out of the business. The irony wasn't lost. Six years as an escort in LA, she'd screwed stars, moguls and icons and not once, *not once* did she cross the boundaries and fall for them. Here? A few weeks with Lori and she'd blown it.

Coco threw her head back and gave a spontaneous loud shriek of happiness aimed at no one and nothing in particular. God, it felt freaking great just to be out in the fresh air, just the two of them. It had been so long that Coco had almost forgotten what it was like to just hang out together and chill.

A blaring horn cut through her thoughts and she jerked the steering wheel to take them back on to the right side of the road. Dax took a long drag on his joint and whistled, 'We're gonna die but at least we'll die stoned.'

Coco giggled and slapped his arm. 'Cut me some slack, it's years since I drove.'

'And it shows, baby, it shows,' Dax laughed.

How great did this feel? Cruising down the highway in a convertible Spitfire, roof down, the whole wind-in-the-hair experience. It was her special treat to them now that they were back on the East Coast but it had been a bizarre experience putting it into action. First of all, she'd had to dig out her chequebook for the first time in a year. Since they'd been on the road her expenses had been zero. They'd just lived off the money Dax earned, leaving her allowance to accumulate in the bank, with just the odd withdrawal for clothes and personal stuff.

No driving, no rent, no bills – nothing to organise and everything arranged for them. She could see why it would take some people to the brink of insanity but for Coco it was a pretty cool way to live. It was all about the music baby and she'd live any way, any how as long as it was all about the music.

And love.

She cut a sideways glance at Dax. He was so freakin' fit. He was broader now than he'd ever been, since he'd started working out between gigs. Hotel gyms, morning runs – sure he still partied like a demon, but the spotlight and the craziness of life on the road had made him more conscious of taking care of himself. He wanted to be sharp out there, to kill it every night and he knew he did that best when he was in shape – unlike the rest of the guys who were embracing nocturnal debauchery like it was the lifestyle they'd always aspired to. Which, in the case of Muff, String and Spank, was pretty much true.

However, even Dax hadn't completely avoided the consequences of the Spikes' lifestyle.

'So how are our little friends these days?' she teased, lowering her stare to his crotch area and then swiftly readjusting as a huge truck blasted its horn when she strayed into its path. Her powers of concentration needed serious work.

Dax rolled his eyes and grimaced. 'Still there. Clinic said another couple of days till they're gone.'

Two weeks ago after their first East Coast gig in Miami, Dax had picked up a girl who performed in a sex show in the kind of club that the tourists didn't frequent. Entertainment over, he'd invited her back to the hotel. Ten days later she was still on the road with him and Coco had come back to their room one morning to find tiny little furry friends crawling on the sheets.

Exit one exotic contortionist. Enter a heavy dose of ointment that Dax swore burned like fuck and smelled even worse.

Coco was just glad that it wasn't an equal opportunities infestation. The girl had done nothing for her and to be honest, she was kinda over the whole threesome thing so she'd taken to hanging out more with Randy Storm and the Decomp guys while Dax had his fun. It was no sweat. Freedom was what she and Dax had signed up for and she was enjoying herself elsewhere so it was no big deal other than she kinda missed him sometimes. It had been so long since they'd just had a day together and it felt great to be having that now. No management, no Decomp, no Steel Spikes, no . . . no . . . Sly.

Beeeeeeeeeeeeep.

Another truck, this time only inches from their bumper.

'Fucking hell, I'm gonna need more than just weed if I'm gonna get through the rest of this day. Got any sedatives in your purse?'

Case in point! Coco giggled. That was the thing about Dax. He made her laugh. He was fun, easy, all about the good times. He was the other half of her heart and she adored every crazy, immature, irresponsible, hedonistic bit of him.

He was good news.

Sly was bad.

There was a darkness in Sly, a danger that had shown itself more and more the longer they'd been on the road. He was getting seriously fucked up every day and it was beginning to cause damage. His performance was still majorly hot, but he'd started missing some lyrics. Sometimes, his timing was a little off. He was becoming ever more arrogant. Erratic. Insular. Egotistical.

Sometimes she saw him watching her and every instinct she possessed made her want to run, to escape from the malevolence that now radiated from his soul.

He was bad news.

And yet . . . he just wouldn't leave her mind.

She watched him every night on stage. She breathed his air and got hot just by closing her eyes and listening to him sing. When she was fucking Randy Storm she thought about him.

But it had to stop because it was a road that wasn't going to end anywhere good.

Just as deception wasn't her thing, neither was delusion. It had taken a long, long time to admit it to herself but Coco knew now that if she went to Sly Rammer she wasn't ever coming back. Marny. Dax. No one else would survive the fall-out and that's why she could never let it happen. Dax was her love, her heart. Marny was her friend, her sister in this whole crazy, beautiful world they were living in. So, much as there was a force that was pulling her to Sly, she would never go there. She couldn't. Because hurting other people wasn't her thing either.

What the fuck had just happened?

Lori kept her eyes fixed on the landscape in front of her, a repetitive question ricocheting around the inside of her head.

What the fuck had just happened?

So much for Miss In Control, Miss Cover All The Frigging Bases – that one was a sucker punch that had completely taken her by surprise.

And Lori hated surprises.

She could hear Diana picking stuff up behind her. Good. Time she was gone because she'd suddenly become a distraction that wasn't welcome around here. A frickin' lesbian. Why hadn't she spotted that before? Sure, Diana hadn't shown any interest in the guys in the band but Lori had just figured that was a combination of them being clapped-out, pox-risk whores and Diana having seen enough cocks in her previous career to last her a lifetime.

A lesbian.

Girl on girl.

Since she'd been on the road with the Spikes she'd seen strippers and models with huge plastic tits suck each other off in sex joints all over the country, but it had always been for the entertainment of the hordes of yelling guys who'd paid to be in the audience. It wasn't real. It was pure theatre and it had left her mildly amused but sexually cold.

Nothing new there.

But this? Aaargh, this made her fucking furious, because if she was honest with herself her life had been a whole lot easier since Diana had been around and – contrary to a lifetime of conditioning – she'd come to depend on her, as much for the company as for the practical help. The fury was twisting her guts and her fists were tightly clenched balls.

What the fuck had just happened?

And what was going to happen next?

Still staring out of the window, her mind threw up an image of Diana walking out of the door and her guts twisted even tighter. No. It was that simple. No. She didn't want her to leave.

But . . .

Damn, her head felt like it was about to explode. This was a new kind of anger, a whole new sensation that was as alien to her as the touch of someone else's lips.

No one had ever got that close before, physically or – she was beginning to realise – emotionally. This wasn't anger, it was fear. Fear of what had just happened and fear of letting Diana walk out of that door.

Lori knew that there was a whole aspect of her psyche that had been switched off long ago, ignored, banished for the sake of total control and achieving what she wanted to achieve.

Now, for the first time someone she genuinely cared about was reaching out to her. And her twisted gut was telling her that it didn't have a fucking clue what she should do.

It was strange to see what the world looked like in the daylight: businessmen striding across the foyer in their JCPenney suits and the briefcases their wives had bought them for Christmas. Families checking in for a few days of sightseeing in the city. A group of teenagers in matching tracksuits, in town to compete in some kind of sports tournament.

And Marny. Limp hair, grey complexion, red-rimmed eyes, her underfed frame drowning in dishevelled, baggy clothes, shaking uncontrollably as she stared at the payphone.

'S'cuse me miss, is everything OK?'

Shit! Another one! Was it national Marny's Welfare Day?

'I'm fine,' she whispered to the young guy in the bellboy uniform. He couldn't be much younger than her – maybe nineteen or twenty, yet he had a real job, an income, a plan. What did Marny have? Sly and a case of the tremors that wasn't going to go away if she didn't get back up to the room to score.

The thought jolted her into action and she snatched up the receiver before she changed her mind.

'Information, what name please?'

'Ramone.'

'Street and city?'

'Mission Street, Philadelphia.'

The knives come out and go through the hearts
Because the love is ending, why did it ever start?
Down on Mission Street.

It was part of the lyric for 'It's Over', one of the songs that the Spikes had recorded and that Sly had revealed was based on his old life there with his family. OK, she was kidding herself. It wasn't just about his family – it was about his fiancée, and the break up and how that relationship should never have been. But that was OK, wasn't it? He loved her now. He'd had the choice all those years ago to go back or be with Marny and he'd chosen her. The song said it was over. She just had to believe that was true and that nothing would change.

But if it did . . .

Well, she'd just have to face that because that was the thing about Sly Rammer – she loved him so much that she would sacrifice anything for him. What she was about to do could have consequences that would tear them apart but it was a chance she was prepared to take because she knew how much this situation was hurting him and she knew she was the only one that could fix it.

Take the love, that is given to me,
The pain inside, gotta let it go free.
It's over.

More lines from the same song. She just had to have faith that revisiting the past wouldn't change their future in any other way than to make Sly whole again, repair the little bit of his soul that was missing.

She breathed a sigh of relief when the operator gave her the number and she hung up quickly, mentally repeating it as she punched it back into the phone.

It rang. And rang. Another ring. And another. No answer. Probably just as well because her whole body was shaking so hard that she seriously doubted she'd be able to speak.

The handset was almost back down in the cradle when she heard the voice.

'Hello? Hello?'

No saliva. None. Her throat had completely constricted, her mouth was totally dry and she was paralysed with fear.

This was a bad idea. Such a bad, bad, idea.

'Who is this? . . . You should be ashamed of yourself! Have you got nothing better to do with your time than make disgusting phone calls? Have you got your wiener out? Well let me tell you, I will hunt you down and I will cut that off and dangle it outside my door so that you and all the filthy beasts like you will know that you can't go around doing this to decent . . .'

'Mrs Ramone?'

Marny wasn't sure who was more surprised — her or the woman who'd just realised that she'd accused another female of being a perverted reprobate in the midst of masturbation.

'Who is this?' Isabella Ramone blustered.

Speak. Speak. Marny was trying everything to make the vocal chords work but they were still stunned into incapacity.

'I'm gonna hang up if you don't tell me who this is. D'you hear me?'

She had to do this. For Sly. It was for Sly.

'Mrs Ramone, I'm calling about Sly.'

'Sylvester?' Mrs Ramone slid up by about three octaves and her speech was coming fast now, like bullets from an automatic weapon.

'Wha'd'ya know about my Sylvester? Who are you? Is he in trouble? Where is he? Where's my boy?'

Not since she was a child had Marny ever felt so terrified.

'Mrs Ramone, I'm Sylvester's friend and I'm calling because . . .' Mouth drying up again, voice shaking. '. . . because he is here in Philadelphia and I wondered if you would like to come and see him.'

As she gathered up her stuff, Diana was so busy remonstrating with herself that it was a moment or two before she realised that there was a hand on her arm.

'You don't have to pack. You're the best assistant we've had and besides, if we let Spank drive the bus he'll stop so often to score that we'll never get anywhere on time.'

Diana sensed that Lori was forcing some levity into her voice, but still she felt an almost overwhelming surge of relief. OK, she'd dodged a bullet. Wouldn't make that mistake again. From now on it was strictly all about business. The urge to leave while she was ahead was cancelled out by the hand that was still on her arm.

'I don't know how to do this,' Lori said softly. What? Fire her? Bullet un-dodged. Perhaps she was still history after all.

But when Diana's gaze met Lori's, she saw eyes that were swimming in pools of water. Nothing could have surprised her more. Lori was fearless, hard, always in control. Suddenly, her heart yearned to make it personal again. Fuck the job. She leaned over and gently traced a soft line down Lori's cheek with the tip of her finger. When Lori didn't pull back, she slid her hand down to the side of her neck and stretched up on her toes. Heart thudding once again, Diana kissed her, a long, tender kiss that felt like it made time stand still.

Lori was the first to pull back, not sharply this time, just a hesitant, tentative pause.

'You have to show me . . . I've never done this before.'

Fireworks exploded in Diana's head and heart as she realised that this was on. Thank you, Lord, it was on. Wasn't it? Perhaps time to double check that she was reading this right. 'You've never made love to a woman?' she asked tenderly.

Lori shook her head.

'I've never made love to anyone.'

'Babe, ain't this where we're going?'

Flicking on her signal, Coco quickly veered off the highway, the car rumbling as it cut across the white lines.

Five minutes of intense concentration later, they pulled into the car park at the Philly helipad, twenty minutes later they were in the air and within the hour they were looking down at the Belmont ranch, the ground getting closer by the second as they descended to land.

All thoughts of Sly Rammer were dismissed as the scene in front of her replaced everything with sheer joy.

Home. Standing a hundred yards away was her mama, waving like crazy, still so beautiful that Coco bet the other Connecticut wives must spit nails when they saw her coming. Even now, dressed in jeans and a white shirt that was tied at the waist, holding back her long dark hair to stop it from going wild in the gusts from the helicopter blades, she was still strikingly beautiful.

Ducking down, Coco charged out of the 'copter and straight in to those outstretched arms. The joyful shrieks could be heard loud and clear despite the whirl of the blades.

'Colette, oh my darling Colette.'

Seemed so strange to hear that name that it almost felt like her

189

mother was talking to someone else. Stranger still that her daddy wasn't standing there waiting too. All those years she'd been away at school she'd fly back in at the end of every semester and there he'd be, waiting at the edge of the landing strip, Stetson on his head, leaning against a big gleaming truck. Hero worship hadn't even begun to cover it. She'd been a daddy's girl through and through, until . . . Until after he was gone and the tragedy had given her a new connection to her mother, a new respect for the woman who was now squeezing her so tightly, and dear Lord, it felt good.

'Mom, this is Dax,' she announced when the embrace eventually ended.

Darcy Belmont had welcomed world leaders, movie stars, music legends to her ranch – but she'd never before shaken the hand of a rock star with waist-length jet-black hair, wearing a vest that exposed a neck, shoulders and arms that were completely covered in tattoos. Oh, and there was the hat. The trilby. It was an incongruous addition to an already startling image.

'Love the hat,' Darcy said with a genuine smile.

Dax laughed as he nudged his girlfriend. 'Hey man, your mama is kinda cool.'

Coco winked at her mother. 'It's a good start, Mom.'

They walked over in the direction of the car.

'So how long can you stay?'

'Just a couple of hours. We need to get back for a sound check at four. You still gonna come over with Grey later?' In the weekly phone calls they'd shared since Coco left, Darcy spoke so often about Grey that there was now an unspoken understanding that they were together. No big announcement, no drama, no ties. Coco decided that she had more in common with her mother than she'd ever realised.

Darcy Belmont nodded. 'Sure, wouldn't miss it. I hear you boys are doing great,' she said to Dax.

He shrugged. 'Yeah, well, it's kinda frustrating, y'know? The crowds are digging it man, but the record ain't hitting the numbers yet.'

'But honey, that's all gonna change and you know it's coming.' Coco jumped on his back and let him carry her to the car. Those five-inch heels just weren't made for grass. 'Mom, we've got some news – the band is going to be making their first video. We start filming tomorrow.'

Darcy grinned approvingly at Dax. 'Congratulations!'

'And we wanted to give you a bit of warning about it Mom, because there's going to be a woman in it who gets all up front and naked.'

Darcy opened the car door, giving her daughter a rueful smile. 'Colette, do you think I'm such a prude that I'd disapprove of something like that? Maybe I'm not as straight as you think I am young lady. And hey, Dax thinks I'm cool.'

Coco jumped down off his back and slid into the front seat.

'I'm glad you're saying that Mom – because the naked woman? Well, that's gonna be me.'

It hadn't taken much for Lori to persuade her to do it. In fact, 'Hey, Coco, wanna be in the video butt-naked?' had just about covered it.

It was going to be fun. A blast. Something to tell the grand-kids about. Or at least, that was the plan.

It turned out to be three minutes of film that would destroy the thing she loved the most.

SEVENTEEN

'Man, that was fucking awesome,' Muff screamed as they piled back into the dressing room after the Philly gig. 'Hey there sweetie, did you see us?'

Muff's celibate groupie replied by leaning over and tousling his hair, while everyone else tried to pretend that they hadn't seen her staring at Sly the whole time.

Everyone except Marny, who was already on the floor taking a hit – one long, glorious line and she knew that the knots of anxiety in her stomach would come undone. She was wired.

So wired she'd been grinding her teeth for the last two hours and now her jaw ached.

Eighteen-thousand fans had been there for Decomp, but the Spikes had totally taken the crowd and won them over until they were screaming for the boys from their home town. Sly had stayed on his game all night, hitting the crowd with hard energy right from the start, working them up until they were going crazy, then slowing them down with the gut-wrenching emotion of 'It's Over', before ramping them right back up again with the mind-blowing combination of 'Four Ways Till Sunday' and 'Suicide Now'. 'Sly, baby, you want some . . .?' Marny slurred as she pointed to the lines of white in front of her. Maybe those pills she'd been taking all day hadn't been such a great idea. She wasn't even sure what they were but Sly said they made him real mellow. They hadn't had that effect on her, despite her taking . . . shit, she couldn't even remember how many. Maybe another line would help her brain work better.

'Lock that fucking door!' Lori shouted to Chuck, the security guard. Marny kept her head down low. Sure, she should have waited until later before she hit the nose candy but, man, she was desperate.

'Hey, Lori, chill babe,' Dax said, pulling a ten-inch joint out of his right boot. 'Last night with Decomp, man, too late for them to kick us off the tour.' The rest of the band gave their unofficial spokesperson a cheer and a chorus of stamping feet.

Lori, however, gave him her now famous stare-of-death. 'Dax, have we been paid yet?'

Penny. Dropped. Sudden. Clarity.

'Chuck, fucking lock it, man,' Spank echoed, while Strings took the more direct route and threw himself against the door, before sliding down and acting as an official rock-star draught excluder. Nothing was gonna stop them getting paid. After all those months of surviving on Lori's handouts they were all desperate to get their hands on some dough, shoot the video the next day, then get back to LA and start finding out what it was like to chill out as bona fide rockers.

As for Marny, she just wanted peace. Quiet. Just long days and nights for her and Sly to lay low and chill out. They'd kick the drugs, tell Dave Lopez they didn't need any more. They were just a nasty habit that they'd picked up on the road and she knew that when it was just the two of them again, they wouldn't need the chemical highs. Leaning down, she snorted another line and then felt Sly's arms catch her as she swayed.

'You OK baby?' he asked, transforming the hug into a grope by playfully shoving his hands up the front of her T-shirt. She could tell he was happy. For now. The euphoria of the gig would wear off soon and that's when it could go one of many ways, all of them featuring belligerence, most of them ending in some form of fight/drama/chaos that would inevitably require the services of Dave or Lori to put right.

But that was just temporary. Once things got back on an even keel they'd be fine. Perhaps it was best that his mother had refused to come over to see him. 'That boy left here and he knows where I am, so he can damn well find his way back to me!' she'd yelled before setting off on a tirade of Italian that Marny couldn't understand. She was fairly sure it wasn't complimentary, though.

The effort had been made and she'd left their names on the guest list just in case they changed their mind. She'd tried. If Mama Ramone couldn't see her way to sharing her boy's life well that just made more room for Marny. No loss. And the most important thing was that Sly didn't need to know what she'd done or that his mother had rejected her invitation.

The banging on the door interrupted her thoughts, as did the rush to conceal everything that could constitute booze or drugs. They could hear that Decomp weren't on stage yet so it was probably them coming to say goodbye. No time for an end-of-tour party – Storm and the rest of the band were heading off to London that night to join Springsteen, Sting, Tracy Chapman and Peter Gabriel on the Amnesty Rock 'Human Rights Now' tour. It kicked off the following night, September 2nd, at Wembley and was scheduled to span six weeks, twenty cities and five continents.

Lori scanned the room to check nothing illicit was visible before she opened the door and was thrust to the side as a troop of people stormed in.

It wasn't Decomp.

Sly gasped as the small, very round, dark-haired female pushed past, marched straight over to over to him and . . . Slap! The sound of flesh on flesh reverberated around the room.

'Eeeew, gross – look at the blood,' Muff's celibate groupie sneered.

Marny didn't understand what was going on. Who were these people? What had just happened? Did someone just hit Sly? And where was the blood? In fact, nothing was making sense. The walls were undulating, faces were coming in and out of focus, the ground was moving from side to side.

The next thing she felt was the ground as she hit it. Then the choking began, there was some kind of liquid stuck in her throat and . . . shit, what was happening to her?

Lori's six-inch steel heels paced back and forth on the concrete floor of the deserted dressing room. Decomp were still playing and the echo of their performance reverberated around the walls. She had to stay until they came off stage so that she could meet with their promoter and manager to collect the cheque for their share of the night's merchandise. The tour fee would come to them via AC in the next few days, but she'd insisted on merchandise payments on gig nights all the way along the tour. Their tour costs including the travel, hotels and roadies were paid directly by AC. As the band's assistant driver, Diana's salary came from the Spikes' account, as did Chuck's monthly cheques for personal security and all the day-to-day expenses. It made sense to keep the cash flow as liquid as possible.

However, finances had nothing to do with why she was pacing. The door opened and Coco rushed in. 'Freaking hell! I was saying goodbye to my mom and I just heard what happened. Any word yet?'

Lori shook her head. 'Diana was driving Sly to the hospital behind the ambulance so hopefully we'll hear something soon. They wouldn't let him ride with her.'

'And his family?'

'Went with him. I don't think it was the introduction to their son's girlfriend that they were expecting.'

Coco chewed on her bottom lip. 'You know, Lori, I feel kinda responsible. I saw that she was getting messed up . . .'

Lori cut her off. 'We both did. I'm every bit as guilty. I saw it and didn't stop it. I should have stepped in sooner but . . .' She didn't finish the sentence. The truth was she hadn't wanted to get embroiled in the drama while they were still on tour. She'd wanted to wait until after tonight before making any moves. Too little, a few hours too late.

'Do you think it would be OK if I went over to the hospital now?'

'There's no point, hon, they won't let you see her. And anyway, Sly is there and I'm guessing that it's probably best to stay out of any confined space containing him and his mother. She packs a mean right-hook.'

For the first time, Coco gave a hint of a smile. It was just another day, another snapshot of life in the orbit of a rock band: two women, one dressed head to toe in rubber, the other in gold hot pants, a string vest and gold stilettos that were partially obscured by thick white woolly legwarmers, discussing the overdose of one of their closest friends.

'So at the risk of being a mercenary bitch,' Lori continued, 'I think you should go home and get some sleep – you've got a video to shoot tomorrow morning.'

Coco wrapped her arms around Lori and squeezed. 'You are truly shallow.' She didn't mean it. But somehow the banter was easier than dealing with reality. Lori might act like she was hard and ruthless, but Coco knew there was a heart in there somewhere.

'Should I be getting worried?' The voice came from the doorway, as Diana appeared in the doorway. Coco and Lori broke up the embrace and looked at her with expressions that sat between apprehension and panic.

'Don't worry, there's nothing to report,' Diana reassured them. 'Sly sent me back to collect a change of clothes for him. Although the truth is, I don't think he wanted me to witness his mother kicking his ass. Where are the rest of the guys?'

'Wringing their hands with concern and devastation while trawling the titty bars.' Lori replied.

'Excellent. Good to know they can keep their heads in a crisis.' As Diana spoke, she reached behind her to close the door only to have her actions prevented by a woman who was standing there, backstage pass around her neck.

'Can I help you?' Diana looked at the newcomer, eyebrows raised as she waited for a reply. Hell, now that she was living the full-on same-sex life, she had to admit that if it all went wrong with Lori tomorrow, then this would definitely be the kind of babe who would appeal for a meaningless rebound fuck. She was petite, dark, jet black hair falling in waves to a tiny waist, her huge dark eyes piercing, her manner bold and confident.

'I'm looking for Sly Rammer.'

Lori shrugged. Like this was exactly what she needed now – more desperate fans. 'And you are . . .'

The mini-babe jutted out her chin, clearly refusing to be intimidated by Lori's height or attitude. 'I'm his fiancée.'

'Of course you are, sweetheart,' Diana interjected, gently putting her arm around the stranger and attempting to turn her around and guide her back out the door, while Lori and Coco turned to face each other, eyes rolling at yet another crazy groupie with a story.

The girl slapped Diana's hand away. 'Don't fucking touch me.' That got Lori's attention.

Miss Groupie might be beautiful but she was about to get her ass kicked if she dared to lay a finger on . . .

'I've got it!' Diana put her hand up to stop Lori's approach. 'I've got it, hon,' she repeated in a calm, conciliatory tone. 'Missy here is just a little bit over-keen to see the band and didn't realise that they're already long gone, isn't that right?'

'Don't fucking patronise me,' came the hissed reply. 'Just tell Sly I was here and I'll catch up with him soon.'

With that she turned, hair flying and stepped back into the corridor and strutted off.

'But who the hell *are* you?' Diana shouted after her incredulously. Always good to get names so they could add them to the blacklist of crazies and girls that had been screwed and discarded and weren't taking it kindly.

'I told you already!' came the muffled reply from halfway down the corridor. 'I'm his fiancée – Gloria Bagstock.'

'What did she say?' Diana asked the others.

Lori shrugged. 'No idea, but hey, forget about it. Just another one of life's crazies. You OK, baby?'

Something in Lori's tone made Coco's eyes narrow in curiosity. The flush in Lori's cheeks as she said it made them narrow even more.

'*Baby*?'

Lori immediately stared at the floor, while Diana broke into a raucous cackle. 'Yeah, we're erm, taking it personal.'

'No way!' Coco giggled. 'Oh, I frigging love it. You two together? The image of that? Muff and Strings may never get rid of their hard-ons.'

'Right, no more.' Lori was clearly uncomfortable with her personal life being open for discussion. 'Didn't you have a bag to collect?'

'Yes *baby*.' Diana wasn't letting her off the hook. Lori remained unamused. 'Good. And if you meet that chick again on the way out, get her name and add it to the barred list. Only crazies I want with that kind of access are the ones in the band.'

EIGHTEEN

'Not here, Ma,' Sly groaned.

'Sylvester Ramone you will listen to me and you will listen now. You're coming home tonight and that's final. Uncle Sol still has a job for you and you can stay in your old room until you get some money in the bank. And you'll get that muck off your face. Santa Maria, if your father was here they'd have to make up a bed for him in the ward. His son! His own son! Wearing make-up like a . . . a . . . *puttana!*'

'Ma!' Sly's sister, Francesca Anna, reprimanded her mother, but no one was surprised that she went completely ignored by everyone at the table. However, the priest and the dishevelled young girl huddled in the corner of the canteen did turn to glance at them, before returning, heads almost touching, to their own conversation.

Even for the canteen at St Joseph's Hospital, the group that was sitting around the table was an unusual one. Two beautiful Italian girls in their early thirties, both dressed casually in jeans and T-shirts. Two older women, same colouring, one stick thin and puffing relentlessly on a cigarette, the other one clearly fond of her pasta, her bosom stretching the black kaftan that covered it.

The larger one's finger was wagging in the face of a slightly emaciated guy with wild, teased-out brown hair that hit his shoulder blades, dramatic eye make-up, his skin-tight leather pants matching the biker-style jacket that he'd thrown casually over one shoulder. Oh, and his skinny torso was bare. No T-shirt, no vest, nothing. Just a multitude of tattoos that his mother was doing her best not to look at because there was definitely nudity involved.

Sly's head was clear enough to wonder if he should get that priest over to perform last rites because his mother was so pissed she could self-combust at any second. The whole scene back at the gig had been seriously fucked up. Marny had just fallen right over, blood everywhere. Lori and Diana had jumped in, called one of the ambulances that was sitting outside the stadium in case of casualties, and within half an hour they were here – no time to stop, think or piss. And of course, where he went, the female contingent of the Ramone hit squad had followed. Now that they were in front of him it was impossible to deny the truth – for the last three years he'd missed them so much, wondered what they were doing, thought about coming back. It was unresolved business and it had sat on the edge of his mind every day since he'd stepped on that bus out of town. But now? Now they were together again and they were coming out with some seriously bad shit, he remembered all the reasons that he'd left in the first place. He wasn't ready for this. Not yet.

How had this happened to him?

How had they even known how to find him? New name, first night in town – and let's face it, his mother wasn't exactly front of the queue waiting for her copy of *Rolling Stone* every month.

And . . . aw, fuck, she was blessing herself again.

'In the name of the blessed mother, as if there wasn't enough shame when you disappeared like that. Your father has never been the same, has he, Maria Christina?'

The head that sat atop the black mountainous kaftan shook wearily from side to side.

'And Gloria, oh what that girl went through.'

That jolted Sly just a little. Gloria. The baby. 'So . . . so . . . where are *they*?'

On the way to the waiting room with a bag of clothes for Sly, Diana stopped at A&E to get an update on Marny and found a doctor standing next to her bed writing on a clipboard.

After introducing herself and telling a small white lie regarding their relationship (sisters – let him have the balls to ask why one was black and one was white) he shrugged non-committally. Diana had a hunch that he saved his best bedside manner for the cases that weren't self-inflicted.

'The next twenty-four hours are crucial. We've pumped her stomach, done everything we can; now it's just a case of waiting to see how she reacts. Has she been suicidal for long?'

The doctor's question took Diana completely by surprise. 'She wasn't suicidal – this was, er, recreational.'

The doctor's eyes widened, 'Well that was one hell of a recreation that we pumped from her stomach.'

Diana felt the weight of his disapproval and judgement and bristled. Hell, this was nothing to do with her. 'So when can we take her home?'

The doctor shook his head. 'No idea – depends how she reacts in the next few hours. But Miss – I have to tell you that given the amount of toxicity in her system, it's not a case of "when" you can take her home, but "if".'

The lights hurt her eyes every time she tried to open them even a little, adding ever more depth to the thudding that was already going on in her head. Pain. Too much pain.

'I'm sorry, I don't know her date of birth. Marny. Yep, Marny . . . damn, what's her second name? Tucker! Marny Tucker.'

'Mama? Mama?' Marny whispered.

Pain. Throat. Footsteps. Fingers on her hair. Stroking it. Who? Where? The smell. What was that smell?

'Oh thank you Jesus! Marny, it's Diana. Do you know where

201

you are?'

What? Marny didn't understand. More pain. Everything hurt. Just everything. Her throat. Her head. Her face. Her stomach. Confused. Why?

'Marny, you're sick, sugar. You had a nosebleed and then you fainted and we had to bring you here to the hospital.'

Marny tried to speak but . . . nothing except pain.

'They had to put a tube down your throat to pump your stomach though so that's gonna hurt for a while. Oh, thank God. Thank God. This is good, right?' she heard the words, but she had no idea who Diana was talking to.

Hospital. She was in hospital. The smell. Scared. The smell. Noooooo. Voices. A man now.

'It's . . . positive. But she's not out of the woods yet. Is there someone who can give us details of her insurance?'

Diana nodded, 'Sure, I'll sort that out.'

Not mama. Diana. Taking care of her. The smell. No. Couldn't be.

'She's trying to say something.' The man's voice again.

'What is it Marny?' Diana asked softly.

'What . . . hosp . . .?'

'What hospital?' Diana repeated. Nodding. Hurt. Pain.

'What hospital is this?' Diana to the stranger again.

'St Joseph's.'

St . . . no. The pain, the incomparable pain that gripped her now. She couldn't be here. Anywhere but here. Not again, it couldn't be . . .

Despite a throat that was raw and burning, the patient started to scream.

'Where's . . . Gloria?' his second attempt at the question wasn't much more coherent than the first. He wasn't sure if it was fear or that last handful of pills that was messing with his head.

'Left! Gone! The whole family! Took off, moved out of town, cut off all contact. Her mother couldn't stand the shame and blessed mother above no wonder. That's what you did, Sylvester Ramone! I'm a grandmother and I can't even hold that *bambino* in my arms because of the shame! Your shame!' Hysteria was elevating her cackle to a screech.

'And for what? For that scrawny little thing that collapsed back there? That's the best you could do?' Sly clenched his jaw to stop himself saying something he'd regret. He knew the drill. Remonstrations. Outrage. Laying on the guilt. And any minute now she was going to clutch . . . Yep, there it was, the clutch of the heart and the heavenward eyes. Martyrdom was alive and well and living in the canteen of a Philadelphia hospital.

'Dear God, what did I do to deserve this? What did I do?' she wailed.

Francesca put her arm around her mother and grimaced at Sly over the top of her head.

He bowed his head so he didn't have to look at the fury in their eyes. Guilt. More fucking guilt. He'd had a lifetime of it and he realised now that it was never going to stop. Like he needed any of this shit now. Five sisters, a mother and too many aunts to count and they'd all clucked over him, loving him to the point of suffocation while constantly reminding him of all the ways that he was failing them. To see the hostility in his sister's eyes now was seriously freaking him out. Time to get out of there, any excuse.

'Going to the john.'

'That's right, run away from your responsibilities. Just like you've always done. I blame myself. I spoiled that boy, didn't I Maria Christina? I know it's true – spoiled from the minute he came into this world. Too much love. Too much freedom. And how does he repay me?'

He was tempted to answer, 'by becoming a musician, doing a national tour and selling fifty-thousand records with a kick-ass rock band.' But what was the point? This was never going to work. Never. As always, anger made his temple throb as he suddenly realised that he had no idea why he'd missed any of them. They were poison, pure fucking poison. Years of resentment and rage hit his brain and he could hear it fry. He bolted up, not caring that his chair toppled over or that once again everyone turned to stare.

'Why the fuck did you come to see me? Huh? Why the fuck are you here?'

His mother's snivelling stopped instantly as her face contorted into a familiar expression of blind bloody fury. 'Don't you dare speak to me like that Sylvester Ramone.'

'Rammer! Sly fucking Rammer! And you know what, Ma? I remember now why I ran the first time. We're done. You can take the name, you can take the guilt and you can all fuck off.'

The slamming of the door as it closed behind him prevented him from hearing her reply but he didn't care. Like he said, he was done. He hadn't asked them to come to the gig. Still didn't understand why they'd come. And didn't give a fuck. He'd told Marny he never wanted to see them again and now he meant that even more. They were done. Now he just wanted to get Marny, get out of here and go get high.

Which way? Right. Left. Right. Shit, he should know this place like the back of his hand after spending almost two weeks here after the dumpster incident. How ironic was this? The hospital that he and Marny had met in and now they were here again, three years later, with completely different lives.

Left. He was sure it was left to A&E. He'd go check on Marny then go for a smoke.

ER. The sign was above a set of grey double doors thirty yards in front of him, a large EXIT sign to the left. Maybe he'd go for a smoke first and then check on Marny later. Or shit, maybe he'd just head back to the hotel after he made sure she was OK. And when she got out of here he was gonna talk to her about the coke and the pills. She'd been hitting them way too heavy lately and it was time to cool off. Chill. Not that he needed to – he could handle it no problem. But she was just a chick, man, and lately she'd been so wired she was bringing him down.

Smoke. He'd have a smoke first, then he'd go see her.

Empty. They'd gone. Forcing her eyes open, she could see them through the glass panel in front of her, all huddled around a desk, a nurse writing on a clipboard, Diana on the phone, pacing, with her back to her.

Move. Had to move. She couldn't stay here. Couldn't let them keep her here. And they would. If they knew, then they'd keep her here for a long, long time.

Wincing with the pain, she pushed herself up into a sitting position then gingerly swung her legs over the side of the gurney. Go. Had to go. Had to get away before they realised . . .

On her feet now, grabbed the gurney, legs too weak to hold her. Steps. Little steps. One. Two. Three. To the side. The door at the side. They wouldn't see her. She just had to make it to the door.

Four. Five. Out the door now, turn left, double doors in front of her. The way out. Six. Seven.

Pain. So much pain.

Eight. Nine. Almost there. Another few steps. Hand on the door. Push. Out. Out. Falling. Help me. Falling.

The arms grabbed her just in time. Rising up now. Safe. Safe. Holding tight.

'Baby, where the fuck are you going?' Sly. Her Sly. Saved.

'Get me out of here.' Whisper. Sly. Her Sly. A nod.

'Whatever you say baby. Let's go.'

Her Sly. He still loved her, even though . . .

'Sly.' Her voice was croaky, a whisper. 'Sorry . . . phoned . . . your . . . mom.'

205

NINETEEN

'OK, baby, we've got you. Dave, give me a hand here will you? Diana, can you get me some water and some towels?' Sly heard Lori take control as he stepped back and leant against the wall, gasping for breath from the exertion of carrying Marny out of the cab and then along the corridor from the elevator. Shit, his lungs were fucked. Maybe there was something in all Dax's exercise shit after all.

'You're OK, honey, we're gonna take care of you.' Lori was telling Marny now, although she was wasting her breath – Marny had been out cold since the hospital when she . . .

'Sorry . . . phoned . . . your . . . mom.'

The voice was going around and around in his head, repeating itself to the beat of his gasping breaths. Bitch. She'd done this. She'd told them where he was, allowed them back into his life for what? So they could fucking lay it all on him again?

'Sly, why don't you go sleep in Dave's room, we'll take care of her and I need you up early for the shoot.'

Dave Lopez, ever obedient, was nodding at Lori's suggestion as he fumbled in his pocket. 'Sure, Sly . . . I'll get the key.'

Sly hesitated for a second. He should stay but . . . she'd betrayed him. They were supposed to have each other's backs, total trust, soulmates. It was a fucking betrayal. Well, screw her. He wasn't going to sit around holding her hand after what she'd done. Forget it. And Sly Rammer had had enough of this bullshit.

Dave Lopez pulled the curtains in his room shut and put the Do Not Disturb on the door. Then he picked up the phone and made a quick call to reception.

'Sorted, man?' Sly asked him impatiently.

Dave nodded. It was all sorted. Just as Sly had asked. He took a small bag of brown powder out of his pocket and threw it over to Sly. 'It's a sample. Just got it today.'

There wasn't even a thank you in return. Dave didn't mind. He'd thank him later, when he realised how incredible that stuff was. Sly deserved it.

Right now what was important was that he took care of stuff, made sure everyone got what they wanted.

'OK man, cab will be there by now – concierge said ten minutes.'

Sly didn't even say goodbye.

From her crouched position on the floor beside the bed, Lori sat back on her heels when Dave came back into the room.

'Is he in bed?'

Lopez nodded. 'Put a Do Not Disturb on the door so he could get some sleep – he's pretty done in.'

'He'll be more than fucking done in if I ever see him letting her get in this state again.'

Gently placing a cold towel on Marny's head, Lori turned so that Dave got the full effect of her next words.

'And Lopez, that goes for you too. Do you understand me?' Icicles formed on every clearly enunciated word. 'The shop is shut. If I ever catch you giving anything to Sly or Marny again, you will leave here with your *cojones* in your mouth. Do you get that?'

No response.

'Lopez! Look at me, not her. Do. You. Get. That?' It was almost a whisper now, but volume was unnecessary as he finally switched his gaze from the woman on the bed to Lori.

'From now on you don't do a fucking thing without running it past me first. Not a thing. Got it?'

He finally found his voice. 'Understood, boss. Loud and clear. Whatever you say, it's done.'

If Lori hadn't turned back to her patient, she'd have seen the smile that crossed Dave Lopez's lips.

Sly watched the flames as they licked around the bottom of the spoon, fire on metal, dancing flickers of red and gold that twisted and turned as they made the bubbles rise to the surface.

There was nothing else – no people, no music, nothing. Just the sweet, sweet smell and the flames, hypnotising him, beckoning to him to come closer. Closer.

'Fucking hurry up dude, you're like, blowing it here.'

The dancing flames beckoned again and Sly moved in to meet them, inhaling deeply as he'd watched the others do before him. The flames were his now. Suddenly they were inside him, searing through him, and he was with them, getting higher, and higher – taking him somewhere that he'd never been. Somewhere incredible. *So fucking incredible.* This was it. Everything else was gone and he had all he needed right here. This was how he wanted to feel forever. Just like this. Just like . . .

The suddenness of the pain took him by surprise. It came from his stomach, a wave that twisted and turned like the flames but brought none of the pleasure. His body rebelling, objecting to what was happening, refusing to accept the ecstasy of the hit.

And there was no holding it back.

'Fucking hell, you prick! You fucking filthy prick.'

The girl in front of him, the one that was now covered in his vomit, was smacking the side of his head. But it didn't matter. All that mattered now was sleep. And then tomorrow, he'd be back to watch the flames again.

TWENTY

The pager on Lori's waistband emitted five loud beeps – by beep number three she'd already snatched it up.

'Come on, come on,' she murmured as she waited for the message to appear on the screen. Fucking inefficient thing. Cut the fanfare; just get straight to the message.

'ETA 5 MINS.'

'Lori, where's Mr Rammer? We're ready for him,' Beck Styler called to her from the other side of the roof. Yep, the roof. November. New York. On a roof. Even the floor-length leather coat and gloves were no protection against the icy cold and wind. Frostbite had claimed the feeling in her fingers ten minutes ago and her ass was currently applying for extradition to a hotter climate.

'He's on his way, Beck – five minutes.'

She went for carefree and reassuring, but cold and stress hijacked the message and delivered strained and nervous. The only consolation in this whole fucked-up situation was that she wasn't Coco. She crossed over to where her Coco was standing, visibly shivering under a blanket that one of the make-up girls had kindly given her. 'C'mere hon – I've heard body heat helps.'

'Lori, a week in the frigging Caribbean wouldn't help right now.'

They both smiled and Lori pulled her a little tighter so no one could overhear as she whispered in Coco's ear.

'Diana found him and they're on the way.'

'Is he OK?'

'Not sure – but if he's still breathing I'm gonna fucking kill him when he gets here.'

'And Marny?'

'She's still pretty out of it. You know, Diana said it was touch and go for a while and some doc was laying on the gloom – probably the reason Marny decided to do a runner as soon as she could stand. Dave Lopez is with her until we find a nurse to take over. I've left him a list of agencies to call.'

'Lori, we're losing the sunrise.' Beck's irritation was obvious. Well, join the club. At least he was getting paid for freezing his ass off and he'd get all the glory when it was done.

For fuck's sake! If she didn't know better she'd have sworn Ari Covet set this whole thing up just to torture her. It had seemed like such a great concept but now the drawbacks were becoming clear. To begin with there was the whole November/New York/temperature-at-daybreak issue. Then there was the impatient director (once a big shot in action adventures until the combination of alcohol and a fifteen-year-old porn star had destroyed his career) who was currently riding her metaphorical ass. But then, that was hardly surprising considering it was a one-day shoot. One day. It was fucking unheard of, but apparently that was as far as Styler's schedule and AC's cash would allow.

At least she'd solved the casting issue by drafting Coco in as the hot eye candy, but by the looks of things all that was going to achieve was double pneumonia and a chill in a place where Coco definitely didn't need it. And that would no doubt lead to more hospital bills Lori could do without. Marny's little stunt the day before had cost them a fortune. In one way it was just as well that she'd checked out early, because apparently the medical institutions of America charged by the hour. As it was, as soon as they'd discovered she'd disappeared, a ferocious woman who had trained for her role as a hospital administrator by being a fascist in a past life had cornered Diana for eight hundred dollars before the security guards would allow her to leave the building. Just as well they took cheques. But if the hired goons had been more efficient in the first place they might not have lost the frigging patient.

So all in all, today was already a challenge – and not just due to the trials of scheduling and co-ordinating the equipment, the instruments, the clothes, getting Sly and Coco here before dawn, arranging for the rest of the band to arrive by 10am and attempting to achieve a full-day shoot with a climax shot at sunset. In theory? Great. In practice, it had already been sabotaged by the minor matter of the missing leading man. Feckless dickhead. She couldn't believe the fucker had taken off in the middle of the night. He'd obviously pretended to Lopez that he was crashin' out, then did a runner.

Thank God for Diana. A little surge of something sweet took the edge off the cold for the first time that morning. Diana had headed up the search party and come up with the goods as always. Although, if Lori knew her fiery little lover she'd probably kicked him all the way up the street first. A warm tingle ran down Lori's spine and she felt the urge – for the first time in days – to laugh. Her lover. Her. Lover. Would she ever get used to that?

The door from the stairs burst open and Lori felt Coco jump. 'He's here!'

'Thank . . .' Lori's voice trailed off. It was Sly. Definitely. But holy fuck he looked like nothing she'd ever seen before. His skin was grey, the colour of the November sky, his eyes the colour of the sun that was coming up fast. A clump of matted hair was stuck to the side of his face and let's not even go there with the clothes. Torn, crushed and covered in stains she didn't even want to think about.

What the fuck had happened to him in the last few hours? He hadn't been a picture of health when he got back from the hospital, but clearly he'd been dealing with the shock of his girlfriend's near-death experience by . . . she checked him out again . . . by rolling in muck before imbibing the entire illegal narcotic quota of the average rock band and then engaging in unarmed combat with a bear.

'Even I wouldn't wanna sleep with that,' Coco whispered.

'Shit, it's even worse than I thought then,' Lori sighed.

Why did she do this job? Why? Hairdressing. That was sounding like a pretty good career about now. Or maybe something in the hospitality industry. Hell, she'd take flipping burgers over this crap.

'Sorry, Lori – I said I found him, I didn't say I could perform miracles.' Diana dragged him over.

'Where was he?'

'Alley behind Hot Pants down in the village. Rest of the guys went in with him, left without him. Apparently he disappeared with the new love of his life right after she climbed off the stripper pole.'

'What the f . . .' Sly mumbled to no one in particular.

'Oh, it speaks – that's a bonus.' Lori gave the stare of death to her investment. Great. Fantastic. Would you like fries with that, Sir?

Sly was swaying in the wind, held upright only by the fact that his full body weight was leaning on Diana.

This had to be sorted and it had to be sorted fast. She wasn't having it get back to Covet that she'd fucked up, couldn't control her band. There was no way she was going to allow him to say that she'd blown the thousands of dollars that this set up had cost.

A revised plan clicked into place. She'd fix this. That's what she did. She took care of situations, sorted everything out, made it happen. McDonald's would have to wait.

'Hey,' she shouted to the make-up and hair girls. 'Come over here.'

They teetered over to her in their six-inch heels, all Lycra dresses and leg warmers, saved from certain hypothermia only by the ankle-length cardigans with weird Picasso designs. They'd obviously been told they were going on a music video shoot and dressed to impress the band. There were large breasts and barely covered crotches – Lori didn't doubt their strategy would work.

'Emergency situation – this is yours,' she grabbed Sly by the scruff of the neck, ignoring his spaced-out objections, and thrust him in their direction. 'Take this six foot of idiot down to the room you're using for hair and make-up, shower him, work your magic and be back here in twenty minutes. Any longer than that and I start amputating limbs.'

Despite several aghast faces no one objected. 'Diana, you go too,' she added after the girls were out of earshot. 'I want chemicals and coffee administered until he's a functioning human being.'

'Got it.'

'And Coco, sorry hon, but it's time to take one for the team. The director is yours. I need him distracted and amused until Sly gets back and I don't care how you do it.'

In fairness, Coco's groan was fairly muted, compelling Lori to give her one last hug of thanks.

The laws of stereotypes would have her and Coco at each other's throats – two women living in the same world, one looking at it as a business, the other viewing it as the biggest playground in the world. But that would be a real dumb approach. Coco was part of the deal with the Spikes – kept Dax happy, was like a sister with perks to the rest of the guys, genuinely liked Marny and occasionally acted as unpaid help.

A case in point being right there, right then.

'Wanna hold this for me?' Coco shrugged out of the blanket and tossed it to Lori, pulled the string at the back of her stars and stripes thong out of her butt-cheeks and threw back her shoulders.

'The things I do for you Lor. But I warn you, if my tits drop off in this frigging cold, you're buying me new ones.'

213

Lori was still laughing as Coco strutted off in the direction of Beck Styler.

'Beck, can we shoot Coco's solo scene first?' Lori yelled. She could see that Beck was about to throw a major strop, so as planned, she immediately softened the blow with, 'She's absolutely ready to do whatever you need.'

Ah, a groupie with absolutely no scruples – every band should have one.

'Action!'

Coco clenched her teeth together to stop them chattering, not easy when she was lying on the precipice of a rooftop, almost naked, in freezing temperatures. A six inch movement to the right would result in headlines the next day stating that an actress shooting a music video had plummeted nineteen storeys to her death. Pressing her back against the cold stone, she stretched her arms out above her head, her only protection against the elements being the bikini consisting of the three tiny triangles of sequinned stars and stripes that had been handed to her when she'd shown up that morning. Just as well she kept her bush down to a minimum.

She could sense the camera just a few feet away from her, Beck Styler beside it, his focus alternating between Coco and the monitor in front of him. The remit had been clear: stretch out, smile playing on lips, and slowly move body in sexual, erotic fashion to the rhythm of the music. Easy in theory, difficult when hypothermia was setting in, only a few misjudged inches separated her from a loud splat, and the stone was having the effect of dermabrasion on her ass.

OK, let's do this. Forget the cold. Forget the fear. Just . . . listen.

The opening bars of 'Suicide Now' blared out of the huge speaker behind the camera. In the finished promo, a clean version of the track would be cut in, but blasting out the song now would ensure that everything was done in synchronicity to the track.

Tye's drumbeat was rhythmic, almost hypnotic.

'Come on, baby, give me a sex face,' Beck Styler whistled. She thought she already had. Consoling an irate former Hollywood hotshot by administering a blow job in the glamorous surroundings of an air-conditioning duct was definitely a first. And hopefully a last. Neither extreme temperatures nor a man who liked to scream 'I'm the almighty' when he came were ever a turn on.

The rhythm section had kicked in now, Muff and Strings' guitars stepping up the pace a little, until . . . BAM! Dax crashes in on lead, with a solo that – she truly believed – was every bit as incredible as the one thrashed out by the incredible Slash on 'Sweet Child o' Mine'.

Dax and Slash – now there would be a threesome. Suddenly she couldn't feel the cold any more.

'That's it baby – you are so fucking hot. Oh, yes, check out those tits.' Beck Styler, world champion in the category of 'Middle-aged Sleazeballs'.

Coco blocked him out. Dax. Slash. Hormones took over from the cold now and forced her nipples to strain even further through the shiny fabric.

Dax. Slash.

Eyes closed, nothing else existed now. Suddenly her very favourite tingling sensation was alive and well in her clit, forcing her pussy to clench tightly, looking for something that wasn't there.

She started to move, slowly, tiny gyrations as she danced where she lay.

There was a low whistle near her head. 'I've got a fucking hard-on,' Styler announced.

Coco didn't care. This was about her. And Dax. And Slash. And . . .

'Cut!'

What?! Noooo.

Her huge green eyes snapped open, her beautiful face furious at the abrupt end to her party. One of the runners threw a blanket around her and she managed a mumbled 'thanks'.

Beck Styler was in her face now. 'You are fucking sensational.'

'I was just getting started.'

'Really? Marry me,' he joked to the amusement of the rest of the crew, several of whom were now adjusting their genitals in an attempt to conceal their raging boners.

Coco considered the offer. 'Can you play guitar?'

Styler shook his head.

'Then sorry – I'll have to pass. I'm looking for the whole package,' she smiled.

'Well, you can have my package any time you like,' he leered. When she didn't respond, he snapped back into work mode. 'OK, next set up. If Sly ain't here in five minutes we're fucked.' With that he was off – sorting out the blocks for the next scene, this one involving a singer who was missing in action.

'You were great hon.' Lori handed her a hot cup of coffee, with a straw sticking out of it.

'So that you don't ruin your lipstick,' she explained.

'Thanks. How's he doing?'

'Diana is just about to bring him up – apparently he's now 50 per cent human, so it's half way better than before. We're gonna have to leave the lift until the end of the day, though.' The lift was the climax shot. Sly was supposed to raise Coco above his head, before clever editing would be used to make it look like they fell off the side of the building.

The core storyline was that all the scenes were dream sequences. Sly sees Coco on the edge of the roof, but every time he tries to reach her she slips off the side. Again and again, he falls asleep, sees her in his dream, and every night he almost reaches her, closer and closer every time, but never getting there before she slips away from him.

Until one final time . . .

He can't take the pain any more. Can't live without touching her, can't handle the guilt that he is the one who is causing her to fall. So on one dark, final moment, he walks over to the edge, steps up on to the precipice, throws his arms out into a crucifix position. Suddenly she's beside him, takes his hand. She's his soul, his heart and now she's with him. They look at each other. Smile. He pulls her towards him, kisses her, lifts her up . . . and they fall. And as they plummet to the ground in slow motion, the scene is overlaid with a transparent image of them in his bed, on white satin sheets, making love, finally together.

Coco had a hunch that it wasn't exactly *The Godfather*, but it was the best they could do in twenty-four hours and on a tight budget. And Lori had seemed confident that the combination of the music, Sly's looks and Coco's body would make it fantastic, so she was happy to go along with it. Anything for the band, baby.

The door that led to the stairs slammed open as the wind caught it and swung it 180 degrees, stopping with a thump against the wall.

Despite the cold, despite the anxiety that they were running behind schedule, Coco couldn't help but grin as he strutted towards them. Jesus, he was beautiful. His long dark chestnut hair, clean now, was blowing behind him, as he swaggered – a walk that was more cool than stoned now – his torso naked, every muscle clearly defined. Dax was so dark and broad that he looked like he'd been carved from oak. Sly on the other hand was leaner, thinner, taller but damn, he looked great, especially as from the waist down his leather pants were so tight she could see the outline of his dick.

Marny was a lucky woman.

'Still wouldn't fuck him?' Lori asked, amused.

'If it wasn't for Marny I might have to revise that statement.'

Suddenly the high of just a few minutes before was gone, replace by a knot of anxiety in her stomach. What was it with this guy? She'd met others who were more attractive, more danger-ous, smarter, but Sly . . .

'Hey Lori, sorry about earlier. Got a bit fucked up.'

The chemicals and caffeine had obviously worked – he was wide awake now, alert and only a little wired.

Coco could see that Lori wasn't letting him off lightly. 'Next time I'll get my gun and use it,' she drawled. 'Luckily Coco used her talents to distract the director and save your butt.'

Sly threw an arm around Coco's shoulders and unleashed his crooked, killer grin.

'Have I told you how much I admire your talents?'

Coco kissed him on the nose. 'Kiss my ass.'

'Any time, sister,' he laughed. That was it. They had a brother/sister thing going. Just like the rest of the band, they were a clan and her feelings towards Sly were nothing more than familial. She just wished that someone would let her pussy know that because right now it was screaming for attention.

They caught the last of the sunrise with the next scene. Remarkably, the ravages of the night before that were still visible on Sly's face actually added to the authenticity of his desperation and he gave a pretty hot performance, screaming into the sun as he tried to reach Coco. She was on her front this time, bikini off, every curve of her silhouette jet black as the sun rose behind her.

'Cut! Great shot people. OK, let's go again.'

It was a relief when the rest of the band showed up at ten to relieve the monotony of waiting around, one-minute shoot, waiting around, one-minute shoot, waiting around . . .

Dax was the first to liven things up, cornering Sly as soon as he heard why the shoot was running so late.

'Come on, man – what the fuck is going on with you?'

The hairs on the back of Coco's neck stood up. She knew Dax was getting more and more pissed at Sly's inconsistency and unreliability. What was the point of a lead singer and songwriter who was regularly too stoned to sing and hadn't written anything worth jackshit in months?

Thankfully Muff – oblivious as always to any drama – came in with a well-timed jibe on the recent developments in his manager's personal life by shouting, 'Hey Lori – heard about the muff diving – that's my job, man!'

Everyone within earshot buckled with laughter except Lori, who had an altogether different reaction. If that knife that flew from the buffet table had been just an inch to the left, Muff would have needed sutures and a tetanus shot.

Coco got to take a break as the focus of the shoot switched to the guys. Ten run-throughs of 'Suicide Now', multiple cameras, various lighting shifts, it was near sunset by the time Styler was happy.

'Here, baby, you hungry?' asked Dax. He'd sent one of the runners downstairs to get her a sandwich and some hot tea. Only when she took a sip did she realise it was laced with brandy. Her kinda guy.

'I'm OK, but I'll be glad when this is over – my muscles are killing me and I think my internal organs have frozen.'

He reached out and pulled her towards him and she tossed the drink and food to one side. There were other ways of heating up. She slid her arms around his neck, taking the blanket with them so that the two of them were cocooned against the cold and the glare of twenty sets of eyes. Dax's tongue met hers as he pressed her against the wall, his hand reaching down inside her thong until she felt the sheer sweet joy of two fingers slipping inside her wet pussy. Oh, yes. This was it. This was her man. This was what he did to her and . . .

'OK people, last scene up here before we move downstairs. I need Coco, I need Sly.'

Perhaps if they just ignored him and . . .

'Now, now children, keep it for later. And Dax, remind me not to shake your hand before you've been to the washroom.' A video director they could ignore, but Coco knew better than to risk the wrath of Lori.

'You guys gonna hang and watch?' Coco asked a decidedly unsatisfied Dax. He glanced over to the rest of the band, who were already heading in the direction of the stairs.

'Nah, we're shooting over to the Village. Gonna catch up with some of the old crew.'

Coco's bottom lip jutted out. The old gang. The bands. The clubs. Last she'd heard Sheedy had changed her name to Swayze and taken up dirty dancing with anyone who had the strength and the stamina to keep up with a two hundred pound mid-op transgender with tits like watermelons. There was nothing she wanted to do more right now than go hang out at their old haunts, cruise the East Village, track down old friends and party into the night. Nothing.

'OK, Coco, Sly, we need you for the bedroom scene,' Styler yelled.

Well, almost nothing.

Her tongue danced with Dax's as she kissed him goodbye. 'You be good. We don't need a second coming of those little critters,' she teased, then laughed as he playfully gave her the finger. Rock 'n' roll. She lit a cigarette and took a deep drag. The bedroom scene. With Sly. Maybe there was something that would be more fun than cruising the village after all.

Beck Styler took a deep drag on a joint as he waited for the lighting guys to finish. Fucking lame that his career had come to this. Shooting jumped-up, wasted rockers in a hotel room that stank of corporate expense accounts and cheap sheets.

He'd been huge once. His Kevin Costner movie had grossed over a hundred million and he could have had the pick of any script in town. Until that little bitch arrived. Sure, she was fifteen, but her mother had pimped her out to him the first day they met. It was all 'please give her a role in your new movie Mr Styler, and she'll be so, so grateful.' The innuendo wasn't lost. As it happened she was perfect for the part and a couple of weeks later he discovered that she was also perfect in the role of sitting on his cock all night long.

He should have known the mother would turn nasty. $500,000 she wanted to keep her mouth shut. Oh, and the money for her little girl's abortion too. He'd told her to fuck off. As if some fat, hick mother from the sticks was gonna hustle Beck Styler.

It turned out to be the biggest misjudgement since he'd stuck his dick in the daughter.

The *National Enquirer* paid her $100,000 for the story, he'd had to settle the lawsuit out of court for a million, the sweet little Lolita was now one of the hottest porn stars in LA and her mother had built up a reputation as the most kick-ass agent in Hollywood.

And he was over. Career gone. He'd practically had to suck off Ari Covet to get this gig. They went back a long way, him and Ari. Years ago, before either of them had reached the top of the ladder, they'd both had a fondness for the kinds of clubs that had rooms in the back that specialised in alternative forms of pleasure. Ari was a twisted fuck. But he was the only twisted fuck in the business that was still prepared to throw Beck a bone.

Or should that be boner?

This bitch in front of him was the most gorgeous thing he'd ever seen. A young, voluptuous Christie Brinkley with the cool edge of Linda Evangelista. And she could blow like the kind of high-class hookers that required four zeros on the cheque before they'd even get down on their knees.

She was up for anything. He could see that. Since the day those tabloid bastards had put his face on the newsstand his creativity had been lost. Today was the first day he'd felt that old buzz again. He'd have to wait to see the rushes, but he was pretty sure that what he'd already shot was fucking blinding stuff.

And now, as he watched her climb on to the white silk sheets, he realised that this could be it.

This could be the shot that reminded everyone just how fucking good Beck Styler really was.

Shit, this was weird. Sure, he'd seen Coco naked more times than he could count, but this was more . . . intimate. Thank fuck

Marny wasn't here or she'd be freaking out. Not that she'd do anything about it, of course. In fact, if the last few weeks were anything to go by she'd be so wasted she wouldn't even notice and after last night . . . Fuck, that was heavy. Drugs and betrayal. Well, her fucked-up stunt had been repaid in full and more, he mused, putting his hands out in front of him and inspecting them. At least the shakes were gone now. The couple of tabs of Valium that he'd dropped a few hours ago had mellowed him out.

Last night he'd seriously thought he was going to die. The last thing he remembered was puking his guts out and the next Diana emptying a bottle of Evian over his face in some stinking alley. But the high . . . dear fucking Lord the high had been like nothing else he'd ever felt. That was some serious shit right there. No fucking way was he going near that again. Too good, man. Way too good. He could get seriously into that stuff and he was smart enough to know that wouldn't end anywhere good.

He leaned down and stuck a straw into the white pile of Peruvian dust that was sitting on top of the mini-bar. Top blow. Whoever Dave Lopez was getting his gear from was giving him the best stuff.

'Sly, we've checked the angles and this is only going to work if you're naked. That OK with you?'

Coco's eyes met his and for the second time that night the thought crossed his mind that this was going get, like, seriously weird.

But then . . . maybe this film with Coco wouldn't be such a bad thing. Man, she was hot, but he was traditional enough to consider her seriously out of bounds. Her and Dax had a messed-up scene going on. If Marny had ever screwed around he'd have gone fucking mental, yet Dax treated it all like it was totally cool. No jealousy. No ties. That was way too much for Sly to get his head around and he'd never been tempted to go there. He liked a woman who was only going to get it on with him and no one else. And fucked up or not, Marny loved him and would never even look at another guy.

It was the way it should be.

Movement over on the bed caught his attention – Coco, wearing just a tiny nude coloured thong, all wild, tangled hair, big eyes and pouted lips.

Yep, she was his buddy's old lady . . . but fuck, what a view.

Styler threw a clipboard across the room, almost decapitating Dave Lopez, who was slouched against the faraway wall. The crash made Coco jump.

'It's not working. It's not fucking working,' he ranted. Either Styler had dropped a bad tab or he was experiencing serious creative anxiety, Coco decided.

'I'm not feeling it. It's just not believable, not fucking believable. What's wrong with you people?'

Coco flopped back on the bed and let out a frustrated groan. If it wasn't good enough he ought to come and frigging try it. Two hours they'd been there, sweltering under the heat of the lights, with the delightful aroma of at least a dozen sweaty, tired bodies all crammed into a room that was so frigging small she could starfish and touch at least two of the walls.

She'd never been shy about having spectators but that was when the audience was turned on and into the vibe. Having a crowd of people carrying various items of equipment, observing things on a professional level, while Beck Styler yelled *'Put that hand there, now kiss her there. Her tits! Feel her tits!'* was having more of an inhibitive effect.

But maybe that wasn't such a bad thing. In all the countless times she'd imagined herself in this situation with Sly, being unable to act like she was turned on had never been part of that picture.

'Out! Everybody get the fuck out!' An assorted gaggle of production people downed tools and made for the door.

'Not you, you fucking imbecile,' he raged at the cameraman. 'You stay, everyone else, gone.'

Coco could see that over in the corner Lori was hesitating. 'It's

OK. Go,' she nodded, despite the fact that she was saying good-bye to her safety net. Having Lori around always kept a lid on things, stopped any situation from getting out of hand. Coco liked the security of knowing that someone had her back. But Beck Styler was close to foaming at the mouth and she wasn't prepared to contradict him.

'What the fuck is up with you? Aren't you supposed to be some big fucking hot-shot rock guy? You look like you're having a fumble behind a fucking gym hall.'

Coco felt Sly tense under the barrage of criticism.

'And you! You were much fucking hornier than that when you blew me this morning. What the fuck's going on with you?'

And this year's Oscar for services to the word 'fuck' goes to . . . Beck Styler.

Coco closed her eyes. This was so not working and getting way, way too intense. Ironic. The first time in her life that getting turned on was a struggle and it was in a public situation with the clock running. But the truth was that she'd been fighting this situation for so long that even though this was a work gig she just couldn't relax. It was still Sly. And he was lying next to her with only a sheet covering the dick that she had fantasised about since the first time she set eyes on him all those years ago on a crappy stage in a deadwood bar.

Styler was pacing now, his freaked-out energy infecting the room.

'Look man, she's my buddy's chick – it's just way too weird,' Sly argued wearily.

'I don't care if she's your fucking mother! We've got another hour to get the scene and then we're out of here. You're about to be the first band in history with a promo that ends thirty seconds before the end of the song.'

Coco jumped up and opened a window. Fresh air. They needed to get some fresh air in here.

Styler was rummaging in a bag at the side of the bed. 'I want this to be so fucking believable that I feel like you are fucking right in front of my face. What do we have to do, huh? What do we have to do?'

His volume was ascending with every screech and completely freaking Coco out. She hated conflict, hated stress. And it didn't look like they were gonna get away from either any time soon, unless . . .

'I need music. I need to hear music,' she said softly. He wanted real and that was never going to happen without a soundtrack. Sly took a large glug of Jack straight from the bottle as the cameraman was dispatched to find a boombox. Coco lit a Camel and inhaled deeply, letting the soothing powers of the nicotine filter out to her nerve endings.

By the time she'd finished, the cameraman was back and Styler's joint had taken the edge off his temper.

'Look, you gotta trust me here. I can make this fucking kill but you gotta trust me.'

Right at that very moment Coco would have donated an internal organ to get them out of there, so trusting Styler seemed like a reasonable option.

'Lose the thong,' he told Coco. 'Trust me, I'll make the angles work so the entire video-watching world doesn't get to see your snatch.'

Whoa – this was a request for trust too far. Sex was her thing – acting in porn wasn't. But then, this was for MTV and there was no way that they'd show anything explicit so maybe . . .

She looked at Sly.

'Too weird?'

He shrugged helplessly and she could see that he just wanted to get out of there as much as she did. Oh, fuck it – so they'd roll around a little, he might even get a hard-on, Styler would get what he wanted and it would be over. Time to suck it up and get on with it.

She stood up and dropped the thong then climbed back on to the bed.

Styler pressed play and as Tye's drums cut in for about the

thirtieth time that day, she lay on her back and assumed the position. Sly was beside her and the script was that the camera would follow his finger as it traced a line from her neck to her stomach then back up again, this time reaching her mouth. His hand would slide slowly to the side of her face as his mouth came down on hers. Then he would lean down, kiss her, slowly at first, then . . .

'OK people, let's do this. Here.'

Styler was holding a small vial in front of her face and by the sickly, stringent smell she knew exactly what it was. This was a bad idea. A real bad idea. Poppers turned her on and gave her a rush like no other, ramping up every sensation, making her heart pound so fast that it felt like it would explode.

'Trust me.'

Shit.

She closed one nostril with her finger and inhaled deeply with the other. The sensation was instant, the most incredible turn-on in the world, so unbelievably erotic that she barely heard Styler as he demanded 'action'.

Sly's finger was travelling now and as she looked into his eyes she could see that the amyl was having the same effect on him. The whole length of his body was pressed against her and she could feel his hard-on, urgent, huge, digging in to the side of her hip.

Nooooo. She didn't want to go here. This was so wrong. So wrong. But yet, stopping just wasn't an option.

The kiss that only half an hour ago had felt perfunctory and awkward was now hard, insistent. His tongue dancing with hers, probing every crevice of her mouth.

And then his hand was on her breast and her fingers were in his hair, grappling, holding him to her, her eyes not even aware of the camera that had moved above them.

'Yes! Oh fuck yes! This is what I'm talking about. Now move above her Sly – I need it to look like you're actually fucking her. Make it look real, man, make it real.'

Sly's lips left hers as he pushed his body on top of hers. Don't panic. It's just acting. It's for the cameras. It's not real. It's just acting. Acting.

He was above her now, looking down on her. His erect dick lying just below her navel, trapped between their hips. Acting. Just acting.

'Coco?' he whispered. And when their eyes met this time, she knew that the acting was over.

She could see it. The look that Dax had when he made love to her. The look that she knew was on her face too. Whatever barriers they'd both put up had just been demolished, wiped out, and now all that was left was the raw truth of what was really happening.

No more words were required for her to understand the question or reply. Only actions.

Their eyes still locked, she opened her legs and gave him the answer. He slipped inside her and she gasped as she realised it felt every bit as perfect as she'd always known it would.

No stopping.

No stopping either of them.

The track had finished now, looped around and started again, and there was no sound other than the music and their gasping breaths. There was no fast action or complicated moves. Just the two of them, slowly moving as one, completely lost in each other.

'Holy fuck,' Styler murmured and if Coco had seen the cameraman's face she'd have realised that his mouth hadn't been closed for the last five minutes.

Sly Rammer was making love to her. And that's what it was. This wasn't a meaningless fuck or a quick screw. It was everything . . . Everything except right.

He was moving faster now, eyes still locked, needing to be deeper inside her, to possess her, keep her. More. More. Her ankles twisted around his, their calves entwined, her hands pressed deep into the flesh of his shoulders. Movement. An incredible crescendo of movement that rose until she could feel that he was losing control.

It was enough. The orgasm started in the depths of her soul and rose to the surface and as it did, her hands dug deeper into his back, her nails leaving ten trails of red from his shoulders to his waist.

And as he came inside her, she knew.

She knew that she loved him.

She knew that there was no going back.

And she knew that she had to leave.

TWENTY-ONE

Rock-a-bye baby . . .

Miss Molly was looking lovely today. Her hair was gold like the corn in the fields. Her big brown eyes were wide and happy.

She had been happy once. She remembered that she would wake up and she would smile and think it was going to be a beautiful day.

But that was before he came.

Before he brought the pain and left it with her and now it would never go away.

Now only Miss Molly understood.

Rock-a-bye baby . . .

She hugged Miss Molly to her chest and squeezed her, promising without words that she would take care of her, keep her safe for ever.

It was always just going to be the two of them, they both knew that.

'You do understand, don't you?' she whispered into Miss Molly's ear.

'You understand why Daddy has to die.'

TRACK 5

TWENTY-TWO

1989

'Like, shit man, how do we follow that?' Dax was pacing back-stage, unusually anxious and wound up.

The Spikes were in the artists' area and on the huge screens that lined the walls of the room, they'd just watched Jon Bon Jovi and Richie Sambora do an acoustic medley of 'Livin' on a Prayer' and 'Wanted Dead or Alive' that had brought the house down. Everyone had expected the big talking point of the MTV Video Music Awards to be the Stones' first live performance in years, or maybe Madonna's crotch-grabbing routine on 'Express Yourself', but going by that last performance, all anyone would be talking about the next day were the two guys who sat in the middle of the stage with their guitars and sang their hearts out. The crowd was still going nuts.

'Relax.' Lori switched into managerial ego-massage mode as Arsenio Hall stepped back up to the podium to introduce the next award. 'They were just gettin' them good and warmed up for you.'

'Yeah, that's exactly what Jon and Rich were doing. They woke up this morning and said, "Hey, let's get the crowd creamed up for the Spikes".' Muff put two fingers against his head, cocked his thumb and mimicked shooting his brains out. Lori wasn't sure that anyone would notice the difference.

On the other hand, it would be hard not to notice that Dax was seriously altered tonight. Wired. Hyper. His normal laidback, easy-going nature replaced by serious tension. Since the rest of the band had the emotional intelligence of a mic stand, they hadn't sussed out what was going on. The only one that might have had a clue was Sly, but he'd gone AWOL an hour ago. Lori was giving it another five minutes before she sent out the search party. Frigging hell, sometimes she wasn't sure if she was a manager, a babysitter or their mother. Cancel that. If she was their mother she'd slap the shit out of them for their behaviour. In the true spirit of rock 'n' roll they'd taken to excess with the dedication of true pros. The drugs. The parties. The girls. Even Muff was getting laid on a nightly basis.

But at least they'd had the success to back it up.

'Hey, Lori, great to see you. Great! Have I told you how fucking awesome you are?'

'Yes, but you have my permission to do it again.'

Bill Simpson, head of Ark Records. He'd been trying to take the Spikes from AC for the last six months but their contracts were watertight and anyway, he was only one of many.

1989 had been their year. Only a year ago Covet had been ready to write off their album, but that had been before the video for 'Suicide Now' had become the most requested video ever on MTV, giving them the kind of worldwide publicity and profile that money just couldn't buy. Over a million copies of the album had now shifted and The Steel Spikes were the biggest new act in the business.

Best-selling rock band of 1989.

Halfway through a 250-gig global tour.

A photograph of Sly and Dax, torsos bare, rocking out at the Spectrum, had been turned into the most popular poster of the year.

They'd even been drafted on to the bill at the Moscow Peace Festival the month before, playing with Bon Jovi, Ozzy Osbourne and Mötley Crüe in front of 120,000 screaming fans at Lenin Stadium. Their livers had yet to recover.

The Steel Spikes were a phenomenon and it was down to killer tracks and the fact that every teenage rock chick in America was in love with either Sly or Dax. And every teenage boy was in love with Coco.

There was absolutely no doubt that the catalyst for their success had been the 'Suicide Now' video. It had also made a star of the woman who wasn't sitting here with them. The one that was at the root of Dax's anxiety. The one that was out in the auditorium, with another band, back in the same building as the Spikes for the first time since Beck Styler had called 'Cut'.

'No, baby, don't do it. You don't . . .'

'Shut the fuck up!'

Marny obeyed. There was no point in arguing when he was like this. Three fortnights in rehab in the last year hadn't got him off it so the chances of him responding to her asking nicely were slim. Better just to let him get on with it and at least then it would be over. Until the next time.

She took a vial from her bag, tipped a little mound of snow on to the back of her hand, snorted it. She'd learned her lesson in the hospital that night. No more pills for her – she was strictly a coke girl now. An involuntary shudder enveloped her as she remembered that night. It had been so close . . . so close in more ways than one.

Resting her head back against the toilet door, she watched Sly through half-closed lids. It wasn't the kind of image MTV would pay to put out: Sly Rammer, sitting on the john, black vest, ripped up jeans at his ankles, his dick swinging in the wind. If the moral majority of America didn't object to the nudity, they'd definitely have an issue with the syringe of brown that was being discharged into his groin.

Shit, Lori would kill him. And her. But she'd tried to stop him, she really had.

Suddenly his head fell backwards and his whole body went limp. She knew the score. He'd stay like that for a few moments and then he'd clamber to his feet, swear he was fucking indestructible and stagger out to do the gig. This man was so far removed from the one that she'd fallen in love with that it was difficult to believe they were the same person. Her sweet, romantic Sly was gone. She didn't recognise this guy's selfishness. She didn't get his obsession with junk. She found it hard that he no longer cared about taking care of himself: no showers, the same clothes every day and twice this week she'd woken up to find him lying in his own piss.

The only thing she understood was the pain that started it and it devastated her that she was the one who had caused that. No matter how many times she told him, over and over, that she'd been trying to help, trying to do something good for him, he refused to accept it. All he could see was his family's rejection of who he was. All he could feel was the pain.

Now, though, the drugs were as much about pushing it to the edge as they were about healing the hurt. He was looking for something, always trying to break boundaries, take the high to another level, party harder than anyone had ever done before. It had become obvious that there was some kind of void in his psyche and only the thrill of the next hit could fill it.

Sly Rammer had a self-destruct button and his finger was pressing down hard.

Marny just hoped she could prise it off before they both went under.

'And the winner is . . .'

Coco felt Randy Storm's fingers dig into the back of her neck. It was impossible to call. Best Heavy Metal video had a line-up that could be classed as either music heaven or the starring cast of her wildest fantasies:

Guns N' Roses – 'Sweet Child o' Mine'
Aerosmith – 'Rag Doll'
Decomp – 'High'
Def Leppard – 'Pour Some Sugar on Me'
Metallica – 'One'
'Guns N' Roses, Sweet Child o' Mine!'

'Motherfuckers. C'mon, let's get out of here.' Storm was pulling her arm, but Coco sat firm. Sometimes her leading man was just a little too demanding for her liking. Actually, that was the understatement of the year. Sometimes Randy Storm was just a megalomaniac asshole. Moody. Temperamental. Arrogant. Narcissistic. Asshole.

The flashback to that night the year before still kept her awake at night. When she'd left the hotel she'd had three obvious choices: join Storm on the Decomp tour, go back to her mom's home to chill out and get her head together, or stay in New York and hang around the village. Heading back to the ranch was the first one to get crossed off the list. She loved her mother but she'd escaped from the constraints and memories in Connecticut once and she wasn't going back – she'd moved on slightly from fucking the Lawson twins in the back of their daddy's car. And besides, she wasn't up for that kind of isolation.

It would have been cool to hang out in NY for a couple of days, but she knew it wouldn't be enough. She'd lived the life now. As far as Coco was concerned hanging with a band was like losing her virginity – once she'd done it once and realised how great it was there was no going back.

Storm had been ecstatic when she'd showed up in London the next day, although Coco had a hunch that his enthusiasm was born as much from the ego boost of winning the girl from the young, hot new band on the block as it was from affection for her. Not that it mattered. Being on the road with Decomp had been great: fifteen countries, incredible experiences and she'd learned more about the business than most industry insiders. Oh, and she got to screw the hot lead singer every night.

The sobriety rule was a downer, but she'd never needed outside influences to get high. In fact, she'd discovered another aphrodisiac in the last few months: success.

The Spikes' video had turned her into an international star overnight. There had been requests for modelling shoots, acting offers, and more then a dozen approaches from extremely rich men who wanted to either buy her, fuck her or marry her.

All offers that involved the exchange of bodily fluids had been politely declined. Instead, she'd worked with the merchandising and publicity guys at AC to rush out a calendar that had sold out in a week. Five reprints later, she'd just finished shooting the pictures for the second one and it was going to be incredible.

She'd also taken the modelling jobs that suited her interests and Decomp's schedule. The fur coats had been a definite no, posing naked while straddling a motorbike wearing Harley Davidson boots had been a definite yes. Draping herself over the bonnet of a '65 Spitfire while playing a Stratocaster had been a job she'd have done for free, while there was no amount of money that would make her star in anything to do with any other band. Her loyalties would always lie with the Spikes – much to the annoyance of Storm, who'd been trying without success to get her on Decomp's new CD cover.

It was strange and kinda cool being a recognised face in her own right and she was grateful for it, but she realised there were definite drawbacks. The tabloids seemed obsessed by the dichotomies of her life and there had already been several 'wild child daughter of billionaire' and 'If Daddy could see her now' type headlines. They'd even tracked down a Mrs Katherine Lawson, former seamstress to the Belmont family, who had spoken at length about how young Colette had been a sweet, God-fearing young girl who'd been a close friend of her sons, Dale and Mack – both of whom were now in full-time employment at the local video store. Cindi and Kimmy had posed in their Ivy League preppy clothes and claimed Colette had always sworn that she was going to marry a rock star. Her mother had given many polite 'no comments'. But still the hacks kept on running the stories: some true, some trippin'. Well, screw them. She wasn't going to go chasing fame and fortune but if it chased her then she was going to enjoy it. After all, there had to be some consolation prize for losing the man and the life that she loved.

'C'mon, let's split,' Storm repeated. It was a good idea. She should definitely go. But Arsenio was back up on the stage now talking about the 'Best New Act' and if there was any justice in the world then it would go to the Spikes. She'd promised herself that she wouldn't contact them tonight. Strictly no face time. No hugs, no 'great to see you'. No fond reminisces. Her heart couldn't take it.

But that didn't mean she couldn't watch to see if they won.

'I'm staying, baby. You split if this is freaking you out.'

'Fucking shit,' Randy murmured, but he didn't get up to leave. No surprise. In a weird way it seemed like the more off-hand she was with him the more compliant he became. For a narcissistic, megalomaniac pain in the ass he could also be a real pussycat sometimes.

'And the nominations are . . . Johnny Deviro!' The new poster boy for white teeth and sultry ballads.

'Candy Cass!' A fifteen-year-old who'd spent forty-four weeks in the charts with her debut album of sugary pop.

'The Whites.' New romantics. All frilly shirts and flicked hair, riding the synthesised wave that started in the UK and was now sliding its way across the Atlantic.

'And The Steel Spikes!'

The crowd's favourite was obvious as a roar of thunderous applause filled the stadium.

Coco had to smile. Her boys. She missed them so much but she'd done the best thing for them all when she left and now she'd moved on. Cut ties. Put the drama behind her. Dax never knew the truth about what happened, and neither did Marny. She just called them, told them that it was time for her to move on, that she'd decided to be with Randy instead. Sly got to go back to his life and she got to avoid destroying the lives of two of the people she loved most in the world. Missing them was her penance, her punishment – and not a day went by that she didn't remind herself that she deserved it.

A camera moved to her right and she reminded herself that – unlike Randy – she should smile and clap no matter who won, especially as she was sitting only twenty feet from the stage so any of the dozen cameras that were being used to film the show could catch her reaction.

'And the winner is . . .'

Shoulders back. Carefree expression. Smile.

Damn, she could do with a drink.

Sly's ass hit the chair just as Arsenio opened the envelope. Talk about cutting it fine. They'd been marched out front to hear their nomination and then afterwards, win or lose, they had to get straight backstage because they were performing in ten minutes – dependent of course on whether Sly had completely numbed his brain cells yet again.

The knot of tension and apprehension in Lori's stomach felt like it could snap at any second. Shit, she was going to beat him four ways till Sunday when this night was over. Marny caught her eye and gave what Lori recognised as the closest thing to an apologetic shrug that someone who'd just snorted a line could manage. For the umpteenth time she resolved to get them back into rehab. She'd tried everything to keep Marny off the coke, short of putting a twenty-four-hour guard on her, but since Sly had started treating her like crap after the Philly incident, it was like the girl was lost and the cocaine was all she had left. She'd heard there was a clinic in Santa Barbara that was using the latest techniques and philosophies – maybe Marny would respond to that. At least she hadn't succumbed to the brown stuff so maybe there was still some sense and willpower in there.

But Sly? If it was up to her he'd be subjected to a padded frigging cell and cold turkey. As far as she was concerned, Sly's heroin addiction was nothing but pathetic self-indulgence. This guy had everything he'd ever wanted, millions would sell their grandma for a week in his boots and yet he was too busy shooting it up or pissing it against the wall. Enough. Diana had found a hardcore dry-out centre in Arizona and she'd have him in there by the end of the week.

She was so busy contemplating that she lost focus for a split second and was only brought back to the present when Muff jumped in the air, screamed 'Right fucking on!', then flew onto the lap of Steven Tyler at the next table and simulated a dry hump.

Thankfully, Dax dragged him off by the considerable mop of hair before the Aerosmith boys had a chance to formulate a plan to kill him.

They'd won! And going by the audience reaction it was the most popular decision of the night.

The guys were following Spank's lead now, heading for the stairs at the side of the stage, Dax practically dragging Sly behind him.

Dear God, don't let him speak. Her silent plea was cut off by the arm that slid around her waist. 'You did it, baby,' Diana whispered as she nuzzled into her neck.

Spontaneous tears sprung to Lori's eyes as she realised – without an ounce of smugness – that Diana was right. Just short of five years ago she'd stood over her daddy's corpse in a stinking bar. Now the world was recognising the band that she'd created and it felt great. The thought that ran through her head whenever her emotions went to any extreme came along right on cue.

'See, Mama? See what I did? And it was no fucking thanks to you.'

The camera zoomed right in on the stunning female at one of the front tables, on her feet now, clapping and cheering, oblivious to the tears that were dropping down her face. The silver vest-dress was moulded to every curve of her killer body and stopped just below her perfectly formed butt, exactly the same length as the waves of thick ash blonde that streamed down her bare back. Her tanned, perfectly toned legs seemed to go on for miles before they reached the six-inch-high strappy sandals.

The next day journalists would comment on the scowl on the face of the rocker sitting next to where she stood. But right now that didn't matter. All that she cared about was the band on the stage and the two men who were in the middle of the scrum. The only two men that she'd ever loved.

It took several moments for the applause to die down, enough time for Dax to lean into Sly's ear. 'You are a fucking disaster, man. Fucking get it together.'

Dax stayed out of other people's dramas but Sly was pushing it way too far. The band was suffering and lately he'd been getting the urge to kick his ass on a daily basis. Right now that urge had never been stronger. It seemed like every discussion escalated into a debate, every debate into a disagreement, the disagreements into screaming arguments. He gestured to Spank to take over the official task of holding Sly up. Fuck knows, they'd been through some shit in the last year but this was the most deranged stunt he'd pulled so far. Idiotic fucker.

Muff, Tye and Strings automatically stood one step back from the podium to let Dax through. They'd rather amputate digits than speak in public. It was one of the reasons that the band worked. He and Sly took care of front of house, the rest of the guys brought up the rear. At least, that was how they'd rolled until last year when Sly became the smacked-up dead weight that they were all dragging around.

As Dax leaned over to speak into the mic hundreds of screaming females showed their love. He rewarded them with a wink and a grin, setting off a second cacophony of appreciation.

He stood there, looking like a Navajo warrior returning from battle – not that Navajo warriors customarily dressed in black leather studded pants and nothing else but a matching waistcoat, sleeveless and left open to show every single inch of his perfectly carved abdomen and football-sized biceps.

A lot of energy and commitment went into keeping his body looking like that and shit, it was worth it. Not that he was on a path of abstinence or moderation. He still smoked a pack of cigarettes a day. He still liked his Jack. He was never far from a large reefer packed with blow. But he always ensured that he balanced out the body karma by training most days. It was working just fine.

And of course there had been an ulterior motive for stepping up his regime: for at least a couple of hours every day, the pain took his mind off missing Coco.

He'd tried everything. Everything. Letters, telegrams and phone call after phone call, but nothing worked. Blank. She'd ignored them all. Left him. Over. And he still didn't understand why. Could it be as simple as she'd claimed – that she'd fallen in love with Randy Storm and didn't want to be apart from him?

He'd given up hoping that the situation would change. Now was the time for him to draw a line under it and move on.

'I'd like to thank two people for this award.' The choke in his voice was as unexpected as it was dramatic.

'We have the most kick-ass, awesome manager in the business. Miss Lori Wyatt, we love you!'

Cut to camera three, a fiercely beautiful Amazonian woman in a black rubber catsuit smiles as she bows graciously to the soundtrack of wild applause. The next day the journalists would speculate as to whether she had an inkling as to what was about to transpire.

Dax leaned into the mic again. 'And of course we have to thank the other person who put us here today . . .'

Back in his office in LA, Ari Covet snorted a line of coke the thickness of a slug as he watched the screen, waiting for his moment of glory. It was his policy never to attend funerals or awards shows. The first, because there wasn't a single person

243

whose death he would give two fucks about, the second because he didn't believe in risking the humiliation of losing. There was no way he was going to stand there with a fake grin on his face if some other cunt's band went up to take the trophy. Far better to watch from the background, reap the glory when it came. Which was right around now.

'And of course, the other person we owe so much to. Someone who's been with The Steel Spikes from the beginning and who is responsible for us standing here today.'

Ari unzipped his pants, slid his palm around his cock and started to chug. Fuck it, he was so turned on he was going to come right as Dax shouted out his name.

Yesssss! He was the fucking king!

'And we are so grateful . . .'

The spunk flew from Ari's dick.

'. . . to the beautiful Miss Coco LaBiba.'

Time stopped.

Stopped.

Everyone was on their feet now, all who were within viewing distance of her watching as she stood there, stunned, more perfect tears falling down her perfect face.

Dax was holding his hands out, signalling her to come up on the stage. Suddenly, at her side, fingers surreptitiously slipped around her wrist and she felt the heat of Randy's breath on the side of her neck.

'Don't you fucking dare,' he whispered.

His hold was tight, making it obvious that if she wanted to break free of him she would have to wrench her arm away and that would just be downright humiliating for all concerned.

Instead, with her free hand, she blew Dax a kiss and shook her head, clearly but gracefully rejecting the summons to the stage.

If it had just stopped there it would have been fine. A little uncomfortable but unremarkable.

Nothing to see. No more to discuss. But then it wouldn't have been rock 'n' roll.

Coco. Where was Coco?

Sly didn't understand. Dax was talking to Coco but where was she and what was all that noise? And the lights – why were all those lights shining in his face? His head was seriously malfunctioning.

Spank's arm tightened around his shoulders as he swayed dangerously close to toppling in the other direction.

That was some seriously good shit. Lopez always got him the best gear and he just hoped there was some more for later because it was gonna be major party time.

But where was Coco? Where had she been, man?

Quite involuntarily, his head lurched back and as his neck muscles struggled to right the imbalance he caught something out of the corner of his eye. Something shiny. Something sparkly. Coco.

She was there. Standing next to that preachy asshole from Decomp. Call himself a lead fucking singer? The guy was a fucking idiot. A self-righteous, drug-shunning motherfucker.

And he had Coco.

Time to do something about that.

A moment ago, Marny had been thrilled. Now she wasn't sure if the coke was wearing off or if it was just that the anxiety was so strong it had wrestled control of her senses, but she was suddenly seriously scared. And she hated that feeling. It was too familiar. Too evocative.

She couldn't take her eyes off Sly's face. He had that expression – the same one that she saw when she tried to stop him going out for a fix. Nothing was going to stop him.

'Lori, get him out of there. You have to get him out of there.'

The situation had deteriorated in the click of a finger and she knew that Lori had seen it too.

'They'll cut it dead now and take them off to the side. Come on. Come on.' Lori murmured to no one in particular.

It was too late.

Up in the gallery, the producer, momentarily absorbed in the sight of the closest thing to sparkly, shiny female perfection he'd ever seen, took his eyes off camera one for a split second too long. Almost ten million people watched as Sly Rammer pushed Spank out of the way and made a break for the edge of the stage, staggering with surprising speed before he practically fell down into the auditorium. It was one of those bizarre moments that seemed to play out in slow motion as he half limped, half swayed over to where Coco was standing.

Marny put her hand to her mouth to stop the scream. Why was he going to her? What was going on? No, Sly, please no.

She saw Coco's face, surprised, clearly unable to comprehend what was happening.

Three feet. Two feet. One foot. He was there. The action was being shown in glorious Technicolor on the two mammoth screens at the side of the stage and she was sure that every single person – unaware of Sly's wasted state – was expecting an *Officer and a Gentleman* moment. He was going to somehow lift Coco up and whisk her on to the stage to receive the recognition she deserved.

Marny knew different.

Instead, he produced a bottle of vodka from the inside of his leather jacket. He held it aloft, to the cheers of the crowd.

And then he smashed it over Randy Storm's head.

Sly Rammer had achieved the impossible – he'd just unwittingly ensured that the next day no one would be talking about Jon and Richie, the two guys who sat in the middle of the stage and sang acoustic versions of their biggest hits.

Instead, everyone would be talking about how Sly Rammer of The Steel Spikes attacked Randy Storm of Decomp on live television.

Even Bon Jovi couldn't deliver that kind of rock 'n' roll.

TWENTY-THREE

LA Times, September 7th 1989

ROCK STAR ASSAULTED AT GLITTERING AWARDS

Controversy rages after Randy Storm, lead singer with rock band Decomp, was assaulted by Sly Rammer of The Steel Spikes.

The incident took place at last night's MTV Video Music awards, a star-studded ceremony that was beamed out live to almost ten million viewers. After outstanding performances by many of the biggest stars in music, events took a rather more sinister turn when platinum-selling newcomers The Steel Spikes took to the stage to accept the award for Best New Act.

As many will know, the video for The Steel Spikes' smash hit, 'Suicide Now' caused a sensation over the last year, a success story that was largely credited to the video starring the beautiful Coco LaBiba, the former girlfriend of Spikes guitarist Dax Rice. Since splitting with Rice, LaBiba has been in a relationship with

Storm, a development that insiders claim was devastating to the guitarist.

In a moving acceptance speech, Rice thanked LaBiba before inviting her to join the band on the stage.

The invitation was declined, a rebuff that appeared to upset a dishevelled Sly Rammer, who then left the stage and smashed a bottle of liquor on Randy Storm's head.

The live show then cut to commercials, leaving the viewing public unaware of further events. However, according to eyewitness reports, the remaining members of The Steel Spikes then left the stage and joined the fracas, resulting in a mass brawl between the two bands. The scheduled performance by The Steel Spikes was cancelled.

As of going to press, no further details are available. Representatives of AC Records, the label to which both bands are signed have so far issued an unequivocal 'no comment'.

LA Times, September 8th 1989

A CUNNING STUNT BY NOTORIOUS RECORD CHIEF?

A statement released today by AC Records claims that the mass brawl between members of The Steel Spikes and Decomp was a display of friendly rivalry exaggerated in the name of entertainment.

According to the company spokesman, 'The stunt was planned all along as an amusing play on the rivalry between the two bands. We do, however, concede that it escalated slightly and gave the impression of being a conflict situation. Furthermore, we understand that this could be upsetting for fans of both acts. For this, AC Records, Decomp and The Steel Spikes apologise unreservedly.

AC Records have been in discussion with both the police and MTV officials throughout the day and we can confirm that no charges will be brought as a result of this incident.

Regrettably, MTV have informed us that they are considering action against the bands and we await confirmation of this decision.

Both The Steel Spikes and Decomp wish to thank their fans for all the support they have received over the last 24 hours.

LA Times, September 9th 1989

A spokesman for MTV confirmed today that no further action will be taken against rock acts The Steel Spikes and Decomp after the mass brawl at the Video Music Awards on 9/6/89. According to our sources, this decision was taken after an unprecedented barrage of support from viewers, leading to the MTV telephone system crashing for thirteen hours yesterday. There has been no comment from within the camps of either band.

TWENTY-FOUR

If Lori had one wish right there, right then it would be that someone should shut that fucking phone up. For three days it hadn't stopped ringing and if she was getting any sleep she was sure it would ring in her dreams too.

'Can you get that?' she asked Diana. God knows what she'd have done without her since the minute Sly lost his fucking mind and decided to play at Smash The Bottle On A Rock Legend.

He was so messed up. So freaking messed up she didn't even know where to start to fix him. The clinic in Arizona didn't have a free bed for another three days, so right now he was under lock and key, with Dave Lopez in charge of ensuring he didn't escape. Oh, and Lopez had also been warned that if Sly managed to obtain any more smack Lori would carry through on her promise to remove his balls and fry them in front of him, whether he had supplied the drugs or not. It wasn't an idle threat. There was a thin line between keeping the band happy and enabling addiction and as far as she was concerned Lopez's inexperience had taken him right across it.

Diana stretched the cord over to where Lori was lying on the camel peach-skin sofa. Her first week in the new house she'd

250

bought at the foot of Laurel Canyon and all the enjoyment had been completely destroyed by the biggest challenge in her career so far.

'It's for you.'

'Who?' Lori mouthed. Diana didn't answer so Lori threw her an irritated scowl as she snatched the receiver.

'Hello?'

'Lori, it's me.'

'Coco! Fucking hell, where have you been?'

'Don't ask. Listen, I'm so sorry, babe. I didn't mean for any of that to happen. Is he OK?'

'Dax or Sly?' Well, with Coco you just never knew.

'Both of them.'

'Dax went into the gym the next morning and hasn't come out yet. Sly is a complete mess. I'm waiting to move him to a clinic in Tucson.'

'Shit, I'm so sorry Lori.'

'Hey, it isn't your fault. You can't help being attractive to misfits and junked-up imbeciles.'

For the first time, Coco's voice lightened just a fraction. 'I know, I'm just lucky that way.'

'How are things at your end?'

'Not great.' Coco sighed. 'Randy got sixteen stitches, all of which burst when Ari told him he had to go along with the stunt line or he was pulling their finance. He's going nuts. Heard him on the phone last night asking someone how much they wanted to put a hit on Sly.'

'You're fucking kidding!' Lori gasped, astonished.

'Nope. Don't worry. One, he's too tight to part with the cash and two, he's already had one run in with the law and doesn't want a repeat performance. I'll keep an eye on him.'

'Thanks Coco. You know, we miss you around here. Muff says he'll give you free head every day for the rest of your life if you come back.'

There was a pause and when Coco finally spoke her voice was

thick with emotion. 'You've no idea how much I miss you guys too. But . . .'

'Come back. Come on. I need you here, Coco. I've no one who can be relied upon to provide sexual favours in times of crisis.'

From the other sofa, Diana feigned outrage and then stretched her foot over and pressed it into Lori's crotch, immediately igniting a fire that had been extinguished three days ago by an unexpected soaking with a combination of vodka, blood and drama.

'I can't, Lori, it's too . . . complicated.'

'I know,' came the sad reply. She understood. Really she did. But the guys missed Coco and Dax was hurting so much that she couldn't help wishing for a happy ending. Shit, what was happening to her? One relationship with a gorgeous black lesbian ex-hooker and she was already on the slippery slope to romantic mush.

'Listen hon, I gotta go, but you know the offer's always there. You take care of yourself and call me if you need me.'

'I will, Lori, thanks. And . . .' There was a loaded pause. '. . . take care of both of them for me.'

As his eyelids finally closed, Marny slumped back and collapsed with exhaustion and relief, thankful that the doctor Dave had procured from some very expensive clinic had managed to knock Sly out.

'That should keep him quiet for a couple of hours, but I can't give him any more than that. Too risky.'

Marny wasn't sure if the risk was to Sly or the doctor's career, given that doling out opiates on the side wasn't necessarily standard practice for a respectable MD.

Dave Lopez shook the doctor's hand and ushered him out before coming back and slipping an arm around Marny's shoulders.

'Hey, how you holding up?'

Marny shrugged. 'OK.' She pulled a mirror out from under the sofa, four straight lines of cocaine already chopped and prepared, and snorted one clean up. This was nothing to do with what was going on with Sly. This was harmless. Fun. Anyone could see that the brown was killing him and she didn't ever want to be accused of sharing his addiction. OK, so she couldn't get through the day without the vital help from her snowy friend, but she never touched the junk. She knew better. She just wished she could stop him too.

'Don't say anything to Lori about Doctor Dope being here, OK?'

Marny nodded. 'I won't. And thanks, Dave. Thanks for helping.'

Jeez, he was so, so kind to her. With his new rock look he was hardly recognisable as the old Dave, but compared to the rest of the crazy guys in her world, Dave Lopez was the sweetest, most reliable man, always there for her the second she needed anything. He'd make a great husband for someone one day. She watched him head off in the direction of the door, stopping only to collect the paper bag that Doctor Dope had left for him. As the door closed behind him, she thought about calling room service for a bottle of vodka then remembered that there was some Jack Daniel's under the bed. That would do. She poured a glass then lifted the remote control for the television before throwing it back down on the bed when nothing grabbed her attention. The thought of making something to eat in the tiny kitchenette had no appeal either.

There was absolutely nothing she wanted to do. Nowhere she could go. No one around to talk to.

Like most of the band, they'd been staying in the suite at the Carlton Inn just off Sunset since they'd arrived back in LA the week before. It was supposed to be a temporary measure. Lori had sat the whole band down and given them a lecture on property investment, telling them all that they should buy somewhere even though they were going to be pretty much constantly on the road for the next two years. Sound business sense, Lori had called it. A waste of good drugs money, according to Sly. And he'd lived up to that by spending the whole week loaded while rotating between the Cathouse, the Whisky, the Rainbow and the Troub, leaving the clubs only to sleep or to grab something to eat in Canter's Deli over on Fairfax. The rock lifestyle baby and nothing was going to stop him living it, with or without her.

As the Jack began to kick in she felt a deep feeling of calm wash over her. It wouldn't last long. A couple of hours maybe. In the early days she'd have sought out Coco and chilled with her, but obviously that wasn't possible now. The tears sprung to the back of her eyes and she sniffed them away. She missed Coco. Sure, she'd got a shock when she saw the video and the sight of her and Sly up there doing . . . well, whatever. But she soon got over it when Sly had explained that it was only acting and that the room had been full of people. They hadn't actually had sex for real – the lighting and camera angles just made it look that way. Even when he was kissing Coco, he hadn't felt a thing, he'd said. He loved Marny. The action in that hotel room was purely for the cameras, end of story.

The letter from Coco had come a few days later, saying exactly the same thing, and telling Marny that much as she loved the Spikes it was time to move on. Time to see what else was out there. Time to give it a shot with Randy Storm. *Take care my little mouse*, she'd written. *Don't forget that I love you and take good care of yourself and Sly. Your friend, Coco.*

It proved there was nothing to worry about because if there was anything going on then Coco wouldn't have left, would she?

Nope, the problems with Sly had nothing to do with anyone else and everything to do with whatever was going on between him, his mind and the drugs.

Marny knew where she stood. Over the last year she'd been reminded of it countless times. Music. Junk. Her.

That was the order. Although the first two were interchangeable depending on when he'd had his last fix.

Everything about their relationship had changed. The intimacy had gone, the intensity had evaporated and the physical side was dead. They hadn't had sex in months. But the loss that she grieved for most was their friendship – that too had been destroyed and she just wished that she knew how to change it.

Her early life had been tough for her, a solitary existence where happiness and security were difficult to find. Being on her own used to be second nature. That had all changed the day she met Sly Rammer. But now, as she inhaled a couple more lines, she realised something.

Marny Tucker felt lonelier than ever.

The kick sent the bedside table flying across the room, stopping only when it crashed into the TV and caused a crack to run right across the screen.

Shit. That'd be another cleaning bill. Story of his life, wasn't it? Dave Lopez: responsible for cleaning up. Cleaning up the fuck-ups and lives of the band. Cleaning up their dramas. Cleaning up the communications between the record company and the management so that they didn't kill each other. This wasn't what he had signed up for when he came into the business. He'd wanted the music. To be part of the scene. But then . . . things just got a little out of control.

He still remembered the first time he got drugs for Sly. Shit, he'd had nothing but judgemental contempt for him. It was just so clichéd, the rock star with the drug habit. Deep down, he'd enjoyed being part of the gang, helping the big guy out.

It was like being back in school all over again. He was the music nerd, the guy who was always on the edge, never quite hip enough to hang with the cool guys and get the coolest chicks.

But he had had a plan. First, he'd made himself indispensable to them. He was the fixer, could get anything, do anything and clean up their crap. Then he'd grown his hair long. Traded the shirts and thin ties for messed-up black vests and leather jackets. Lived in boots and battered jeans that he washed only when absolutely necessary. He became one of them. Or rather, he became the closest thing he could be to Sly.

But everything had changed that night.

That night, a year before, when Sly had brought Marny home from the hospital, half dead, and then left her. How could he do that? How?

That's when Dave realised how much he loved her. He also realised that the chemicals might just be the only way to remove Sly from the picture so he'd taken the opportunity to promote him to something a little more pharmaceutically interesting and now Sly needed him, needed his supplies just to function. The power was exhilarating. He was in the inner circle – and that meant he got even closer to the prize.

He'd loved her vulnerability, her sweetness, from the moment he'd met her, but now that had grown to a full scale obsession. And if Sly wasn't around then she'd see him, it was up to him to give her the life she deserved to have. He just had to stick to the plan.

He picked up a Beatles album from the bed and put it on. Marny couldn't see it yet, but one day she would realise that she loved *him*, Dave Lopez. He knew she would. And until then he could wait, because he absolutely knew that one day he would have Marny . . . and all Sly would have left was the high.

The Rainbow was a heaving mass of bodies from the front door to the bar.

But Randy Storm was Moses.

As he walked in at the front of the Decomp posse the crowds parted, practically genuflecting as he passed them. And this was in a club where rock stars came as standard. Dave Lee Roth was already ensconced in one booth with eight scantily clad model-esque beauties. Somehow Coco doubted they were talking politics and current affairs.

Over at the bar, a couple of the guys from the Scorpions – she'd met them before, back in Germany when Decomp were playing the Frankenhalle in Nuremberg – were tying one on. And rumour had it that Mötley were going to jam later. Randy had used that as the reason for coming but Coco had her doubts. This was about proving a point. It was about showing his face and proving that he had nothing to feel embarrassed about after the shit at the VMAs. And Coco suspected it was also about hunting down Sly and the guys for a rematch.

She'd tried to talk Storm out of it but he was on a mission and nothing was stopping him. Even a call to Bob, the sobriety counsellor, hadn't been able to stop them. In fact, Bob was probably right this minute at the airport booking a ticket to his home town of Nebraska after Storm had threatened to eat his children if he didn't get out of his face.

It was safe to say that the serenity and spiritual karmic Zen had fucked off right around the moment that the bottle had come crashing down on Randy's head. He'd been a simmering powder keg of rage ever since. And Coco had a horrible feeling it was about to blow, right about . . .

'Put six bottles of Jack on the table and make sure they never run out,' Randy ordered a pretty little waitress with breast implants that were barely covered by a tiny, pale blue Lycra minidress.

. . . right about now. Coco flicked him a sideways glance but knew better than to say anything else. That would be the end of the sobriety phase, then. She half expected someone else in the band to object, but nothing. Instead they all sat there, arms slung around an assortment of girlfriends, watching to see what would happen next. It was the Decomp way. Unlike the Spikes, where Sly, Dax, Lori, even Spank had a legitimate voice, Decomp was a dictatorship that took no prisoners. And Randy was the guy who gave the orders. He was sober? The whole band was in abstinence mode. He was drinking? They all were. And going by the eager look on their faces, she knew which they preferred.

It was something that she never thought she'd ever even contemplate, but this was one night that Coco LaBiba just wasn't in the mood to party. Too much tension was screwing with her vibe. If the Spikes came in here tonight there was going to be carnage.

And she knew what side she would have to be on.

The sweat trickled off his brow as the pain kicked in. Fuck, it hurt. It hurt so much and that was why he liked it. His arms were trembling now, buckling under the pressure of the weight and just at the very moment when he knew he couldn't hold it up a second longer, he jerked the dumbbell back on to the rack.

That's when he realised that the roar he could hear was his.

The gym was always dead at this time of night. The only other guy in the place, a muscular misfit who sat behind the desk over at the door, eyed him warily. Usually Dax would give him a wave, crack a joke, tell him to chill, nothing to worry about, but tonight he didn't care. It hurt. Something inside just hurt.

It was bad enough that she'd left him but last night he'd finally realised why. He'd seen the look on her face as she'd watched Sly coming towards her and it was eating him up. Sex was one thing, love was completely different. That fucker. He was destroying everything.

They'd been friends. Brothers. The first two years they'd been a partnership that had been second only in importance to his relationship with Coco. They'd fucking rocked it. Sly's lyrics, his music − it was poetry, man.

But Sly was pushing buttons now. Fucking up the band by being late for rehearsals, getting so doped up before gigs that he could barely stand on the stage, and shit, he hadn't written anything decent for months. Dax had called him on it every time at the beginning, challenged him to clean up his act and get the Spikes back on track. One hit album wasn't going to sustain a lifetime. He'd soon realised, though, that it was pointless. Sly had retreated to somewhere that he didn't even hear voices anymore, couldn't take the criticism or heat without going straight for another fix.

Dax had always viewed it as a professional problem. Nothing personal. Now? He wasn't gonna kid himself on any longer. There was something going down between Coco and Sly and Sly hadn't even had the decency to give him a heads up. Brothers? The guy was a fucking snake.

And it was time someone straightened him out. In every way.

Invisible. She wanted to be invisible again.

Nothing going on here. Nothing to see.

That way she wouldn't have to look at the expressions that were shooting her way from the stage, a humiliating mixture of pity and scorn. Wasn't it supposed to be the other way around? Weren't the strippers the ones who were to be judged and sympathised with? Or treated with contempt? Not tonight. Tonight Sly received a welcome like the high school quarterback at the homecoming parade and she'd been ignored, other than those few fleeting glances. She shouldn't have come, but she was worried that if she didn't he'd end up in yet another dumpster. It was only a matter of time. Every day he was sliding further and further into the gutter and she was powerless to stop him. Better to stay by his side, even if it meant hanging out in a dive strip bar called Legs Open. Why the hell had he wanted to come here?

At least they'd been seated in one of the VIP booths against the back wall, a black leather-lined semi circular booth with red velvet curtains that draped at both ends of the arc.

After a waitress had served up a bottle of Scotch in an ice bucket with two glasses, she felt Sly's hand take hers. Her heart beat a little faster. It was the first time he had touched her in months. Maybe there was still hope, maybe . . .

'She gets me so fucking hot.'

What? She must have misheard. Be confused. Must have . . .

'So fucking solid.'

Marny felt her hand being pulled on to his crotch. Nope, nothing had been misheard – there was definitely heat and it was definitely solid. It was only then that she noticed the small bottle in his left hand. Poppers. He'd used amyl a few times, back when sex was high on the priority list for them, but not like this. Not when he was looking at some girl on the stage, while his free hand was going up her back, releasing her bra clip, moving round to the front to . . . He couldn't. He couldn't want to do this here. In this sleazy room with sleazy guys all around them. At last his eyes left the girl on the stage and met hers. 'Fuck me,' he whispered.

'Sly, I . . .'

'Fuck me.'

People were staring so she quickly leaned over and flicked the curtains closed. She'd never said no to him and sure they'd made love in more public places than she could count, but that was when they were still good, still happy, when he still adored her.

Maybe . . . maybe that was it. Desperation, hope, washed over her. Maybe things were changing back, back to the way they used to be. She could be that person again and so could Sly. They could start again, dry out, reconnect.

There was a slight pressure as he pulled her on to his knee, both of them still facing the same direction, her back to his front. No, she didn't want it like this. She wanted to kiss him, to look into his eyes, to see his soul.

'Bend over baby,' he whispered it while his hand slipped under her ass and pulled down his zip. In seconds, her black leather miniskirt had been pushed up around her waist, her panties pushed to one side and he was inside her, the discomfort as he pressed against her taughtness making her wince. OK, so it wasn't going to be slow and loving and tender, but at least he still wanted her. She felt herself begin to loosen, to welcome his thrusts, his . . .

'Fuck!'

It took her a second to realise that he'd come, shot inside her then slumped back, done, finished. He lifted her off and plonked her back down on the leather seat, then used the table to lever himself to his feet. 'Back in a minute babe, just gotta slash.'

He flicked open the curtains and took off. Now she was sitting alone in a huge booth, looking and feeling like a twisted freak while a dozen naked women danced in front of her.

Invisible. She just wanted to be invisible.

Ten minutes. Twenty. Thirty. Where was he? A guy in a baseball cap in the DJ booth in the corner flipped the music and Marny recognised the first few bars of 'Need You Tonight'. INXS. Coco had made her listen to them night after night on the tour bus, giving Marny one of the ear pieces from her Sony Walkman. They'd lie there, like twins, conjoined by wires and a deep appreciation of the singer's voice. He wasn't Sly but he was close. Tears pricked her eyes and she had no idea why – the choice was too great. Humiliation. Self-loathing. Loving Sly. Missing Coco. The miserable existence she'd somehow become trapped in. Sitting alone while strippers wiggled their snatches in her face.

God, she couldn't do this any more.

'S'cuse me, but do you know where the guy I was with has gone to?' It was mortifying that she had to ask, but at least this waitress had been one of the ones who were treating her with gentle pity rather than full blown hatred.

'Honey, if you don't know . . .' The waitress drawled. Southern accent. Texas? Alabama? From a distance, in the dim, smoky atmosphere of the club she looked twenty. Up close Marny could see that she was closer to forty. '. . . then I ain't gonna tell you.'

Marny's stomach lurched. What the hell did that mean? Where was he?

Realisation dawned – he was scoring. She thought Dave had given him enough stuff to see him through the night but obviously he'd come here looking for more. Why else would Sly Rammer, lead singer with The Steel Spikes, be laying low in a dive bar so sleazy her feet had been sticking to the carpet since she got here?

Grabbing her purse, she headed in the direction of the red velvet curtain in the corner of the room. People had been going in and out of there all night and Sly had gone that way too so she figured the toilets were back there. She was right.

She'd just stepped through when a fat Middle-Eastern looking man in a cheap, shiny suit staggered out from a room that emitted such a stomach-wrenching stink that it had to be the toilets.

He reached out and grabbed her left breast, sticking a ten dollar note down the front of her top with the other hand. 'C'mon then sweetheart, show me what you got.'

She slapped his hand away.

'Ooh, I like a girl that plays it rough. Whassa matter – not enough dough there for you? Well sweetheart I got plenty more.'

As he spoke he moved towards her and now his gut had her pressed hard against the corridor wall, so close that she could smell the garlic on his breath as it mixed with the putrid stench of his sweat.

Then the hand came. Podgy, damp, probing fingers that slipped right under the hem of her skirt and grabbed her bush so tight the scream was out before she could stop it.

'Hey, Andros, enough! She's not one of our girls,' the Southern waitress gently pulled him away. 'Come on my big hunk o' love, I've put another drink on your table. On the house.'

The deviant perv gave Marny yet another pathetic look to add to the many she'd already received and backed off. 'Keep the money,' he told her. 'An' if you change your mind I can up the dough – you're so uptight, you gotta be needin' a good fuck.'

The noise that came from the back of her throat was almost guttural as she slid down the wall. The waitress didn't bend down to comfort her. There was a limit to what she'd do for a stranger and that little stunt could have got her fired – Andros was one of their biggest spenders and he knew the boss. One word and she'd be out on her ass and that was no good when she had bills to pay and mouths to feed. So right now, all she cared about was getting the young thing outta there before there was any more trouble. She figured there was only one way of doing that. It would do her good in the long run. Really, she was doing her a favour, the poor bitch.

'In there, honey,' she told Marny, gesturing to a door further down the corridor. 'And if I was your mom I'd tell you to start walking and don't stop.'

Curled in the foetal position now, Marny gasped for breath. Had. To. Get. Out. Of. There. Had to get Sly and go. Now. Right now.

Summoning every ounce of strength that she had, she pulled herself up and staggered over to the door, pulled on the handle and opened it.

For the rest of her life, every single day, she would wish that she hadn't.

Sly, lying on the black carpeted floor, head up against a bed the colour of blood, empty syringe at his side.

Oh, and he was wearing something new. Five foot five of blonde stripper, the one that had been on the stage earlier, was on all fours on top of him, her mouth around his cock, her ass sticking in his face. And going by the fact that his mouth was buried in her crack, he seemed to be enjoying the snack.

He didn't even look over.

'Sly?'

Still the only noise came from the female who was groaning as she sucked.

'Sly,' she repeated, louder this time.

He finally broke away and when she saw his face she knew. His eyes were heavy, his sneer obvious, his skin glistening with the female's juices. She knew he was lost to her.

'Marny,' he murmured wearily, irritated. 'Can't you just fuck off?'

Coco had never seen the Rainbow so busy. Obviously word that some of the guys from Mötley might jam had spread like wild-fire and the bodies were piling in desperate to hear some of the tracks off their new album played live. Dr. Feelgood had only been out a fortnight and already it was obvious it was going to be huge – a subtle twist of irony that the craziest band in the business had put out their best album when they'd finally cleaned up and got sober . . .

Unlike her friend beside her.

Randy was hammered now – majorly agitated, loud, belligerent and acting like the second coming of Christ, greeting his devoted worshippers as they flocked around him. The rest of the band were sucking the faces off an assortment of girls: some girlfriends, some bar chicks who had come to their table and never left. At least half a dozen had tried to hit on Randy but he'd swatted them away. She'd like to have believed that it was out of courtesy to her but she knew better. Tonight he was intent on two things: falling off the wagon in spectacular style and waiting for Sly Rammer. Word was that Sly was out on the town tonight and Randy was like a loaded missile: armed, explosive and ready to go to war.

'What the fuck are you looking at?'

Coco spun to see Randy screaming in the face of some young girl clutching a pen and a cocktail napkin. 'Get the fuck outta my face.'

Oh this was not going well and it was going to end even worse.

'Leave it, hon,' she said gently, putting her hand on the arm of the teen and smiling apologetically. 'Leave it for now.'

Wide-eyed, the fan backed away, equally mesmerised, thrilled and horrified. Wait till she told the girls back in Galveston about this! One week in LA and already she'd been screamed at by Randy Storm.

Coco watched her and saw her younger self reflected right back. That optimism, the eagerness for excitement, the carefree attitude of someone who had just stepped into the big world and who was determined to conquer it – or at least have a damn good time screwing her way around it. Where had that person gone? When had she settled for less than her dreams and become so jaded?

'Coco?' the bouncer, Big Rick, had appeared at the booth and was crouching down in front of her. She liked Rick. Bald, big as a brick shithouse and the best line in vulgar jokes she'd ever heard. 'Can I have a word?' With that he faded back into the crowd. Obviously whatever needed to be said, needed to be said in private.

'I'll be back in a minute baby,' she told Randy, who didn't even hear her; too busy screaming at his drummer's girlfriend that she was a whore. This guy had some serious frigging issues with women when he was loaded.

It took a few minutes to slink her way across to Big Rick at the door, and she was sure she passed Lita Ford and Chris Holmes on the way there. Awesome. Holmes had been keeping a low profile since he left W.A.S.P. and everyone on the scene was waiting to see what both of them did next.

'Hey Rick, what's up?' Faking a smile had started to come easy. She'd been getting plenty of practice lately.

'Coco, Sly is downstairs with some chick. We know what went down with him and Randy, man, so we're stallin' him, made him some dinner, giving him some drinks. He'll be up soon though. Is it cool? I don't want no shit up here.'

Her heart sank. There was no way they could knock back Sly Rammer – the club thrived on rock 'n' roll and Sly was today's poster boy. There was no way they could throw out Randy Stone either – he was rock royalty. The restaurant downstairs would be closing soon so they were running out of options. Sly and Marny would only wait for so long before he'd get bored and come up. If only she could speak to her, warn her to get Sly out of there, but it was too risky. She was going to have to come up with another plan.

'Do me a favour, Rick, keep him there a little longer. Half an hour max. Can you do that?'

Rick nodded. 'Leave it with me.' He scanned the crowd standing nearest to him and then clicked his fingers. 'You, you and you,' he said, pointing to three tall, scantily clad girls, each of them with hair that was wider than their hips.

'Sly Rammer is downstairs. How about you go keep him amused?' They were gone in a flurry of screams before he finished the sentence.

'Thanks Rick.' Coco slid past him, saying a silent prayer that Marny wouldn't mind her night out with Sly being hijacked by a gaggle of over-enthusiastic fans. A surge of longing overtook her. Marny. What she wouldn't give to be back on the tour bus, lying on a bunk, sharing a Walkman with Marny.

Shit, what was happening to her? She used to fantasise about fucking rock stars, now she was fantasising about lying around just listening to the music. She really had to make some changes in her life.

She found the payphone on the wall outside the toilets, took a piece of paper from her purse and punched in the number that was written on it.

Two rings. Come on, answer. Six rings. Answer. Ten rings. Come on, come on. Fourteen rings. She hung up. No answer. Shit! How the freaking hell was she going to stop a loaded missile all by herself?

The banging on the door was relentless but she ignored it anyway. No big surprise that he'd lost his key. He'd lost his frigging mind.

She leant over the coffee table and did another line. Shit, she just wished she could remember how many she'd had today. Ten? Twelve? Yet still the pounding in her head wouldn't stop and neither would the tears or the flashbacks. Sly doing that . . . thing to that female. Breathe. She couldn't breathe. Couldn't breathe.

Thud. She threw her head back and banged it against the wall. Divert the pain. How could he do that to her? And she was smart enough to realise that going by his attitude it wasn't the first time. Bastard.

Breathe. She had to breathe.

This was so much more painful than the loneliness, the worry, the devastation that he'd been treating her like shit for months. This was actual, physical pain, like her soul had been ripped out and taken some internal organs with it.

Make it stop. Another line. Got to make it stop.

Because what else could she do? There was absolutely nowhere else she could go. This was her life. Her family. Everything. She had no job, no money, no friends outside the band – her whole life pretty much added up to this. So how should she deal with the fact that it had all just slipped away?

But then, hadn't it slipped away the moment she'd picked up that phone and called his mother? It was her fault. She shouldn't have done that. She should never have brought his family back into the picture. She should have spoken to Lori. Stopped Dave Lopez giving him the junk. Stayed clean herself. Taken care of him. Tried to keep their sex life alive. It had been so important to them once and she'd allowed it to dissipate because, well, because Sly wasn't bothered and if she was truly honest she didn't want to have sex with someone who'd spent the last night sleeping in his own piss and couldn't remember the last time he'd had a shower.

Why hadn't she done something about that too? She could have bathed him, taken care of him, made sure he ate. What kind of girlfriend was she to have neglected him like that? Everything was messed up and it was all her fault.

It was over. She knew that now. Sly had moved on, left her a long time ago.

Her throat constricted even further. Breathe. Couldn't breathe.

The banging started again. She knew she had to answer it. The night was bad enough without getting thrown out of the hotel for disturbing the other guests. The rest of the band had most of the other rooms on this floor but there could be families, children, anyone below them.

Swinging her legs around off the bed she attempted to walk, but . . . thud. Her legs wouldn't carry her. God, what was happening? Why wouldn't her legs work? Half crawling, half dragging herself along the floor, she managed to get to the door, reach up and open the handle.

Thud. Again. This time it sent her sprawling across the floor. If only she'd had time to move before the door was pushed open. Sorry Sly. So sorry. Right now there was nothing, nothing she wouldn't do to feel his arms around her, to feel the security that she used to bask in, that knowledge that someone was on her side, someone would take care of her.

'Marny? Holy fuck, baby girl, what happened to you?'

Through the pounding, her head struggled to keep up. Not Sly. Dax. Poor Dax. So sad since Coco left. He sunk to his knees next to her. 'What happened?' he repeated.

Speaking was impossible. Her throat was closed, her head was pounding and there were so many tears that she was choking on salt water.

Dax was getting exasperated now. 'Where is he? Marny, where's Sly?'

His arms were around her now and he was holding her tight, running his fingers through her hair, being sweet to her like he always was. He was the good guy. Always the good guy.

'He was . . . having sex with . . . someone,' she spluttered.

'Coco?'

Shaking her head made it even sorer. Why would he say Coco? Sly would never sleep with Coco. He was . . . breathe. Had to breathe.

'Club . . . Sex . . . Stripper.'

'Bastard.'

Suddenly, she was moving, upwards. Dax was carrying her. Good guy, Dax. So sweet. He took her over to the bed and gently placed her down, pushing her hair back, drying her tears, shushing her with soft words and smiles.

Soft words and smiles . . . and a kiss.

A gentle kiss. Like Sly used to do. Soft. Like he adored her, loved her. A long kiss, still there, and it felt so, so good.

Someone had their arms around her again. And for the first

time in a long time, Marny remembered what it was like to feel safe.

'Are you going to get that?'

'No.'

'It could be important.'

'More important than this?'

Diana laughed as she ran her hand down her lover's back, both of them grinning at each other, their limbs a tangled web of familiarity and love.

This was the Lori that other people didn't get to see and in a way, she was glad. This was her Lori: soft, giving, and even – although only occasionally – vulnerable.

It had taken a long time for Lori to drop her guard, really let Diana in. She didn't blame her. When it came to fucked-up childhoods they'd both taken star prizes and those kind of scars didn't heal.

'I love you,' Lori whispered.

'And I love you sugar. And not just because you have the hottest ass I have ever seen.'

Lori giggled. 'No, but I bet it helps.'

'Sure does, baby – sure does.' Diana's hand tightened around Lori's left buttock and she dipped her head down to take one of Lori's nipples in her mouth, then felt a wave of pleasure as her lover gasped. Three years and the sex was still as hot as ever.

Lori was up on one elbow now, nudging Diana onto her back before moving on top of her. But not for long. With a long, incredible sensual trail of kisses and bites that worked their way down her body, she reached the bush of wiry hair and then moved beyond it. It was Diana's turn to gasp. Her legs automatically opened wide and Lori moved between them, her tongue now running along the lips of Diana's pussy. When it slipped inside she had to stop herself from letting the orgasm build. Not yet. Oh sweet lord, not yet. Because, damn, this girl could do things to her that she'd only been able to dream of before.

Lori's tongue was on her clit now, circling it, flicking across it, stroking it, moving in perfect synchronicity to the two fingers that had now slipped inside her, taking her closer and closer to . . . If they'd had direct neighbours they'd have heard the scream. Sweet Lord, it was incredible: pure, utter ecstasy that came in wave after wave. Don't stop, don't ever stop, don't . . .

The phone cut right through the moment. Aaargh!

'That fucking thing!' she reached over to snatch it and whatever asshole was on the other end of the line had better run because she was going to hunt them down.

'What?' she barked.

'Diana? Oh, thank God. Diana, listen – you gotta come get Sly out of here before Randy kills him!'

Ten seconds later the phone was back in the cradle and they were both hurriedly throwing their clothes on, to a soundtrack of 'Fuck, fuck, fuck!' from Lori.

They were almost out the door, when Lori doubled back and opened a drawer in her bedside chest.

Diana saw the gun come out and go straight into the back of Lori's waistband.

The questions could wait.

Right now there was a lead singer about to get his ass kicked. Or worse.

TWENTY-FIVE

The girl felt both his hands go around her neck. Jeez, she never figured Randy Storm for the kind of guy who liked it rough, but then, he was seriously loaded.

And kinky.

Wow, the things he'd wanted to do were pretty twisted.

The things he was saying to her . . . It was, like, really dark but totally incredible.

This was the best night of her life. She'd got into an incredible club and she'd met loads of amazing famous guys like Randy Storm. The only thing better than that would have been meeting Sly Rammer from the Spikes. Someone had said that he was downstairs in the club, but by the time she and Randy were leaving he'd already gone.

They'd come back to Randy's house on the beach and had the craziest sex, the wildest time, something that she'd always, always remember as being the most amazing thing she'd ever done.

She could hear the waves crashing against the rocks outside. She knew they were there because he'd already taken her from behind over the rails around the deck. My God, his stamina was incredible. This was the real deal: dirty, raw and so horny that she knew she was going to want to do this again and again and again . . .

Until the pressure on her neck tightened a little.

That was starting to hurt and bummer, it was eating into the buzz. She wanted to bring her hands in to pull his arms back but she couldn't slip them out of the ties that were harnessing them to the posts of the bed.

'Baby, that's . . .' It was really hurting now. Couldn't get the words out.

And the look on his face had changed. His eyes were bulging and his lips contorted so that they bared his teeth.

Too tight. Too tight. Too . . .

Then everything went dark.

TWENTY-SIX

LA Times, September 12th 1989

ROCK 'N' ROLL HOMICIDE

Randy Storm, lead singer of the rock band Decomp, was arrested last night after the body of Julie Chapman, 21, was discovered floating in the swimming pool on his property.

Cause of death has yet to be confirmed, but according to sources Miss Chapman's body bore similar injuries to that of murder victims Mary Jo Taylor and Candy Rays, the two 19-year-old prostitutes who were murdered in the grounds of Storm's Santa Monica estate after a party in June 1986. Mr Storm was provided with an alibi on that occasion by several other members of Decomp.

Miss Wendy Cole, 21, a friend of Miss Chapman, confirmed that the two girls had travelled to LA together three weeks ago from their homes in Galveston, Texas, with the intention of seeking careers in television. Since arriving in the city, they had been living in the Two Flags motel in Hollywood.

Miss Cole has also confirmed that Miss Chapman left the Over the Rainbow club on Sunset last night with Mr Storm and several other members of his party.

LAPD is expected to release an official statement later today.

TWENTY-SEVEN

The room was sparse; whitewashed walls, blue plastic tiles on the floor, twelve seats in a circle in the middle of the room. Not even comfortable seats. Just those brown plastic ones that made your balls hurt after you've been sitting in them for ten minutes.

'So Sylvester, do you wish to speak to the group today?' There were two members of staff in the session – a male counsellor and the woman in the white uniform who was now looking at him quizzically.

Sylvester. Did this broad think she was his mother or something? Because, he thought with a snigger, if she was his mother she'd have whipped his ass all round the room by now.

He shook his head and grunted. He backed it up with a sneer, but his hair had become such a thick, overblown tangled bush that it hid most of his face. He kinda liked it that way – rockin' the Slash vibe.

These group therapy sessions were the worst part of the day. It was all bullshit. Sitting there with bloated corporate types whose septums had crumbled long ago and upper-class bitches that were too fond of the gin. Waste of time. Complete waste of time. How dare those bastards throw him in here, treat him like some delinquent kid? Fucking Lori – how could she do this to him? If it wasn't for him she'd have nothing. Nothing. And Marny – she hadn't exactly come charging down to rescue him either. OK, so from what he remembered the scene in the strip joint hadn't ended well but she'd still be pushing a slop trolley around a hospital canteen if it wasn't for him. Man, he was glad it was over. She'd stifled him for years – all that 'stop taking dope' shit and the constant presence, always hanging around, like a parasite just sucking the life out of him, just like Gloria had done all those years ago. Well, history was repeating itself because now he didn't want or need Marny either. From now on he was flying solo and his head was clear enough to see exactly where he was going.

Man, the first two weeks in here had been brutal. He'd never felt anything like it in his life, like the worst dose of the flu ever, compounded by the worst pain – a gnawing in his guts and a crawling under his skin that he'd seriously thought was going to drive him insane. He never, ever wanted to repeat that experience. But he didn't want to be here either.

He was on top of this shit now. Hand smacked. Lesson learned. Delinquent reformed. Time to go.

'Sly, can I ask where you're going?' The counsellor, Jay, a bearded throwback in an orange kaftan who'd survived the sixties only by luck and the implantation of a pacemaker, kept his voice calm and even. Desert Hope wasn't a lock-down facility. The whole premise behind it was that it had to be voluntary; although they did keep the patients locked in their rooms in the first couple of weeks of detox for their own safety.

Sometimes it worked. Sometimes it didn't. Jay had seen guys like this dozens of time before and he had a hunch that the latter would be the case here. This guy wasn't ready to let go. Wasn't ready to be here.

'Just going to the john,' the patient murmured.

Sylvester Rammer walked out of that room . . . and just kept on going.

'Hey, you're awake. Brought you some coffee.'

Coco stretched up, not in the least self-conscious that she was completely naked. Well, when the whole world had already seen pretty much every inch of you, there was no point in being bashful in front of your mom.

'It's a beautiful day,' Darcy said as she placed a cup of coffee and a toasted cinnamon bagel on the chest next to where Coco was lying, before wandering back round and sitting on the vacant side of the bed. Nothing had changed in the room since the day she left it. Same crazy pink and white colour scheme, same huge posters of Van Halen, Twisted Sister, KISS and Aerosmith. The irony was that she'd met all of those guys now. The seventeen year old who left here would have been ecstatic about that.

Coco smiled. 'Autumn has always been your favourite time of the year.'

'You remembered.'

Her mother moved a couple of pink silk cushions out of the way and lay down beside her, just like they used to do when she was younger. Mom didn't look any different now. Still beautiful – those high cheekbones and crazy bright green eyes, a figure that any sixteen year old would die for. Class. The one word that always came to mind when Coco thought about her mother was 'class'.

The silence that followed was comfortable, easy. The complete opposite to every day of her life for the last five years. She hadn't realised how much she needed this until she got here, barely a week ago after the longest night of her life.

And one of the worst.

After she'd called out the mayday to Lori, she'd gone back to Decomp's table and seen that she'd already been replaced by the tweenie Randy had blown off earlier. To be honest, it was a relief. The curtain had already come down on that one and it was time to leave, so instead of rejoining them, she'd headed downstairs to see Marny. Only Marny wasn't there. One of Sly's hands was holding a spare rib; the other was on the thigh of some gorgeous, sexed-up chick who definitely wasn't her old friend. He was beyond wasted. A mess. Freakishly skinny, greasy limp hair, wrecked clothes. A total mess.

They'd spoken for a few awkward minutes before – thank God – Lori and Diana arrived and dragged him out – shouting and cussing the whole way.

Drama. Too much drama. Where had all the fun gone? It was all falling apart; going sour and getting seriously messed up. As she'd stood there, watching him getting dragged into the car, she realised that she wanted out. So she'd done the one thing she'd always sworn she would never do: opted for quiet isolation.

She'd come home.

For the last two weeks she'd seen no one and talked to no one except the police, who'd tracked her down and called her two days after she'd left LA. They'd already spoken to witnesses – the cab driver who took her from the club, waited until she'd packed some clothes, then taken her straight to the airport. They'd seen the camera footage of her sleeping in the departure lounge for four hours as she waited for the first flight to New York. They knew she wasn't involved in Julie's death but they had a hundred questions about Randy.

Randy was in jail. And that hurt. Not that the murdering son of a bitch was imprisoned, but that she'd never realised he was capable of killing. That poor girl. Coco's heart ached for her and she'd spent hours recriminating with herself for leaving. She could have saved her. She hadn't.

But there was still time to save herself. Things had spiralled out of control – the break up with Dax, the situation with Sly, Randy, Julie . . . the universe was telling her that it was time for change.

There was a hand on her hair now, stroking it, slowly, tenderly, like her mom had done every night when she was a little girl.

Before she left this ranch as a teenager, she'd slipped into a messed-up situation that had seemed like the end of the world. That time, with the help of her mom, she'd pulled it back together, healed and moved on.

Now the question was, where would she go to this time?

'Tell me again – how long ago was it that I was on top of the world, totally psyched that I'd conquered the music business?'

Diana looked at her watch. 'Approximately four weeks, five days and erm, four hours ago.'

Lori nodded thoughtfully. 'D'ya think that's a world record time for everything turning to shit?'

Diana roared that sexy, husky, low laugh. 'Could be worse. We could be searching the gutters and alleys of Hollywood for some punk-ass singer.'

Lori tucked a couple of dollars into the pocket of the tramp who was lying on a pile of garbage. In an alley. In Hollywood. And yes, her punk-ass singer was missing. Raising her right eyebrow, the one she kept for only the most cynical occasions, she gave Diana the filthiest look she could muster and was rewarded by another sexy, husky low laugh. Reluctantly, the scowl turned to a faint smile.

'You keep me sane, do you know that?'

'I do.' Diana replied. 'Now come on, hustle – the night is young and there are some gutters I'm just dyin' to get to.'

Lori shook her head and once again thanked whatever power existed in this messed-up world for giving her Diana. She hadn't been exaggerating when she said that Diana kept her sane. If it wasn't for their relationship she was pretty damn sure she'd be curled up in a corner in the foetal position, refusing to deal with all the shit.

Although she still might get to that, if she ever found Sly Rammer. Fuck, she should just have let Randy Storm kill him that night in the Rainbow – at least they'd have shifted even more albums. Look at Elvis – hadn't he made more money after he died than before?

Then she could wind up the Spikes, take Diana to some island in the Indian Ocean and spend all day making love and drinking margaritas. There were worse ways to spend your life. Like trawling through LA's low points looking for a . . . Urgh, a garbage bag split and spewed its contents all over her new Lucchese leather boots. She clearly hadn't thought through the dress code for searching for missing jerk-offs.

Still, at least it took her mind off the rest of the shit that she was dealing with this week.

If problems were really opportunities in disguise, then this moment was about as full of opportunity as things got. Ever methodical, she even had them listed on her mental blackboard.

1. Sly Rammer, her lead singer, had vanished. Gone. Walked out of rehab and last seen on a flight heading back to LA a week ago. Currently presumed incapacitated in a gutter.
2. The absolute peach – and this was the one that she would never have seen coming in a million years – her guitarist was screwing aforementioned lead singer's ex.
3. Dave Lopez, the guy who was meant to be her right-hand man, had phoned in sick seven days out of the last ten, and when he did show up he just played Beatles records all day long.
4. One of her few female friends had gone AWOL after her rock star boyfriend murdered a twenty-one-year-old fan.
5. Muff, Strings, Spank and Tye all had the clap after a night with a particularly adventurous groupie.
6. Ari Covet was asking questions and reminding her that the Spikes were due in the studio in four weeks to start writing and recording the next album.
7. Eight weeks after that they were due to leave for their first European tour.
8. With the exception of Dax, the whole band now spent the major part of every day completely wasted.
9. She had a 'To do' list so long it could be rolled up and used to wipe her ass.

10. Oh, and her brand new, $300 Lucchese boots were covered in shit.

Happy days.

'Hey!' Diana called out from about fifty yards further down the alley. There was only one streetlight and it was at the other end, so Lori struggled to make out what her girlfriend was looking at. Obviously some kind of garbage because she'd nudged it out of the way with her foot.

Kicking the crap off her boots, she wandered over. Yep, it was garbage all right – in the form of one depressingly familiar rock singer.

'Is he dead?' she asked, trying to keep her voice calm.

Diana shrugged. 'I ain't touching him to find out. Ain't had my vaccines. But his chest appears to be moving so I'm guessing there's still life in there.'

No wonder Diana wasn't on her knees and administering mouth to mouth. Just like last time, and too many times before, Sly Rammer was lying there in his own vomit and piss. Going by the overwhelming stench, they should have been able to sniff him out from miles away.

'What the hell are we gonna do with him, Lori? You know, this is just gonna keep on happening until he goes too far.'

Lori nodded. Diana was right. And much as she looked great in black, the last funeral she'd been to was her daddy's and she didn't want to be going to another one anytime soon.

They'd tried punishment. They'd tried restrictions. They'd tried rehab several times. Nothing worked.

But . . .

An idea started to formulate in her mind. There was one thing they hadn't tried. And it just might save his life and her career.

'Mornin' baby girl, how you doing?'

Marny stretched and slowly, gradually opened her eyes, at the same time giving him a sleepy smile. She was still unaccustomed to waking up without a fog in her head, however, the heaviness in her stomach? Well, that still came as standard.

Dax. Dax was taking care of her now. Making her well.

He laid out two plates on the small white wooden dining table next to the kitchenette.

'Scrambled egg, bacon, juice,' he told her. Her favourites. She'd told him that when they'd arrived here a couple of weeks ago and he'd had it ready for her every morning when she woke up. Dax rented an apartment just north of Malibu, in a tiny community by Zuma beach that was home mostly to surfers, aging hippies and struggling artists seeking solitude from the world.

She padded over to breakfast wearing just one of his old grey ripped-up T-shirts. It drowned her frame, even though she'd definitely put on a few pounds since she . . . well, since Dax found her. Picked her up. Cleaned her up.

'How you feeling?' he asked, his voice so sincere. It was what she loved, no, *liked* most about him. On the outside: fierce, wild, rock guy. On the inside: kind, genuine, mellow.

There was no comparison between Dax and Sly. Everything was different. With Sly, the main focus of the relationship had been on her taking care of him – his needs, his agenda. With Dax it was all about him taking care of her. First step – he'd flushed away all of her coke. All of it. And then he'd held her when she screamed as she watched it go. He fed her. They went for walks. They played on the beach. He was even teaching her how to surf. For the first time in years she was stepping out of the Steel Spikes bubble. They were like a normal couple, holding hands, kissing, creating incredible, sweet sensations that she'd never felt before. They hadn't made love yet. It was a step too far for her, a physical barrier that she wasn't ready to cross.

But in her head? It still felt like she was betraying Sly. It didn't matter that he didn't want her anymore. It didn't matter that he was away doing those . . . *things* to other women. All that mattered was that she still felt like she belonged to him, not the guy who was standing in front of her with a pan full of bacon. She wanted Sly back so much – the old Sly, the one who loved her. However that guy had left a long time ago and she knew that he was never coming back.

'You're still feeling weird.' It was a statement not a question. She shrugged. 'Kinda.'

'You know, it's OK.' He sat down opposite her in low-slung jeans, his deep golden torso bare, every muscle clearly defined. 'Marny, I get it. When Coco left I felt like I was gonna die. She was like the other half of me and then she was gone.'

As she watched him she saw the feeling that was gnawing at the pit of her stomach reflected right back at her. 'But, you know, what can we do?' he shrugged. 'They make their choices.' There was no bitterness in his voice, only sadness and resignation. After a few silent moments of staring at the tablecloth, he seemed to push away the melancholy. Leaning towards her, he brushed his hand through her hair. 'Look, Marny, I'm not promising anything. I don't do monogamy. You know that. Coco and I both believed in total freedom and I won't pretend to have changed.'

A burning sensation began at her neck and began to work its way up across her face. Don't cry. Don't cry. He was going to tell her to go. She'd known it was coming and sure, it was for the best, but what would she do? The trembling started, kicked in big time, her whole body shaking, her stomach threatening to relieve itself of its contents. It was the thing that scared her most, made her lie awake at night: without Sly and the others in the Spikes universe, she had no one. No place to go and not one other person on this earth that cared if she lived or died.

'Hey, hey, hey,' one step and he was at her side, crouched down, hugging her tightly. 'Baby girl, I'm just being truthful because I don't want any secrets here – they mess with the head, man.'

'I . . . know . . . I get it too,' she whispered, struggling to get the words out past the massive lump that was stuck in her throat. 'I'll pack up and get out of here.'

He pulled back, placed a hand under her chin and lifted it so they were face to face, his deep black eyes burning into hers.

'No, Marny, that's not what I'm saying. Stay. I want you here. What I'm saying is that we both have to know what's happening, what's real. If you want to go, I like, totally understand. But you're family Marny – and if you want to stay then I'll always take care of you.'

She stared at him, so beautiful, so open. He had a spirituality that she couldn't even begin to understand. He wasn't Sly. He so wasn't Sly. But he was going to take care of her, give her a place to be. And right now that was all she had.

The exquisitely perfect lyrics of 'She Loves You' blared from the record player. He hadn't bought it on CD yet – preferred the way his old 45 crackled as it played.

There was a thumping noise from Mrs Beaker downstairs. The old bitch was supposed to be half deaf but the minute he put a record within five feet of his stereo system there she was, banging on her ceiling, shrieking at him to keep the noise down. Dave sighed as he leant over and flicked the knob down a couple of notches on John, Paul, George and Ringo, telling him again how much she loved him. Yeah. God forbid Mrs Beaker's peace and quiet should be sacrificed at the temple of the Beatles.

She loved him. He knew she did. So why, when Sly had finally disappeared, had Marny gone to Dax instead of him? It shouldn't have played out like that. She should have realised what they had, seen that they were meant to be together. They were. In the last few weeks, he'd sat on his sofa, listening to Lennon and McCartney describe his feelings for her. He'd played 'Something' until the disc had warped. They knew. They just knew how he felt about her and she should too.

The silence made him crazy. He had to keep his mind working, keep it going, keep thinking about her and eventually she would come to him.

He opened the top drawer of the beech veneer bedside cabinet and gently, like he was handling a priceless, fragile object, he took out a black journal and pen. His novel. He was writing a novel that would be dedicated to Marny. These were his private thoughts, the messages that came from his soul and belonged to him and him only. No one would ever see this apart from her. One day.

He opened the book and flicked to the last page that he'd written. OK. Time to do more. Time to put pen to paper. He thought for a moment, then started to write.

A few moments later he paused to check his progress. Yep, it was classic. His best page yet. He couldn't wait for the day he would show it to her, then she would realise that he'd thought about her every moment of every day.

He glanced back down at the page.

Dedicated to the love of my life, Marny Lopez.

Yes, one day he would show it to her. When she was his.

'What's up, baby girl, can't sleep?' Marny shook her head. She'd been sitting out on the balcony, smoking cigarette after cigarette for the last two hours. And she didn't even smoke. In the absence of coke and vodka, it just seemed like something useful to do with her hands, something to think about, something to take her mind off the fact that Sly wasn't there. He hadn't come looking for her. Hadn't come to explain, to ask forgiveness, to make it right.

Dressed in just a pair of old Levi's, his hair hanging loose and flowing down his back, Dax sat down next to her, took the cigarette from her hand and inhaled.

'I don't know what to do.' It was a simple statement, whispered, barely audible above the sound of the waves in the distance.

'You're going to have to find a way to move on from him, Marny.'

She nodded. He was right. This wasn't any kind of life, it was an existence. Survival. Purgatory. Stuck in a warped limbo, unable to go forward, unwilling to go back.

Sly had made his choice and it didn't include her – now she had to find a way to live with that.

It was time.

As if reading her thoughts, Dax stood up and reached down to her. Her hesitation was brief.

He leant down to kiss her as he'd done many times over the last couple of months, but this time it was different, more insistent, their breathing heavy, their hands searching.

When he gently pulled her T-shirt over her head, leaving her body exposed to him, she didn't stop him.

It was time.

TWENTY-EIGHT

Rock-a-bye baby . . .

Miss Molly was happy. She'd been a real good girl and said her prayers and it was time to sleep. Sleep. She pulled the drapes closed really tight. The shadows wouldn't come tonight. If she squeezed her eyes shut and didn't look then they wouldn't come.

The minister had told her that. 'Do not tempt them,' he had said. 'For if you look into the valley of darkness the shadows of Satan shall claim you.'

The shadows of Satan scared her, so she would just keep her eyes closed and then they wouldn't find her.

Sleep.

Rock-a-bye baby . . .

At first she wasn't sure what she was hearing.

Sleep.

There it was again.

Sleep.

She couldn't. She had to know. If the shadows of Satan were here then she had to know what they were saying.

She opened her eyes, terrified, more scared than she had ever been.

But there were no shadows, only Miss Molly.

And she was smiling.

'I know,' Molly whispered. *When did she learn to do that?* 'I know how we should do it.'

'Do what?' she asked, so excited that her friend had found her voice.

'I know how we're gonna kill him.'

TWENTY-NINE

8am. Coco didn't remember when she had last been up and out at 8am. Staggering home? Yes. Awake, refreshed, and ready to start the day? Definitely not.

It was yet another beautiful autumn Connecticut day and her mother had persuaded Coco to join her on her regular sunrise ride. The horses, two beautiful Appaloosas, were loving the workout. The jury was still out for Coco.

'Mom, is this really necessary? Isn't there a law against partaking in healthy pursuits at this time in the morning?' she yelled as Darcy streaked away in front of her.

Her mom laughed as she slowed down and waited for Coco to catch up and come alongside her, then they both steadied the horses down to a slow trot in companionable silence. The peace still felt strange to Coco. After living in chaos for so long, the wide open spaces and silence were alien to her. Comprising of thousands of acres of crop land and forestry, they could ride for hours on the ranch and never meet another soul. Back on Planet Spikes, Coco couldn't go to her own bathroom without encountering at least two strangers.

'What are you thinking about?' Darcy asked with an inquisitive smile.

Coco sighed dramatically. 'River Phoenix. I think it's a tragedy that he's only eighteen and I'll therefore have to wait at least five years before our age difference no longer seems relevant and he can marry me.'

The trees rustled with a cackle of laughter that Darcy couldn't repress. Coco joined in. It was good to hear her mom laugh, good to be with her. This time together had been great, allowed them to reconnect and get to know each other as two adults instead of as mother and child. She had always loved her mom – now she realised that even if they weren't related she would really *like* her too. The night before they'd watched Mr Phoenix in the Indiana Jones movie and agreed that the boy was seriously handsome.

'Coco Phoenix – kinda got a nice ring to it, don't you think?'

'Colette Phoenix,' her mother corrected her with a smile. She'd never bought in to the name change. 'Anyway, I thought you only liked bad boys?'

'For Mr Phoenix I'd make an exception. Didn't you see how he could move? All that and positively clean living – it's persuaded me to leave the dark side.'

Distracted by the banter, she didn't notice that the horses had naturally followed the trail around a sharp bend. Coco suddenly realised where they were. She pulled up the reins and steered her horse around a 180 degree turn. As soon as Darcy saw what she was doing she followed suit, her expression quickly transformed from amused to grave.

'I'm sorry sweetie, I didn't even think. Are you OK?' Coco nodded, counting to ten to distract herself from the tears that had suddenly, out of nowhere, sprung to the back of her eyes. One. Two. She would not cry. Three Four. Five. Would not. Six. Seven. No damn way.

'Do you ever think about him?'

Coco shook her head. Eight. Nine. Ten.

'Colette, you know he loved you, don't you? And what happened will never change that. You were his princess and he adored you from the moment you were born. He loved both of us.'

'But we weren't enough, were we?'

The pain that flashed across her mother's face made her immediately regret the outburst. For better or worse, her mother had loved him – and as she rode on in silence, nothing could stop the memories of how it all ended at its worst.

'Come on Boston, come on boy,' Coco nudged her heels into the flank of her 15th birthday present and he sped up to a gallop. How lucky was she? A horse and a car for her birthday, a gorgeous little Spitfire that Daddy had custom-sprayed in pink. Of course, she would only be allowed to drive it on the ranch until she was old enough to get her licence, but even that would be way cool.

If it were possible, though, the horse had excited her even more. A stunning jet black Quarter Horse with a glossy raven mane. She'd immediately named him Boston, a tribute to the birthplace of Aerosmith, her favourite band – and taken off singing 'Mama Kin' at the top of her voice.

Her mom and dad had beamed as they watched her go and Daddy had promised that once a week he'd make time to ride over to the pony club with her. It was going to be their time together, he said. Their special time. For the first few weeks he'd kept to his word, but now, well, it seemed he was too busy for her today. She'd waited at the house for over an hour but he hadn't shown. He was an important man, her daddy, so she shouldn't mind. Actually, she didn't really. It would give her the chance to ride there by herself and she could tuck her tape recorder into the saddlebag and play her new John Cougar album real loud. Her favourite track was 'Hurts So Good' and she already knew all the words. And anyway, she'd heard the whispers around the house about Daddy running for governor and that would be incredible – just think of all the people she'd get to meet! Bruce Springsteen. She would surely meet Bruce Springsteen.

After saddling up Boston and pressing play on the tape machine, she'd taken off across the ranch, unafraid and completely confident. She'd been riding there since she was three and knew every inch of it. Down across the main paddock, through the woods for a few miles, past the lake, then another mile to the boundary, through the gate and the pony club was across the road. Easy.

The time passed quickly and Boston enjoyed the gallop. Daddy always made them canter real careful so it was great to let loose a little. She was just clearing the trail through the woods, just about to turn sharp right out to the side of the lake when she heard the noise. Voices? Animals? Maybe the ranch hands were working on the fencing – there'd been a whole lot of poaching going on around here lately. Daddy had told Grey Masters, the ranch manager, to shoot them with the big guns the ranchers always carried.

It was only when she turned the corner and the whole lake was laid out there in front of her that she saw the horse tied up to the side of the lake house.

Daddy's horse.

Why was it there? Then it came to her – he'd ridden ahead and waited for her. Maybe he'd already been out on the land and decided to meet her here? Yay!

She shackled Boston up next to Trigger, Daddy's horse, and bounded on to the porch, swung open the door and . . .

Daddy was there. And so was Jed, one of the ranchhands.

But they weren't waiting for her. Jed was on his knees in front of Daddy and he had Daddy's penis in his mouth and Daddy was making this noise that . . .

'Colette? Colette? Darling, you're in another world.'

'Sorry, Mom, I'm just . . . distracted. It's nothing.' Coco slid off her horse and handed the reins over to Manuel, the lovely man who had been in charge of the stables since she was a child.

'*Gracias*, Señora Coletta.'

Coco rewarded him with a kiss on the cheek and then smiled as he blushed bashfully. For ten years she'd been doing that to him and for ten years he'd beamed with embarrassment every time.

But even the warmth of the exchange couldn't rid her of the chills the memories of her father had left behind. She'd thought she could handle being here, thought she'd moved on. She was wrong.

Her mind flipped on to the next time she'd seen her daddy, just seconds after he spotted her and shoved Jed away from him. Grappling to pull up his pants, he'd chased after her, unaware that he was in the last moments of his life. 'Colette?' he'd croaked as he lay on the ground, his hand stretching up to her. There wasn't time to take it. Her daddy took his last breath, right there in front of her.

'Colette?' She heard the name again. This time, however, it was a woman's voice.

Coco turned to see Lisa, Manuel's daughter, coming towards her, a cordless phone stretched out in front of her.

'Colette, it's a call for you – lady says it's urgent.'

Sighing, she took the phone, expecting it to be the police again. How many questions were they going to ask her?

'Coco? Oh, thank fuck – you've no idea how hard it was to find you.'

'Lori!' It was a surprise, but a welcome one.

'How are you doing, honey? Still thanking god that psycho Storm didn't make you a very dead legend?'

It was harsh, nasty and in such bad taste – and Coco couldn't help but giggle. Oh, how she missed Lori.

'Yeah, I've definitely found religion but so far I'm sticking to the missionary position.'

Lori cackled uproariously on the other end of the line and a wave of homesickness washed over Coco – ironic, since she was standing in front of the only place she'd ever actually been able to call home. Dax would find a song in that somewhere.

'So, seriously, babe – how are you doing?'

'Honestly?'

'Honestly.'

'Not so good.'

'Excellent.'

'Pardon?' Coco mentally re-ran that conversation and yep, got to the same point of confusion. 'Lori, why does that fact that I'm not so good sound excellent to you?'

'Because it means you're not too busy skipping through meadows for me to ask you for a favour.'

'What kinda favour?' Coco asked, her suspicion and dread balanced by the fact that she knew there was nothing Lori could ask of her that she would refuse to do.

'A big one. Honey, I need you to take care of Sly.'

Marny pulled her cardigan tighter against the early morning sea breeze and dug her feet into the sand, enjoying the sensation as the grains found their way into the crevices between her toes.

'You sure you don't want to come in?'

She shielded her eyes as she looked up at Dax, standing in silhouette against the sunrise on Zuma beach, his wetsuit hanging loose around his waist, a surfboard under one arm. If there was a Greek God of Rock Star Surfer he would be it, standing there in front of his worshippers, long hair blowing in the breeze, his perfectly formed body a tattooed work of art.

'Is it OK if I don't?' she asked. She didn't want to disappoint him but she was feeling grim this morning. In fact, she felt a million times better when she existed on a staple diet of Marlboros, vodka, coke, downers and the occasional bit of gourmet junk food. The heaviness in her stomach just wouldn't shift, she felt tired all the time, and so, so emotional. It seemed like since the minute Sly left she'd cried a river and – as she felt that familiar tightness in her throat – the river wasn't showing signs of drying up any time soon.

Dax leaned over and ran his fingers down the side of her face. 'Baby girl, you don't need to do anything you don't want to do.' OK, cue tears. He was so nice to her all the time and it inevitably set her off because it just reminded her how unlike Sly he was. Crazy. Stupid. She wished she understood it. With Sly there were no options – they did what he wanted to do, when he wanted to do it and she just went along with everything he said because that was the way that it had always been. No decisions, just everything laid out for her and taken care of. And, bizarre as it sounded, that was the way that she liked it – the way she *wanted* it to be. It had been so long since she had made her own decisions that she'd forgotten how to. Dax's laidback democracy freaked her out. But she'd never tell him that. He'd been so kind to her and she was deeply grateful.

She watched him run into the ocean with a backwards wave. He was just so . . . tender. Both in and out of bed. She'd only ever been with Sly and with Dax it was an entirely different experience. In the beginning Sly had been sweet, gentle, tender . . . but in the last couple of years the sex had become more perfunctory, more disconnected, until it had tailed off to an occasional meaningless fuck and then that night . . . She didn't even want to complete the thought.

But with Dax? Wow, the feelings were incredible. He took his time, touched and kissed and licked every part of her, hungry to please her and to make every moment count.

No wonder Coco had loved him – they were both such open, decent, uncomplicated spirits.

'Here boy! Here Loggins!'

The source of the voice was coming from behind her and as she turned . . . aaaargh! Two feet of tongue slapped from one side of her face to the other. OK, so maybe two feet was a slight exaggeration, but it felt like that. She was guessing she'd just met Loggins. Only the panting and friendly bark hinted that it was a dog. On first glance it reminded her of the mop she used to clean the floors all those years ago at St Joseph's. That's exactly what it looked like – a large mop without the stick, just masses and masses of black cords emanating from an invisible central core. It was the most adorable thing she'd ever seen.

'Hello gorgeous!' It was officially irresistible and clearly loving that she was rubbing its neck. Or it might have been its ass – it was difficult to tell which was which. Thankfully the tongue came out again to give her a clue. Neck. Phew.

'Sorry, I'm so sorry! Loggins you're grounded – do you hear me?'

Loggins didn't seem too concerned as he flopped down on Marny's feet and refused to budge.

'Sometimes I wish I'd gone for a cat,' said the smiling blonde woman with a leash in her hand. In white cut-off shorts and a long, baggy grey sweat top, she looked so fit that it was only when she moved around to the front of her that Marny realised that she was heavily pregnant. 'I used to jog with him every morning and he hasn't quite sussed out that we've suspended the running part,' she said, gesturing to her bump. 'Mind if I sit for a moment?'

Every pore of Marny's being went in to panic mode. Dogs were fine, but she didn't do strangers, she didn't do casual conversation. What would she say? As always, crippling shyness shut down her faculties and her motor skills. Mouth not moving. No words coming out.

Thankfully, the woman didn't seem to notice as she lowered herself down until she finally plumped on to the sands. 'I'm gonna need mechanical intervention to get back up again,' she smiled, then pointed to the bump again. 'Eight months and three weeks. And let me tell you this thing is so heavy I want a shopping cart to wheel it around in.'

Marny suddenly realised that she could sit there all morning and say not a single thing and this smiling, chatty female probably wouldn't even notice. The thought eased the panic just a little, enough to stutter out a few words.

'I like your dog.'

'Thanks. He's a Hungarian Puli – completely insane but devastatingly handsome. Just like all my men. Named him after Kenny Loggins – must have watched *Footloose* fifty times. Hear that, Loggins? You've got a fan, you big love machine.'

Loggins responded by flopping his head back down with the

rest of him on top of Marny's legs. Marny suddenly realised who the woman reminded her of – the Kelly McGillis character in *Top Gun*. It was Sly's favourite movie and they used to watch it all the time before . . . before . . .

'It is so beautiful here in the morning. We don't usually see anyone else at this time though.'

Marny realised there was a question in there. 'I'm just waiting for my . . . erm . . . boyfriend. He likes to come early. He's over there,' she replied, gesturing into the surf.

Her new companion put her hand to her eyes and squinted just as Marny had done a little while before. 'Oh, I see him. Wow, cute guy.' Her eyes squinted a little more and Marny glanced up to see Dax coming out of the water.

'Oh dear God, a woman in my condition shouldn't see a man looking like that first thing in the morning – it could bring on childbirth.' Then, as if she realised she'd just blurted out something out of turn, she laughed and put her hand on Marny's arm. 'I'm sorry, sorry – I shouldn't be saying things like that about your boyfriend. I'm . . .'

'No, no – it's OK. He has that effect.' For the first time, Marny was starting to relax and realised that she liked this strange, loud lady with the strange over-familiar dog. In fact, if she wasn't feeling so nauseous she'd even be enjoying the company.

'No wonder, he is seriously hot.' Dax was about a hundred yards away now, headed in their direction.

'In fact, do you know something – he looks a bit like Dax Rice from The Steel Spikes. God, I love that band. Seen them four times. The things I could do to . . . Oh. My. God.'

Dax was fifty yards away now and the woman was nudging Marny frantically. 'He is *so* like Dax Rice I could take him home right now and even in my condition I could . . .'

Twenty-five yards.

Silence.

For the first time since Loggins had bounded on to the beach, there was complete silence.

'Hey baby girl, surf's awesome.' Oblivious to the fact that the woman's chin was now resting on her rotund belly, Dax grinned at them both as her reached down for a towel and dried off his face.

There was a considerable pause before the woman regained the power of speech. 'Excuse me,' she murmured, almost deadpan, 'but do you know that your friend is Dax Rice from The Steel Spikes?'

Marny laughed. 'I noticed.'

'Holy crap, this could put me in labour.'

Dax had tuned into the situation and was finding the whole scene amusing too. 'Well could you name your baby after me 'cos I always thought that'd be kinda cool.'

'Ouch!' Surprisingly, the exclamation of pain came from Marny and not the woman who could quite easily experience her first contraction at any minute.

'Sorry, pins and needles in my feet. Sorry, Loggins you'll have to . . . ouch!'

Her legs spasmed and Loggins reluctantly took the hint and slid off them.

'Aw, aw, aw, aw, aw,' Marny was rubbing furiously, causing Dax to lean down and pull her to her feet. 'C'mere baby girl.'

'If you would do that to me I'll *give* you this baby,' the woman grinned.

Dax never got to try.

Because as soon as she was upright, Marny swayed, lurched, and slid right back down on to the sands.

'Oh my gosh, she's fainted,' exclaimed Dax's biggest fan. 'Quick, run to the tap and get some water. And don't worry – I used to do this all the time at the beginning.'

The jet made a perfect landing on the airstrip, a testimony to the pilot's skills and the ideal weather conditions. As soon as it came to a stop, the expanding steel staircase slid out from its storage space and the door opened. Lori came first, looking hot as ever in torn-up jeans and a black waistcoat with nothing but toned flesh underneath. Diana was behind her in sweats and sneakers. Between them was a mound of mess that practically had to be rolled down the stairs.

Lori was mortified. 'Sorry, Coco – we thought we'd searched him good but he must have had some gear hidden somewhere . . .'

'Don't even wanna think where it was,' Diana interjected.

'. . . because he went into the toilet half senseless and came out completely senseless.'

'Coco!' a senseless Sly mumbled. 'Baby, it's Coco.' They all turned back to look at him, sitting on the bottom step, head in hands, hair looking like a demented bush, his grey complexion matching his grey jeans and his grey T-shirt.

'Oh, and we think he's got an imaginary friend,' Lori added ruefully.

Diana nodded. 'Perhaps the imaginary friend was stashing the dope.'

At that point, the three of them broke into simultaneous grins and Coco realised that her mother was standing observing the whole situation wide eyed and bewildered.

'Sorry, Mom – you remember Lori and Diana from the Philly gig?' Darcy reached out and shook their hands. She'd only met them for a split second at the concert but Coco had filled her in on all the details and history over many of the long nights they'd sat out back talking.

'I have to say ladies, it's a strange world you live in,' Darcy observed, not unkindly.

'You're welcome to join us – the pay is pathetic but you get free tickets for Spikes concerts,' Diana grinned.

Darcy feigned regret. 'Tempting, but I think I'll pass.'

'Mrs Belmont . . .'

'Call me Darcy.'

'Sorry . . . Darcy. So sorry to do this to you but we were running out of options. He skips rehab every time, insists he wants to do it his way, and we just thought that having Coco with him might help. She doesn't take any crap from him. Am I allowed to say "crap" in front of you?'

'I think given the circumstances we'll allow it,' she teased. Meanwhile, Coco was looking pensive. 'Lori, you know I'll try, but . . .' she couldn't find the words. Lori reached over and hugged her. 'That's all we're asking honey. He needs to be back at the AC ranch in four weeks to start recording the next album. Ari thinks it's already written. I swear I'm never going to heaven. Anyway, if you can keep him alive until then we'd be grateful – if you can clean him up that would be a bonus.'

'The doctor is already back at the house,' Coco said. After they'd agreed to take Sly in, they'd made a confidential call to a trusted family friend, an ex-army medic who now specialised in drug treatments for vets. He'd been willing to help and had agreed to come every day to administer the medication Sly would need to get through his second detox in just a couple of weeks. Hopefully this one would last a little longer.

'Would you like to stay for lunch? You're more than welcome.' Darcy offered. Coco had a hunch that she was secretly intrigued by the drama and the craziness of it all.

'We would love to, but we have to get the jet back – we had to beg AC to let us use it and they only agreed because I told them that Sly was making a live appearance at the Stones gig tomorrow night at Shea Stadium. When Ari finds out he didn't show he'll have a stroke.'

'Every cloud . . .' murmured Diana.

Coco hugged them tight, Diana first, then Lori. 'I know how hard this is for you, Co, and I can't tell you grateful I am.'

A few hours later, Sly's mood had undergone a radical change. 'Get me the fuck out of here!' he screamed.

The doctor didn't even flinch, just loaded up another syringe with something and injected it into his arm. 'Fuckers! You fuck-ers! You . . .' Silence.

His eyes rolled and the fog came back down.

Then it was all black again.

It was difficult to argue with facts. And the two blue lines on that stick were definitely facts. Marny's stomach twisted even tighter, her heart was thudding out of her skinny chest and she felt like sudden contact with the ground could happen again at any moment.

Pregnant.

How could she be pregnant? Her periods had always been wildly erratic, stopping for months on end, a situation she put down to her woefully poor diet and the effects of drugs.

Pregnant. She couldn't be a mother. Jeez, she didn't even know how to take care of herself. She had no home, no stability . . . A wave of wooziness overtook her and she clutched the table as she fought to breathe.

Pregnant.

She couldn't have this baby. She couldn't. There had to be somewhere she could go, where this whole nightmare would be brought to an end. Lori would be a good mom, organised and smart. Coco would too – she was the nurturing kind. Look at the way she had stepped in to take care of Sly. Lori had told her that she'd just called Coco up and she'd agreed to help. Somehow it made her feel better that she knew he was with Coco and not lying on the floor of some strip joint. Coco would keep him safe, she knew it. Yep, the women she knew would make great moms, but not her.

The panic and the fight to stay upright had distracted her so much that she hadn't heard the door open. She jumped as Dax appeared in front of her, holding out a large, clear plastic cup full of fresh orange juice.

She took it gratefully and started to sip – the cool liquid soothing her as it slid down the back of her throat. He spotted the stick on the table, lifted it up and stared at it for several seconds, then calmly put it back down again.

'Baby girl, you know we need to talk.'

Marny nodded. It had been a week now since that morning at the beach and she'd put off doing the test for as long as possible, convinced that denial would make the whole situation disappear. Now it was clear it was going nowhere.

Dax pulled out a seat and slid into it, throwing his spiked-up cowboy boots up on one of the other chairs. So cool, so chilled, Marny marvelled at his ability to deal with everything in such a laidback, together way. He'd be a good dad one day. Any kid would be lucky to have him. Wow, the wooziness took a grip for the second time.

'So I need to know . . .' Dax's voice was warm, calm. 'Is there any way that this kid could be mine?'

'Have you noticed anything weird about Dave lately?' Diana asked Lori.

'Dave's always been weird,' she shrugged, 'it's part of his charm.'

'I know but I'm just thinking he seems a little . . . wired. You know, like *altered*.'

Lori put her pen down and pulled Diana down on to her knees, slipping a hand inside the top of her shirt and cupping her breast as she kissed her playfully.

'So let's get this straight. Dax and Marny are screwing, Sly is in solitary, the rest of the guys have the most indestructible dose of the clap that the medical profession has ever known, Ari Covet is a raving psycho and yet you think Dave Lopez is 'altered'. Diana, he is positively fucking normal around here.'

With practised ease, she flicked open Diana's shirt buttons one by one, then pulled down her bra cup and flicked her tongue against her nipple, before taking it inside her mouth and gently sucking.

Diana pretended to ignore the action.

'I know but I just gotta . . . *feelin'*.'

Lori broke off and raised her head to make eye contact with

302

her lover. 'Look, he is weird. He's always been weird. But he's in the music industry, so that makes it perfectly normal. So will you please stop your damn worrying and take care of this feelin' I've got instead.'

'Yes, boss,' Diana murmured sexily as she slid off Lori's knees and on to the floor, then hooked her hand into the front of Lori's waistband and pulled her on top of her. Within seconds, they were both naked, hands groping, pinching, slipping inside.

'Stop!' Diana whispered insistently. Lori did what she was told. She might be the boss in the day job but outside of work they were strictly equal opportunities.

'Kneel there,' she pulled Lori up so that she was balanced on her knees, then lay flat on her back and slid her head into the void underneath Lori's pussy, pulled her down closer and began to run her tongue along the soft pink lips.

Oh holy fuck, that felt good. Lori threw her head back and instinctively brought her hands up to mould and caress her own breasts. Already the tingling was starting in her buttocks and she knew it wouldn't be long.

She glanced down at the sight in front of her, Diana's torso and her thick black bush, left long and natural the way Lori liked it. Her huge round tits sliding just a little to each side, looking sooooo gorgeous but neglected down there on their own. It wasn't fair that she was having all the fun, now was it?

Definitely not.

She bent forward at the waist and slid her hands between Diana's thighs and opened them wide, then moved in, letting her tongue trail a tantalising line from Diana's hip bone down to her clit. Now this was much better: both of them licking, nibbling, both eating pussy and it felt so, so freaking incredible. The tingling was getting stronger for Lori now and she could tell by the way that Diana's muscles were throbbing and tightening that it was for her too. Oh, yeah baby, this was so good. Nothing else mattered to Lori but right here, right now and the orgasm that was ripping through her . . .

'Yeeeeees!' Their screams were simultaneous, two backs arching in unison, two bodies, both dripping with sweat and juices electrified with sheer, unadulterated pleasure.

Yep, Lori thought as she slid to the floor, exhausted but oh so satisfied – equal opportunities were definitely the way to go.

Sly realised that the monsters had gone now and all that was left was the spot on the ceiling. So tired. Why was he so tired all the time? He stared at the spot a little longer. Sometimes it moved. Sometimes it got a little bigger. Sometimes it spun around and around and when it did that he could hear his mama's voice, singing.

So tired.

Maybe he'd just sleep a little longer.

'So, you wanna tell me why I'm hearin' rumours that your boys are fucking freakin' out?'

'Good morning to you too Ari. Pleasure to see you.' Lori drawled as she crossed his office and pulled back the chair on the opposite side of his desk.

Fuck, that broad got fitter every day. Not that he'd tell her that of course. She'd fucked him over and he hadn't forgotten that. Never would. But there was only one thing that Ari Coyet cared about more than dignity and pride – and that was money. So he'd taken a calculated decision. He'd decided to park the little stunt that her and that bitch slut whore had pulled on him and take the dough. For now. But it wasn't over. One day he'd fuck her good and proper . . . in every way.

And in the meantime, he'd ride her ass about every fucking little thing that he could.

Bitch. Look at her now, slouching in the chair like she didn't have a care in the fucking world. Well, she'd better start paying attention because he'd heard through the grapevine that the Spikes were messed up and he wanted to know the truth.

'So?' he asked again, waiting for her answer.

'So what, Ari? Look, ask Dave – he'll tell you things are cool.'

'That little fucker is so pussy-whipped by you two cunts that he wouldn't tell me if the whole fuckin' lot of them were on fire.'

He was getting agitated now. Where was his medication? Where had Rita May left it this time? He pulled open the drawer on the left-hand side of the desk and there it was – a gold saucer with a perfect, two-inch high peak of white snow. Hell, it was so perfectly displayed she shoulda put a flag in the top.

No time for chopping – he just stuck a straw right in the middle and hoovered up as much as his nostril could take.

Better. He could concentrate now.

'Where are they?'

The bitch shrugged again. 'Most of them are here in LA. Dax has gone up to Carmel for a coupla days and Sly is over in Connecticut chilling out and getting some new songs together. They work better when they're on their own. It's a creative thing.'

'He wasn't being very fucking creative when he missed the Stones gig.'

Lori nodded gravely. 'I know – still can't believe the irony. Kidney stones. Laid low by kidney stones when he should have been playing with the Stones. Couldn't make it up.'

Was that bitch smirking? 'Cos if she was he'd wipe that smirk right off her face with a ten grand bill for using the AC jet for a waste of fucking time.

He bent down for another snort, just to even up the left/right balance.

'Yeah, well they'd better be ready to go next week 'cos I ain't wastin' more dough on the studio time. Four weeks, that's all they got. And don't even think about screwin' up because let me tell you something, Miss Smart Ass – one album ain't a career. This time next year they could just be a bunch of has-beens that some kids used to wank off to. Ya hear me?'

Lori stood up. Shit, she just kept on going that girl – like an Amazonian fucking goddess. He'd definitely screw her one day –

her and that other one, both of them together. One on his face, one on his dick.

'Don't stress it Ari – it'll be done, I'm telling you. Don't I always deliver?' she was definitely smirking now. Smug bitch. He watched her go, that tight ass poured into the tightest leather pencil skirt, her long legs bare until they slid into stilettos with six-inch steel heels. And he bet she wasn't wearing any panties.

Cock-teasing bitch.

As the door slammed behind her he flicked a switch on his desk that locked the door, then pushed his chair back from his desk to reveal his angry, red throbbing dick.

Who was smirking now? It hadn't been a meeting – it had been a good reason to sit there, naked from the waist down and feel his dick grow hard while he screwed with her.

He pulled his new toy out of his bottom drawer – a rubber cunt that he'd picked up in a sex shop off Hollywood and Vine. He placed it over his dick and pressed the button then gasped as it contracted and squeezed the spunk out of him in seconds.

His kinda woman – cheap, always open and didn't fucking talk back.

THIRTY

The sea breeze was blowing in through the open window, making the white muslin curtain billow and relax, billow and relax, billow and relax. The simple beauty of it was almost hypnotic, Marny thought.

They'd arrived at the cottage yesterday. Only a few hours drive up the 101 and yet a million miles away from LA, it was a tiny white clapboard building nestled into a cove between Carmel and Pebble Beach. They'd eaten, talked, slept and woken and she'd now lost track of how many hours she'd been lying there, just thinking. Every now and then she'd panic, stretch towards the long French windows and check that Dax was still out there, sitting on the deck, a pen and pad on his lap. She hated to be alone. As long as he was there she was fine.

A baby. It had gone from 'pregnant' to 'a baby'. In her mind, it was a person now, someone who would grow and be hers and . . . yes, it had crossed her mind that with a baby she would never be alone again.

Dax appeared in the doorway and smiled at her. 'I'm just gonna throw together some lunch. Hungry?'

'A little.'

The truth was that she wasn't at all, but she knew she had to eat, had to keep her strength up no matter which way the decision went.

As she watched him walk over to the kitchen, wearing nothing but a pair of surf shorts, she mused for the millionth time that the situation would be oh so different if the baby, her baby, was his.

They both knew it wasn't. The doctor had said that she was almost twelve weeks gone, way before she and Dax ever got together.

Her baby. Sly's baby. Conceived on the most humiliating night of her life.

Dax had spoken to Diana on the phone that morning and she'd said Sly would be back in a few days. The familiar panic started again. She'd have to tell him – about her and Dax, about the baby, about everything.

Not that she thought for one minute he'd be upset that she was with Dax now – he'd made it quite clear that he wanted her out of his life and now she was. But the baby? In the early days they'd talked about having children, fantasised about what they'd be called, what they'd look like, but that was a long, long time ago – before the Spikes and the drugs and the chaos.

Dax came over and placed a plate of fruit on the bed: strawberries, melon, thick, juicy slices of avocado. He was on a mission to inject as many vitamins as possible into her at every given opportunity. 'I'm just going back outside, but I want you to read this.'

He put a sheet of paper down next to the fruit, a leaf from the pad he'd been working on all morning, then wandered back out to the deck.

'Make it Mine'.

That was the title and below were three verses and a chorus that didn't need music behind them to make her cry.

I'll be there, I'll be the one you need,
We don't have to turn back time.
You and I can keep the truth
We just need to make it mine.

A huge dollop of a tear fell down her face and plopped on to the avocado. She pushed herself off the bed and crossed to the deck, standing in the doorway to watch him for a few moments before she spoke.

'Do you mean this, Dax? You want to say the baby is yours?'

He stopped writing, then rested the pen and pad on the table and looked up at her.

'Marny, I've no idea if I'd be any good as a father, and Lord knows I didn't wanna find out this soon – but if you're looking for someone to be a dad to this baby then I swear I'll do the best I can.'

'And us?'

A flash of something made his brow furrow for just a second before he shrugged.

'We'll . . . we'll get by. The way we do now. No promises, no lies.'

His beautiful face was so earnest, so kind, and even now she could see that he was being as completely truthful as he always was, without saying the words that might hurt her.

He didn't love her.

But then, the truth was that she didn't love him either.

A tune suddenly assaulted her senses and she heard Dave Gilmour's haunting vocals flood into her head, singing 'Wish You Were Here'.

It was Sly's favourite Pink Floyd song. It had been one of the tunes on his Walkman the night she'd found him and for months he would listen to it every day. Now she realised it could be her and Dax. Just two lost souls, neither of them with the person they really wanted to be with.

Always afraid that the other person would go back to the one that they really loved.

The song was the ultimate declaration of love. But when she listened, it wasn't Dax she thought of.

It was the father of her child.

'How's the patient?'

'Closed. Sullen. Uncommunicative. A pain in the ass.' Coco replied, 'So I think he's getting back to normal.'

Darcy playfully nudged her daughter with her shoulder as she took her place next to her at the side of the corral, then watched as Grey patiently coached Sly, who was trying and failing, to lasso a fencepost.

It was progress. It had taken him almost two weeks to even master the art of putting his clothes on. The withdrawal had been brutal, horrific to watch, a gruesome cautionary tale that made Coco thank God that she'd never used heroin. It just wasn't her thing. She wanted to be in the moment, enjoying every day, not zombied-out chasing an unattainable high. And she definitely never wanted to go through the agony that she'd watched Sly endure.

He'd finally turned the corner after a fortnight or so, and since then he'd been incredibly subdued. Like he'd finally gained clarity and didn't like what he saw. He was beginning to look like the old Sly again on the outside, but it was the inside that was still worrying her. She'd tried to talk to him, get him to open up, but he was largely uncommunicative. Brooding, even. The only time she saw any joy or enthusiasm was when he was working with the horses.

Darcy broke the silence. 'Have you two ever had, you know, *a thing*?'

'Mom!' Coco gasped, shocked.

Her mother replied with a rueful expression. 'Oh come on, my little purist angel – I don't need details, just a general overview.'

Coco sighed sadly. 'OK, there was a "thing". Once. But he was so wasted that I don't even know if he remembers.' She laughed at the absurdity of it. 'There you go Mom, I'm a class act – are you proud?'

Coco feigned embarrassment but somehow she didn't think Darcy would be too shocked, given that she'd met the band, been offered sexual favours by Muff, had a nice cosy chat with the lesbian managers, and spent the last month hosting a drug-addicted lead singer who had told her to fuck off at least twice. Although he had apologised a few days later when the worst of it was over. And none of that even came close to the most shocking thing that had happened in their lives.

Cleaning Sly up had been a real group effort and she so appreciated her mother's help. But . . .

'You're going to leave, aren't you?' Damn, it was like she had psychic powers.

'I have to, Mom, I can't stay. The memories . . .' She didn't need to say any more. Darcy understood. She'd been there, lived it, seen what her daughter had been through.

'Where will you go?'

Coco shrugged. 'I honestly don't know. Maybe New York, do some more modelling. Or LA. Lori has asked me to take Sly back just to make sure he doesn't fall off the wagon on the way, but after that? No idea.'

'You couldn't go back to Dax?'

Coco rested her head on her hands and watched Sly have another try with the lasso.

'I couldn't, Mom. I miss him so much but he doesn't know about the "thing". And if I told him I think it would break his heart.'

'More than leaving him?'

It was a good point. Coco shrugged. 'I know that when I left he was hurt, but I'm sure he's over it and he's OK – he's still got the band, his music and probably a queue of groupies waiting outside his door all day long. But if I told him how I felt about Sly . . .'

'How do you feel?' Darcy asked gently.

'I love him, Mom. I don't understand why. He's an arrogant fuck-up but I love him.'

She felt an arm go around her shoulder and pull her tight. 'And Dax wouldn't be able to deal with that. It would split the band and then what would he have? Me gone, career over. I couldn't do that to him.'

'You know, maybe that choice should be his.'

Coco didn't have time to object, because Sly had just lassoed his first fencepost and was punching the air and hollering.

'Coco, did you see that! Did you?'

'I did, Roy Rogers. You may have a career in rodeo if you ever decide to give up singing.'

Still whooping, he ran over to where they were standing and hugged Darcy, then enveloped Coco in the tightest squeeze. As she made eye contact with her mom over Sly's shoulder, she saw her own sadness reflected there.

Sly finally released her and then took a step back and looked at them both.

'Listen, I know we're leaving tomorrow and I just wanted to say thank you. I can't tell you how much I appreciate everything you've done for me. I guess I was pretty messed up.'

Neither woman objected.

'So thanks. I kinda . . . Well, I kinda guess I love you guys.'

Coco dug her nails into the palms of her hands.

He loved her. But then, she already knew that. What she didn't know was if it was the right kind of love.

Lori was pacing. Back. Forward. Back. Forward.

'Sugar, we just got that floor done and I'm not paying out another $5000 to get a new one.'

Lori picked up an apple from the fruit bowl and launched it in the direction of Diana's head. Thankfully, her lover had the reflexes – as well as the flexibility – of a cat.

The clock chimed 9pm. She stopped pacing long enough to pour a shot of brandy into a crystal glass and throw it back in one.

The thought suddenly struck her that problems and anxiety aside, it was incredible that she now lived in a house surrounded by nice things. Most of it, she had to admit, was Diana's doing. She'd decorated the place herself, spending day after day in paint-spattered dungarees, applying subtle coats of cream, white and mushroom to the walls. Then she'd furnished it simply – dark wood and white furniture, an old mahogany table in the kitchen that the auctioneer had sworn once belonged to Ava Gardner. Lori doubted it but decided not to break the myth – especially after they'd christened it that first night with champagne that wasn't drunk from a glass.

If old Jack could see her now he'd damn well split a gut. House, Car. Career. Success. Hot black lesbian lover. Wherever he was in hell, she hoped he could see her and weep. Bastard.

'Lori, you're pacing again.'

Diana had pulled herself up to sit on the granite worktop and now she was taking a huge chunk out of the apple. 'He'll be here. Have some faith, sugar.'

Lori stopped and stared at her, expression deadly. 'Yeah, you're right – I'll have some faith. Because let's face it, The Steel Spikes are so notoriously fucking reliable and trustworthy in every way.'

Fuck! Didn't Diana understand? This was her career on the line – her life, their home, her reputation, their future. She'd worked damn hard to get them this far and they were so close – so, so close – to fucking it all up.

And she knew that moment could come anytime.

Dave Lopez had been dispatched to the airport to collect Sly and Coco. Dax and Marny were on their way back from fucking God-knows-where. The rest of the guys were under instructions that if they weren't packed and ready to leave for the studios the next morning they'd have to start looking into the help available for ex-rock stars who were now missing their kneecaps.

'I should have gone to the airport to get them,' she said, just fretting out loud.

'Lori, you have to start trusting other people. Dave will get him and he'll bring him back safely. Anyway, what could go wrong between here and the airport?'

'The Roxy, the Troub, the Whisky, the Rainbow . . .'

Diana laughed. 'Coco is with them, she'll keep them straight, don't worry.'

'I miss her, you know? Think she'll stay?'

Diana shook her head. 'No idea. Does she know about Dax and Marny?'

'No. At least, she didn't hear it from me. Christ, what a mess. I've got visions of Sly taking Dax out, Marny going into melt-down, and Coco spending the rest of her life trying to put Sly back together again.'

Diana tossed her apple core in the garbage. 'Has anyone ever told you that you're way too cynical and jaded? Maybe it'll play out great. Sly and Marny were done, he made that clear. So maybe Marny and Dax will live happily ever after, Sly and Coco will get it together, they'll all accept it as responsible, mature adults and go on holiday twice a year to a cabin up in Big Bear. It could happen,' she cackled.

Lori rolled her eyes. 'Great. Now I find out my girlfriend's obviously on crack.'

Diana jumped off the counter and slid her arms around Lori's waist, then playfully bit into her earlobe. 'C'mon, sugar, let me take your mind off all this anxiety. It's getting extremely uncool.'

Tempting. Very tempting, but . . .

They both jumped when the doorbell chimed.

'Oh, thank fuck, they're here. Saves me shooting Dave.'

'See! Told you everything would be OK. You just need to get yourself some faith, girl.'

A minute later Lori was back, but it wasn't Coco and Sly who were walking behind her.

'Hey Marny, how you doing?' Diana asked.

Marny shrugged and fidgeted awkwardly with the sleeves on her jumper, before replying.

'I'm OK. How you doing?'

'Good, sugar, I'm good. Are you here to see Sly?'

Marny suddenly transformed into a deer caught in headlights. 'Why, is he here?' she gasped, panicked.

'No, but he's coming in soon. We think.' Lori added pointedly, looking at the clock.

'I . . . I didn't know. I thought he wasn't back for another few days.' She was clawing at her own hands now and Lori realised that she was seriously upset. Faith. Have faith. Diana's words jolted her consciousness. Whatever it was they could handle it.

'Are you OK, honey? Is there something you need?'

Marny shook her head and when she stopped Lori could see that her eyes were swimming with tears.

'I . . . I . . . just came to tell you that . . .' she broke off as the tears avalanched down her face.

Diana immediately put her arms around her and shushed her until the sobbing stopped.

Lori subconsciously tapped her foot, anxious just to get to the crux of the problem. Was it Dax? Was something wrong? Dear fucking Lord if he'd taken off too she was giving up. That's it, she was officially giving up. This shit wasn't worth it.

'I'm . . . OK,' Marny spluttered, between the tears. 'But I'm . . . I'm . . . pregnant.'

Yep, you just gotta have some faith, Lori realised . . .. Faith that things would go incredibly fucking wrong every time.

'Half an hour until landing,' the flight attendant told them as she made a final sweep through the cabin, clearing away used crockery and trash. The flight had been delayed for two hours back at JFK so they were running way behind schedule. They were the only people in first class and a couple of years ago they would have drunk the bar dry, danced in the aisles and smoked in the toilets. This time they'd spent most of it in silence, Sly lying across three seats sleeping, Coco staring out of the window, listening to Bon Jovi's *New Jersey* album. Actually that wasn't strictly true. For the most part she'd been playing 'I'll Be There For You,' over and over and over again. As she watched the attendant return to the galley, she finally snapped it out of the machine and slipped in a mix tape instead. Aerosmith's 'Angel' was the first track. He knew. Steve Tyler knew what this felt like. She could hear it in every note of his voice.

Her mom had told her to tell Sly how she felt, but she knew it would be a mistake. Sly Rammer was the kind of guy who hated to be backed into a corner. Besides, she would never, ever do that to Marny. Sly had refused to talk about her but Lori had mentioned that they were going through a rough patch. They'd get back together. Marny must be going freaking crazy without him there. In fact, she was probably at the airport waiting for him. So better just to let it be. Drop Sly off, move on. Her agent had called to say there had been a few work offers in LA so she'd check them out, see what happened. In fact, she still thought it was hilarious that she even had an agent – so much for shunning the material life and living off music and free love. What kinda commercial cop-out had she become, she thought with a smile.

A sudden tug from the side made her earpiece fall out.

'What you listening to?' Sly asked, in a tone that was the closest to happy she'd heard in a month.

She leaned over and slipped the earpiece into his ear, causing him to grin as his head immediately started nodding to the beat. When he started quietly singing along, she thought her heart would snap in two. Tyler in one ear, Sly in another, both professing their love for her – in previous times she'd have been on her second orgasm by now.

When the song stopped, she clicked the tape off. No more. She couldn't take it.

There was a pause for a couple of moments, before he reached out and took her hand. 'You've never mentioned it.'

It. The weather? The state of the political system? The . . . fuck it, she knew what he meant, but surely he didn't want to talk about that now. They'd been together for a frigging month,

316

albeit for half of that he'd been borderline insane, and now they were twenty-five minutes away from LAX and he'd decided he wanted to chat? Noooo, not going there.

But apparently, he was. And he was stroking her hand while he did it.

'Why?' he asked.

Coco sighed. 'Why did it happen or why did I never mention it?'

'Both.'

She shrugged. 'It was for the cameras – artistic integrity they call it.' Her attitude was breezy – she wanted to close this down. It hurt too much and she'd be damned if she'd ever show it.

'Bullshit.'

'Sly, leave it.'

'Why?'

'Because I'm asking you to.'

For a few long seconds, he stared at her and she was terrified that he was going to push her, make her admit what was really going on. He was a smart guy. He probably knew already, but he'd had enough drama lately to last a lifetime and she was guessing that he wasn't ready to deal with any more.

'I need to talk to Marny. I've been thinking about everything a lot and you know, I treated her pretty rough back there.'

'Then you'd better beg for mercy because she loves you, Sly.'

Dear Lord, make this stop. Right now she'd take an emergency landing over this. However, she had to do the right thing. Marny loved him and she deserved better than he'd given her.

'I know, Coco. I know she does.'

When they touched down they were still sitting in silence. And it was only when the exit doors slid open that he turned to speak to her again.

'Thanks, Coco, for taking me in. I'd never have cleaned up without you. I was way too far gone, man, but you gave me the space to get sorted and get my head right. I owe you.'

It was a debt she didn't know if she'd ever collect.

★

Lori pulled the suitcase out from under the bed and flicked the combination. When it snapped open she reached in and gently eased it out. She had no idea why she felt the need to do it, but she just did.

'Are you ever gonna tell me?'

Lori jumped as Diana's voice jarred behind her. Too late to hide, perhaps time to divert.

'Where's Marny?'

'Sleeping on the sofa. Poor thing, she's exhausted. And pregnant. Shit, didn't see that one coming. What do you think she'll do?'

'No idea. Trust Dax to play hero though. If I was straight you'd have competition honey.'

'Yeah, whatever.' Diana smiled as she came towards Lori and then knelt down beside her at the edge of the bed. 'Oh, and before you ask, I called LAX and their flight was delayed. They should be here soon. Not ideal that his pregnant ex is lying sleeping on the sofa, but I couldn't exactly toss her ass out in the street.'

'Some faith, huh?'

'Stop changing the subject. So . . . are you gonna tell me?' she gestured again to the item in Lori's hands.

Lori put the doll down on the bed and stroked its hair as she spoke.

'This doll is the only thing I have left that my mother gave me. Jack threw everything out when she left but I hid this under my bed and he never found it'. There was no self-pity in her voice, no martyrdom or self-indulgence. Just the facts. The cool, calm facts.

'Why didn't you tell me about it before?'

'What's the point? It's past. But then when Marny started talking about the baby I just had an urge to dig it out. I miss my mom, Diana. I don't even know her, yet I miss her.'

The sob came so quickly and violently that Diana almost didn't have time to register what it was before Lori buckled, doubled at the waist, her face contorted with raw, searing pain.

Diana fell beside her, scooped her up and held her tight, shushing her, rocking her, whispering words of comfort, of love. This was a side of Lori that she'd never seen before, a vulnerable soul that let her feelings out, no control, no restraint.

They sat like that, wrapped tightly together until Lori was still, then Diana felt her take a deep breath, compose, gather. The control was back, and with it came the habit of using humour to deflect emotional situations.

'Am I turning into a sentimental old sap?' Lori asked her.

'Nope, just dispelling the rumours that Lori Wyatt is in fact an emotion-free android. If this gets out in the business you could be ruined.'

'You're right, and we can't go making Ari Covet happy – I'd have to kill myself.'

Diana pushed back up on to her feet. 'Come on, I'm gonna require at least a half bottle of Jack to deal with the rest of the night.'

As the two women left the room, the doll's eyes watched them go.

'You coming in, Dave?' Coco asked as they pulled up outside Lori's house. He shook his head. 'Nah, I'm gonna head home. Got a project I'm working on – want to get back to it.'

'No problem,' Sly retorted. He slapped his old supplier on the back. All the way from the airport it had felt strange having a conversation with Dave that didn't include a shopping list of chemical enhancements. Probably why Dave seemed so pissed and uncommunicative – he'd just lost his best customer. 'Thanks for the ride.'

'No problem.'

He drove off and Sly picked up Coco's case as well as his then followed her to the door. They hadn't even got to the bell when it swung open and a clearly loaded Diana welcomed them with open arms.

'Sugars! Come on in, come on in. We'd have put the flags out but we weren't a hundred per cent sure you'd make it. Whole lot of gutters between here and LAX.'

'Thanks for the confidence,' Sly grinned.

Diana put her hands on her hips and gave him the mock-raised-eyebrow-stare-of-death. 'Sugar, last time I saw you, you had drugs hidden up your ass.'

Sly at least had the decency to look embarrassed, and Coco was just about to add to the roasting when a force hit her at speed – a force with arms that were now tightening around her.

'Fuck, I missed you!'

And that also, seemingly, had a good line in profanity.

Coco laughed, 'Well, fuck I missed you too.' Their embrace lasted for a few minutes before Lori pulled back and looked at Sly, then at Coco, then at Sly again. 'You two OK? You didn't like, elope or anything?'

Coco slapped her hands away. 'Yeah and our six kids are out in the station wagon. Don't be crazy, Lori.'

'Yeah, 'cos that would be considered crazy in our lives,' Lori threw back.

'Lori, we're cool. Apart from the fact that we've been here two minutes, man and we're still standing in the hall.'

'OK, OK, look – we've got a bit of a situation on our hands. Marny is in there.'

Coco felt Sly tense beside her, while she was caught between rushing in to see her friend and getting the hell out of there so that she wouldn't have to see Sly and Marny face each other again.

Stupid. Stupid. Stupid. It was only one night. She was just going to stay here one night and then she'd be gone and she never had to deal with this scene again.

'Great,' she said – it probably came out a little too brightly but she figured that Diana had consumed one too many drinks to notice, while Lori was so busy scrutinising Sly that she would be oblivious too.

Diana made a sweeping 'after you' gesture and Coco heard Sly

320

take a deep breath as Lori opened the door into the open-plan ground floor.

The first thing Coco saw was Marny and she could barely mask her surprise. The last time she'd seen her Marny had been thin, deathly pale, her hair limp and face drawn. But even though she was obviously just waking up, this girl was positively breathtaking. She'd gained some weight, her blonde hair fell in gleaming wisps around her face and she looked exactly like the girl Coco had first seen sitting beside the singer back in Lori's bar in Rackstown.

Wow. Just wow.

'Marny, you look incredible!' All reservations, all worries, all strains gone. All that mattered at that moment was that her girlfriend was there and she was so, so happy to see her.

Marny clung to her long and hard and when she pulled back Coco saw the tears. She also saw that Marny wasn't looking at her any more.

She was staring at Sly.

And he was staring right back at her.

This wasn't how he'd expected it to play out. He thought they'd see each other, talk, he'd apologise to her and then they'd go their separate ways. He'd been so sure it was over, so determined that he wouldn't make the same mistakes again. And Coco. There was something there, unfinished business, but he'd resolved to get to that later. One situation at a time. Now that he'd cleaned up he wanted to stay that way and to do that he had to stop himself from overloading. That place he'd been in was somewhere he never wanted to go back to. One situation at a time.

Now, this situation was waiting for him to make a move. He suddenly had no idea what his next move was going to be.

Invisible. Once again, the terror was too much and this was worse than ever before.

Invisible. She just wanted to be invisible.

He was standing there in front of her, and he looked amazing. Clean. The skeletal face transformed back to beautiful.

She didn't know what to do. The one thing she did know was that she couldn't stay with Dax. She couldn't be around Sly every day, seeing him, hearing him. There was still time to disappear, just move on without ever confessing that anything had ever happened while he was gone. If she didn't tell him she knew that Lori, Diana and Dax wouldn't either. She'd make them promise. Then she could just go, Dax would help her with money and she'd set up somewhere quiet, peaceful. Carmel! She could move to Carmel. Lease a little house by the ocean and live her life, just her and their child.

Their child.

She was going to keep it. Because right there, looking at him, she knew there was no way she could do anything else. This was Sly's son or daughter and she couldn't end that life. She'd known too much death already.

She wouldn't tell him. She'd just go. Yep, that was the best idea. He hadn't asked for this, didn't plan for it to happen and he'd already told her that they were over.

The trembling cranked up a gear as he moved towards her.

'Marny, I'm so sorry. I was a prick and I just want you to know that I'm sorry.'

She couldn't believe what she was hearing, but her heart soared. At least they'd part on good terms – he didn't hate her, didn't really think she was a parasite. She knew that had been the drugs talking and he'd just confirmed it.

He was sorry. Now she should tell him it was OK, make peace and then go, leave him to live his life. The knowledge that everyone else in the room was staring at her made the heat start to rise in her chest. Time to go. Time to say goodbye and . . .

'I'm pregnant.'

Well that was one way to tell him, Lori decided. Probably the worst way, but at least it was done. And she had to admire Coco's

322

considerable acting skills, because she'd practically pushed Sly out of the way to hug Marny again and tell her how happy she was for her.

Coco. Four words. Promiscuous, wild, decent, kind. She'd take it up to six words with 'almighty fuck' but she only had the word of half the names on the Billboard chart on that one.

Coco's reaction was a distraction that gave Sly time to breathe and Lori time to grab her jacket. There was somewhere she had to be. And she had to take one of her little friends along with her.

If ever he needed to score it was right now. She had to be shittin' him, but as he stood there looking at her terrified face he knew she wasn't.

This couldn't be happening again, just like before, just like with Gloria. Another kid. Shit. Fucking hell.

But . . . he focused on the eyes in front of him. This wasn't Gloria, this was Marny.

Flashback. That same face, terrified, years ago, watching him as he woke up on a hospital bed. She'd saved his life. For a while there he'd forgotten that. If she'd delivered this news when he was messed up he'd have lashed out, told her to forget it, but his head was clearer now. And even though doing the right thing didn't always come easy to him, he realised that this was one of the times that doing it right mattered.

His mind had been made up for him.

Call it fate. Call it God. Call it some fucked-up crazy universe, but it had decided what he should do.

His newfound freedom was over already.

Lori was halfway down the hall when the doorbell rang again. Probably . . . Nope, she couldn't even guess. It could be anyone. Nothing surprised her anymore.

She pulled open the door and stood to the side to let the caller in. 'Welcome to Dodge,' she grinned.

'Is Marny here, Lori? Just getting a bit worried about her, man. She split hours ago.'

Nope, nothing would surprise her.

'Dax, she is but you need to hear the update. You want me to spare your feelings or give it to you straight?'

'Straight.'

'Sly and Coco are here too. Marny has just told Sly she's knocked up. It looks like they're gonna work it out. I asked Coco and Sly if they'd got it together and they denied it and I believe them. Sly has no idea you have been playing hide the drumstick with his girl, so I wouldn't bring it up. And if you wanna turn right around and go back out the door then it would probably be the smartest move you ever made.'

She could see it was taking him a few moments to process and wondered which aspects he was having the most difficulty with.

'Coco is in there?'

There it was. In a way she was happy for him. Taking care of Marny had been done out of responsibility. Shit, he was a crap rock star – where was the arrogance, the self-destructive behaviour, the gargantuan ego? If it wasn't for the fact that he could play guitar like no one else on earth this guy would be out of a job.

'Look, I gotta go, but . . .'

'Dax?'

The hallway door had opened and Coco was standing there.

OK, there was only so much of this heterosexual shit she could take. There were far more important things that needed to be done.

'Where are the guys?' Diana asked, giving a bottle of beer to Coco and a glass of milk to Marny.

'Out back having a smoke. Apparently Lori would string them up by the balls if they smoked in here,' Coco said.

Diana nodded. 'Very true. She's dangerous when riled.'

'I get the feelin' you kinda like that.'

'Yep, got a thing for psychopaths – always been my downfall. What are the chances that by the time they come back in they'll have written twelve killer hits? Lori has told Ari Covet that they're ready to lay down the tracks.'

'Sorry to disappoint you hon, but I don't think Sly's written anything this last month,' Coco warned her.

Marny put the milk down on the side table. On a coaster, lest Lori punish her too.

'Don't worry, Dax has at least a dozen. He's been obsessed.'

Coco looked up, surprised. 'Marny, that's so sweet that you've been checkin' on him. Thanks, hon – I know he will have appreciated it, especially given how you've been feeling.'

Diana threw back another shot of Jack. Hell, she should just grab the bottle and a straw. It was all about to go right up shit creek and she intended on using a JD bottle as an oar. But then she saw the red heat rise in Marny's neck and she knew it was safe.

Telling Sly was the first brave thing Marny had done in years. She wasn't due another act of boldness this decade.

'What about you and Dax? Any chance?' Diana asked, deflecting the opportunity for confessionals.

The reply was a hesitant shrug. 'He wants me to stay but I'm gonna leave tomorrow. Time to move on.'

Marny welled up again and sniffed loudly. 'Sorry, the doctor says it's the hor . . . hor . . .'

'Hormones,' Diana helped her out.

'Yeah, them.' Marny turned back to Coco. 'Co, I know I've got no right to ask you but stay. Please stay. I need you here. Coco, I'm so scared to do this. And Dax . . . he loves you.'

Diana suddenly realised what was going on. This was Marny's way of righting things, of bringing Coco and Dax back into the same world. Maybe the kid was smarter than she had given her credit for.

Coco avoided answering. 'Back in a second. Diana, where's the washroom?'

'It's down the hall, but the floor is being retiled so we're not using it. Black marble. Expensive but so gorgeous I may lie on it every night. Use the one off the bedroom, sugar, first door at the top of the stairs.'

It was only a few moments until she was back again, and this time she was in possession of an astonished expression and a slightly beat-up kid's toy.

'Oh my God, Diana, who does this belong to?'

'Lori.'

Coco couldn't take her eyes off it. 'A Miss Molly doll. I had one exactly like it.'

'Yeah, I had one too,' Diana nodded, 'Until my sister swapped that and her virginity for a bag of weed.'

It seemed Coco was still wrapped up in the nostalgia of it all.

'I got mine for Christmas and I loved it so much. I think every girl in America got one that year.'

The memory baton passed to Marny, who shook her head sadly. 'I didn't.'

Dax took a deep draw on his Marlboro and followed it up with a slug of Jack. He held it out to Sly and watched, astonished, as Sly waved it away. Shit, this whole scene was seriously weird. For months he'd had the image in his head of Coco and Sly at the awards ceremony. He'd tortured himself with thoughts – not of them fucking, but of Coco telling Sly that she loved him. He wanted confirmation of what he knew and then he wanted to start punching Sly and never stop. The guy was poison – he'd fucked up Coco, fucked up Marny, fucked up the Spikes and for what? For the sake of his arrogant, overblown ego and the junk he'd been pumping into his veins. Dax had never been a violent man, but he'd absolutely wanted to kill Sly Rammer. Until now . . .

He looked at him and for the first time he saw some humility there, a glimmer of acknowledgement of what he'd done. Coco had brought him back and despite them having been holed up for the last couple of months there was no sign of a relationship. Maybe, just maybe, he'd been wrong about that one. And Marny . . . the way Marny had looked at Sly had sealed the deal. She loved him. She wanted him back and all Dax had ever wanted for her was that she was happy. The only way that was going to happen was if she went back to Sly.

'You know, man, I just wanted to say that . . .' Sly stumbled over his words. More humility. Hesitation. This was like the old Sly, the one that was a decent guy until the ego and the drugs had turned him into a monster. 'I'm . . . I fucked up, man. I'm sorry.'

Any remnants of animosity that Dax was holding on to scattered in the breeze. He was also aware that this would be the perfect time to let Sly in on the fact that he and Marny had been together for the last while.

'Sly, I . . .' No. The guy was sober, had just got clean. This wasn't the time to deliver an announcement that could fuck him up again. It could wait. Instead he threw his arm around his old partner and kissed the top of his head. 'Forget it man. Shit happens.'

Lori opened the door to the suite with the key she'd coerced the old guy at the front desk into giving her. It was amazing what fifty bucks could do. Of course, knocking on the door would have been an option but she knew they'd only answer if they thought she was a whore or a dealer and if they had already been visited by both then she'd be standing there all night.

She didn't have that kinda time to waste. For all she knew, Dax and Sly could be back at the house killing each other right now.

Surely no one would be so fucking stupid as to blurt the truth? Diana she could count on. Coco didn't know. Marny wouldn't dare. And she knew Dax cared about Marny too much to screw things up for her. No, she was pretty sure that Sly would remain oblivious – just as long as she took care of the four other possibilities.

The light on the door clicked to green and she pushed it open. For a moment she wished she'd knocked. It was utter carnage.

On one bed, Muff had his head between the legs of a screaming girl who was handcuffed to the bed and clearly loving it. That boy took his life's work seriously.

On the other bed, Strings was snorting coke out of the ass of a female that even at that angle Lori recognised as one of the interns at AC.

Seven or eight heavily made-up naked chicks were lying on the floor with Tye, two of them fucking him, the rest of them fucking each other. Several of the band's road crew were dotted around the room, some of them unconscious, others sticking their dicks into willing recipients.

Through the open door of the bathroom she could see that Spank was using a razor blade to slice a thick, red line down the forearm of some Goth chick he'd been dating for the last couple of months. Diana had been called to rush her to hospital a fortnight before when Spank had inadvertently gone too far and removed a large part of her nipple.

Chaos. Carnage. A brutal fucking mess. Yet she'd still rather deal with this than all that emotional shit back at the house. The drugs and the relationships had bogged them down but it was time to get this band back in the studio and then back on the road, doing what they were supposed to do. Even if it meant spilling blood.

She slid the gun out of her waistband. The first shot sent a chair flying across the room, the second reduced the TV to spare parts.

'Everybody get the fuck out.'

She noticed Muff sprinting towards the door. That boy was never gonna be an astronaut.

'Except the Spikes,' she roared. He froze. Excellent.

In less than a minute the room was cleared, Spank's girl leaving a trail of blood behind her.

Maybe she should consider sending him on a first-aid course.

'OK, here's the deal,' she began, then became distracted by something in her peripheral vision.

'Strings, can you put your pants on, your dick is winking at me.'

Strings pulled a sheet across his still-erect penis.

'As I was saying . . . Sly's back and he's cleaned up so we're set to leave tomorrow for the studios. Dax's on board too.'

They were all watching her with unusually rapt attention – maybe she should conduct all their meetings while brandishing a deadly weapon.

'Problem is, Sly doesn't know about Dax and Marny's little . . . *friendship* over the last coupla months.'

Lightbulbs pinged on over Tye and Spank's heads. Muff and Strings would need a little longer.

'Now, the only other people who know about them are you four, so I'm gonna make you a deal. Any of you tell him and I use this on your person. Hear me?'

'Lori, you are, like, seriously outta fucking control, man.'

'Spank, are you volunteering to be my first victim?'

He tutted in total disgust, but clamped his mouth firmly shut.

The image kept a smile on her face all the way home. By the time she opened her front door she was feeling chilled for the first time in weeks.

They were back on track. Everything was cool. The Steel Spikes had a future again and she was going to get them back on top – no personal shit, no distractions, just business.

It took her a few moments for reality to catch up with her brain and for her to realise that she was standing in the middle of the room and everyone – Diana, Marny, Coco, Dax, even Sly – was staring at her.

'What? What's happened now?'

More silence. She stared directly at Diana this time. 'Di? What's going on?'

'Lori, I don't know how to tell you this, but . . .' Pause. Diana struggled to finish the sentence.

'Just fucking tell me – you're freaking me out.'

'A woman just called here.' Diana blurted.

'If it's Spank's slut and she says he's cut her other nipple off she's lying – I've just seen her and she still had both.'

'What?' Diana clearly had no idea what she was talking about.

OK, so it wasn't Spank's slut.

'Doesn't matter. So who was it?'

She watched as Diana inhaled before answering. What was with all the freakin' dramatics tonight?

'Lori, she said she was your mother.'

TRACK 6

THIRTY-ONE

1990

Marny pushed herself out of the chair and waddled over to the kitchen window to watch the surfers ducking and gliding in the late afternoon waves. While she was there she absent-mindedly pulled a couple of browning petals from the lilies on the windowsill. It was her only indulgence – fresh flowers from the weekly farmers' market that she scattered in brightly coloured pottery vases throughout her house. *Their* house. Hers. Sly's. And – she thought as she rubbed her rotund stomach – the baby's. 'Just two weeks to go, little one,' she said, and was rewarded with a sharp kick just below the right-hand side of her ribcage.

She still found it incredible that she had adapted to living alone. Some might look at her life and think it was a lonely one, a solitary existence, but after a period of adjustment it had turned out to be pretty close to perfect for her.

It had been her choice to stay behind when she moved into the later stages of pregnancy. Being on the road with a rock band wasn't the ideal place to prepare for a new baby and if there was one thing that Marny had realised when she decided to keep the child it was that the baby must always come first. Unlike her mama, she wouldn't care more about her husband or the parties or the liquor – it was going to be all about the baby now, with Sly a very close second.

Coco had helped her find the house in Manhattan Beach, forty-five minutes south of downtown LA. It was a great place to live – right on the sands and unlike in LA she could walk to the store, to the coffee shop or to the library. Nobody interfered with her life, yet there were enough people around who knew her now and would stop to chat and pass the time of day.

It had been hard at first – the loneliness had been crippling then, but that had been solved when Coco had come to stay for a few days and never quite left. Not that she was there all the time: Milan, Paris, Tokyo, London, she modelled all over the world. However, when she was in California, sometimes one night a week, sometimes two or three, her home was in Marny's house and it suited them both. They understood each other, understood the world that they had lived in, shared a history. But one part of their recent history had not been shared, and she'd never told Coco about her time with Dax. She couldn't. In Marny's mind it was almost like it had never happened. She was with Sly again, back where she should be and she wasn't going to rake up anything that could jeopardise that.

Coco would be home tonight, coming back to keep her company for a week before Sly got a break in the tour. The timing was perfect: a two-week hiatus that started two days before the baby was due. It was gonna be the most exciting, incredible . . . Wow – another kick, this time on the left. Surprise more than pain made her yelp as she put both hands on the edge of the sink, leaned over and took a deep breath. One. Two. Three. Another breath. As the water began to pour from between her legs she snatched the phone from the side and dialled. Punching in the numbers, she fought to keep calm as she realised that she was going to need Sly home sooner than that . . . Like right now.

★

'Arch that back, baby – arch that back. Oh, yes, that's it. Hot. Hot! Hot, baby hot!

Coco's expression immediately flicked from fierce to amused. Gilbart was a legendary photographer and he was lying on the floor in front of her, wearing nothing but a pair of silver spandex shorts and a mahogany tan, salivating not over her, but over the $10,000 Balenciaga that was draped over her body. The Balenciaga definitely came first, the hot topless tech guy who was working the lights and the fan came second, and she was third. She'd been in the industry for six months and already she'd picked up the need-to-know basics:

1. It wasn't as glamorous as it looked.
2. It was a lonely existence.
3. Most of the guys in the fashion business were gay.
4. The straight ones were so saturated with sexual activities that they were lazy, smug and self-important. Therefore, they were – almost invariably – lousy screws.

What she wouldn't give right there, right now for Muff to walk in that door and give her head until her back arched for real. Now that really would be hot, baby hot.

'Oooh, yes, Coco, that's it – loving the face. Loving it! What are you thinking about you filthy little tiger?'

Her laughter rose over the sound of Madonna's 'Vogue'. That had been Gilbart's choice – after her selection had been vetoed. She'd slipped Bowie's new *Changes* compilation into the CD player, only for Gilbart to clutch his heart and pray to the Virgin Mary for the salvation of her soul before taking it right back out again.

He shot off another dozen frames and threw his arms out wide.

'Darling, darling, darling, that's a wrap! Good work people! Powder in ten minutes for anyone who has the need.' Gilbart's talent was legendary, his sexuality was a matter of public record, and his raging coke habit was taken for granted. How else could he stay that skinny? Still, at least he was generous with it.

She didn't bother to close the curtain in the corner of the room as she changed. Horse bolted. Stable door shut. There wasn't a person in the room who hadn't seen her naked at some point today and nudity was nothing more than an occupational necessity. Modelling might create images of beauty and lust for magazines, but the reality was that on the shoot it dehumanised the body to such an extent that when the lights were on all sexuality shrivelled in the glare.

This so wasn't the right career for her, she thought for the thousandth time.

To her absolute astonishment, that first job her agent had hooked up for her after she brought Sly back to LA had turned out to be the cover of *Sports Illustrated*, one of the top gigs in the modelling world. If starring in the Spikes' video had sent her shooting to the stars, the *SI* cover had kept her in orbit. After it hit the newsstands she could pretty much name her price. Turned out her price was fairly high, yet the jobs still kept on coming in and she kept on taking them. What other choice did she have? She didn't want to stay back in Connecticut, she didn't want to live permanently in LA and she couldn't go back into the place she really wanted to go: the world of The Steel Spikes.

Living with Dax again just wasn't an option – she loved him too much to lie and he'd never accept that she was also in love with Sly, even if it was a feeling that she would never act on because of her love for Marny.

So instead she'd become a butterfly – going where the jobs took her, living a life that was all about schedules and shoots instead of sex and sounds, shacking up with Marny when she was working in LA. Marny was the little sister she'd never had – but it didn't stop her missing the old days so bad that it hurt.

There had been countless affairs along the way – all of which had been emotionally void and sexually disappointing. Nothing even came close to the freedom and love she'd known when she was with the Spikes, on the road with her best friends, being able to be totally herself and let loose without judgement or consequence. That was living – this was just existing.

Her wisp of a thong was just sliding over her hips when she felt the curtain close behind her. 'Gilbart, I'll be . . .'

The rest of the sentence stuck in her throat right around the moment that she realised that hot topless tech guy was now sharing her space.

Raising her eyes heavenwards, she said a silent thank you to the gods of well developed pectoral muscles. He looked at her inquisitively, obviously asking for permission to proceed.

The rip as she tore her thong from her hips gave him the answer.

'Marny. Marny! Calm down honey, calm down, I get it. Who is there with you? Oh for fuck's sake. OK, I'm going to call an ambulance and I will get him there for you honey, I promise – I will get him there.' Lori slammed down the phone and turned to Diana, who was lying on the bed, just coming out of a six-hour sleep. 'Need a flight and need it now, Marny has gone into labour.'

Diana sprung to her feet, pulled an old Stones T-shirt over her naked torso and with a mantra of 'Shit, shit, shit' slid into the seat that Lori had just jumped out of and snatched the phone back out of the cradle.

'Where is he?' Lori asked, already at the door. Diana shrugged. 'No idea – haven't seen him since we landed.'

Great. She had only minutes to find Sly Rammer, somewhere in Mexico City at 4pm, which for the Spikes was the middle of the night. He could be anywhere: hospital, jail, gutter, morgue – but just this once, just this once dear God, let him be in his room.

Grabbing a pile of keys, she stormed down the corridor. Anyone who said rock bands were rowdy should come to their hotel in the afternoon. Silence. Complete silence. They'd flown in at 3am, after leaving straight after last night's gig at the Stadium

Caracas in Venezuela. Tonight was free while they waited for the crew who were travelling by rail and road to arrive and set up the production, and tomorrow night they were playing to a sell-out crowd of twenty thousand at the Palacio de los Deportes. Of course, the sensible thing to do would have been to get straight to the hotel, chill back and catch up on some sleep. That would have been wise. Conscientious. And that's exactly why the band slipped a thousand dollars into the hands of the customs officials who had greeted them, jumped into the two limos that they'd arranged to be waiting for them on the runway and headed off in search of debauchery, Mexican style.

Arriving at his room, not for the first time, she acknowledged the efficiency of having the hotel give her copies of every room key when they checked in. The guys had grumbled at first but she hadn't cared – there had been way too many incidents when it had been invaluable. The time Muff slipped into an alcohol-induced coma that almost resulted in him choking on his own vomit. The time in Spain that Spank OD'd on acid and trashed the room, launching a sofa through a sixteenth-storey window. Thankfully Lori had seen it fly past, got into the room and got him out of there before the police arrived. With no proof as to the culprit, they'd had to let him go, despite $26,000 of sofa-inflicted damage to the waterfall in that Barcelona square.

After sliding the key in the door and opening it to see a wall of darkness, the first thing that hit her was the smell. It was a good sign. Toxic odours and members of The Steel Spikes often went hand in hand. As she flicked on the switch and light flooded the room, she re-evaluated the 'good sign' theory ever so slightly. Sly was lying face down in the middle of a king-size bed, a puddle of sick on the floor beside him. The room looked like it had been ransacked (which it very probably had) and the only other occupant was Chad, the security guard that Chuck, now head of their security, had assigned to look after Sly. Chad was now 'protecting' Sly from his vantage point on the floor, where he was passed out and naked with a love heart drawn in lipstick

338

on his chest – a subtle pink shade that matched the colour of the fleshy part of his scrotum where she assumed pubic hair had once lived.

Picking her way through the debris, she reached Sly and pushed him over on to his back. Yep, same fate. Bald. Chest, pubes, legs. All hair gone. That was gonna cause a mighty uncomfortable stubble rash when it started to grow back. And right now she hoped it would hurt like the fires of hell.

There was no point in trying to wake him on her own. She picked up the phone at the side of the bed and summoned Dave Lopez. He was about to have a very bad day. He had to get Sly to Manhattan Beach and back in twenty-four hours, fire one security guard and explain to her why the fuck her lead singer was devoid of his body hair. Yet another new addition to his job description . . .

She threw open a window and almost immediately there was a grunt from the bed as Sly thrashed around, perhaps looking for a cover since his bald balls had just been exposed to the cool morning air. Look at the fucking state of him. OK, so he wasn't back on the junk, but his smack habit had been replaced by raging alcoholism that was so out of control it was a miracle his liver hadn't applied for transplant. The guy was a total fuck up. And he was about to become a father.

An image of old Jack immediately came into her head and she felt the hairs on the back of her neck stand up. All these years later and the hatred still hadn't diminished. Neither had the contempt. Or the disgust. And in her case that applied to both parents. That was why she had never returned the call from the woman who claimed to be her mother. Maybe it was her mom, maybe it was a crank – she didn't want to know. Instead of finding out, she'd changed her number and filed the whole incident to the back of her mind under 'Shameless Bitch'.

Mommie Dearest had walked out and left her with Old Jack when she was six years old – it was a bit fucking late to realise that she'd missed a few birthdays.

There was another groan from the bed and she lashed out with one leather biker boot and aimed a kick to the side of Sly's hip. It connected with the kind of brute strength that she hadn't even realised that she had and shit, it felt good. Although, clearly not for him. He immediately buckled over into the foetal position and put his hands over his head to protect himself. He needn't have bothered. She'd never touch the face – it was worth too much money to her.

His eyes were flitting open now, the pain obviously working its way through the fragmented neural pathways to the fried brain. What did Marny see in this guy? What did Coco think there was to love? As far as she was concerned, other than a voice and stage presence that was designed by God, he was a waste of a good pair of leather pants.

She couldn't help herself. She aimed another kick at the ribcage and this time Sly's eyes flew open again and stayed that way.

'Wake up sleeping beauty,' she drawled. 'This is the day some poor kid finds out that you're its daddy.'

'OK Marny, we're going to start pushing soon,' the pretty young midwife's voice cut through the pain and as Marny gripped the metal struts at the side of the bed, a roar came from the very depths of her soul. Eight hours and still no baby. And where was Sly? Where was he?

'Did you call her again? Did you call Lori?' Marny spat each word out through gritted teeth. Nurse Linda calmly nodded her head. 'I did and she said he was on a flight and would be here . . .'

The door swung open and a figure gowned in green rushed towards the bed and grabbed her hands.

'Coco!' Marny wept, sweat flooding her face. 'Oh thank God. Where's Sly, Coco, where is he?'

'He'll be here soon hon, he landed at LAX five minutes ago. Oh baby, I'm so sorry I wasn't here for you. I got home and I called Lori and . . . it doesn't matter. How are you doing . . .?'

340

Another roar cut the conversation short and this time Marny was squeezing on Coco's hands so tightly she yelped.

Nurse Linda's head disappeared under the green gown that was covering Marny from the waist to the stirrups that held her ankles. 'OK, Marny, it's time. I'm going to ask you to push on the next contraction.'

'No. No. No.' she sobbed, 'I have to wait for him. Can't. Do. It. Without. Him.'

'I'm here honey and we can do this,' she heard Coco say, and then she felt a hand gently brush her damp hair back from her face. Coco was here. She was with her. She wasn't alone.

'Aaaaaaargh!'

'OK, Marny, now push. PUSH!'

The pain sliced through her, an inconceivable agony that was tearing her in two.

'Marny, the head is out and I've got the shoulders. Now come on, just one more push. Just one more . . .'

'Aaaaaaargh!'

Suddenly the sensation changed from pain to a sliding, slippery feeling, then . . . nothing. Everything stopped and there was silence. Complete silence. 'Coco? Coco what's happened?' she shrieked.

A piercing scream cut through the air as the midwife suddenly stood upright, clutching a tiny creature covered in blood and gore, its mouth wide open, repeating the scream that had announced its arrival into the world.

Nurse Linda immediately brought it to the top of the bed and lowered Marny's gown, then placed the baby on her naked chest. The crying stopped instantly.

'Congratulations,' she beamed, 'you have a beautiful little girl.'

The emotion was instant. And as Marny's tears slid down on to her daughter, she knew right there and right then, that this was the defining moment of her life. She had a daughter.

A beautiful daughter. She belonged to someone. And someone belonged to her.

Raising her eyes, she saw a reflection of her tears as Coco wept, then leant in to kiss her.

'You did it, Marny, you did it. She's incredible. And she has lungs like her daddy,' she laughed.

The sentence was barely out when the door swung open once again and another tall, gowned-up figure joined the mix. It couldn't be a doctor. There wasn't a medical man in the world that had that kind of swagger.

In one swift action he snatched the mask off his face and tossed the green cap to one side.

Coco immediately took a step back and let him take her space.

Marny watched him as he stared at the bundle in her arms, then at her, then back at the baby, as if trying to compute what was going on. All thoughts of what she'd been through were gone now, and all she could think was that he looked exhausted. Beat. She felt a pang of guilt that she hadn't been on the road with him, taking care of him, making sure he was OK.

'Sorry I didn't get here . . .' he'd finally found his voice, but she put her fingers on her mouth to shush him.

'It doesn't matter. It's a girl, Sly – we've got a baby girl.'

Marny held the baby up to him, so he could take her, hold her, love her.

A few seconds later an astonished midwife picked up the phone and punched in three numbers. 'Need some help in here – Mr Rammer has just passed out.'

In the ensuing bedlam, no one noticed that another person had entered the room and that he was standing, perfectly calm, at the side of the bed, one hand on Marny's shoulder, the other stroking the face of the beautiful baby in her arms.

'She's perfect,' Dave whispered to Marny. 'Just like her mom.'

THIRTY-TWO

The crash made everyone on the same floor jump, most of all the three men sweating in suits in front of him. 'I will kill every one of those fuckers before I let them walk away – do you get that?' he roared. 'What do I employ you braindead cunts for? Now get it sorted or my foot and your colons are gonna get mighty fucking acquainted.'

He watched them back out of the office, their sphincters so tight with fear that that they could barely walk. Harvard. Princeton. Yale. What the fuck good were these Ivy League educations when not one of them could do the fucking job he asked them to?

All they had to do was keep the Spikes at AC and make as much money out of them as possible. Was it really so difficult? He'd done the hard part. He'd found them, he'd signed them, he'd made them global fucking superstars, outselling every other band in the world over the last two years. *Suicide Now* had shifted twelve million copies worldwide and the follow up, *Don't Touch The Spikes* was on track to beat that. They'd been on tour now for six months, the first stage of a campaign that would see them play 341 concerts in forty-four countries over the next eighteen months. And the gigs were already sold out. The Spikes were as big as it got and it was all down to him: Ari Covet. Fucking genius.

He'd got it right. Not that he'd ever doubted he would.

The rock genre had changed over the last couple of years, with these new grunge guys coming in – Soundgarden, Alice in Chains, Pearl Jam and Nirvana were all creating a buzz – while the old names crumbled. Look at Decomp. They were all fucking toast now that Randy Storm would be living it up with Charlie Manson and Sirhan Sirhan at the COR for the next sixty-two years without parole.

But despite the trends, the splits and the corpses, Ari was still riding way high and that was because he'd got it so, so right with the Spikes. The only thing he'd have done different was . . .

'Mr Covet, your 10am appointment is here.'

Still agitated, he pressed the button on the intercom. 'Tell her to wait.'

Shit, he wasn't in the mood now. Nothing made his dick shrivel more than the prospect of losing money. He wanted to go punch the crap out of the bag in the corner instead and every jab would be aimed at Lori fucking Wyatt. There were no words left to describe how much he hated that bitch. She was trying to screw him and there was no way she was gonna get away with it.

Sliding open the bottom drawer on his right-hand side he pulled out a bottle of tequila. Maybe throwing the first bottle of the day at those imbecile lawyers had been an error of judgement – now he'd have to get Rita May to send out for more as it had been a long time since just one bottle was enough to get him through the day. But first, he had to take care of the more pressing issues at hand.

Standing up he dropped his pants, then picked up the white tab that was sitting beside his phone. The cocaine had gone long ago, as soon as he stopped being able to get it up on command. Instead, for the last couple of years a little Mexican friend with contacts in the pharmaceutical industry down there had been supplying him with something far, far more enjoyable. With a practised ease, he slid the white tab up his ass. Methamphetamine suppositories. Smoking it stank the place out, he wasn't going down the injection route, so this was the next best thing. It would take a little while to kick in but when it did? It made him capable of fucking for hours. And he intended to.

'OK Rita May, send her in.'

The door opened and in strutted Desire – who was no doubt named Betty or Jane when she was born in the backwoods of Fuck Knows Where. But now she was Desire, $500 an hour, double jointed, tits the size of watermelons.

'Hey Ari baby,' she purred as she shimmied across to his desk. Good – she'd followed orders. He usually only saw her at home, but he'd had a little idea that required an office visit so he'd told her to dress smart. The sight of her didn't disappoint. Shiny patent high heels, a black skirt suit, briefcase. Perfect. He could already feel the boner coming to life. Oh yeah, baby this was gonna be a blast.

'Strip.'

No domination shit today – since he'd started on the meth his MO had switched and now he preferred to be in charge. He opened the bottle of tequila and slugged some back while he watched her.

The jacket was the first to come off, after she slowly opened each button, never breaking eye contact, a teasing smile on her face the whole time. When it finally slid off her shoulders and those magnificent tits sprung free his dick reacted likewise. OK, now they were in business. He slugged back some more tequila and settled back to watch the show, enjoying every second of it.

This girl knew how to earn her dough. She was swaying her hips from side to side now, licking her lips as she did it, like there was some song going on in her head that she had to move to. One hand was around at her back, undoing the skirt zipper, the other was caressing her voluptuous left tit, a one-inch long purple nail tracing circles around her nipple.

Suddenly the skirt dropped and although he'd seen it a dozen times before, he still let out an involuntary little whimper of surprise. She was perfect. Absolutely fucking perfect. Perhaps just a little too short, but the sight in front of him made him overlook that. Her long, black hair pulled back tight into a ponytail that hung down to the small of her back. The piercing green eyes. Those perfect tits. The scalpel-sharp cheekbones. The legs that went on for miles, every inch of them perfectly tight and toned. She looked so like Lori Wyatt she could be her sister. But right now, as the meth started to take effect, Ari chose to believe it was her who was standing there, bold, defiant, her hands on her hips, legs wide apart, showing him that beautiful bald pussy. The one he had paid for.

He slid back in his chair and removed his pants, then signalled her to come forward.

She was his to do with as he pleased and it was time, time to remind her who the boss really was. He could feel two things happening now; the urge to fuck was getting stronger and stronger and the room was starting to move in and out of focus.

The thought that had been driving him insane for weeks slipped back into his head, the one that had resulted in at least a dozen meetings with his legal team that had all ended with frustration, fury and threats. It had been his only regret and his biggest mistake, signing the Spikes to a five-year, three-album deal. He should have gone for double that. Now that bitch Wyatt was threatening to switch labels. It would be over his dead fucking body. Didn't she know that he was in charge? That no one, *no one* shafted Ari Covet? Little Miss Wyatt was gonna have to learn that and learn it fast. And as her lips slipped around his dick and started to suck he decided that maybe the Spikes' betrayal wouldn't be over his dead body.

Maybe it would be over hers.

THIRTY-THREE

The chattering of the cleaners out in the corridor was giving Sly a fucking headache.

Chinese? Japanese? Where was he? Shit, what did it matter? Another city, another gig, nothing changed.

His hand automatically reached down and gave his balls a scratch. Fuck, he felt rough. Last night had been . . . Wow – shooting pain across the temples. His hand moved from scrotum to head and began rubbing. Last night had been interesting.

'Hey, singer man, I do that for you?'

He felt a hand move across his forehead from the right and take over the administration of strokes. When the pain eased he eventually had a go at cranking one eye open. Female, young, black hair, beautiful. It would have been rude not to smile.

'I do that for you,' the voice repeated. Hang on, that voice came from the left. He cranked open the other eye. He was seeing double. It was definitely time to give up the booze.

The combination of a racking cough and double-vision panic pushed away the worst of the fog and that was when he remembered. Oh, yes, baby. He opened both eyes simultaneously this time. Sisters. It was all coming back now. Two sisters and they

347

could do things to a man that could give them the most popular family business on earth.

Maybe they could extend their kind strokes to another part of his . . .

The slamming on the door made them jump, especially when it was followed by loud male voices and the screeching of hysterical cleaners. Sly didn't even have time to cover his modesty when the door burst open and Dax and Lori stormed in.

'Fucking hell, you're a peach,' Lori whistled in a voice that made it clear it wasn't a compliment.

However, even in his compromised, befuddled state, Sly realised that much as Lori could be terrifying, a pissed-off, muscled Dax was the bigger threat to his imminent wellbeing.

'You are a fucking shambles, man!' Dax shook his head, disgusted. So 'Good morning' was out of the question then. And he was guessing they hadn't come to bring him some coffee and a couple of Tylenol.

Dax launched a kick at Sly's leg that got him right on the kneebone.

'Dax!' Lori exclaimed. Doubled over, Sly watched as Lori pushed Dax back.

'What? You think he doesn't fucking deserve that?'

Lori looked at Dax, at Sly, and then back at Dax. 'You're right,' she shrugged. 'Go ahead.'

The next kick was even sorer.

Man, this wasn't good. But Sly had no idea just how much worse it was going to get.

Lori removed the two wide-eyed Japanese girls with a wedge of notes while Dax paced the room. He'd had it. He'd had it with carrying Sly, he'd had it with the lies, he'd had it with the fact that Sly hadn't written a damn thing since he came back on board after drying out. Shit, what was he talking about? He hadn't written anything worth a crap since the *Suicide Now* album.

But most of all, he'd had it with the broken promises. Sly had sworn he'd take care of Marny and this was how he did it? Forget it.

He wrenched Sly out of bed by the hair – not difficult since he was once again near-skeletal – and dragged him to the bathroom where he dumped him in the shower.

This stopped here and now. No more. Dax had stood back for Marny's sake and waited for Sly to do the right thing, but it was clear he was going to need a little more instruction on the matter.

'What do you want from me? What?' Sly screeched as the cold water rained down on him.

'Do the right fucking thing and be a fucking man about it.'

The right thing. Do the right thing. Why the fuck was the whole world obsessed with him doing the right fucking thing? Well, he'd show them. What did he have to lose?

He'd show Dax, he'd show Lori – then maybe they'd get off his freaking back and let him get on with living his life the way he damn well pleased. Hell, he needed a drink.

But first he had to Do The Right Thing.

One trans-Pacific phone call later, Marny was at the newsstand buying a whole big pile of wedding magazines.

THIRTY-FOUR

Wistful Weddings magazine, December 21st, 1990

Hitting the High Notes – a round up of this year's music industry weddings by Jan Johnston

Some captured the romance of the sweetest ballad, some had the passion of the most dramatic aria – of course we can only be talking about the gloriously glamorous and unforgettable weddings of music industry stars this year. Back in April there was the dramatic Las Vegas union between Guns N' Roses frontman Axl Rose and Erin Everly, stunning daughter of Don Everly and Venetia Stevenson.

June saw the summer wedding of rock goddess Lita Ford, to former W.A.S.P. guitarist Chris Holmes. Fast-forward to September and Mötley Crüe were in celebratory mode with the marriage of Mick Mars and backing singer Emi Canyon.

Rolling Stones legend Mick Jagger broke off from an Asian tour in November to wed beautiful supermodel Jerry Hall in a breathtakingly romantic, Hindu ceremony in Bali. This oh-so-famous duo have two young children and have already been together for thirteen years – the perfect preparation for a lifetime of togetherness.

The bagpipes rang out over Beverly Hills, Los Angeles last week when British rocker Rod Stewart married twenty-one-year-old model Rachel Hunter in front of an impossibly glamorous audience of music makers, models, friends and family.

However, all of these fabulous weddings might just be overtaken in the romance stakes by the ceremony that is scheduled to take place this week between Sly Rammer, lead singer of The Steel Spikes, and his beautiful long-time love Marny. Details are confidential, but we do know that one mile of beach on the Malibu coastline will be cordoned off and lit with flaming torches. Shortly before midnight on 31st December, the bride and groom will arrive by boat from their home further along the shore. It is thought that the ceremony will be performed to the sound of the Spikes' hit ballad 'Act of God' and the vows will be made on a bed of flowers in front of a hundred guests. The couple's newborn daughter Daisy Colette will be tucked up in bed, however many household names, including the other members of The Steel Spikes, countless rock legends and of course top model Coco LaBiba are expected to attend. 1990 – One year, six couples and a whole lotta love.

THIRTY-FIVE

Dave Lopez dragged the knife across the old vinyl 45 of 'Something'. It was *their* song, *had been* their song. It had meant everything to them. So why? He grated the blade back and forward across the black plastic. Why was she marrying Sly? Why would she marry someone who treated her like that when she could have so much better? He'd seen what Sly Rammer got up to. OK, so he'd quit the smack, but ever since then he'd been fucking his way around the world, treating her like shit, forgetting to show when she flew in with the baby to see him, scoring acid, pills, coke in every city they played. The guy was scum. Total scum and he didn't deserve her.

It was wrong. He picked up his prized copy of *Revolver* and gently traced his finger around the edge of it. It couldn't go ahead. Marny couldn't marry Sly because she should be with him.

The question was, how long did he have to wait?

'You look incredible, honey – just absolutely incredible.'

Marny smiled, doing her best not to let the tears fall and spoil the make-up that had taken her friend an hour to apply.

'Are you sure? I definitely look OK?' She turned back to the mirror and she knew that what she saw there had more to do with Coco than with her. How many girls got styled for their big day by one of the most successful models in the country, the only one of the new crop of supermodels who had actually turned down a spot on George Michael's 'Freedom' video?

Marny's dress had come from Vera Wang, a champion ice skater turned *Vogue* fashion editor turned designer that Coco had modelled for in New York when Wang had launched her design salon in the Carlyle Hotel. It was the most beautiful thing Marny had ever seen – a simple white silk-pleated sheath that gave her curves she didn't have, before gently flaring out below the waist and falling to a hem that was gathered at random intervals by tiny ivory silk rosebuds. Afternoons sitting on the deck of her Manhattan Beach home had left her skin a sunkissed shade of gold and her hair was tied back in a loose bun at the nape of her neck, leaving tendrils of white to frame her face.

It was the image that every little girl dreamed of, that every parent looked forward to seeing. Except hers, obviously. It suddenly struck her that not one member of her family would be there to see her marry.

Tears welled up and again she had to fight them back. Other than Daisy, her biological family didn't matter. Coco, Lori, Diana, Dax, Dave and the band would be there. They were her family now, the only ones who mattered.

They were the people who were in her life and it was a simple life that she loved. Of course, she wished that Sly was home more. Snatched weekends once a month or so were no substitute for a life together, but she'd never stop him from doing what he had to do – and what Sly Rammer lived to do was go on that stage every night and feel the adulation of the crowd. That was enough for him though. He wasn't one of those guys who needed the groupies and the wild times any more – he called her every night after the gig and told her how much he loved her and the baby. And wasn't he proving that by marrying her? It didn't matter that he only had a month off before going into the studio to record the next album. What mattered was that they loved each other and she and Sly would have the rest of their lives to spend together.

One more glance in the mirror. At last, she was the princess who was going to get the happy ever after.

Where was the Jack, man? Sly opened another cupboard in the kitchen with one hand, while he lit up a Marlboro with another. The bastards had hidden everything from him and he was sick of gettin' treated like some fucked-up kid. He'd agreed to this, hadn't he? Done the responsible thing, taken the decision to make it legal. OK, so he'd only done it to get Dax and Lori off his case. His relationship with Dax was so shit now that they couldn't even stand to be in the same room as each other. Who the fuck did he think he was, Mr High and Fucking Mighty with the morals and the 'You gotta do the right thing'? As far as Sly was concerned he was already doing the right thing. He'd bought Marny and the kid the house, flew her out every now and then, made sure everything he did was kept discreet and didn't complain when Diana appeared with the phone every night and made him call Marny up. What else did they want from him? He wasn't built for conventionality and domesticity. If he was he'd have been a fucking country and western singer and written songs about lonesome nights on some frigging porch.

But shit, what did it matter? So he'd marry her, get Dax off his case, give the kid his name, keep Marny happy. She'd saved his life once so it was the least he could do, he reminded himself as he pulled a bottle of Jack Daniel's from the back recess of the cupboard.

The very least.

'David Geffen is here.' Diana wandered up behind Lori and rubbed her shoulders as she sat at the dressing table drawing on two dramatic sweeps of eyeliner. Lori smiled. Geffen had just sold out Geffen Records to MCA but he was still a major player who turned every act he touched into gold. Lori talked as she worked. 'Good. Clive Davis from Arista is on his way too. I've put them in the same row as Bill Simpson from Ark. We've also got Warner, EMI and Def Jam there. And Ari is in the back row so he gets a perfect view of all the others. Mr Covet is gonna shit a brick.'

'Thought this was a wedding, not a business deal,' Diana said, already knowing the answer. Lori lifted the eyeliner away from her face and grinned. 'Honey, everything is business.' Every minute of every day, except the ones spent naked.'

Today had been a typical example. Up at 5.30am, a few hours on the phone to Asia tightening up deals on their next tour there and on a dozen or so merchandising licences that she was negotiating. Then she'd spent the morning with Dax over at the Guitar Centre on Sunset signing the new 'Dax Spikes' guitar that Gibson had launched in his honour. The kids had queued around the block, real fret-heads who had gazed at him like he was some kind of god. It was good to see him taking centre stage instead of Sly for a change. Not only did he deserve it, but he appreciated it more too.

Around lunchtime she'd left Dax with Diana while she raced back to the house to check that Sly was still under lock and key. Just a few weeks before they'd traded the house on Laurel for a three-bedroom, white and glass art deco ocean pad in Malibu and that was the venue for tonight's wedding. Just to make sure nothing went wrong, she'd had Sly staying there for the last two days and on her orders Dave Lopez had posted two guys at each entrance to make sure it stayed that way. To be honest, she didn't know whether or not she was doing Marny a favour by keeping Sly on the straight and narrow, but she just hoped against hope that he would one day sober up, grow up and come to his senses. He'd been getting more and more unreliable with every passing week – the drink, the partying, and while he wasn't back on the junk, he was definitely using again. Relations with Dax were at breaking point. Lori spent way too much time refereeing or keeping them apart and the rest of the band was feeling the pressure. Dax and Marny had always been the ones that grounded Sly, kept him relatively functioning as a human being, but without either influence he was just a belligerent prick and it was only a matter of time before Dax, or maybe Spank, reached the end of their patience and took him out.

She just had to make sure she got the new deal signed first.

Finally, *finally* she was saying goodbye to Covet and it felt great. The old bastard was still in there fighting and threatening, but Lori knew she wouldn't go there again. She was only keeping him in the game so that his offers would force the negotiations as high as possible. He wouldn't lose them without a fight and that's what Lori was counting on – a fight with lots of zeros at the end that would force his competitors to follow suit. The irony was, the man who'd once been the ultimate hustler didn't even realise that he was being played. He'd lost it. His meth habit was well known in the industry now and the guy looked like he was dying in front of them. His teeth were rotten, he'd aged ten years in the last twelve months and he was taking risks with the hookers that were extreme even for a fucked-up deviant like him. Only last week a young journalist from *Rolling Stone* had shown up to interview him only to find a naked Russian female lying on his desk. Ari had proceeded to give the guy an hour's worth of face time while stopping every now and then to pour tequila over the woman and lick it off. When he'd suggest the journo might want to fuck her before he left, the poor guy had bashfully declined and hastily departed.

No, Ari was done. She had created the biggest band in the world and now she was on the cusp of signing the biggest deal in music history and she knew that all she had to do was play it smart, get this wedding over with and try not to let any of these fuckers kill each other.

'Baby, have you been shopping again? Honestly, how many toys can Daisy have? She's not even one and you've pretty much filled her room.' Diana's question snapped her back to the present.

Puzzled, she followed Di's gaze. 'Oh, not guilty. That came over with the wedding presents that fans had sent to AC,' Lori replied.

'Sweet Jesus, there are some strange-assed people out there. Was there a card?'

'Nope, just a note pinned to it that says 'To Sly Rammer.' That was it. Otherwise I'd have thought it was a mistake. I mean, who sends a doll as a wedding present?'

'Are you ready?' Coco asked Marny, 'And don't cry 'cos you'll start me off again.'

She held Marny's hand as they stepped on to the cruiser for the short trip from Manhattan Beach down to Malibu. Coco, Marny, a couple of security guys and Dave Lopez, who'd gallantly volunteered to escort her to the ceremony. Although, given that he looked like he was totally spaced out, it might be a case of Marny leading him. Poor Dave – he was unrecognisable as the eager young thing they'd travelled to LA with all those years ago. He'd gone from being a relatively bright-eyed, enthusiastic – if slightly nervous – guy with ambitions and dreams and turned into an introvert who always looked completely miserable. Coco guessed that was what several years in the music business could do to you. Maybe he just needed to get laid. Yep, that was it. After the wedding maybe she'd set him up with a cool chick who would put a smile back on his face.

She smoothed down the silk of her Chanel dress, a strapless, body-skimming column of emerald that fell to just above her ankles, cinched in at the waist with a belt of crystals. It was stunning, but she wouldn't be making any plans to bend, dance or breathe deeply. The captain flicked on the switch on the deck heater and she also pulled a thick wool blanket around her and Marny. It would have made far more sense to travel by car, but somehow this had just seemed much more romantic.

The boat pulled away slowly from the end of the pier and started to make its way along the coastline, travelling at a speed that was quick enough to get them up to Malibu on time for the ceremony but not so fast that the breeze would mess up their hair.

'How are you feeling?' she asked Marny, thinking that for someone so beautiful on her way to the happiest event of her life, she was looking mighty worried.

'I hate leaving her, Coco, even for the night.'

'She'll be fine, babe. You know that it would be crazy to take her.'

As Marny nodded reluctantly, Coco slipped her arm around her and squeezed her tight to reassure her. They'd deliberated whether to bring little Daisy but it was a crazy idea. For a start it was the middle of the night and she'd been tucked up in bed for hours, and secondly there were going to be fireworks at midnight and that would be terrifying for her. In the end, Marny had been persuaded to leave her with Bernadette; the housekeeper Coco had hired to help Marny out and keep her company while she was away. Lately that had been pretty much all of the time. If anyone had told her that one day the most significant thing in her life would be work she would have laughed. But it was true. When the wedding was over she really had to think about what she wanted in life, make a plan, get it sorted.

The funny thing was that she was so aware of how it looked from the outside – the glamour, the beauty, the success – but the reality was that she had never, ever been unhappier. Except of course when her daddy . . .

'Thanks for being here Coco,' Marny whispered.

'I wouldn't be anywhere else.'

Only Coco knew it wasn't quite true. This wasn't easy for her. Other than the night of Daisy's birth (and let's face it, he probably didn't even register that she was there) her path hadn't crossed Sly's since the night they'd come back from the ranch, when he was clean, sober and subdued. She didn't pine for him, or lie awake thinking about him any more, but every now and then she'd hear him sing and the physical reaction was instant. It was like the last five years had never happened and she was hearing him for the first time and nothing, *nothing* made her heart beat faster than the sound of his voice. She was wasted. Gone. Consumed by a feeling she didn't want or understand.

They'd come around the bay at Marina del Rey now and watched the lights in the condos of the Santa Monica shoreline drift past. In the distance were what looked like thousands of tiny lights, little fireflies darting about on the horizon, lighting up the darkness, drawing them towards their flickering flames.

Marny's eyes filled up again.

'Don't you cry, you'll ruin that make-up,' Coco warned her warmly. The tears that started to fall were clearly not paying attention.

'I'm getting married,' Marny whispered, as if the reality was just dawning on her for the first time.

'Yes, you are my darling,' Coco whispered. She pulled Marny's head down on to her shoulder in an embrace designed to give the nervous bride comfort and support . . . and so that Marny wouldn't see that her bridesmaid was crying too.

'Tell me you're kidding me. TELL ME YOU ARE FUCKING KIDDING!'

'Do I look like Eddie Murphy?' Diana replied, with just a little more attitude than was probably required.

'How the fuck can he be gone? That bastard is gonna be the fucking death of me!'

'He told the security guys he was going to check on the flowers . . .'

'THE FLOWERS!! And they believed him? Does Sly Rammer look like the kind of guy who gives a flying fuck about FLOWERS?'

She thumped her fist down on the granite counter top and then winced as a flash of pain assaulted her. Flowers. Those dickheads that were working for the security company obviously had chest measurements that were higher than their fucking IQs.

Focus. Focus. She knew she shouldn't be yelling at Diana, but if she didn't shoot the messenger then there was every chance she'd end up doing fifteen without parole.

'How long have we got?'

Diana looked at her watch. 'They should come ashore in about twenty minutes.'

'And how long has he been gone?'

'About half an hour. Oh, and he took the bottle of Jack that I'd stashed at the back of the laundry cupboard. Bastard must have sniffed it out.'

Lori let her forehead fall forward on the cold granite while she tried to regain her will to live. After a few moments she shook herself off and sat back up straight. 'He doesn't have any transport, does he?'

Diana shook her head.

'OK, then there's only one place he will have headed for. Give me the phone.'

Diana tossed the cordless handset over to her and Lori caught it effortlessly. She then flipped open the Filofax she'd just pulled out of the kitchen drawer and flicked through it until she found the right number.

There was a pause after she'd dialled.

'Hi, can I speak to Jenna please? It's her mother and it's an emergency.'

Out of the corner of her eye she noticed that Diana was grinning now. Lori loved her girl: unflappable, calm, smart – and the great ass and those huge brown eyes were an added bonus.

'Jenna? No, it's not your mom, it's Lori Wyatt. Listen, girl, it's worth a hundred dollars – is Sly Rammer there? . . . You are a star, my darling. OK, two hundred dollars if you can get him to the back fire exit in ten minutes' time. Don't care how. Tell him there's someone out there dealing coke – that ought to do it. OK, thanks.'

She snatched up the nearby walkie talkie and pressed the button on the side to summon the head guy on the security team. 'Chuck, can you get your ass in here, like now.'

The back door immediately swung open and a hulking figure filled the space.

Lori, hands on hips, looked at him with utter scorn.

'Flowers?'

He shrugged and shook his head. 'I know boss, couldn't believe it either. I plan to take the guys who were responsible and personally drown them just as soon as there are no witnesses.'

The tension slipped down a notch or two. Poor Chuck, his task was an impossible one. Securing multi-billion dollar corporations? Easy. Guarding presidents? No problem. Keeping five sexed-up, doped-up degenerate rock stars alive, out of jail and in the right place at the right time? Mission Impossible.

'It's a good plan. In the meantime, Sly's at Girl Town. It's ten minutes away – you've got fifteen to get there and get him back here in one piece.'

The door was swinging behind Chuck before she'd finished the sentence.

One way or another this wedding was going to happen and it was going to be a success. She had too much riding on it to let it fail.

The lights of the boat were getting closer and he could see the faint outline of the two women sitting on the deck. Marny. She'd be beautiful, of that Dax had no doubt. He picked up a pebble and tossed it into the water. There was a part of him that wanted to save her from Sly, stop this fucked-up excuse for a wedding from going ahead and rescue her. But then, hadn't he done that before? The truth was that no one could rescue Marny but herself and she was in too deep to have even a hope of seeing what Sly had become. There was no breaking her away from him. It was a lifetime thing for her whether they were together or not. And at least the whole band had formed into some kind of warped protective cushion, shielding her from his behaviour while forcing him to give enough to keep her happy. It wouldn't end well, but it was the best option for her right now because she'd finally be Mrs Sly Rammer – so when he fucked off and killed himself, or ran out on her or destroyed her life in whatever way his woefully ineffectual mind could come up with, at least she'd be left with the impression that he'd once loved her and she'd be financially taken care of for life.

The outlines were even clearer now and his gaze switched to the mane of ash blonde hair that was being backlit by the deck lights, making Coco look like some kind of ethereal Greek goddess. In the last few months he'd seen her on billboards, in magazines, and even on a two-foot square canvas that he'd commissioned from Frankie Marinaro, a hot new artist who worked in thick oils. But he hadn't seen her in the flesh. Now, as she drifted towards him, he felt his heart constrict with every inch of her approach.

He loved her. The last two albums had been twenty-four tracks of heartbreak and pain, each one inspired by the fracture that she'd left when she'd packed her bags. He pushed himself up to his feet and walked towards the water's edge, his white shirt, open to the waist, billowing in the breeze from the water.

As the deckhands jumped off and tied the boat up to the end of the small jetty, he put his hand out to help them on shore. Marny came first.

'You look stunning,' he told her, his rasping East Coast voice deep with emotion. As she leant up and kissed him on the cheek he saw that her eyes were glistening with tears. 'Thanks Dax. For everything.'

Dave Lopez had slipped onshore and was waiting to escort her across the beach. Dax turned back to the boat, to the woman standing there and he held out his hand . . .

Bastards! What the fuck had just happened to him? One minute he'd been headed out back with some hot waitress who promised him a couple of ounces and a one-way ticket to pussy heaven, and the next he was on his face in the back of a Jeep with the mighty fucking weight of his security chief holding him down.

He'd changed his mind. They couldn't make him do this. Didn't they know who they were fucking dealing with here? He wasn't some lowlife jerk that they could slap around. He was Sly fucking Rammer. And he'd do whatever he damn well wanted to.

Ari Covet could feel what was left of his teeth grinding together. What asshole had planned the seating here? The call had gone out for them to move to the chairs for the ceremony and when he'd given his name to the young kid in the penguin suit he'd been shown to the very back row. Ari Covet did not sit in the back fucking row.

In his peripheral vision he caught sight of a familiar face a few rows ahead of him and to the right. It was . . . It was . . . What the hell was wrong with his memory tonight? He leaned over and whispered in Desire's ear. 'Hit.'

Right on cue, she opened her purse, slid out two small pills and surreptitiously slipped them into his hand. However, he was less than inconspicuous as he threw them back. What did it matter what this bunch of losers around him thought? Some jerk further up in front of him who looked a bit like Dave Geffen turned around and checked him out with a smug fucking grin. Yeah, well the smug grins of every asshole in the music industry would be gone when he re-signed the Spikes to a deal that would keep them locked up until they were being wheeled out of care homes.

It suddenly came to him – that guy a few rows ahead over on the right looked a bit like Clive Davis. Couldn't be. Last he heard Davis was over in New York babysitting Whitney.

Another familiar face strutted down the aisle and slipped into the same row as those other guys. Bill Simpson of Ark Records.

Ari felt his temperature begin to rise.

The back of Clive Davis' head was coming towards him now, then away again, then towards him, zooming in and out of focus as it moved. And that guy . . . the one that looked like . . . fuck, it *was* Geffen. David fucking Geffen and he was sitting here at the wedding of one of *his* acts. So was Clive Davis. And now that fucker Bill Simpson who'd been trying to get his hands on the Spikes for years was playing the big shot up at the front too.

All their heads, coming towards him, away, towards him, away, all laughing, laughing so loudly it was making his eyes rattle.

They could only be here for one reason – that bitch Lori Wyatt. So she thought she could play him. She really thought she could play him? Well she was gonna learn a lesson. Nobody played Ari Covet and nobody took away anything that was his.

He slid his hand down the front of his pants and then moved it off to the side, stopping only when he hit cold hard metal.

It was all going to come to an end . . . even quicker than he'd planned.

It had taken Coco by surprise. When he put out his hand and helped her off the boat she'd felt a spark of . . . of what? Of whatever it was that made her so unstoppably attracted to him in the first place. That was unexpected. But then, a woman would have to be dead not to feel a surge of something when Dax was around. Damn, he was the most magnificent-looking man she'd ever seen. Somehow the years were making him look even more handsome, more noble, more absolutely, incredibly freaking fuckable. There were a million sensible reasons to avoid this and she had to hang on to those. Her time with Dax had passed. Besides, although she knew from Lori that he hadn't had a serious relationship with anyone else, there was nothing to suggest that he was still in love with her. Nope, they were definitely past tense. The break up with Dax and all the shit that went with it had been so painful that she'd promised herself she wasn't ever going to go back there. Living back in the world of the Spikes, with Sly nearby, was way too complicated a situation to deal with. She'd moved on and he'd almost certainly moved on too.

So why was he holding her like he never wanted to let her go?

'Hey Lori, what's up?' Dave Lopez sauntered into the kitchen behind the security guard who had been sent to fetch him.

'Nothing – unless you want to count the fact that there are two hundred guests out there, including every music mogul in Hollywood, dozens of celebrities and a blushing fucking bride, yet the groom has decided today's not the day to get married.'

He tried to hide the smile. He had been right all along.

'Is Marny still down in the cabana?'

He nodded. 'They're just touching up her hair and make-up – said she'll be ready in five minutes.'

'Shit. I need you to get out there and stall, stall, stall while I sort this asshole out. Or kill him. Right now the second one is looking good.'

No, he wasn't going anywhere. This was the perfect opportunity, his chance to claim what was his, to take Marny and little Daisy and be a family. They deserved that. They deserved someone who would love them the way they should be loved.

'Lori, why don't you let me talk to him – come on, he listens to me. We've been through a lot of shit together and I can, you know, *relate*.'

Lori sighed, then gestured in the direction of the bedroom.

'Dear God help us if you're our last hope.'

Dave kissed her on the cheek as he passed.

Their last hope was about to get exactly what he wanted.

Was this what it had come to? He was the biggest rock star on the frigging planet and they had him trapped in a room with a guard outside the door. Well, they could all go fuck themselves. He'd get married when he was good and damn well ready and that wasn't right now. Right now was about the bottle of Jack he had hidden under his jacket and the ounce of blow that was in his boot.

He was just about to reach for the latter when the door swung open and Dave Lopez appeared. Dave. Boring jerk but hey, he served his purpose.

'Hey bud, how you doing?' Lopez asked.

'Can't do it man,' Sly replied, rescuing the bottle of Jack and taking a slug from the bottle. He couldn't. Why was everyone always trying to trap him, to back him into a corner, to make him do shit he didn't want to do? And why was Lopez looking at him real weird? Shit, he wanted some of whatever he was on.

'You know, man, you're right – you shouldn't do it.'

Even through the fog, Sly recognised that that wasn't what he'd been expecting.

'Wha . . .?'

The question wasn't even out when Lopez cut him off. 'She's far too good for you, you arrogant prick. Far too good. She deserves better than the shit you put her through so just . . .' Stunned into inaction and silence, Sly didn't even react when Lopez reached into his pocket.

'. . . do us all a favour and die.'

And at that moment, Sly Rammer found himself staring at the most lethal weapon of all.

Marny looked at her reflection and felt the tears gush to her eyes. She blinked them back. The make-up artist had just spent five minutes working on her eyes and probably wouldn't be amused if she had to repeat the process.

'Ready?' Coco asked her, their hands clasped tightly.

As Marny nodded, Coco leaned in to give the bride a hug and whispered, 'OK, Mrs Rammer, let's go get you married.'

Diana burst in the door. 'Security just radioed to say that Marny is heading up from the cabana. Is he ready?'

Lori stopped pacing and shrugged. 'Dave Lopez left five minutes ago – said Sly would be out soon but just needed some time to get himself together.'

'Well sugar, I'm thinking that time has just come to an end.'

It was there. Just sitting there. Ready for him to pick it up. And if he did it would be over. Sly knew that, but, man, he fucking wanted to do it so bad.

Lopez was right – Marny deserved better. In a weird way that statement had been like a physical slap, waking him up to exactly what was going on here. It wasn't just about him, it was about her too. She deserved better. None of this was Marny's fault. She didn't deserve to be stood up, humiliated in front of all those people.

Running wasn't an option this time. He'd run out on his family, he'd run out on Gloria, he'd even come close to running out on the Spikes when the smack and the sex became more important.

It was time to stop running.

His gaze returned to the thing Dave had left behind. One syringe, fully loaded, ready to go. He wanted it so bad he could taste it. But . . .

An image of Marny was in his head and he couldn't shift it; he'd managed one day home in the last three months and when he'd arrived she'd been out front, sitting on the sands, playing with Daisy, both of them laughing.

Picking up the syringe, he knew exactly what he needed to do.

The door swung open and there was Lori, looking about as pissed off as he'd ever seen her.

'Ready?'

He knew she was furious and fuck, she'd make him pay for this. Closing his hand around the syringe so it was hidden from her view, he slid it into his pocket.

Yep, he knew what he had to do: marrying Marny was first on

the list, and right after that he had a long, long-awaited reunion with Mr Brown.

Dave slid into a seat at the end of the back row and a few seats further along spotted Ari Covet, looking like he was about to explode. No big surprise. The head of every major record label was here and that had to be sending Ari into orbit. Well, start the countdown because tonight wasn't gonna go like any of these dudes expected and he planned to keep a low profile when the shit hit the fan. Over at the entrance to the path that led to the cabana and the shore, he could see a security guard talking frantically into his walkie talkie. Marny must be on her way. He checked his watch. Ten minutes since he left Sly. The fix would already be in his bloodstream, working its way around, reacquainting itself with all those little nerve endings and shutting them down. The dose hadn't been huge – no point killing him, but hey – if that's how the dice rolled then Rammer only had himself to blame.

Sure, Marny would be disappointed. Devastated. It would take her a while to come to terms with being so badly let down, but in that time he would show her what real love was. He would be there for her, take care of her, love her back to life and happiness. They would be a family: him, Marny and Daisy.

The guests were starting to fidget now, to look around, wonder what the hold up was. There was a noise behind him and he turned to see Lori striding towards them, her expression focused, deadly serious.

They'd found him. They'd found him whacked out, comatose, maybe dead . . . whatever. The important thing was that she was coming to tell them that it was time to go home. As soon as Lori had broken the news, he'd go to Marny, take her home, look after her like she deserved.

There she was, that fucking bitch! Ari Covet stood up and started making his way along to the end of the row. It was time to put her fucking straight. Think she could fuck with him? He had a little friend that would persuade her differently. He would put the fear of fucking God into her and her signature would be on that new contract before he could flick the safety off. And if she refused? Well that could have a whole other ending but he'd worry about that when the time came. He was Ari Covet and he ruled this town – there was nothing he couldn't do and nothing he couldn't get away with.

There were exclamations of annoyance and pain as he trampled on feet all the way along the row and he'd just reached that waste of space Lopez as Lori got within touching distance.

What the hell was Ari doing? He was stomping towards him, but even Dave could see that Covet's eyes were only on Lori. Shit, he was going to speak to her. He was going to corner her and go off on one of his rants and no, Dave couldn't let that happen. Lori was on her way to announce the wedding was off and she had to do that so he could go to Marny. Marny needed him. She was waiting for him.

Ari was right next to him now, about to pass him, so he instinctively threw his leg up to stop him. It would get him fired but hell, he didn't care. He'd have Marny – that was all that mattered. 'What the fu . . .' Ari had no idea what was going on but his reflexes were slow and caused a delayed reaction – long enough for Lori to pass and for him to . . . Man, he didn't look right. Instead of pushing to get past Dave's obstruction, he was standing stock still, his face purple, a thick layer of sweat oozing from his pores.

Time to get him outta there before he did any damage. Lori had to make the announcement, send everyone home and then he could rescue Marny.

Covet's legs were buckling now and his mouth had gone in a weird direction, way off to the side, and he was making a gasping noise. The guests immediately next to them were starting to stare. Couldn't have that. Couldn't have a scene. Wasn't part of the plan.

He sprung to his feet, grabbed Ari and, practically carrying him, swung him around and headed away from the seats. Luckily, everyone's attention was now on Lori, who had reached the front of the aisle.

The catering tent. He'd head for the catering tent. Shit, Ari must be well stoned – he was practically having to carry him. They crossed the twenty yards away to the marquee and he'd just pulled back the flap on the front when he heard her voice rise over the crowd.

'Ladies and gentlemen, I apologise for the delay, but as anyone who has ever been to a Spikes concert will know, Sly never likes to start things on time.' There was a murmur of amusement from the audience. Why was she joking? This wasn't a time for jokes – she should be breaking the bad news, telling them straight that it was all off.

'So ladies and gentlemen, without further delay, I'd like to present Mr Sly Rammer.'

No! It couldn't be! Sly should be out of it by now! Through the open canvas doorway, Dave listened as the opening bars of 'Act of God' filled the air, he watched Sly swagger up the aisle and stop at the front, and then his heart stopped as Marny appeared and slowly, gracefully walked towards Sly.

It was only when the young waitress shrieked 'Oh my God,' that he realised he'd let go of Ari Covet, and his boss was now unconscious on the ground beside him.

Marny couldn't take her eyes off Sly as she walked up the sandy aisle. How had she ever got so lucky? Sure they'd been through their tough times like any couple, but they'd come through it and found their way back to exactly where they should be: together.

Sly Rammer was her soulmate.

Her life had only begun on the day that she found him. Before that there had been no one, not a single person who cared whether she was alive or dead, much less loved her. Sly had taught her what love was about and she knew that's why they'd got through the bad times and made it all good again. They were going to have an incredible life together; her, Sly, Daisy and hopefully more babies to add to the family.

Her family. For the first time in her life she was going to be in a real family.

As she stopped in front of the minister who was performing the ceremony, she couldn't see anyone for the tears that filled her eyes. Except her soulmate.

Sly watched her come toward him, her veil framing her beautiful face, the soft lighting illuminating her eyes. For a moment she looked exactly like she had when he'd met her: scared, worried but so fucking beautiful. The emotion stuck in his chest as he suddenly remembered how much he'd loved her. Soulmates, that was what they used to say. But that was before he'd sold his soul in return for the intoxicating thrill that only Mr Brown could give him.

'Are you crying?' Diana's voice was an incredulous whisper.

Lori rolled her moist eyes. 'Sand. Allergy.'

'You are crying! Aw shucks, my girl is a romantic pussycat after all. Who knew?' Diana joked.

The fake smile that was plastered on Lori's face camouflaged a long, sad sigh.

'It's got nothing to do with romance,' she whispered, staring at Marny as she took Sly's hand and turned to face the minister. 'I just feel so, so sorry for her.'

This was all wrong. This was Sly and Marny's moment, the first Steel Spikes wedding, the epitome of romance in a stunning setting in front of an incredible cast of guests . . . and all Coco could think about was getting laid.

Looking heavenward, she silently appealed for divine intervention. Dear Lord, I promise this request is a one-time thing, but please, please switch off my sex drive and allow me to get my urge to jump him right here and now under control.

This was excruciating. Marny was beautiful in white, Sly looked like a rock god in his black leather pants and flowing white shirt, and the moment was all about them. It really was. But unfortunately no one had informed her nipples, which were most definitely standing to attention and pointing in Dax's direction.

It would be the easiest thing in the world to fuck him tonight. They'd been so good together. So, so good. And she missed him. But she'd been with the Spikes, done that and she wasn't going to go there again. With the two of them it could never be a meaningless fuck, and after everything that had happened in their world, that was all she wanted.

There was a movement on her left-hand side and she realised that Muff was leaning forward from his seat in the row behind her and his mouth was only inches from her ear.

'Hey Coco, looking hot, babe,' he whispered. She winked and smiled in return. They were at a wedding – they shouldn't be having a little chat among themselves while the bride and groom were pledging everlasting devotion. Unfortunately, Muff had missed that class in etiquette school.

'So I was thinking that maybe later we could, you know . . . you, me, the dive of your life.'

Coco's gaze went heavenward for the second time as she fought not to laugh out loud.

God did work in entirely mysterious ways.

'I now pronounce you husband and wife.'

The entire audience burst into an uproarious cheer, with loud exclamations of celebration coming from the direction of the Spikes.

For once, Marny didn't care that all eyes were on her as Sly lifted her up and kissed her hard and long.

They'd done it.

Mr and Mrs Sly Rammer.

Marianne Tucker was gone and Marny Rammer had taken her place.

It was the happiest moment of her life and she knew that it was only the beginning. No more pain, no more loneliness, no more fear, no more drama – from now on she was going to be just . . . *happy*.

Her mind hadn't even put the full stop on the sentence when she heard the wail of the approaching sirens.

THIRTY-SIX

Rock Out magazine, January 3rd 1991

MUSIC MOGUL CLOSE TO DEATH AFTER ROCK STAR WEDDING

Exclusive insider eyewitness accounts and photos by Bobby Sofranko.

The wedding of Steel Spikes singer Sly Rammer and his girlfriend of five years Marny Tucker was thrown into chaos by the collapse of Ari Covet, head of AC records.

Covet is believed to have suffered a stroke and is presently in a critical condition in Cedars-Sinai Medical Centre. A representative from AC Records issued the following statement yesterday morning:

It is with deep sadness that we confirm the illness of our founder and president Mr Ari Covet. His condition is currently extremely serious and we have put our trust and faith in the medical professionals at Cedars-Sinai, who are working to ensure Mr Covet receives the best possible care. We would also like to thank the general public, Mr Covet's associates, and the stars of both the music and movie industries who have been so thoughtful in sending their condolences and prayers.

According to insider reports, Mr Covet collapsed just moments before the ceremony. However, organisers and guests were unaware of this as he left the wedding area after complaining of feeling unwell.

Gilly-Ann Strong, personal make-up artist for supermodel bridesmaid Coco LaBiba, revealed that the situation only came to light when paramedics arrived on the scene after being alerted by a member of the catering staff. This was shortly after the bride and groom had completed their vows. 'I saw everything,' said a traumatised Ms Strong. 'He just fell over right in front of me and I immediately rushed to his side and put him in the recovery position. I then called to staff and informed them that medical help was urgently required. But I'm not a hero – I only did what anyone else would do.'

The following photographs of Mr Covet fighting for life, taken by an anonymous source, show the gravity of the situation.

There has been no comment as yet from the Steel Spikes spokesman. However, it is believed that Mr and Mrs Rammer are currently spending their honeymoon at home in their Manhattan Beach mansion.

THIRTY-SEVEN

Rock–a–bye baby . . .

Someone put the light out. Who did that? She didn't like it when the light went out.

'Miss Molly?' *she whispered.*

The arms came around her neck and hugged her close. It was OK. Her friend was right beside her.

'I know how to make the lights come back on,' Miss Molly *whispered.*

'How?' she replied, trying not to think about that horrible feeling in her stomach, the one that she always got when she felt real sad or real afraid.*

'We have to think happy thoughts,' Miss Molly *said.*

Rock–a–bye baby . . .

Happy thoughts. Nice thoughts. Ice Cream. Sunshine. Swings. Ribbons.

And how long it would take him to die.

THIRTY-EIGHT

Lori reached out and shook the hand that was being offered to her. 'Pleasure doing business with you. And I'm glad we have an agreement on the announcement. Not that I'll lose any sleep over Ari Covet, but I'd rather not risk any kind of backlash by being perceived to have screwed him over when he's on his deathbed.'

Bill Simpson lifted his Montblanc pen from the desk and slipped it back into the inside pocket of his $2000 suit, then nodded to the four lawyers – two from each side – who were gleefully rubbing their hands under the table in anticipation of their fat commissions. Lori's representatives looked to her for confirmation that they were dismissed and she replicated Simpson's nod. The four of them left the room, no doubt heading straight over to the Polo Lounge to celebrate their windfall. When only Bill and Lori were left, he held his hands up in a gesture of agreement. 'Totally understand. *LA Times* asked me for a tribute yesterday – had to gargle with mouthwash afterwards. Any word on his condition?'

Lori shook her head. 'Apparently they put him into a coma as soon as he was admitted to try to minimise the damage to the brain. As far as I'm aware, that's still the situation. Five days isn't long enough for them to get a clear prognosis.'

Simpson nodded thoughtfully. The Massachusetts Institute of Technology graduate hadn't taken Ark Records from his mother's garage to the third biggest record company in the country by dealing in emotions and feelings. 'Look, I have no problem keeping a lid on the deal just now, as long as I know that our plans are proceeding as we agreed.'

Lori nodded as she stood up and began to pack her copies of the paperwork into the Gucci file case Diana had bought her for Christmas. It was the perfect finishing touch to the organ-crushing Vivienne Westwood rubber dress that gave her a twenty-four-inch waist and a cleavage that bordered on mountainous. She was playing in the big leagues now and had dressed accordingly. 'Not a problem. The Seattle studio is booked out for eight weeks February and March, so by May you'll have yourself an album, and we're ready to get back on the road come the fall. The Spikes are a touring band, Bill – it's what they do best.'

'And Rammer's little . . . issues?'

'Like I said, those were over a long, long time ago,' Lori reassured him, flashing a confident smile. 'He's been clean for years. You saw him at the wedding, Bill – he's a family man now. Strongest chemical he goes for these days is caffeine.'

Simpson lifted his black Louis Vuitton briefcase from the floor beside him and slid the contracts inside. They'd hired a boardroom at the Beverly Wilshire so that Lori wasn't spotted going into the Ark head office. As the 'insider reports' from the wedding had shown, the tabloids were getting more and more creative in the search for a good story.

'Glad to hear it. Because trust me, the last thing I'll tolerate on my label is a band that lets their habits get in the way of making records.'

'Understood. But you don't have to worry about the Spikes, Bill. Taking care of them is my job – and I make sure I do it right.'

They said that the first high could never be recreated but hell, this came close. This was good shit. Really, really good shit. He tried to focus on Dave but his eyes kept rolling and the fog was coming down. Down. Down.

It was the best feeling in the world, like real love, or the most incredible fuck, or watching eighty-thousand people screaming your name. This was the best, man. His old friend had come back . . . and it felt like he had never been away.

Marny poured a coffee out of the pot that sat ready and waiting from the moment she got up until she got ready for bed. Over the last few days it had only been off for a few hours. Sleep was impossible. How could she switch out the lights when she didn't know where he was, didn't know if he was alive or dead? She was worried sick, but she didn't want to call Lori or Dave, because that could land Sly in real serious trouble with the band. Besides, how humiliating to admit that you'd married the love of your life and hadn't seen him since.

The coffee splashed into the mug and she took a long sip, not even noticing the scalding sensation on her lips. This was supposed to be her honeymoon, but instead she'd spent the last five days alone with Daisy, wondering where her husband might be. This anxiety was worse, much worse than when he was on the road, because this time he had an option — and he'd chosen something else over being with her. She just wished she knew who, or what it was.

The wedding night was a blur now. They'd barely passed the 'kiss the bride' bit when they discovered what had happened to Ari and all hell broke loose. Paramedics and cops arrived and that had been enough for at least half the guests to flee the scene. Most of the rest only stayed out of curiosity. After Ari had been taken away it seemed too weird to carry on with the mass celebration so they'd called a halt and dismissed the staff that had been hired for the occasion. They'd then said goodbye to what was left of the guests and the band and their partners had just all headed back into Lori's house with supplies from the bar. They'd drunk champagne until dawn to the sound of the guys jamming on their guitars. In hindsight she'd been grateful it had turned out that way as it had been the perfect way to end the night, and much more comfortable than spending it with two hundred people she barely knew.

She just wished she'd had some warning that her happily married bliss would end right there.

Next morning she was leaving to get back to Daisy when Sly announced that he wasn't coming with her. Some business to take care of he said and no, he didn't know how long he would be. She hadn't seen or heard from him since.

A yelp from the bedroom told her that Daisy was awake and she went to her, smothering her in kisses as she did every morning. This is what Sly was missing. His daughter was a few months old and he'd only woken up in the same house as her a handful of times.

But then . . . she supposed this was to be expected. It wasn't that Sly didn't love her or his daughter, it was just that the whole concept of staying in one place was alien to him. Yes, that was it. It was just going to take him a little time to adjust to not being on the road and if he needed to go have a blow out before he could settle down and spend time with them, then that was OK. Understandable. She would just have to wait until he was ready.

She just hoped for all their sakes that he'd be ready soon.

'Any word yet?' Coco shouted into the phone, straining to make herself heard over the searing guitar riff on the Red Hot Chili Peppers' 'Under the Bridge'. It was day two of a shoot for Victoria's Secret in New York and she was working with Millie Jacks, her favourite photographer for two reasons: she took killer shots and she liked the music real hard and real loud. Today Coco needed some Kiedis, some raw, hot, sexed-up Kiedis to put her in the mood to give the kind of vibe that Millie needed.

'Nothing. But Dave called and told me not to worry – says he knows where Sly is and that he's fine. Why can't he be fine *here*, Coco?'

The pain in Marny's voice made Coco's stomach flip. 'Honey, you know it's just the way he's always been. He needs space, time. Needs to do things his way.' Coco was trying to say the right things but inside she was seething. Damn that selfish prick! He was the most self-centred, arrogant, narcissistic asshole on earth. A rage of contradictory emotions washed over her – she hated his guts, really, really hated his guts. But yet . . .

'Do you want to bring Daisy out here? I can arrange the flights – might take your mind off things.' Even as she made the offer she knew what the answer would be. There was no way that Marny would fly to New York when Sly was missing in action in LA.

'Thanks, Coco, but . . .'

'I know, honey – you don't have to say it. Look, I have to go. Give Daisy a huge hug from me and I'll call you later. Try not to worry, OK?'

Empty words. Of course Marny would worry. Ugh, Sly Rammer was such a prick for doing this to her.

'Coco, baby, are you ready?'

Millie Jacks' high-pitched Bronx twang summoned her to the set. At five foot one in her suede slouchy boots, Millie was a throwback to the early days of the New York Dolls. She'd been a teenager in the punk rock days and her sense of self, style and fashion had stayed there. Her hair was shaved on both sides, the Mohican in the middle was bright blue, and she wore a black baggy boiler suit, unbuttoned all the way down to the crotch, with absolutely nothing underneath. Coco adored her and the feeling was mutual.

'Wow, looking good, girl! There are times in life when I wish pussy was my sexual orientation.'

Coco roared with laughter as she made a few adjustments to the tiny silver sequinned bikini top and matching thong. 'Honey, you wouldn't be able to handle me.'

'Maybe not, but I'd die trying,' Millie retorted. 'Oh and I brought in a Spikes CD – want some of what you gave in that video I first saw you in.'

Thankfully Millie was too busy checking the lighting to realise that Coco had stopped dead in her tracks. Other than that one song on Marny's wedding night, she hadn't listened to the Spikes in a while. It was too painful. Hurt too much.

But to say that out loud, in front of Millie and the techs and all of the assistants and stylists that were floating around would just be way too embarrassing. The last notes of the Chilis faded away and Jacqueline, Millie's French assistant, flipped the CD out and replaced it with the new one.

Even if she hadn't had any warning, she'd have known. Those first chords, a complicated riff played high up on the fret board, a fast-paced, heavy rhythm that locked the listener in and made their heart beat faster – it could only be Dax. A tingle started at the top of her spine and arrived at her clit in record time. By the time Sly's vocals came in she was lost. Lost in the sounds, in the lyrics and in the past. She'd missed this so much. So so much.

Her body was moving almost independently of thought or reason, completely surrendered to the music.

'Sweet freaking Jesus, Coco – you are sex on legs, girl.'

Coco didn't hear her. In her head she was hearing her boys, her two boys, and she was seeing that vision that had greeted her when she stepped off the boat that night. Dax. Beautiful. Fuckable. Dax. She hadn't received the requested action from God, or taken Muff up on his generous offer, so all night, the sexual tension between them had been so strong that she'd actually been relieved to call a cab at 4am and head off to LAX to catch the first flight to New York.

Now he was playing for her, making her move, turning her on. An hour, four changes and twelve tracks later Coco was still in the zone, her legs weak, her emotions drained, every inch of her screaming for some kind of release from the exquisite agony that only Sly and Dax could cause.

She was on her knees now, head thrown back, just a sheer white thong covering her as she thrust her hips towards the camera, her breasts shielded from the lens by her arm.

'Hell, I think my sexuality just flipped all by itself. I swear I've got a hard-on,' Millie whistled. 'Coco, you are giving it, girl, givin . . . Holy shit.'

It took Coco a few seconds to realise that the clicking of the camera shutter had stopped, the studio had grown still and the final bars of the album had played out to silence.

Pulling her head up, she realised that Millie was no longer focused on her. Instead, she, like everyone else in the room, was staring off to the side, towards the door, where . . .

'Dax.' As if it were the most natural thing in the world, there he stood. Or rather, leaned. Propped against the side of the door-frame, in a pair of beat-up black jeans and a white T-shirt, his hair tied back from his perfect face.

There wasn't a sound in the studio as every single person there waited for the next move. Everyone knew their history. Their relationship was legendary, written about in the music and tabloid magazines, speculated over in bars, gossiped about between friends. She was the model who had left him for Randy Storm and – the story went – broken his heart. He was Dax Rice. Rock god. And he was there, right there in front of them.

Coco was the first one to break the silence. 'What are you doing here?' she asked, her voice soft, choked with emotion.

He didn't skip a beat, didn't add drama or bluster. He just locked eyes with her, spoke, explained.

'I've come to get you.'

Diana peered out of the window, checking where Lori had gone to. There she was, halfway between the house and the waves, lying on a sun lounger with a huge pile of paperwork on the table beside her. She had a one-track mind, her lover. Actually, there were two tracks but the second one that featured Diana in a starring role only got used on a sporadic basis these days. She didn't mind. Lori's focus, drive and ambition had been a huge part of what had attracted her in the first place so it would be hypocritical to criticise it now. However, she was smart enough to know that Lori needed more in her life if she was to sustain any kind of long-term contentment. Scratch just a little of the surface away and it was obvious that Lori had demons, ghosts from the past that manifested themselves in everything she did, in the way she acted, in the hard shell that she wore to protect herself from the rest of the world.

Lori had made her happier than she could ever have believed possible. She'd rescued her and saved her from a life that didn't bear thinking about.

Now it was her turn to repay the love.

Groping around in the pocket of her white denim shorts, she located the piece of paper she was looking for and pulled it out. Ten numbers. Ten expensive numbers, paid to the private investigator out of her own savings. Ten numbers away from changing Lori's life for ever.

Now she just had to persuade Lori to use them.

Sly! That had been her first reaction when the doorbell had rung, and she'd taken the stairs two at a time as she'd run to the door.

As soon as she got into the hallway, she could see through the centre glass panel that she'd been wrong. Heart thudding, she'd pulled open the door.

'Dave. What's wrong? What's happened? Is he OK?'

It all came out in a rush, along with a whole-body tremor and tears that had shot straight to her eyes. He immediately wrapped his arms around her. 'Hey, hey, calm down, it's OK. Everything is fine,' he said gently, squeezing her tightly and shushing her with soft tones and strokes of her hair.

'Where is he, Dave? Where has he gone to?' she sobbed.

'I don't know, Marny, but I know he's OK. I met a guy who was with him last night – they had a few beers and Sly told him he was just chillin', taking time out.'

Marny wasn't sure if the relief or the heartbreak would win. The relentless sobbing that just wouldn't stop gave her the answer. Five days of stress and tension and worry exploded into racking, heaving waves of grief that were utterly unassailable.

Dave helped her over to the limed oak dining table in the middle of the kitchen, pulled out a chair and sat her down. 'Where's Daisy?' he asked. 'Sl . . . sl . . . sl . . . ee . . . pp . . . ing.' The word fought its way out through the choking tears.

'And Bernadette?'

'St . . . ii . . . ll. O . . . f . . . f.'

'Marny, how can he do this to you? I'm here now, and I'm going to take care of you.'

Dave stroked the tears off her face and waited, holding her all the while, until she'd calmed enough to speak. This couldn't go on. He couldn't let Sly go on treating her like this. She had to see what he was doing to her, had to break away from him and Dave was the only one who could help her do that. It was for her own good.

Reaching into his pocket, he pulled out a small silver box and opened it.

'Marny? Marny, I brought this for you.'

He tipped the box over and let the contents fall onto the counter top. The surprise stunned her into silence and it was a few seconds before she found her voice.

'No, Dave, I don't want it. I can't. Not again.'

Even as the words that came out of her mouth objected, he could see that not once, not even for a second, did her eyes leave that little mountain of white powder in front of her.

How could she have forgotten how good this felt? They hadn't even made it to her room at the Plaza. Steve Tyler would have been proud. Oh yes, they'd made love in an elevator all the way from the first floor to the twentieth, and down again. Then back up. Then down again. Coco reckoned that the elderly woman who'd twice attempted to get on at the third floor was probably on the phone to her therapist already.

As for Dax, there hadn't been a damn thing she could do to stop herself. The moment he'd touched her she'd realised that the time for the Dax-abstinence was over. Every bit of her demanded that she give in to him and she wasn't for arguing.

The elevator, the corridor and then as soon as they'd burst into her room, they'd torn the clothes from each other – pulling, biting, kissing – and then they'd fallen to the floor in a tangle of limbs and sweat.

She'd opened her legs wide and allowed him to push inside her, his breath on her neck as he told her every little thing he was going to do to her, all of them involving words she would never say in front of her mother.

Her pelvic muscles spasmed as they gripped him, not relaxing even for a second as he thrust in and out of her, tenderness gone, leaving just raw, frantic passion.

She felt that glorious sensation in her clit as her third orgasm of the day began to build and she tore her mouth away from his. Not this time. This time she wanted it to be on her terms, the way she liked it best.

Using all her strength, she pushed him to one side, forcing him on to his back and then rolling on top of him. Her desperate gasps of breath were interrupted by his gorgeous low, sexy laugh as he realised exactly what she was doing. Pushing herself upright on to her knees, she slid backwards then raised herself up above his huge upright cock. Then slowing things right down, she gradually, inch by excruciatingly sexy inch, lowered herself down on to the tip of his dick. She took a little inside then raised herself up again. Both hands on her breasts now, kneading them, playing with them, she lowered herself down again, just a little further this time, then pulled back up. A low, loud groan escaped from his lips as he lay there, defenceless, unable to do anything but surrender to exactly what she wanted.

Downwards, she was moving downwards again, taking more than last time inside her, then letting the muscles in her pussy squeeze him as she moved back up again. Up, then down. Up, then down. She repeated it time and time again, each time she lowered, taking a little more of him inside then letting go. Her eyes were closed, her head thrown back, completely absorbed in the ecstasy. Again. And again. And again. Until she felt his juices explode inside her and she knew, knew she was ready to feel it again – that complete and utter magnificence of thrusting down on Dax Rice's dick.

Taking one final deep breath she let herself push all the way down, the movement making him immediately spasm inside her as he came hard, fast, her screams telling him that she was doing the same. And when she fell forwards on to him, their bodies sticking together with the sweat and tears and the kisses that wouldn't stop, she knew. She knew that she had to go back to him. She also knew that she had to tell him the truth.

THIRTY-NINE

'Mrs Rammer?'

The surfers were out again today, bobbing up and down in the waves like little ducks. Little yellow ducks that went to and fro, to and fro . . .

'Mrs Rammer?'

. . . lots of them all in a row, just to and fro, to and fro . . .

'Mrs Rammer!'

Marny jumped as Bernadette appeared at her side, looking decidedly unimpressed.

'So . . . sorry, Bernadette. Still can't get used to that. Please, let's just stick to Marny.'

The nanny's expression made it perfectly clear that she didn't approve, but hey, at least Marny was being factual. Was she actually Mrs Rammer yet? Ten days after the wedding and she still hadn't seen her husband. What did that make her? Abandoned? Rejected?

Definitely alone. And this time, the feeling was seeping into her pores. When Sly was on the road she could handle the distance, the emptiness, without sinking into melancholy. But the fact that he was out there somewhere, through choice, probably no more than an hour away, was excruciating. What was wrong with her? What had she done? Why didn't he want to be here?

Thank God for Dave.

He called her every few hours, popped in twice a day, held her when she cried and never came without the little helpers that were getting her through the day.

'Mrs Rammer, it's time for Daisy's afternoon nap. Would you like to read to her today?'

It was usually Marny's favourite part of the day. She knew that reading to a tiny baby seemed like a waste of time but Marny wanted her to know the sound of her mommy's voice, liked her to fall asleep knowing that she was safe, that she wasn't alone. They would lie on the day bed in Daisy's bright yellow room and Marny would snuggle Daisy into the crook of her arm as she told her stories of princesses and castles and clouds and oceans. Then Marny would smother her little one's face in kisses before switching on the pink music box that lay beside Daisy's bed and she would watch as the tinkling of the music lulled her into a soft, dreamy sleep. Sometimes Marny would lie there, just watching her until she woke up. Other times she would snooze with her, wrapped up tightly, their chests rising and falling together with every breath that they took. It was heaven. Real close to heaven.

'Mrs Ram . . . Marny?'

She snapped back to the moment. What was wrong with her? Her head was so cloudy that she couldn't focus, couldn't think. This wasn't right. She had to get straightened out, get her senses back.

'Erm, no Bernadette, could you do it today please?'

Her nanny nodded, her expression puzzled, and for a moment Marny thought there was something else Bernadette had wanted to say, but didn't. Instead, she turned and headed back upstairs, leaving Marny alone with the surfers.

The surfers and her little mound of snow – the snow that was frying her head, making her brain fog. She had to stop taking it. Hadn't she been there before? Hadn't she broken free of its grasp and cleaned up her life? She knew she couldn't function properly – it was clouding her judgement and she had to be alert and clean to be there for Daisy and Sly. Or maybe just Daisy, because right now it felt like Sly was never coming back.

As she reached over to the coffee machine, she realised that the trembling had started again: her hands, her head, her heart. It had to stop. She had to make it stop. She didn't want to be scared any more, didn't want to feel the fear every moment of every day that he hadn't come home to them.

Maybe . . . maybe she just needed a couple more lines. Just a couple. Just until Sly came back. When he came home she would stop, tell Dave not to bring her any more. And that would be soon. Sly would come back real soon.

As she leant down and made a line of the fine white powder disappear, she heard noises coming from upstairs. Bernadette must have finished Daisy's story and her little one's eyes were probably closing now. Yep, the footsteps crossed from one side of the room to the other, and then came the unmistakable sound of the door opening before Bernadette's steps continued on to her own room. All that was left was stillness, perfect peace, just the sound of Daisy's music box lulling her to sleep.

Rock-a-bye baby . . .

The cantaloupe flew past Diana's head and smashed into the wall behind her, a testimony to her quick reflexes and ducking powers. Lori's shoulder ached with the effort of the throw but when Diana pulled herself upright again, Lori realised that she was laughing. Laughing! That hadn't been the intended outcome.

'Seriously? Did you seriously just throw fruit at me?' Diana's grin was as infuriating as her nonchalance. This was Diana's way of dealing with bad situations, making jokes, brushing things off, playing situations down. When it came to The Steel Spikes that was a vital part of the job, it was what made her a shit-hot tour manager. And when it came to their personal life, it was also a skill that occasionally came in handy.

Lori knew she shouldn't be taking her raging anxiety out on her girlfriend, but right now she needed someone to blame.

'Why the fuck did I ever let you talk me into this? Why did you have to track her down? She left, Diana, don't you get that? The bitch left me!'

'So tell her! Tell her that! But you gotta meet her Lori – you gotta get some kind of resolution to this because it's eating you up.' It was the same argument Diana had used over and over again.

There was still half a fruit bowl of ammunition left but suddenly Lori no longer had the energy. She couldn't do this. Her mother had abandoned her when she was six years old, left her with a violent father in a shithole bar where anything could have happened to her and plenty did. It was unforgivable. She'd made something of her life and she hadn't needed a mother, a father or a family to do it. She sure didn't need them now.

Yet . . . Lori had called her.

Diana had got her at a weak moment, given her the number on a night that she'd been to visit Daisy and Lori had held the tiny baby and wondered – wondered how her mother had felt when she'd held her in her arms.

It had made her realise that she needed to face it. Later that night she'd downed half a dozen shots of Jack and picked up the phone, her free hand clutching Diana's arm so tightly there was a risk of bruising.

The first set of rings cut through her thoughts and she almost hung up. Her teeth were grinding against each other, her knuckles white around the receiver when . . .

'Hello?'

Hang up. HANG UP!

'Can I speak to Della Wyatt, please?'

There was a long pause on the other end of the line before the voice, a little shakier this time, spoke again.

'The name isn't Wyatt anymore. But I'm Della. Della McBride. Who is this?'

'You don't know me Mrs . . . Della,' Lori stuttered. 'But I'm your daughter.'

But that was then.

Now that the meeting was only minutes away, she was back-pedalling furiously. 'I shouldn't have called her, Diana. I don't have a mother. As far as I'm concerned she's lying with Jack back in that plot in Rackstown cemetery. She's dead.'

'That's not true, Lori,' Diana said softly, coming towards her, her arms ready to wrap around her. 'Sugar, you miss her.'

'I don't.'

Diana reached out and put her hands on either side of Lori's face, her smile sad, her voice soft. 'Then why do you look at that doll every damn day?'

'Coco!' 'Coco, can you stop there?' 'Can you look this way?'

The flashbulbs went off like strobes as they ran the gauntlet of photographers at LAX. Coco was glad she'd worn her oversized Ray-Ban Aviators, otherwise the evidence of her lack of sleep over the last few days would have been captured for posterity.

Much as it was flattering, she knew that the snappers weren't there just for them. Hank, the rotund, over-familiar security guard who had whisked them through the arrivals terminal had filled her in on the reason for their presence. Apparently, a rumour had swept the city that President George Bush was flying in for a whistlestop meeting with newly elected California governor Pete Wilson.

It seemed like every newspaper editor had dispatched photographers to the airport to cover the arrival, determined not to be the only one who missed out if the story was true. The security guard swore it was false – and he'd been there thirty years and knew everything that was going on. If the president was on his way in, apparently he'd have been the first to know.

Coco almost felt bad for them, but she knew the game well enough to realise that the snappers could earn a good few bucks on the side, selling these pictures of rock guy Dax Rice and model Coco LaBiba to the tabloids. It would make a story, the two of them back together again after all these years – and even if it didn't, the tabloid editors would make one up.

'Coco – this way!' 'Coco, over here!' 'Dax, is it true that you two are married now?'

The photograph after that last question was the one that would run in the gossip columns the next day: Rice, dressed all in black, leather jacket turned up at the collar, with his arm slung around LaBiba, looking gorgeous in white skintight denims and a matching fine-knit polo-neck sweater and shawl, the two of them laughing as they walked.

The limo was waiting for them as they exited and they threw themselves into the back, disrobing as they did so. It was impossible to strike a balance. When they'd left New York it had been four degrees, here it was over seventy. The driver pulled away to get rid of the ensuing crowd, before he asked them where they were going.

Dax slipped his hand around the small of her back, his fingers sliding inside her jeans and pulling her towards him. José had been driving long enough to know it was time to raise the dividing window between the back and the front.

It was like coming alive again after a long, long hibernation. The last couple of days had been bliss: sexy, fun, romantic, everything she had been missing since the day she walked away from the Spikes. And from Dax.

'So where to, Miss LaBiba?' Dax whispered as he licked her neck, his free hand reaching inside the front of her sweater and working its way upwards. 'My place? Shit, I can't believe you've never been to my house.'

'Tempting, definitely tempting,' she murmured, reaching around to flick the button open at the top of his jeans. That quickie in the first class toilets just hadn't been enough and she wanted him, *needed him* again right now. 'But I have to go check on Marny first.'

Her free hand stretched over and pressed the intercom button.

'Manhattan Beach please. Ocean Drive,' she gasped, her tone altered by the sensation of Dax's mouth closing on her nipple.

Dear Lord, how had she ever lived without this? This, the incredible thing that happened between the two of them, the sheer raw, sexual chemistry and fire. They were two of a kind her and Dax, and somewhere along the line she'd forgotten that, forgotten how amazing it could be when it was just the two of them and the rest of the world didn't exist. It was time to put her feelings for Sly to one side permanently. They were futile. If she was being completely honest with herself, the Sly who existed now was not the one she'd fallen in love with. It was time that her heart accepted what her brain already knew. There was nothing between her and Sly. Nothing.

'Hey, I'm telling Muff about this,' she giggled as she opened her legs wider and pressed her hands against the armrests on either side of her for support.

He was on his knees in front of her, head buried in the space between her thighs, his tongue slowly, teasingly flicking her clit.

Oh, yes. Oh, yes. Every little movement sent shockwaves through her pelvis and straight up to her brain. This. Was. Sensational.

The muscles in her abdomen tightened and her buttocks clenched as the first wave of the orgasm took hold, but still he didn't stop: licking, biting, sucking, forcing the climax to swell and explode again and again in a release of screams that no dividing window could conceal. Only when her cries began to subside did he raise himself up and slide his throbbing cock inside her. Coco's legs automatically slipped over his shoulders as he thrust inside, coming almost immediately as he pressed hard against her.

Spent, exhausted, ecstatic, they stayed like that for a time that neither of them could measure.

'I can't feel my legs,' Dax said eventually.

'No problem, you can feel mine,' she quipped. It was so easy. So comfortable. So right.

He reached up and kissed her gently on the lips. 'I didn't hear your answer earlier.'

'My answer to what?' she replied, slowly removing her legs from over his shoulders while thinking it might be an idea to take up yoga.

'To the guy in the airport's question.'

Pulling back, she racked her brain, her forehead puckering slightly as she put the events on rewind. Nope, nothing.

'What question?'

'He asked if we were married.' It was impossible not to watch as he pulled his jeans back on, tucked his cock inside and zipped them up. His body should win awards, it truly should.

'Oh. But I didn't answer him. Why would I?' she replied. OK, she had her bra, she had her sweater, now where was her thong?

'What about mine?'

His what? His thong? She was way too tired to concentrate on more than one thing here.

'My question.' What was going on here? And why was he looking at her with that incredibly goofy expression?

'What question?'

His hand curled around her neck and he pulled her towards him, before kissing her softly again.

'Will you marry me, Coco?'

Hell, what a ride! Sly had forgotten how freaking incredible it was to do whatever the fuck he wanted. Month after month on the road, going where he was told to, singing on command, the press, the fans, always on show like some kind of performing monkey. Now he was free. Free to do exactly what he wanted to do. And he had.

Those two little blondes he'd scored with on the first night had been un-freaking-believable. They lived in an apartment over on Hudson with six other girls, all of them in the escort business, all of them queuing up to give Sly Rammer their services for free. His red raw dick was a testimony to their skills and enthusiasm, although if he didn't have the clap it would be nothing short of a miracle.

Not that he could remember all of it. Dave Lopez had showed up as he left the Rainbow on that first night with enough brown to keep him going for a week. He was all right, Dave. Sure, he'd pulled a bit of a fucked-up stunt before the wedding. What was it he'd said again? Sly searched his brain for the answers but no, he couldn't remember. Hey man, what did it matter? Dave was making it up to him now.

The night time traffic on the PCH was light as he raced towards Malibu. How long had it been since he'd driven any-where by himself? When Lopez had shown up with the keys to the black Ferrari, he'd been psyched.

'Try not to kill yourself,' Dave had told him as he'd handed them over.

He leaned over and turned up the volume on the tape deck, then listened as Ziggy Stardust blared from the speakers. 'Life on Mars'. Classic, man – fucking classic. It didn't get any better than this; the music, the car, the two hot chicks that were waiting for him back at their apartment. He just needed some more cash to keep the party going so he was heading over to Lori's house to top up the funds. She always kept cash in the safe and would see him straight until he got his shit together.

Man, this car could move. Through the blur, through the dilated pupils, he realised that the turn that would take him down the lane to Lori's house was right up ahead. But the lights, man – the red lights, they were stationary and right in front of him, just there. There. Not moving. What was that? He pulled the steer-ing wheel to the left, jerked it and – Wow! Shit, what was that? Damn, he must have hit some kind of fucking animal to have made that noise.

The red lights were moving away now as he swerved back on to the road. Hell, he was good. He still had it. No fucking car was gonna go out of control when Sly Rammer was driving.

A space opened up to his left and his tyres screeched as he

turned into it. A few hundred yards more and he'd be there. Quick stop, some cash and then it was back to the party, baby.

Gotta keep the high, keep the buzz.

Sly Rammer had no idea that it was the buzz that had drowned out her screams.

The cab had missed the turning and let Della McBride off too far along the road so she started walking back towards the lights of the house in the distance. The house her daughter lived in. The daughter that she'd waited a lifetime to see again.

She was so fixed on her destination, on what lay ahead, that she didn't see the white lights of the car until it hit her. For Della McBride, the buzz went dead.

Lori's eyes flicked to the clock again, just as they'd been doing for the last hour. 9.10pm. According to Diana, her mother should have been there at nine. Her stomach twisted as she unfurled her legs from underneath her and pushed herself off the sofa. This was exactly why she had never wanted to track down her mother: it hurt. It hurt, made her vulnerable, made her scared, and those were three emotions that were strangers to her, that she hadn't felt since she was six years old.

'I told you. I told you I didn't want to see her. She doesn't give a fuck about me and now you've let her prove it all over again.'

Diana watched her pace up and down the room and Lori could see that she was working up to argue, to make yet another speech full of useless excuses, when the windows lit up.

'See! I told you she'd come. OK, baby girl, now just stay cool, OK? Stay cool.'

How could she stay cool when every single nerve ending had moved to the outside of her body and was screaming with fear? She didn't want to do this. She wasn't ready. Wasn't prepared.

Diana gave her one last wink as she swung the door open and Lori felt her nails dig into the palm of her hand. Pain. Let the pain distract her from what was really going on. Her mother. She was about to meet . . .

'Sly? What are you doin' here?' Diana's surprise was obvious.

'What's with the look?' Lori heard him sneer.

Diana shrugged. 'Nothin.' Sorry, sugar, we were expecting someone else.'

He jumped when the doorbell rang. Edgar was late. It wasn't the kind of service he expected from him considering the amount of business he put his way. He opened the door to see his supplier leaning against the wall. Man, he looked worse every time he saw him. The guy was grey, skeletal, twitching – but he was holding the gear and that was all that mattered.

'Sorry, Mr Lopez, busy night,' Edgar stuttered, handing over the brown bag with Dave's supplies. Further along the hall, he saw one of his neighbours' doors open a few inches and close again. Nosy bastards. He wasn't worried. Other than the fact that Edgar looked like he had, like, Ebola or something, he didn't come off like the typical drug supplier. Young and preppy, Dave had met him when Edgar's father – a major movie producer – had booked the Spikes to sing at Edgar's eighteenth birthday gig a few years before. They didn't usually do private shit, but it was just after 'Suicide Now' had started to really pick up major airplay and Edgar's father was willing to pay a hundred thousand dollars for one night's work. For them, it had been a no-brainer. For Edgar, it had been another step on a slippery slope that had ended with his father cutting him off after he sold everything in their Pacific Palisades summer house to buy smack. The route to dealer's runner had been a short one after that, especially since he still hung with his college buddies, all young guys with way, way too much money to burn. Nothing like hanging out at the country club while off your face on coke and Quaaludes.

He took the bag, checked the contents then handed over the dough. Time to go see his two favourite recipients of his wares. Marny, his beautiful angel, would be over at the house and he'd given those two little blondes from Hot Babes enough money to keep Sly occupied for a fortnight. They were probably in the

Rainbow or the Whisky tonight. He'd go track them down . . . just as soon as he'd had a little smoke of the finest Peruvian weed that money could buy.

The phone rang before he even got the flame to the tip of the spliff.

'Dave? Lori. Listen, we've got Sly at the beach house and he's pretty messed up – can you come get him and take him home?'

The smile was automatic. Sometimes the gods just threw you a bone and let you kill two birds with one stone.

If she'd walked into Dax's new home without realising who it belonged to, she'd still have known instantly. It was Dax. Just everything about him. The white-washed walls decorated with stunning ten-foot square Native American art. A natural oak floor that didn't require rugs or throws to accentuate its beauty. The furniture was the polar opposite of the black, red and glass trends that were so popular at the moment. Every piece was hand carved: raw, thick oak, simple beech and glorious yew that was free of gloss or paint. He told her that he'd left his apartment up near Zuma beach and bought the place for the view and she understood why. It was incredible – facing into the Santa Monica mountains, away from the sea, focusing on the land and its beauty. Rough. Simple. Pure. Wild. Dax.

Coco stretched and then curled back like a cat into the heat of his chest. They'd been home an hour and spent almost all of it in bed.

'What's bothering you?' he asked softly. 'You're tapping your fingers – something's on your mind.'

It felt so, so good to be back with someone who knew her so well, but that had a downside too. She paused for a moment, hesitant to articulate her thoughts because that made her fears somehow real.

'Do you think she's using again?'

Marny. They'd spent two hours with her on the way back from the airport and it was obvious that something just wasn't right. Her reactions were off, her eye contact was minimal, she was slow, a little dazed. She'd helped Coco pack up some of her stuff with robotic, monosyllabic movements and speech.

Dax shrugged. 'Probably just sleeping pills like she said. She's had a rough time – Sly's speciality is causing carnage to all around him.'

'I know,' Coco answered. Wasn't she living proof of that? Marny knew what she was getting herself into but it didn't make Coco fear for her any less. Marny wasn't as strong as her, didn't have the emotional reserves to stand up to him, deflect his behaviour. Her dependence on Sly was painful to watch. Now Coco was worried that Marny had transferred some of that need to another dependence altogether. But then . . . where would Marny get anything like that? She didn't know any dealers, didn't see anyone except Bernadette. No, Dax was right. Maybe a few too many sleeping pills while she waited for Sly to come home.

Coco lifted her head so her chin rested on his chest, her eyes searching his for answers. 'Any idea where he is?'

Dax shrugged. 'Could be anywhere. None of the guys have got back to me yet.'

They'd put in calls to Muff, Spank, everyone they could think of, that afternoon but no one had seen him. 'He'll turn up, Co, he always does.'

He always does.

It rang in her head. It was the unavoidable fact of her life. Sly always turned up – in her head, in her heart.

When Dax had asked her to marry him she'd thought he was joking, but no. He wanted her. Wanted to be with her. Make her his.

'Are you trippin'?' she'd giggled, completely dumbfounded.

His eyes, more than his words, told her that he wasn't. It should have been the moment that changed her life, started a new chapter, made her shriek with joy, yet all of those things were pushed right out of the way by a wave of apprehension and panic that had drenched the moment. She had to tell him everything. He deserved total honesty and if they were going to be together he had to know. She wanted no part of a relationship with secrets. Every married person she knew had a whole extra career going in duplicity. Her daddy had been married to her mom when he'd died with his pants around his ankles.

However, the back of a limo wasn't the time or the place for confessions so she'd answered his question by dropping the clothes that she'd been scrambling to pick up from the limo floor, and climbing on top of him instead.

'Tell you what baby – how about we just keep practising this kinda stuff for a while?'

He'd laughed at her blatant distraction ploy. 'OK, but I'm coming back to that one later.'

Now she realised that later had come.

His arms tightened around her as he kissed her forehead. 'I love you Coco. I love you. Don't ever leave me baby. Not again.'

It was time. She pushed herself up on to one elbow, the fingers on her other hand softly tracing a line across his lips.

'Dax, I want to come back to you. I do. So much so that the thought of not being with you makes me hurt. But you have to know something . . .'

He turned to look into her eyes and they stayed that way for a few moments, both searching, her for the right words, him for a way to stop her from saying them.

'I know,' he said.

Coco felt her heart speed up again as she waited for him to explain exactly what he knew.

'I know why you left. Sly.'

There it was. One word.

Moments passed before she trusted herself to speak. 'I'm so sorry, Dax. I was in love with both of you.'

The silence took over again, until, 'Did you screw him?'

'Only on the video shoot. Never again.'

'Why?'

Coco shrugged. 'You. Marny. Me. Self-preservation. I don't know whether you've noticed but the guy is a total fuck up.'

Oh, she'd missed his laugh, the low, treacly joy of it.

'It was like an illness. Just there. Nothing I could do to stop it.'

'And now?'

Hell, she really wished he hadn't asked that. Now what? How did she really feel about Sly Rammer now? Her voice was soft, her eyes heavy as she answered.

'When I hear him sing the feelings come back Dax, but that's it. It's only about the music now.'

She leaned over and kissed him, a slow, gorgeous kiss that didn't want to stop, but when it finally did she was the first to speak.

'I love you Dax. Music or no music, I love you.'

'Marry me,' he whispered, this time with so much feeling that a single teardrop ran down her cheek. He brushed it away.

'OK.'

'OK?' he repeated, his hands on either side of her face, his eyes intense, questioning.

'OK.'

They both screamed at the same time, rolling across the bed, wrapped in each other, both ecstatic. Eventually, he stopped, kissed her, pulled back.

'No secrets, no lies Coco. Just you and me. Always.'

Holy crap, she felt like her heart would burst. Always. Always. Her and Dax.

'Always,' she grinned.

'Wanna talk?' Diana paused at the doorway, watching her girl as she lay on the bed next to the things that mattered most to her. Lori shrugged, looking as sad as she was exhausted.

'Did Dave pick up Sly?'

'Just now. Came in a cab, so they're both away in the Ferrari. And you know what they say about men with sports cars.'

'Small dicks, big egos, have to pay for it?'

Diana laughed. 'Not quite, but it's close enough.'

Shit, this was horrible. She almost felt better when Lori was throwing fruit at her instead of just sitting there, trying to crack jokes while radiating aching sadness.

'I'm so sorry Lori – I really thought she would show.'

For a long time Lori didn't answer and Diana had a horrible feeling it was because she was trying not to cry. That would be the worst thing ever. Her girlfriend was strong, a powerhouse, invincible – if she broke down now because of something she'd done, the guilt would escalate from huge to unbearable.

'This is all she left, Di. A doll. It was all I had, growing up. No friends, no love, nothing. Just a doll. And if Jack had found out about it, that would have been gone too.'

Diana felt the tears spring to her own eyes now. What a shit life Lori had lived. She wanted to hold her, protect her from the past, yet what had she done? Opened her up to more pain, more rejection.

'I'm not contacting her again, Diana,' Lori said quietly.

Diana lifted the doll, put it back into the case that was lying on the floor, then crawled onto the bed beside her love.

'Don't, baby. Let's just forget about it.'

It had been far too easy really. He'd picked Sly up from the house, listened as Diana bombarded him with orders about taking him straight home, stopping for nothing, refusing to give him cash, etc. etc. He knew the drill. If Lori hadn't pissed off to her bedroom he'd no doubt have been getting it in stereo.

Luckily, he'd tossed his little brown bag of goodies into the Ferrari on the way in. If Diana had spotted that she'd have gone ballistic. He'd only let Sly see it when they pulled out and got back up on to the PCH, going real slow so as not to attract the attention of the two cop cars that were parked up on the road a little further along. Four uniforms were out of the cars so there was obviously some kind of action going on. Just as long as it didn't involve him, then he wasn't for caring.

Sly had been all for going back to party. 'C'mon man, let's get going. Those pussies are wet and waitin'.'

'I dunno dude – Diana will be real pissed if I don't take you back to the house. She said she was gonna call Marny and check.'

'Fuck that. What is she, my mother? It's party time, man.'

That's when the seeds of his idea had started to grow and if he did say so himself it was brilliant. Before he'd been focused on keeping Sly away from Marny, keeping him high, fucking with them for as long as possible until Marny saw the light and turned to him for . . . well, for everything. They were meant to be together. He knew that. Sure, it would cost him his job and all that went with it, but she was worth it.

However, what if . . . what if there was another way, one that would bring this to a conclusion, force Marny to make a choice? And that choice would be him.

He watched as Sly snorted a line of coke off the dashboard. The smack would have to wait until they were somewhere that he could cook it up. He had enough supplies for a speedball tournament and he was ready to share.

'You know, man – I don't understand why you don't have the same scene that Dax had when Coco was around.'

Sly snorted another line, rubbed the excess on his gums, then paused to process what he'd just heard. Lopez took it a sign to continue. 'I mean, come on, man – she should know what to expect when she's with a guy in a band. Should be happy to join the gig. Should be, like, communal, dude.'

Sly was headbanging now in time to the radio. He'd flicked on to KNEC and the sound of The Sisters of Mercy's 'More' blasted from the speakers. Man, he was wired. For a second Dave thought that Sly hadn't heard what he was saying, hadn't got the message, but when the record ended, Sly had flicked off the radio, stretched both arms above his head and roared like a crazy man. Which was pretty close to what he was.

Only when his lungs were empty did he make any kind of reply.

'You're right, man. It's time to get some serious party on.'

He was still laughing when they made their first stop.

Their first instinct had been to ignore the doorbell, but when they heard the unmistakable sound of Tye beating out a tune on the wall, Dax had relented and opened the door.

Muff, Strings and Tye had bounded in like hyperactive puppies – tattooed hyperactive puppies dressed entirely in denim and black – after downing at least a bottle of whisky between them. Spank, never one for exuberance, had trekked in after them.

'Hey man . . .' Strings greeted Dax.

'Hey. Anyone found Sly yet?'

'Yep, Lopez has him. He's taking him . . . oh ya fucker, Coco!'

She was only two steps in from the bedroom when Muff and Strings dive-bombed her, sending her flying across the room. And it was all done from a place of love and excitement.

The three of them crashed to the floor in a flurry of limbs and kisses.

'Great to see you doll. If I wasn't so wasted, I'd get a hard-on,' Strings announced when the action finally stopped.

'So what is this then? You're gonna be hanging again?' Muff asked.

Coco smiled over at Dax, her expression questioning.

'She's gonna be hangin'.' Dax answered.

Muff slouched back, grabbed a cushion off the floor and launched it in Dax's direction.

'Fuck, man – how do you do it?'

If Dax hadn't been high on beer and love, he might have sussed what was coming next, might have pre-empted it, stopped it or at least had a defence ready. But Muff was on a roll . . .

'I mean, shit – first Coco, then Marny, now Coco again – man, you're like a revolving fucking door.'

Coco's eyes immediately flicked back to Dax.

'Dax?' They both knew the question went deeper than one word. His silence answered it.

Ten minutes later, Coco was gone.

As the door slammed behind her, she spat out something about secrets and lies.

Marny had just checked on Daisy when she heard the door bang downstairs. Oh, thank God. Thank God. He was back. But . . . who was with him? A female's voice? Laughing. Giggling. Must be Coco. Dax and Coco. Her grin was automatic. It was just like before – Dax and Coco were back together and now Sly was here and it was all going to be OK. They were all OK. Life would be great again. She just wished she hadn't taken those last few lines because she was feeling real strung-out now.

Daisy didn't even stir as Marny left the room. Her daughter was a heavy sleeper and she was glad because it sounded like the guys downstairs were up for making some noise. Probably a good thing that Bernadette had gone to stay at her sister's for the birthday party of one of her nine siblings.

Closing the door behind her, she headed downstairs, heart thudding with relief. He was home. He was . . .

The sight in front of her made her stop dead. Oh, yes he was home. And Dave was with him. But the other members of the party weren't Dax and Coco.

'Hey! There's my baby!' Sly was slurring now, swinging a bottle of Scotch. His complexion was sweaty, his hair was damp, and he looked like he hadn't showered for a month. Dave, on the other hand, was standing in the corner, hands in his pockets, a weird grin on his face.

'Baby, this is . . . is . . . Megan and . . .'

'Scarlet,' the other blonde added petulantly.

'Megan and Scarlet. C'mon, baby, we're all gonna get real friendly.'

Sly leaned over and pressed play on the CD player. Marny had no idea what was on there. She never listened to music when she was on her own, so whatever disc was in was the one Sly had been listening to last time he was here.

She recognised Axl Rose's vocals immediately – telling her he wanted her to take him down to the Paradise City. The girls immediately jumped up and started to dance, slowly, provocatively, like willows, their limbs moving and curling and stretching.

'Come on, Sly baby, dance with us,' Megan purred. Or maybe it was Scarlet. It was all too confusing.

'Sly?' she blurted, watching with disbelief as he started to grind his hips into the butt of one of the girls. Suddenly Dave was next to her, his arm around her, still wearing that weird expression.

'Hey, Marny, come on – it's just a bit of a party. And here, I brought you a present.'

A present? She didn't need a present, she just needed her husband back here, preferably alone, preferably sober, and preferably acting like he loved and had missed her.

Clearly it was too much to ask.

Instead she had a scene from some twisted porn flick going on in front of her and now Dave, one of her few friends, was holding out the strangest present she'd ever been given. A sugar cube. Why would she want a sugar cube?

'Take it, Marny – I promise you it'll make you feel a whole lot better about this.'

No. She wouldn't do it. She couldn't.

'What is it?' she asked. The others were looking at her now, judging her. Sly was laughing, the girls sneering at her. Her skin began to crawl with embarrassment. She didn't want to be here, didn't want to feel like this.

'It'll make it all better, Marn,' Dave promised. His voice was soothing, caring. Dave always took good care of her. Hadn't he visited her every day, made sure she was OK? Now he was watching her, still holding out the cube.

'Take it, honey – it will make all the bad stuff go away.'

She couldn't. It would be crazy. Look what happened to her last time she used something other than coke. It had been hell. The worst kind of hell.

'Why were they still all looking at her? Why? They were freaking her out. FREAKING HER OUT!'

'Here, hon, I promise it's what you need.'

What she needed? Right now she needed her husband. She needed him to get his hands off these females and get them the fuck out of her house. She needed him to put his arms around her and tell her it was going to be OK. But she knew that right there and then, Sly didn't care what she needed – he was too busy getting it on with another woman right in front of her.

Slowly, almost robotically, she reached out and took the cube from Dave, and put it in her mouth . . . because no kind of hell could be worse than the one she was looking at.

FORTY

Malibu Weekly, January 20th 1991

News Round-up

Police are today appealing for witnesses to an incident that occurred on the Pacific Coast Highway on 12th or 13th January 1991. The victim, an unidentified white female, approximately 45 years of age, was discovered with severe head injuries and was taken to the UCLA Medical Centre, Santa Monica, where she remains in a critical condition. No identification was found with the victim. Police are unclear as to how she arrived at this location, but as she was discovered in an area that would not be considered suitable for walking or hiking, they are currently working on the theory that she was left in this spot by a person or persons unknown.

Any information should be directed to Los Angeles County Sheriff's department, Malibu/Lost Hills Station.

FORTY-ONE

Rock-a-bye baby . . .

The shadows were back. They'd been gone for so long, since she had made her plan, her reason to keep going, but now they were back. They were coming at night, lurking outside, coming in when she closed her eyes. Make them go away, Miss Molly, make them go.

But Miss Molly wasn't listening. She was planning.

Rock-a-bye baby . . .

Everything was in place, everything was done, except . . . how were they gonna get to him?

How were they gonna surprise him?

And how were they gonna get away?

Miss Molly would work it out. She always did. And in the meantime, she'd keep the curtains open and the music on.

Rock-a-bye baby . . .

Because as long as the music was on, the shadows would wait outside.

FORTY-TWO

Was it too much to ask that he got a name plate on his desk? Hell, he didn't need an office with a view, or a swanky computer or even one of those new cell phones. He'd stick with the vista of the roster noticeboard, his battered old word-processor – the one that Noah used to type up his first novel on the ark – and a bleeper that had an unfortunate habit of falling into the urinal when he peed.

Just a name plate would be nice.

Bobby Sofranko. If they were really feeling like spoiling him, they could add 'Features' underneath. But then, *Rock Out* magazine didn't exactly have a reputation for spoiling its staff. It didn't matter. He wouldn't be there long. This was just a stepping stone for him, another shimmy along the path to journalistic stardom. *Rolling Stone* perhaps. He knew that they'd been impressed with some of his Steel Spikes articles over the years because they'd occasionally requested permission to quote him. Yep, *Rolling Stone* would be cool. Or *Spin*. Or maybe even the non-music classics like *Playboy*. Yep, he could definitely handle getting his staff bonus over at the mansion.

He just needed an angle. A story. The big one that would

make his name and that he could use as a springboard to a better life. One that came with a frigging name plate.

It wasn't going to be easy though, as long as he was stuck on bands and gig reviews, spending his whole life travelling to hick towns covering small festivals and obscure performances by bands that split before their self-pressed albums hit the shops.

He needed a scoop. And he had an idea that might just land him one.

'Sofranko! Do I pay you to stare at that fucking wall?' The voice came from his editor's office, the only enclosed area in the open-plan office. Bobby picked up the slim file in front of him. Fuck it, what did he have to lose? The only thing he had was the roster-board view and they were welcome to take that away from him.

His heart started to beat a little faster as he approached Brad Callan's office. When he'd been studying journalism, he had an image of the stereotypical gruff but fair old-school editor, the one who would blast you to your face but defend you to anyone on the outside. Brad Callan fulfilled half of that remit. He was an arrogant, mean, dictatorial old bastard who suffered no fools and wouldn't hesitate to kick your ass out of the door for the slight-est misdemeanour. Wasting his time came high up on that list – which made this walk towards his office either the bravest or most stupid thing Bobby Sofranko had ever done.

'Better be good,' Brad muttered, without even looking up, as Bobby reached his doorway.

Bobby cleared his throat. Jesus, his mouth was drier than Death Valley in a drought.

'I . . . I . . . I . . .'

'Turn around and don't come back till you can speak,' Brad snapped impatiently.

Bobby almost did exactly as he was told, but stopped when he realised that if he didn't do this now there was no way he'd have the nerve to try again.

'Boss, I've . . . I've got an idea for a story,' he said. More of a whimper, actually.

Brad finally lifted his head and gave Bobby the kind of look that he imagined a maniac would adopt right before he pressed a button to eradicate a small country from the face of the earth.

'More.'

'The Steel Spikes.'

'Been done a million times. *You've* done them a million times. Next!' Brad's head went back down again.

He should go now. Definitely. Before the call went to human resources and he found himself on the street with nothing but a damn bleeper to show for his hard work.

'Not this angle, boss.'

Brad raised his head with exaggerated weariness this time.

'More.'

OK, he reckoned he had twenty seconds. Thirty at most. This was going to have to be the pitch of his life. 'I was on background on Sly Rammer's wedding last year, doing the filler research – you know, family, friends, school, all that kind of stuff.'

Brad Callan was now holding his pen like he would, at any minute, deploy it as a missile.

'And the thing is, his wife . . .'

'Who gives a fuck about his wife?'

'No, sir, I know that normally it would be of no interest sir, but it's just that his wife, Marny, she . . . er . . . she doesn't exist.'

For the first time, Brad's face registered a flicker of interest.

'So what are you saying? He married his right hand?'

Brad seemed to find this amusing, so Bobby smiled nervously.

'No, sir, well obviously he got married, only not to someone called Marny Tucker. Marny Tucker doesn't exist. I checked every record, every file I could find. I even called up our affiliates over in Philly, but nothing. No family. No school. No friends before she met the band. Marny Tucker doesn't exist.'

Bobby's ass relaxed very slightly when he saw Brad's pen being put down on the desk.

After the most unbearable pause since Bobby had asked Juliana Jones to the school prom, Brad spoke.

'Sounds like bullshit and we don't have time for you to be running around chasing ghosts. Got a magazine to run.'

Yep, he'd been rejected by Juliana Jones too. Shit.

'But if you wanna look at it in your own time, that's up to you.'

It was all Bobby could do not to punch the air and arrange the rest of the office staff into a Mexican wave. He knew exactly what Brad was saying. It had potential. Definite potential. He just wasn't willing to finance the story. But he was interested and if he, Bobby Sofranko, could put this together then he was on to something. Yes! He was definitely on to something!

He just hoped it was something worth printing.

TRACK 7

FORTY-THREE

May 1991

It had started with a phone call, the most thrilling phone call of her life. The letter had come next. And now, in just twenty-four hours, it would be a reality. The pinnacle of her career and her existence on this planet. Validation of who she was and what they'd accomplished. And it felt great. Diana had framed the letter for her and hung it on the wall beside her desk. When it seemed like it was all going to hell on a tour bus – when Sly was sent to rehab for the seventh time, when Muff got arrested for indecent exposure, when Spank amputated two toes in a cutting experiment too far, when Bill Simpson was riding her ass because of late delivery – all she had to do was look at that letter and it was all worth it.

THE AMERICAN ROCK 'N' ROLL
HALL OF LEGENDS

Dear Ms Wyatt,

Further to our recent telephone conversation, it gives me great pleasure to confirm the induction of The Steel Spikes into The American Rock 'n' Roll Hall of Legends. As you are no doubt aware, this accolade is given neither lightly nor without merit. It is felt that The Steel Spikes warrant inclusion for the following achievements:

Highest sales (USA, albums and singles) by a
    group/multiple-person act over the last five years.
Three successive number one albums (Billboard chart).
Twelve successive number one singles (Billboard chart).

As discussed, the ceremony to honour The Steel Spikes' induction into The American Rock 'n' Roll Hall of Legends will take place at The Shrine Auditorium, Los Angeles, California on the evening of May 19th 1991. Attendance will be by invitation only. The event will feature music industry names from past and present, and will be televised on all major music channels. As part of this tribute, a number of America's most successful acts will perform Steel Spikes hits. I have enclosed a list of provisional suggestions and would be grateful if you could contact me with your comments on these at your earliest convenience.

Thank you in advance and congratulations on this tremendous achievement.

Mr Daniel Donaldson

President – The American Rock 'n' Roll Hall of Legends.

Enc/

The Steel Spikes Tribute – Suggested Participants/Performances

Mötley Crüe – Act of God
Guns N' Roses – Four Ways Till Sunday
Soundgarden – Suicide Now
Nirvana – Take a Dive
Bon Jovi – Black, White And Brown

Alice in Chains – Spike
Aerosmith – The Law Don't Matter

Please note: The above artists will be contacted as to
availability upon your approval.

FORTY-FOUR

Rock-a-bye baby . . .

Ooooh, she was getting that funny feeling in her tummy, the one that always came when she was really excited or happy. They'd found a way. Miss Molly had found a way.

And now she was on her way there, on her way to see him, to do what she'd dreamt of doing for all these years.

Daddy was going to die.

He was going to die.

And she was going to be there to watch.

Then the happy feeling in her tummy would never stop.

FORTY-FIVE

They thought he didn't know what was going on. They thought
he'd lost it. Well, he hadn't. Rita May still came to see him every
day, brought the magazines and the new CDs, told him what
was happening out there. That's how he'd found out. Those
cunts. The Spikes. They were being inducted into The
American Rock 'n' Roll Hall of Legends tomorrow night, the
biggest event in their careers, the careers he – Ari Covet – had
built for them. And had they invited him? Had they fuck! No
word, no contact, not even a fucking card. Nothing. Nothing
from the Spikes or any of the other bastards in the industry. He
was gone. Forgotten.

'Come on Mr Covet, time for physio. Let's see if you can make
it twenty yards tonight.'

Oh yes, he was back on his feet now. And soon, all of those
cunts would remember exactly who he was.

'Mrs Rammer, are you OK?' Marny was sure she could see pity
in Bernadette's eyes. There was an irony. The nanny was feeling
sorry for the woman who paid her salary, who was married to
one of the most successful musicians in the world, who lived in

a beautiful home and who had more money in the bank than she could ever spend. Yet the nanny felt sorry for her.

Marny understood why.

Her life was a sham, a hollow sham that she could only face by blurring it to the point of numbness. Coke got her up in the morning. Coke kept her sane during the day. Valium got her to sleep at night. She saw her husband on the occasional night he was in LA, or when she flew out to meet the band every few weeks in whatever city they were playing in.

Those were the times that she needed more than just the coke and pills, she needed her sugar cubes. Those little cubes dipped in acid that made her feel the way she had to feel to do what they wanted her to do. She'd hated it at first, but now the high made it painless. After a sugar cube, she loved everyone, loved Sly, loved Dave, loved them enough to join the kind of party they wanted her to have. She got it. They were best buddies, spent all their time together, shared everything, including her. Sly had told her there was no choice – it was that way or nothing.

The guilt came the next morning, when she looked at herself in the mirror and despised what she saw. The feeling was a familiar one. Growing up she'd felt that way every single day, and it had only stopped the night she'd found Sly Rammer in a dumpster. He'd healed her that time. Now he was sending her back to her own personal hell.

And she was alone in it.

Even Coco had gone, left months ago, came one night, packed up her stuff and left. Said she had work in Europe. Marny hadn't heard from her since, but Lori had explained – so now Coco knew that she'd been with Dax and she hated her. Wouldn't speak to her. Wouldn't take her calls. Had just vanished into thin air.

Figured. Everyone left her eventually. All she had, *really had,* was Daisy.

But lately she'd come to see that history was repeating itself.

When Marny was a little girl, she'd realised that she'd be better off without a junkie mother. Now she was starting to think that Daisy would be too.

Bobby Sofranko's heart had officially stopped beating. Any minute now he would fall to the floor and Brad Callan would call reception and tell them he had a corpse lying on his office floor. He had to breathe. Yes, breathing was essential. Brad had been reading the piece now for what felt like hours – probably less than two minutes – and so far his reaction had been zilch. *Nada.* But . . .

The head slowly came up and Brad was now looking at him square in the eye. 'You sure about this?'

Bobby nodded. He was sure. It had taken him months of research, endless nights, weekends and holidays, obsessively searching for answers and explanations. He'd travelled from coast to coast more times than he could count. He had credit card balances that could sink a small country's economy. Yes, he was sure.

Brad whistled. 'This is fucking unbelievable.'

It was. But was it good enough to run? Was it going to be the scoop that made his career?

That was when Brad Callan did the most unexpected thing of all: he laughed. Actually it was more of an evil villain-type cackle.

'Next week. We're too late for this week's press, but we'll run it next week. Timing is perfect – we'll be covering their induction in the same issue. In fact, fuck it – let's scrap everything else.' Brad's expression was wide-eyed and fired up now. 'We'll make this whole issue about the Spikes. Yes! Fucking genius! Everything – where they came from, how they got together, the LaBiba shit with Randy Storm, the music, the gigs, the gossip – and how all that time they were living with . . .' With a dramatic flourish, he gestured to the sheet in front of him.

Marny Rammer – Evil Past Exposed!

ROCK STAR'S WIFE IS DOUBLE KILLER
by Bobby Sofranko

For many years she has shunned the spotlight, content to stay in her husband's shadow while he climbed to fame with the biggest rock band in the world, The Steel Spikes. Now, *Rock Out* magazine has discovered the reason for Marny Rammer's reluctance to court publicity – and it's a truth that will shock and horrify the band's loyal fans.

In December 1990, Sly Rammer married Marny Tucker in a candlelit ceremony on Malibu beach. Or at least, we thought he did.

In fact, Marny Tucker does not exist. The woman that Sly Rammer married was Marianne Thomson, a name that will be familiar to most of our East Coast readers.

The case of Marianne Thomson is one that is etched in the memories of everyone who has encountered it, studied by law students and recounted as a scary story around campfires.

In October 1975, in a run-down Philadelphia suburb, the body of seven-year-old Benny Thomson was discovered in his bed by his nine-year-old sister, Marianne. According to police records and court transcripts of the case, Marianne had checked on her brother at approximately 9pm the previous evening and found him asleep. In fact, a post-mortem would later show that Benny Thomson had been in a coma, a condition brought on by ingesting excessive amounts of alcohol.

A police investigation was immediately launched and centred on Benny Thomson's parents, Chad (42) and Dorisanna (25). Both parents had a long history of petty crime and drug and alcohol addictions. However, before charges in this case had been brought, both Chad and Dorisanna were killed when their home burned to the ground. The first officers on the scene found Marianne sitting outside the house watching it burn, DIE written on her forehead with her mother's lipstick.

Marianne Thomson immediately confessed to the crime, claiming she was motivated by revenge for the death of her brother.

Marianne was committed to the Paediatric Secure Unit attached to St Joseph's Hospital in Philadelphia for an unlimited time period. After spending ten years in the unit, Marianne was given a new identity – adopting the surname of her deceased maternal grandmother – and a position in the canteen at St Joseph's Hospital as part of the unit's efforts to re-integrate her into society. Marianne absconded from the unit on 29th May 1985, and despite a nationwide hunt was never traced.

Records show that Sylvester Ramone, who later changed his name to Sly Rammer, was admitted to St Joseph's Hospital on 18th May suffering from a drugs overdose.

Marianne Thomson has now been found and the nation has a new, terrifying story to discuss: The Rock Star and the Killer Bride.

'Sugar, are you ready to go?' Diana yelled. A few seconds later the impatient tone was replaced by a sexy, appreciative whistle. 'Lori, if there was any way I could get that leather suit off you without breaking a nail, then I'd be trying right now.'

Lori laughed and licked the side of Diana's face as she passed.

'You know, maybe we don't have to go right now. Those band guys can wait – spent years waiting on them, so maybe it's time to let them see how that feels.'

'Tempting. Definitely tempting. If I trusted them all to stay in one place, refrain from getting fucked up and abstain from causing each other permanent injury, then I might take you up on that. But hey, it's the Spikes, so let's go.'

She had a point, Diana decided as she followed her to the door. The induction was the following evening and they'd managed to get all of the Spikes to LA in one piece. If they let them loose there was no telling what would happen, so Lori had come up with the very smart idea of having a pre-induction party over at the Chateau the night before the ceremony. That way they'd all be together, they wouldn't be out clubbing and whoring, and it would be easier to keep track of them.

'Did you persuade Coco to come?'

Lori nodded. 'Yeah, but I'm not proud. I tell you that girl is stubborn. Dax has tried everything to get her to speak to him, Marny's tried too but she's just washed her hands of all of them.'

'So what changed her mind?'

'I begged. And lied.'

Diana smiled lazily. 'You are so turning me on right now.'

Lori ignored her. 'I told her that Marny was really fucked up, which is true, that I needed her help, which is true, that Marny could die if we don't straighten her out, also true. Then I said I was doing an intervention on Marny in the Chateau Marmont, tonight at 9pm and she had to be there to support me. One big fat lie.'

'Genius,' Diana whistled.

Lori took a deep bow. Without being conceited, she had to admit it was a pretty smart idea. And it would be followed by an even smarter one. The guys were finally taking a break. A long one. Tomorrow night would be the last night on duty before a six-month break, the first real time off they'd had off since the band formed in 1987. It was long overdue. As was the month in Bermuda that Lori and Diana were treating themselves to as soon as it was over. Just another forty-eight hours and they'd be on a plane and out of there. Easy.

No problem. After all, what could go wrong in that time?

She'd been so distracted that she hadn't realised that when Diana opened the front door there were visitors there who'd been just about to ring the bell. It was only when they spoke that she tuned back in.

'Miss Wyatt?' the older one of the two asked. Lori nodded, her expression somewhere between irritation and despair. Those fucking Spikes couldn't keep themselves out of trouble for even one day!

'LA County Sheriff's Department. We'd like to speak to you about a Mrs Della McBride. I believe she is your mother.'

★

426

Lori was on her second Scotch, but it wasn't the alcohol that had her confused. Her mother?

'So let me get this right – she was hurt? Here?'

'Actually, it was approximately half a mile from here. We've now established that a cab dropped her off and she chose to walk in a westerly direction, believing that she'd already passed your location. As we now know, that wasn't the case. Mrs McBride was then struck by a vehicle and discovered later that night.'

'But . . . but why? Why am I only hearing about this now?'

'There were no witnesses and I'm afraid Mrs McBride suffered extensive head injuries and had no recollection of the events. It's only in the last few weeks that her memory has returned and we have been able to piece together what happened that night. So if you wouldn't mind answering a couple of questions . . .'

Lori nodded as she refilled her glass.

'Do you know of anyone who would want to harm your mother?'

This time, Lori shook her head. 'I don't know anything about her. I haven't seen her since I was six.'

'Yes, we are aware of Mrs McBride's previous hospitalisation.'

'What?'

The officers were looking at her now with quizzical expressions. The younger one looked to the older one for permission to carry on. The slight tilt of his superior's head granted it.

'Mrs McBride was hospitalised in 1970 after being attacked in the . . .' he checked his notepad for the details, 'The Alehouse bar in . . .'

'Rackstown,' Lori completed the sentence.

The officer continued to speak as if he was under oath and giving evidence. In any other circumstances Lori would have laughed at his rookie eagerness.

'Mrs McBride . . .'

'My mother!' Lori blurted.

His face flushed. 'Sorry, your mother was attacked on the

premises and struck several times with a baseball bat, suffering extreme trauma to the head.'

The blood in Lori's veins ran cold. It was the same. The same way Jack had died. Baseball bat. That couldn't be a coincidence. 'How long was she in hospital?'

The rookie checked his book again. 'Almost a year, and then Mrs McBride was a patient in the Pittsburgh Memorial Convalescence Centre for a further eighteen months. She continued to suffer from short-term memory issues until the incident on the PCH, in which her memory was, temporarily, completely erased.'

Nothing made sense. Nothing. Why had no one ever told her all this? Why had no one mentioned that her mother had been in hospital? Why had Lori been told that her mother had run off and deserted them? None of this made sense.

The older cop was speaking again now. 'Before we go, Miss Wyatt, can I just ask what colour of car yourself and your colleague drove in January when the accident occurred?'

'Silver,' Lori replied.

'Red,' Diana said.

'OK, thank you.' The cops got up to leave, but as they did so Lori heard herself asking a question.

'What colour of car hit her?'

'Black.' The younger cop replied. 'We managed to ascertain by residue on Mrs . . . sorry, *your mother*'s clothes that she was hit by a black car. Investigations on the paint suggest it's an Italian model – probably a Ferrari.'

If the sheriff had seen what happened within minutes of them leaving the house, he'd have turned right around and come back again.

'Sugar?' Diana said hesitantly, watching Lori with a wariness that was alien to her.

Lori's head snapped up at the same time as the barrel snapped shut. She tucked the gun into her purse and grabbed her car keys.

'Sugar, let's calm . . .'

'Fuck that, Diana! That junkie bastard almost killed my mother. Now are you coming with me or not?'

Everyone always made way for a wheelchair. No one asked questions. People fell over themselves to help. It made them feel better about themselves. It made him feel shit.

But not today.

It had been easy to find out where they were. *Rock Out* had run an article on their forthcoming induction and mentioned that they were having a pre-ceremony dinner the night before at the Chateau. Yeah, right. You only had to look at the Spikes to realise that balanced diets and nutrition didn't really factor. 'Pre-ceremony dinner' meant party.

As he tucked his pistol under the blanket that covered his legs, Ari Covet smiled. This was a party he'd just invited himself to.

Coco furrowed her brow in confusion as she knocked on the door. Lori had told her to come to Room 121 of the Chateau Marmont at 8pm. Now she was standing outside the door and it sounded like there was a party going on. That couldn't be right. It was supposed to be an intervention, not a celebration.

She knew she shouldn't have come but Lori had sounded so desperate. Five months had passed since she walked out on Dax and then Marny, and the rawness of the pain was only now beginning to subside. Secrets and lies. They'd both kept secrets from her and while they hadn't told her blatant lies, there had definitely been duplicity.

Dax had contacted her countless times since she'd left but she'd ignored him. It was over. He'd crossed a line. Only a couple of years before, she'd crossed the same line with Sly, and paid the price – she'd left the world she loved so that she didn't hurt Dax or Marny. Shame they hadn't given her the same consideration. If they'd had meaningless sex she could just about have handled

429

it, but she'd persuaded Lori to tell her the truth. She knew now that they'd lived together, then kept it a secret and forced the rest of the band to keep it quiet too.

It was a betrayal.

But there still wasn't a day that went by that she didn't miss them, miss the band, miss the craziness and the love, miss Dax.

She knocked on the door again, then gasped when it was opened by Muff. He didn't give her time to think – just dragged her inside, right in to the middle of Steel Spikes bedlam. She had to get out of there, had to . . .

'Coco?'

Dax.

'What are you doing here?'

Shit, he looked incredible. Which wasn't the point. The point was that she was supposed to be here for . . .

'Lori asked me to come see Marny. Said she's pretty messed up.'

Dax gestured over to a bed in the corner where Marny lay, completely stoned and out of it.

'She is. It's good to see . . .'

'Look, I have to go. This isn't what I thought it would be. Lori obviously thought . . . Actually, I've no idea what Lori was thinking.'

'Stay.' A shock of electricity charged up her arm as he touched her.

'No, I . . .'

'Please. No strings. Nothing heavy. I'll stay out of your way. It's just so good to see you.'

It was a terrible idea. The worst. She scanned the room, saw the booze, the coke, the girls, the Spikes, all in party mode and then . . .

Slash. The sound of Slash's intro, the freakin' incredible sound of the opening bars of 'Sweet Child o' Mine'. The feeling started in her stomach, goosebumps came, the hairs on the back of her neck welcomed Axl's vocals as they blasted in with

430

the opening line, the volume rising over the chaos that sur-rounded her.

Coco LaBiba knew that she shouldn't be there. But she also knew that she was home. Maybe it was time for one last party.

FORTY-SIX

Rock–a–bye baby . . . .

Almost there. She still couldn't believe that the plan had worked. She had Miss Molly to thank for showing her the way, telling her how to do it and where to go.

Just a few more hours now and then it would be over.

Daddy would be dead.

And the shadows would never come back again.

FORTY-SEVEN

1991. The Chateau Marmont, Los Angeles.

The Steel Spikes are in residence.

Last night, the puddles on the carpet were Jack Daniel's, sweat and water from the bath that overflowed when one too many rake-thin blondes cast aside their handbags and headshots and climbed in to join Sly Rammer in the kind of bathing session that had more to do with getting dirty than clean.

In the main bedroom all the usual suspects were orbiting Planet Fucked Up. On the floor, the other band members, Dax, Spank, Tye, Strings and Muff, were all coked up, sexed up and letting the action come to them. And come, it did. The girls lined up to please them, desperate to inhale the stardust along-side the white powder that rose in snowy peaks from every surface. On the round, scarlet silk bed lay Marny Rammer, naked, stoned, her legs wide enough to accommodate the long brown locks that were undulating between them, completely oblivious to the fact that if she and Sly were a normal couple they'd be having dinner right now to celebrate the sixth anniver-sary of the day they met.

Over at the huge mahogany dining table Coco LaBiba was performing her party trick – all it took was flexibility, an open mind and three dicks. Tonight two of them belonged to the band and one to a journalist who would forever consider this the most incredible night of his life.

No one paid much attention to the first gunshot – the music was so loud that everyone thought it was a sound effect on 'The Law Don't Matter', the Spikes' global hit that was blaring from the sound system.

It was only when the music stopped and another shot rang out that they were forced to pay attention. Lori Wyatt held the smoking gun; over six foot in her steel stiletto heels, a leather catsuit adhered to every inch of her body, her hair scraped back into a two-foot long black ponytail that reached the small of her back. She had their attention now.

'If I don't know you then fuck off,' she announced, her clipped voice perfectly calm, raised barely above conversational level.

Ten minutes later the suite was empty of everyone except the core players: Marny, Coco, Dave, Diana and the band, a few of them wondering aloud when their manager was going to find a new party trick. It wasn't the first time Lori had shot up a hotel ceiling but shit, there had to be an easier way to clear a room.

All that had happened last night.

This morning the room is silent and the numbers even fewer. One man lies slumped against the window, his pulse long stopped. Near the door, another body, perfectly still. On the bed lies a woman, her motionless limbs splayed like a broken starfish. Only her shallow, sporadic breaths give any clue that she's not already destined for the morgue, an occasional rasp audible over the tinkling sound of the music coming from a wooden box that lies open on the floor.

Rock-a-bye baby . . .

A bored Honduran maid walking by with a large pile of eight hundred thread-count Egyptian cotton sheets stops, listens, smiles, remembers.

On the tree top . . .

Her reminiscence is cut dead by a sudden realisation. As the fluid seeps out under the door and spreads across the deep-pile, monogrammed carpet to the white canvas of her shoes, she understands . . . and the only sound now is the sound of her screams.

Because this morning, the puddles are red.

TRACK 8

FORTY-EIGHT

LA Times, May 20th 1991

THE WORLD MOURNS A ROCK STAR – A Special Report by Bobby Sofranko of *Rock Out* magazine

Tributes have been pouring in today after the brutal bloodbath that took place in the early hours of yesterday morning and led to the death of Steel Spikes member . . .

When she closed her eyes she could still see it all so clearly, like a movie, a horror story, a slash and kill thriller that had over-stocked on blood supplies and decided to use them all up anyway.

It was a nightmare.

Anyone's worst nightmare. It was some kind of twisted act of God.

She saw it now, all of it, and it made her so scared that . . .

BEEEEEEEPPPPPPPPP!

The alarms screeched so loudly that everyone in the Intensive Care Unit felt a shiver of panic. The crash team barged through the door, pads at the ready. In seconds a doctor was by her side. 'CLEAR!' he yelled. The shock lifted her torso off the bed. But it didn't restart her heart.

'CLEAR!' he shouted again.

The second one was worse, so violent that she lurched then flopped like a rag doll.

The movie was still playing in her head.

She was there on the bed and Dave Lopez was doing something to her that she didn't even want to think about now. She watched the top of his head move, felt his tongue inside her, felt her nerve endings tingle as her pleasure sensors sent messages back to her brain.

The guilt. She wouldn't think about the guilt now.

Lori had arrived, shot the room up, cleared it out and only when everyone except the band, Coco, Dave, Diana and her were left, did she realise that this wasn't just any other Steel Spikes party. The fact that Lori was holding a gun to Sly's head gave it a whole other dimension.

'You asshole. You fucking asshole! You nearly killed her!'

Then Sly was screaming, crying as Lori slipped the safety off and cocked the trigger.

'No! Lori, no, come on honey, don't do this!'

Lori was looking at Coco now, watching her as she came nearer, hands out in front, pleading with Lori to stop.

'I didn't kill anyone. I fucking didn't!' Sly was screaming. She had never seen him like that – terrified, so, so scared. It was how Marny felt every minute of every day. Diana was beside Coco now.

'Sugar, put the gun down. Look at him, Lori, he didn't know. He was out of it that night . . .'

'Junkie fucking scum!' Lori screamed, shaking now, trembling, her finger on the trigger of the gun that was pressed against Sly's temple.

Diana was still speaking, her voice soothing, tender. 'Bermuda, sugar. Just me and you, tomorrow. Don't take that away from us, Lori. Don't let this piece of shit take that away. It's me and you, Lori. Just me and you.'

For the first time there was a hesitation in Lori's expression, confusion across her brow.

Coco was still moving towards her, two feet, one foot, she was there now, and she slowly, gently pulled the gun away from Sly's head. He immediately collapsed to the floor and vomited. Not for the first time he was lying in a river of his own sick and piss, but never before had it been caused by fear.

Coco eased the gun out of Lori's hands and dropped it to the floor, then kicked it towards Dax.

'Don't let Muff near it,' she warned, spotting the guitarist moving forwards.

Lori was crying hard now, really sobbing, completely devastated by something that the rest of them didn't understand.

What had Sly done? Who had he nearly killed?

'Take her home, Diana,' Coco handed a shaking Lori over to her girlfriend and watched as they headed for the door.

'OK, guys, let's break it up,' Dax said. The others didn't take any persuading. Despite most of them having homes within ten miles, they'd all booked rooms in the Chateau as per Lori's instructions. A mini bar and a porn flick were preferable to all this drama.

Coco had come over to Marny then, wrapped her arms around her. 'Are you going to be OK?'

She'd nodded: numb, confused, stoned.

'Honey, you can come with me, I've got a room just downstairs for tonight.'

Marny had shaken her head. Her husband was staying here. This was the suite they'd booked for the night. He was staying here and so would she. It had been so long since they'd spent the night in the same room that she would take the chance to be alone with him any way she could get it.

'I'm fine, really, it's OK,' she'd told Coco, then watched as she reluctantly left, with Dax going straight after her.

Sly was climbing to his feet by this point, making for the bathroom, when the doorbell rang. Coco. Dax. One of the boys. They must have forgotten something.

Sly opened the door and for the second time that night he was looking into the barrel of a gun. He backed up, hands in the air, murmuring a mantra of, 'Oh fuck. Oh fuck.'

She'd sat bolt upright on the bed as terror had consumed her.

'Remember me, Sylvester? Ring any bells?'

Sylvester? No one called him that except his family. His mother, his sisters . . .

He was shaking his head. 'What the fu . . .'

Her scream was almost animalistic, a primal rage of pain. It was only then that something clicked in his head.

'Gloria? Oh my God, Gloria!'

Gloria! How many times had Marny wondered what she looked like, thought about whether she would come and take Sly away from her. Gloria – the woman he'd been engaged to all those years ago when she'd found him in the alley, the one who had been pregnant with his child, the one that he'd jilted at the altar.

'This is for Molly,' she spat.

'Molly? Who the fuck is Molly?'

Marny didn't even recognise his voice any more – fear had taken it to an entirely different pitch.

'Molly is your daughter,' Gloria was talking in a weird baby tone now, 'The one you killed.'

The shot went straight through his head, a circle of red popped out the front as he fell to the floor. That's when she remembered screaming, until a bullet came in her direction and stopped the noise. Just as she closed her eyes that last time, she saw Gloria drop the box she was carrying, put the gun to her own head and pull the trigger. And then there was music. Soft, tinkling music. Rock–a–bye baby . . .

Just like Daisy's box. Daisy. She wanted her baby. She had to stay here for her baby.

'CLEAR!' It was the most painful one yet and something changed, something started . . .

Beep. Beep. Beep. Beep. She heard the young doctor, 'We got her. We got her back.' Then he rhymed off a whole lot of instructions that she didn't understand.

She was back.

And for the first time in a long time, she wanted to stay.

FORTY-NINE

It was a perfect, breezy morning, the kind of day that made Bermuda seem like it was a paradise specially designed by God. The music oozed out of the speakers, infusing the audience with warmth and tenderness. It was Coco's choice – Otis Redding singing 'These Arms of Mine' so soulfully and tenderly that it sounded like his heart might break at any moment.

Daisy was the first to walk up the aisle, spreading white rose petals from a white wicker basket. Twelve months after the death of her father, two-year-old Daisy had turned into a mini-Sly – dark, stunning, temperamental, wild, and she sang with the most incredible voice.

Coco came next, beautiful in a soft white one-shouldered sheath that flared gently down to her bare feet, so that she glided like a Roman goddess. Darcy held her hand as she walked, her smile beaming wider with every step.

The only thing that could have been this day any more perfect would have been if her daddy had been walking on the other side of her. She missed him. She missed him so much. That night in the hotel when she'd watched Lori put the gun to Sly's head, she'd known that she had to act quickly because it couldn't happen again. Years ago, she'd watch her daddy die in front of her. He'd run after her, upset, shouting to her to stop, but she'd kept going. Only when the yelling stopped did she turn back and watch as he sunk to his knees. By the time she reached him he was gasping for breath. 'Daddy? Daddy!'

'I'm sorry Coco . . . I . . . I love you.'

The end. That was it. Nothing more. Later she'd realise that that was the moment she'd switched off her emotions, closed them down, detached herself from them, allowing them only to surface when the music was playing, helping her to escape to a place that didn't feature the pain of watching the person she loved most in the world die because of her. She'd made him run, forced him to chase after her and it had killed him.

It was only after she'd prised the gun from Lori's hands that she realised that she'd taken a life back. She'd lost one and then saved one, if only for a short time. And much as losing Sly had been devastating, there had been a healing there for her.

Sly's death came with a reminder that life could be snatched away at any moment. It had put everything into perspective for her. Marny, Dax, life. She loved all of them and she wasn't going to deny that by holding on to a grudge or a hurt. It had finally sunk in.

She'd finally got it.

She was ready.

Dax was her forever guy. The only one she wanted. Call it maturity, call it wising up to reality, but she had realised what was important. It was all about Dax now. She'd bought him a Tiffany ring, a solid silver band, engraved with '*Home to you . . . always*' on the inside.

Coco LaBiba was just about to put it on his finger.

'If you cry I'm trading you in for someone far more butch — two episodes of tears in one year is my limit for a girlfriend.'

Lori's response was to aim a subtle sideways kick at Diana's shin. 'Better. Much, much better. If you carry on like that I might let you beat the crap out of me when we get home.'

Lori tried to stifle the laugh, but everyone within a few feet heard the giggle and turned to see what was going on. Lori Wyatt. Giggling. Shit, the world was going to hell.

She looked down at the woman sitting to her right. Her mother didn't have the strength to stand for long periods of time yet, but it would come. She was a fighter. Now Lori knew where she got it from. The truth had been hard to take. Jack had been the one responsible for the beating that put Della in hospital, but of course it was her word against his. A mugging, he said. No jury would have convicted on zero evidence. Lori knew now that Della had tried to come back for her when she was released from the convalescence centre two years later, but Jack had kept her away. For a start, she was a woman with a brain injury; he said he would prove she wasn't fit to bring up a child. And just in case that deterrent wasn't big enough, he said if she took Lori away he'd track them down and do the same to her daughter as he'd done to her. Fear had made the decision for her. She'd waited. She'd relied on Sheriff Donachy to look out for Lori, while she waited. And when Lori was coming up on her twenty-first birthday, old enough to take over the bar and look after herself, Della had done to Jack exactly what he'd done to her.

The case had never been solved. It never would be.

Bobby Sofranko would get more than a name plate when he got back from this trip. Exclusive access to the rock wedding of the year, interviews with all the members of the Spikes and the inside story on twenty-three-year-old Gloria Bagstock – who, as an eighteen year old, had been taken from her home, moved to a new area and forced by her parents to abort Sly Rammer's baby. She'd then watched as the man who destroyed her life became a superstar.

Gloria had gone on to take bearing a grudge to a whole new level.

Murder. Attempted murder. Suicide. That was some night's work.

After her funeral, her parents had discovered that she'd been planning it for years, writing in her diary to a fictional character called Molly – the same name that she and Sly had picked for their baby before he'd left her. They weren't sure, but they thought it had been inspired by the Miss Molly doll that had lain at the bottom of her bed since she was a little girl.

They'd had absolutely no idea that Gloria had become unhinged, just thought she'd become a loner, introverted, someone who liked to keep herself to herself.

Bobby had found out that she'd tried to get close to Sly before, after a gig in Philly, when she'd used one of his sisters' names to get backstage. Apparently Lori and Diana had just taken her for an obsessed, crazy fan. They'd got the first two adjectives right.

On the subject of crazy, the Spikes were also co-operating with him on his forthcoming biography of the late, un-great Ari Covet. The poor old bastard had been found dead in his wheelchair, the victim of a second stroke, two hundred yards from the entrance to the Chateau Marmont on the night Sly Rammer was killed.

To add insult to fatal incident, someone had robbed him blind, taking his wallet and whatever else he had on him when he died. He wasn't missed. However, his life story would shift books by the thousands and Bobby was the man to tell it – with 50 per cent of the profits going to his named co-writer Brad Callan. Brad hadn't written a word, but it was the price Bobby had had to pay in order to meet the Spikes' demand that the story about Marny's background be canned.

He and Brad had agreed instantly, even though it meant losing their huge splash. The pay-off was worth it. Marny's story might sell some extra copies that week, but their new relationship and access to the Spikes, the book they were planning on Sly's murder, and Covet's biography on top, would make them both very successful and very rich.

Everybody won. Except Ari Covet. And from what Bobby knew of him already, he'd have fucking hated that.

★

Marny watched her daughter and beamed with pride, but even her maternal glow couldn't match the joy of the six women seated in her row. Sly's mother and his sisters were a huge part of their life now, ever since she'd invited them to meet Daisy after the funeral. It was only right. They were the only family she had.

There had been a time when she'd thought that she would need them to raise Daisy for her. Sly's memorial service had been held in the grounds of Lori and Diana's home, on the same beach where Sly had promised to love her for ever. Afterwards, Bobby Sofranko had found her, told her what he'd discovered and given her a draft of the article. It was all in there – every hellish, brutal truth. Enough to devastate what was left of her life.

Lori had come as soon as she'd heard the scream.

The last thing she remembered before she hit the sands was Diana aiming a right-hook in Bobby's direction. By the time she woke up, Lori had taken care of it, cut a deal, made the problem go away.

Marny may not have family, but she had friends who had her back.

And more.

'Hey sweetcheeks'. The man with the great line in hilarious smarm slipped into the empty seat on her left. It had been unexpected. Radical. But after Sly died and Lori fired Dave Lopez with the caveat that if he came within a hundred miles of any of them she'd get the gun back out, Marny had found herself drawn to someone who made her laugh, who let her feel – for the first time – like a kid. Although of course, he did have other legendary talents too. 'Will you fucking sit down – none of us can see past that hair', Strings moaned.

Muff gave the finger to the rest of the band standing in the row behind them, then leaned over to kiss Marny. It was early days, but it showed promise. And promise was more than she'd ever had before. Even if he did keep all matches well away from her when they had a disagreement.

'Do you, Dax Rice, take Colette Belmont to be your lawfully wedded wife?'

Dax nodded, his gaze never leaving hers for a second.

Coco heard her mom choke on a sob in the front row. She hoped they were tears of joy, and not horror that her only child was standing in front of a minister pledging her life to a man who was wearing ripped-up black jeans and a leather waistcoat.

Truth. Honesty.

This was who they were.

Dax Rice, the rock star, and Coco LaBiba, the girlfriend who had always lived by her own set of rules.

'I do.' There was a collective sigh of emotion from the women in the audience.

'And do you, Colette Belmont, take Dax Rice to be your lawfully wedded husband?'

Oh, she did. She absolutely did.

Only the preacher clearing his throat jolted her to the realisation that she hadn't actually spoken the words out loud.

'I do!' she blurted, laughter now joining the sobs in the audience.

'Then I now pronounce you man and wife.'

Before the preacher could get the next line out, Dax's hand was on her face, touching it like it was the most precious thing he'd ever seen.

'Always,' he whispered.

'Always.'

Coco knew with her whole heart and soul that it would be.

The photographer checked the image one more time before pressing the button. He had the shot. Three women, all of them laughing, all of them stunning in their own way.

'Sure you won't stay any longer?' Coco asked Lori when the posing was done. She shook her head regretfully. 'Have to get back to LA. Looking at a couple of new bands back there.'

'Thought Diana had forced you into retirement,' Marny teased.

'She thinks she has,' Lori replied, 'but the boredom would kill me. If I take on another act, don't suppose you two ladies would want to come back on the road? You know, give a bit of moral support?'

'Nooooo, thank you.' Coco exhaled, 'My days on the tours and on tables are over.'

'I have a suggestion, though,' Marny interjected. 'If you don't mind waiting a few years, that is. Daisy announced today that when she grows up she wants to be a singer in a band.'